Mark Barrowcliffe was born in Coventry and gradu-
ated from the University of Sussex. He worked as
a journalist and a conference-organiser before
becoming a full-time novelist.

Lucky
Dog

by Mark Barrowcliffe

First published in 2004
by HEADLINE BOOK PUBLISHING

A REVIEW paperback

10 9 8 7 6 5 4 3 2 1

ISBN 0 7472 6799 5

Typeset in Palatino by Avon DataSet Ltd, Bidford-on-Avon, Warwickshire

Printed and bound in Great Britain by Mackays of Chatham plc, Chatham, Kent

Headline's policy is to use papers that are natural, renewable and recyclable products and made from wood grown in sustainable forests. The logging and manufacturing processes are expected to conform to the environmental regulations of the country of origin.

HEADLINE BOOK PUBLISHING
A division of Hodder Headline
338 Euston Road
London NW1 3BH

www.reviewbooks.co.uk
www.hodderheadline.com

For Jake Barrowcliffe

Thanks to: Wendy Bell, as always, Emily Turner for her advice, Julia Jordan for her poker knowledge, Paul Heathorn for listening to my jokes, Dave Adams, Vikki Pihl and Suzi Skinner likewise. Thanks to Danny Plunkett for the pun.

I meant to thank Dr Jeffrey Handel for his medical advice in my last book but I forgot. Better late than never, Jeff. Well, not in your game, I guess.

Oh love will make a dog howl in rhyme.
Francis Beaumont, *The Queen of Corinth*

The more I see of men the more I like dogs.
Mark Twain

Man is the only animal that laughs and weeps; for he is the only animal that is struck with the difference between what things are and what they ought to be.
William Hazlitt

1

Hot Dog

I wished at the time that Mr Gilbert had picked someone else's office in which to have his heart attack.

Had I known then what I know now, of course, I would have shaken him warmly by the hand. This may have interfered with the attempts of the lovely Lucy to revive him, so perhaps it's better that I did not.

As a card player, I can tell you things come in runs. Just as a poker man may not be able to get arrested at certain points in his career – and if you play cards like I play cards then a career is what it is – and at other times everything he touches will turn to gold, life has its rhythms and themes.

The theme for that particular month of June appeared, without wishing to stray into the disagreeable realm of melodrama, to be death.

And, for that matter, dogs.

That noon, under a heavy sun, I had watched my mother buried.

'Today is the beginning of the dog days of June,' said the moist vicar as we laboured back from her grave, 'traditionally a period of inactivity.'

'Quite a considerable period for my mum,' I said, watching the heat shimmer over the headstones. I gave him a weak smile. My mum would have been pleased to see me bearing up.

I could have done with a break that afternoon, from difficulties, from stress, from other people's problems and from my own. God, however, occasionally plays Jenga with our souls, seeing how much He can challenge the foundations of our beings before they collapse. So He sent me the crooked Mr Gilbert and his heart condition.

And his dog.

You'd think when you see someone hit the floor right in front of you that you'd remember some telling, cinematic detail. The arc of the cigarette through the air, for instance, or the expression on the man's face.

All I remember, though, is the curly-tailed dog looking up at me with what appeared to be a shrug and the sort of expression that says, 'Well, that just about puts the tin lid on it.' This was noteworthy because that was the exact same remark I was making to myself.

I don't want it to appear that this terrible event did not affect me. In fact I think that, short of Mr Gilbert himself, it had a greater impact on me than on anyone else on earth.

I'd decided to return to the office after Mum's funeral as I didn't want to spend the day moping. I needed something to take my mind off it and, because poker games are rare at two o'clock on a Thursday afternoon, my credit card didn't work for the internet tournaments any more, drink wasn't my thing, drugs I wouldn't know where to begin and Lyndsey my girlfriend couldn't get the time off work, I thought I'd return and at least sit at my desk, if do no work.

If you should be moved to sympathy for me at this point, let me offer you something to temper your tender feelings. My job, what I do for a living, my daily crust is . . . Before I go any further, let me say that I am, as was my father from whom I inherited the business, pathologically honest. It's nothing I've been taught and it's certainly not a religious calling. It's just in the bones, something at a genetic level.

I wish I could ditch it, I really do. Like when they underbilled me for my council tax. Do you realise they do not have any facility at all at the council for people to complain about being undercharged? A week of phoning and sleepless nights it took me to be able to pay the correct amount.

I can't cheat, I can't lie, I don't even like disappointing people. I'll admit these are unusual qualities for an estate agent but that's our trade here at Son and Barker – so named because my dad had given my grandad a job briefly before he died. Yes, estate agents and honest too. We're the ones, the exceptions that prove the rule.

You'll find no imaginary competitors for the home of your dreams here, no invitation to submit 'a sealed bid', no wildly over-optimistic assessment of the value of your property.

Son and Barker don't want to get involved in any such shenanigans. And so we lose out. As my father said, though, 'Better an honest poor man than a rich liar.' Or, as my mum said, 'Not really,' as she read the Littlewoods catalogue with longing in her eyes – but it wasn't her running the business, was it?

Honesty may seem an unusual quality for a poker player too, though it isn't if you know the game. You're following the rules, after all, and a bluff isn't the same as a lie, though it's similar enough, I suppose, to provide a little titillation and relief for the honest man. Whatever, we all need a break from ourselves now and again, a safe little zone in which we can be someone else.

We don't get much passing trade in my shop, most of our business responds to our adverts. Anyone will tell you, even if you struggle like Samson at the wheel to prevent them, that the three rules of property are location, location, location. Well, the location of our shop is lousy, lousy, lousy. It used to be OK, OK, OK in the seventies when my dad bought it but it's in that large concrete development outside Worthing station, part of the gleaming sixties brave new world, before people decided they quite liked the dull, cowardly old one and moved all their shops away down the high street.

We try to make it comfortable, decking it out in plants and books so it's more like a living room than an estate agency. I think it's a tribute to our good taste that so many of the decorations have been stolen over the years.

Now it's just me, the ironmongers and the model shop that remain. We're the only ones who bought rather than rented our premises. My dad knew he was on to a loser but bought it anyway, reasoning that we should show faith in property.

'No one will know it's rented,' my mum said.

'I will,' he said.

At this point my mother rolled her eyes and snapped shut the Littlewoods catalogue in what I can only describe as a meaning-ful way.

We had to move and plans were in train for the business to go to the centre to try to cut it up against the big chains. I don't know why I'd been so reluctant to up sticks. I suppose it was because my dad thought he could make a success of it here and I wanted to prove him right, even if he was very demonstrably wrong.

So when the fat man I was to come to know as Paul Gilbert came in, pulling the dog behind him, it was into an empty shop. Empty apart from me and lovely Lucy. I'd given the other staff the afternoon off because I didn't want them to have to look at my long face. The staff were the three Andrews – Andrew, Andy and Drew – young and ambitious and gone in two years if they were half as good as they thought they were. An ideal combin-ation of cheap wages and hard work.

Lovely Lucy the secretary, however, said she had things to sort out and would stay for a while. I think she was just seeing that I was OK, as is the wont of the lovely. This was great in one way but not in another.

I like Lucy very much indeed but she makes me rather uncomfortable sometimes. I don't know what it is but there's something that emanates from her, a kind of frightening warmth, that gives me that feeling you get when you stand at the bottom of a skyscraper and look up – a sort of vertigo.

I think it's because I never feel quite at ease being looked after. Looking after, I'm fine, but I don't seem to be very good when the care's coming the other way. It's not her fault, she's my secretary, that's sort of her job, but still I feel I don't know where to put myself when she buys me one of my favourite Walnut Whips without me asking her to or organises a cake for me on my birthday. She'd just put a Walnut Whip on my desk when Gilbert came in.

'Ah, someone's here,' he said, fedora hat slanting one way, the cigarette-bearing smile the other. The dog turned to go. Even then I noticed something about the animal; he reminded me of a child who'd been dragged into a shop by his mum to get something waterproof and unfashionable and who, on hearing they didn't have it in exactly his size, was making tracks for the toy shop.

The heat was insufferable and the fan inadequate to its task. My shirt was tight and overbuttoned at the neck. This was actually nothing to do with the temperature. It was because the night before I'd managed to put a rust stain up my two best shirts with the iron and so was encased in an Auntie Gillian special. Auntie Gillian always buys me three shirts for Christmas but refuses to accept that I'm a sixteen-inch neck. 'You're more fifteen and a half,' she says, brooking no argument. So I say, 'Thank you, they're lovely,' and I put them in the drawer but before I know it I'm down to the last of the wash and fishing one out to iron in the morning.

Why the woman can't buy me one that's straightforwardly too small I don't know. 'Right on the edge of being OK but actually not,' I'd said to Lyndsey as I put it on, tight as a poultice, one morning.

'Sums up your life,' she said, taking the washing out of her machine where it had been running on Economy 7 during the night. Lyndsey is full of these jokes.

'Black humour!' I say.

'It's not humour,' she says, deadpan, which we both know is even more black humour. We do have a hoot.

Gilbert approached my desk as if under steam, billowing clouds of B&H descending.

'There's no dogs in the office,' I said. I don't know why we didn't allow dogs. We had a 'No Dogs' sign and since every shop has one I suppose we thought we'd be less of a shop without one. 'And no smoking,' I said.

'Right you are, chief,' said Gilbert, not removing the dog, in fact telling it to sit, while lighting a cigarette off the butt of his last. 'But I'm on the horns of a dilemma and I was wondering if you could help me out. You see, my mother has just died and I need to sort things out with the authorities. This is her dog, I'm stuck with him and I need someone to mind him just for an hour. Do you think you could do that? I can't leave him outside, he's quite valuable.'

The questions I might have had, the suggestions I might have proffered were as sandcastles before the tide of his words. 'My mother just died.'

Had I stopped to think, things might have been different. I mean, do we have authorities in England? No, we have incapabilities – the police complaints incapability, the rail incapability. I won't go on as I haven't got all day.

Suddenly I didn't see a strange man in a rather dodgy blazer and grey slacks that had given up trying to contain his girth and had decided to settle for a position of reasonable dignity somewhere around the low hips. I saw myself.

'Of course,' I said, 'yes, of course, yes, he can go in the staff room, give him here.'

'Thanks a lot,' he said, looking at his wrist where a watch

would have been if he'd had one. 'I really must get going, I'll be back in under an hour.'

And then he was off in a puff of smoke, with strange speed for a porker.

I looked at Lucy, she looked at me, we both shrugged and looked at the dog, who seemed to turn down his lower lip in a 'well, don't ask me' expression.

'Do you want a biscuit?' said Lucy, crouching in front of him and talking in that slightly over-loud way older people reserve for foreigners. Lucy's quite informally dressed in trendy shirt and three-quarter length skirt and when she bends, her legs and her back make a shape that I wish an employee's legs and back would not.

'Biscuit?' said Lucy.

The dog let out a noise rather like someone finally giving up in a breath-holding competition and wagged his tail.

'I think that's a yes,' I said.

Lucy stood and straightened her skirt, the bent S of her crouch seeming to unite with another backwards S to make an hour-glass.

I scribbled a note on my desk. 'Get out more often. Out out. Not poker out.'

It was a good tactic of mine, though, to try to think of Lucy as an arrangement of shapes and colours – a curve and some red for the lips, the dark swoop of the hair, a sheen on the skirt, the white of her skin. I didn't want these things connecting into a woman because that way a deal of misery might ensue and so I took her in in parts, which made many of our exchanges similar to those of the spotty schoolboy talking to the sexy teacher.

I was, after all, spoken for and she was my employee and so any suggestion of *that sort of thing* was out of the question. I was thinking this as she moved to the back of the shop and I took my eyes away from a shape at the back of her that it's pretty difficult not to associate with a woman.

I've never got over the suspicion that I employed her because she was so attractive. At the time, though, I thought it was her natural cheekiness that appealed to me.

'How would your friends describe you?' I asked at her interview.

'Oh, go on, rub it in,' she said.

This made me laugh. It takes a kind of courage to be like that and I liked it because her irreverence contrasted with my reverence. I mean, I called a parking warden 'sir' the other day.

The interview was two years ago. She'd be off to another job soon, doubtless. Hey ho.

Lucy went into the staff room at the back of the office, 8' × 6' and with an irrelevant facing aspect as it has no windows, some scope for development though no one will bother.

The dog looked at me and then trotted after her. He was an average-looking dog, really, of medium size – probably tall enough to come just over the knee if he was sitting down.

To me he looked rather like a large piece of lightly burnt toast, a golden brown on the legs and head but with a saddle of black across his back. The tail was curled over towards the back in a bushy question mark and the ears were like those of an Alsatian but more floppy. The eyes were strange too, deep brown but ringed in black, as if he was wearing a light kohl but unselfconsciously and with a strange dignity, like a teenager waking from a drunken sleep to wonder why his friends are laughing and his mum's make-up box is open.

Lucy led him back in behind a biscuit and I noticed the white at his front, like a smart bib. He was certainly a handsome dog, a bit like a small German shepherd but softer looking, with a way of panting that made him look as though he was laughing.

She fed him a biscuit, which he swallowed with a loud slap like a dolphin with a mackerel.

This clearly wasn't the end of proceedings as far as the animal was concerned. I've seen people project expectation before, in light coughs, in meaningful inclinations of the eye, in 'over to you' gestures. The dog, on not seeing another biscuit appear, took on a look of horror like a mother on the *Titanic* hearing there was no space on the lifeboat for her children.

'All gone?' he seemed to be saying. 'Can fate be so cruel?' For some reason I imagined him saying the word 'cruel' with two syllables, like Cruella but with the 'a' knocked off.

'All gone,' said Lucy, showing empty hands. I could see this wasn't true. There were three digestives and a custard cream on the desk.

The dog put his nose into the air and gave a knowing nod. Then he raised both paws in a kind of half begging gesture, dropped one shoulder as if he might roll over and finished by lowering his back legs slightly in a half sit – as if to say that, for the gift of further sweetmeats, he might be persuaded to perform all manner of tricks.

'I think he wants another,' said Lucy, laughing at his capers.

'I think he does,' I said.

The dog made a noise like the person in the breath-holding competition taking in air for a second go.

Another biscuit disappeared as if down a coal chute and he resumed his look of expectancy. For him, it appeared, satisfaction came and went in a tick, a flickering interruption in a life of permanent desire.

I put my head into my hands. Sweet as the dog was, I have to say that I wasn't in the mood.

What I was in the mood for I didn't know. Not for bank statements, though I took one from my desk drawer. When it comes to communications with financial organisations I have the attitude that what you don't know can't hurt you. This isn't true, as the last time the bailiffs came to repossess the office I didn't know I was £70,000 in debt on the business account and it would have hurt me considerably to see my only source of income removed. Luckily I'd had a big win the night before and was able to waft a few wads of cash in their direction as garlic towards the vampire.

Of course this proved a shock to the system and I was no longer £70,000 in debt. No, after weeks of careful play, I was £72,456.98p in debt, which represented a substantial cut in my spending, at least since my mum had been in decline.

I think at this point it would be helpful if I explained my approach to poker.

I am not a risk-taker, it has to be said. True, I have occasionally inserted a cotton bud into the ear canal of life and have used the toilets in McDonald's without having bought anything, but poker is not about increasing your risks, it's about minimising them.

The fascinating thing is that if you play the odds and act sensibly, it's an easy game. Really, it is. So I didn't accrue my £70,000 in gambling debts by taking risks. No, like most people, I got them backing certainties.

It made it rather difficult finding the money to bury Mum.

'Just put me out with the rubbish when I go,' she'd said.

'I've looked into that,' I'd said, 'and technically it's illegal.'

Still, I'd managed to pay for a decent funeral with the cheque her nursing company gave me after they'd taken their money out of the value of her flat. Also, brightly, I was OK for the coming month and could afford to pay the staff. As long as I was prepared not to eat anything for a while. Or drive my car. And to sit in the dark in the evenings. If I did that I reckoned I could summon enough money for about three games in the coming four weeks. Nothing, I know, but better than *nothing*.

I sat looking at the statement: £72,456.98p od. Od being overdrawn. I put my finger over the letters. Now that looked better.

The bell on the door went again and we looked up to see the

second odd-looking figure of the day. He was the first Texas oil baron sort of chap I think I'd ever seen in the shop.

He wore a cowboy shirt, a Stetson and cowboy boots, and I mean wore them. It's possible to have clothes like this on your body, for a fancy dress evening for instance, and not really be wearing them. With your slightly stiff demeanour, your mildly embarrassed smile, you're poking out from underneath them saying, 'Look, it's me really!' This chap fitted his Wild West gear like a mustang fits its skin – which is well, for those of you who have never clapped eyes on a mustang.

'Hello,' I said, 'can I help?'

'You just sit right where you are and I'll click my fingers if I want you to come running,' he said in very much the manner of J.R. Ewing. Despite his clothes I was surprised he had an American accent. Cowboys in Worthing are more common than you might think since the line dancing craze swept the WIs and Rotary clubs.

He went to the window and browsed up at it in the normal way.

Anyone who meets the public on a regular basis will tell you that it contains a heavy slice of scum. I'm reasonably used to being abused, as anyone who can't perform miracles or sell houses for a quarter of their proper value is in this game so his manner didn't really bother me too much.

He wiped sweat from his brow with what appeared to be a piece of toilet paper.

I looked out onto the sun-bleached concrete.

'Hot enough to fry an egg on your tongue out there, isn't it?' I said.

The dog looked sideways at me, as if this was something he was very much willing to try.

The man ignored me and just kept scanning the windows.

'Thought so, thought so,' he said. He turned to me as if he expected me to ask him exactly what it was that he thought but, since he'd been so rude, I didn't see fit to give him the satisfaction.

He looked at me with something approaching displeasure, though that may have been due to his cowboy boots, inappropriate footwear for – well, wearing on the feet really.

'I could buy every property in this window just on my credit card,' he said.

I was tempted to ask him why, if he was so rich, he didn't ditch the comedy clothes. Instead I just sat back in my chair and smiled, as if I was taking him seriously.

'That's got you to sit up and take notice, hasn't it, fellah?' he said. I was trying to place his accent. It wasn't exactly Texan, it seemed cut with something else. Vaguely Romford, actually.

The dog took his eye momentarily off a custard cream Lucy was dangling above his nose to size up the Texan. The Texan in turn sized up the dog.

'That's a good piece of dogflesh you got there for such a pesky little outfit,' he said, slightly intrigued. 'Tell me, where did you get one helluva mutt like that?'

'Are you interested in any of the properties?' asked Lucy pleasantly, the invisible, balancing side of her sentence saying, 'If not, why don't you just fuck off?'

'No I ain't!' said the Texan, 'If I wanted damp I'd go and lie in the Mississippi.'

'Is that in Texas?' I said, not ever being too good on the geography of North America.

'It and Dolly Parton!' he said. 'Now let me hunker down and take a look at this hound.'

He knelt before the dog, and as he did so I noticed that his bootlace tie was secured with a silver dog's head. He lifted an ear and looked within, as if he expected to see light coming out of it. Then he pulled up the flap of the lip and rubbed a finger over a tooth like I'd once seen my dad run his finger over the badge on an E-type. He measured the span of the back with his hand, he brushed the fur one way and then the other, he lifted the tail and ran his hand along its looping curl.

'Well, of all the places to find you!' he said.

The dog rolled his shoulders in what I took for a clear, 'Aw, shucks!'

'Let me introduce myself,' he said, looking at me properly for the first time. 'I'm James T. Wilkinson, you're at my service. Dogs are my life and my business. What is this Monopoly money you use? Pounds, ain't it?' He reached into his jacket and pulled out a bulging wallet. 'I'll give you five thousand for him here and now, what do you say?'

'Hang on a minute,' I said, 'what are you on about?'

'You know what I'm "on about"! Jesus, what language do you folks speak over here? Five thousand pounds for your dog here and now. Let me count it out.' He began thumbing £50 notes onto the desk in front of him.

'What are you doing?' I said.

'Five hundred, six hundred, seven hundred . . . oh, here, you count it, I'm done with this crazy cash.' He tossed me the wallet and I caught it, almost dislocating my wrist. It was absolutely stuffed with cash, overflowing with £50 notes. I was tempted to ask him if he played poker, but I didn't.

'Look,' I said, putting the wallet down on the desk, 'what is this about?'

'Yeah, very funny,' he said. 'I may not know a lot, mister, but I know dogflesh. And there is no way James T. Wilkinson passes up the opportunity to purchase a Sliding Wisehound of that quality. He'd be stud king of Tennessee!'

The dog looked as though this was a reasonably appetising prospect.

'Is Tennessee in Texas?' said Lucy.

'It and Disneyland,' he said. 'Just keep counting, and remember, you owe us one. If it wasn't for us, you'd be speaking German.'

'And if it wasn't for the French you'd be speaking English,' said Lucy.

'What?'

'Lafayette,' she said, rather sheepishly. 'Wasn't it the French that won the American War of Independence?' I recalled she'd ticked off a history A level the year before.

'Bollocks to Lafayette,' he said, which struck me as an un-American phrase and sentiment. 'Just get on with counting. Do you know how rare that dog is? Have you never heard of the Sliding Wisehound?'

'Sort of,' I said, as if I was au fait with the Wisehound, if not what you might call an expert.

He stared at me. 'You don't know, do you? Jeez! Still, I can't blame you. I thought at first he might have been a Creeping Foglemutt, or a Vaunting Storkstalker or even a Rough-furred Poisewoofer, which are quite similar though not as valuable. Some might mistake him for a Wheeling Warg but this is a Wisehound, for sure. There are only about thirty-two pairs of these dogs in the world and this one's about the best specimen I've ever seen. Look at that profile!'

The dog extended his chin proudly.

'Celebrity dog,' I said, which is one of those lame things people tend to say in such situations.

'Celebrity?' said James T. Wilkinson. 'This isn't a celebrity, my boy, this is a star! Do you realise how valuable that dog is? Well, OK, if you do, call it ten thousand. Just count the money straight out of the wallet there.'

I was going to reply but Lucy got there first. 'I'm afraid he's not ours,' she said with a laugh.

'Not yours? Well, whose is he? I want to talk to the herdsman not the steer. Get him out here. C'mon, where is he?' He looked around the office like a meerkat with an eye out for hawks.

'I've no idea where he is,' I said, 'but if you wait here he'll be back in an hour.'

Wilkinson looked at his wrist, although I noticed he didn't have a watch either. 'Nothing in this country works on time. I've gotta get a car in five minutes for business in town.' He reached into his jacket and produced a very impressive-looking card holder in leather. 'Take this and make sure he gets it,' he said, skimming a card towards me.

I picked it up off the desk and looked at it. 'James T. Wilkinson,' it said. 'Cows, dogs and oil – to the stars.'

I passed it to Lucy.

'Which stars do you supply oil, dogs and cows to?' she asked.

'Oh, I couldn't say,' he said, 'it's highly confidential.' Again he looked left and right, as if suspecting ambush. 'But let's just say that if the gentleman here had asked me that question I would have said, "Oh Papa, don't preach!" '

'Why's that?' I said. Lucy gave me a little dig with her foot.

'Must rush!' said Wilkinson, and he was gone in a blink, like a prairie dust devil.

'He knows Madonna!' said Lucy.

'Well, she's getting on but I think calling her a dog's a bit strong,' I said.

'That's who did "Papa Don't Preach"!' she said.

'So it is,' I said, remembering to exclude myself from any invitation to pop quizzes. Why would Madonna need to go to someone for oil? I wondered. Couldn't she get it from the garage like the rest of us?

'I bet he's going to sell this dog on to her for a fortune!' Lucy said.

The dog had a look about him that said he wouldn't be very much surprised if such a thing were to happen; in fact, that he would be mildly surprised if it didn't.

The phone rang. It was Lyndsey, my girlfriend of four years.

'Just checking you're OK,' she said.

'I'm fine,' I said. 'Bit spaced but fine.'

'I know,' she said.

There was a silence and I felt her sympathy coming down the phone towards me.

'Could I ask you,' she said, 'if you could drop in at Sainsbury's for some anchovies tonight? I'm going to be working late and I can't get them.'

'Sure,' I said. 'Do you want me to bring them over?'

'Tomorrow will do,' she said. 'Get some red grapes too. I'm out.'

Lyndsey was a bugger for her antioxidants.

'OK,' I said. 'You don't mind that I want to be alone tonight?'

'No,' she said. 'It'll give me a chance to catch up with the girls anyway. Why don't you go now, you can't be sitting in that office all afternoon in your state.'

'I'm looking after a dog,' I said.

'Whose dog?'

'A bloke just came in and said his mum had just died and could I look after her dog for ten minutes. Then another bloke came in and said it was a Sliding Focusmutt.'

'Wisehound,' said Lucy in the background.

'Wisehound,' I said, 'and offered ten thousand pounds for it. Weird, eh? He's left me his number to put the other bloke in contact with him.'

'I wouldn't do that if I were you,' said Lyndsey.

'Why not?'

'Offer the other bloke one thousand for it and take nine thousand yourself for it. That'd buy me a new Clio.'

She's been saving for a new Clio for about a year now, ever since the plastic wrapping on the seats of the old one had started to discolour. This has meant some very dull nights in.

'Ha ha,' I said.

'Ha ha,' she said back. She's full of these joke suggestions and 'ha ha' is always my response to them. Like that time the car was in for repair for two weeks and the tax ran out while they were fixing it. She suggested waiting two weeks until the new month began to renew it. Madness. I'd have been going around like Harrison Ford in *The Fugitive*.

'Love you like crazy!' she said.

This is something she's got off one of those films and she expected me to say it back, which I did. This is fine because I do love her but I don't necessarily find it easy to say so. Not all women, I know, would put up with this lack of enthusiasm.

We gave kisses down the phone, which revolts me but is the sort of thing some women expect, and I looked up to see the dog's owner coming through the door, like W.C. Fields through a turnstile.

'Hello,' I said. The dog didn't look over-pleased to see him. I wondered if he was as forthcoming with the biscuits as Lucy had been. If the dog was the sort that was fed on leftovers he was going to be a pretty hungry hound from the look of Mr Gilbert, who did not appear to be the sort to leave much over at all.

'Hi,' he said. He looked absolutely exhausted as fat people do on hot days. 'Do you mind if I sit down?'

'Go ahead,' I said. In truth I'd enjoyed the company of the dog and wasn't too keen to see him go. He was a friendly little chap. Plus, of course, I am the sympathetic sort and didn't mind being a shoulder to cry on for Gilbert.

'They found her this morning,' he said, lighting a cigarette, despite Lucy adding a second No Smoking sign to my desk with something of a clunk.

I didn't reply; there aren't many replies to that.

'She lived in the Caterham Flats. She'd been beaten to death,' he said, making a slight beating action with his hand. 'An intruder.'

'What about the dog, didn't he fend him off?' I said.

'Locked in the back room,' said Gilbert. 'He heard the whole thing. Poor little sod.'

The dog didn't look in urgent need of trauma counselling; a biscuit maybe, but counselling, no.

Gilbert started to shake slightly and put his head into his hands.

'I haven't even got the money to bury her,' he said, 'and I'm stuck with her dog and . . .' Big fat tears were coming down his big fat face. 'Where am I going to get two thousand pounds from?'

Lucy brought him a cup of coffee which he took gratefully.

'I lost my mum the other week,' I said.

'Burglars?' said Gilbert, rather like someone surveying the wreckage of his neighbour's cabbages and enquiring knowingly after slugs.

'It's a long story,' I said.

It was a long story. Over ten years, before the death of my dad, before I took over the business, before Lyndsey, before before. 'A terminal illness,' the doctor had told her. 'Interminable, more like,' she said, eight years into the coughing and the shaking and the physio and the medicine. I didn't mind looking after her, though. When my dad went she didn't really have anyone but me and it's rewarding to care for someone.

'I can hear it if you like,' said Gilbert.

'I don't think it would help,' I said. 'It was just a nervous system thing. She died last week.'

Now tears were coming up in me too. 'You'll be with dad again,' I'd said to her, at the last. 'I'd rather banked on going to heaven,' she'd wheezed.

Then she was gone, leaving me alone in a flat whose value had been mortgaged against nursing care and wondering where best to get rid of her eighties flatpack furniture.

'I'm sorry,' said Gilbert, and I felt a bond between us.

'I'm OK,' I said, feeling spaced out. 'I might be able to help you, though.'

'Oh yes?' said Gilbert, pricking up his ears like an old setter who'd seen too much of the game pie.

'Funnily enough,' I said, 'if you want to get rid of that dog, I know someone who would take it.'

'He's a valuable dog,' said Gilbert, through a scarf of smoke. 'I've had an offer of fifty pounds for him. I need all the money I can get for the funeral.' The word funeral seemed to be particularly painful to him and he snivelled into his cigarette.

'We can do better than that, can't we?' said Lucy, clearly pleased to be able to help, although directing the fan at him.

'We certainly can,' I said. 'We had a man in here just a second ago who said he'd pay . . .'

I don't know why I had to do it in gameshow fashion, with a dramatic pause just before the number but I did.

'More than fifty pounds?' said Gilbert, looking like the boy who had only ever wanted a bicycle for his birthday receiving that very bicycle. 'I hope it's not too much because if I get too much I'll be back to blowing it all on drink and my life will be a right mess.'

'Ten thousand pounds!' I said.

Gilbert looked at me in utter disbelief, as well he might. The fan blew the streaming smoke back from his face so he looked as if he was moving forward at speed.

'It's a Sliding Musclebarker,' I said.

'Wisehound,' said Lucy.

'Sorry, Wisehound,' I said, 'and it's worth ten thousand pounds.'

The dog looked up at me in a manner that seemed to convey this was a conservative estimate.

Gilbert had stopped crying and was staring at me with the surprise of the man with the cabbage problem finding that a tiny spaceship had been responsible for all the damage.

'I . . .' He didn't know what to say, I could tell.

'I've got his number here,' I said, handing over the card. 'Just give him a bell and he'll pay you cash. Between you and me I think you might get a bit more than ten thousand. He's loaded and not very nice. I'd screw him for every penny he's got if I was you.'

The dog seemed to nod. There was a bit of a 'natch' to him.

Gilbert looked at the card, and shook his head in total disbelief, like the cabbage gardener peering into the windows of the tiny spaceship to see them drawing up plans for a crack at his carrots.

'I haven't got time,' he said, in a rather strange way. He took off his hat to reveal a bald head troubled by the sort of hair density you normally find at the bottom of a dirty bath.

'What do you mean?' I said. 'You can use our phone right here.'

'No!' he said. 'Er, you call. Look, you're an agent, why don't you take some commission on this? I think it only right.' He held his hat to his chest as if he might at any moment burst into song.

Lucy looked at me with concern.

'I won't hear of it,' I said. 'No, this is your money, it's your dog. You need the money. No.'

Gilbert drummed his fingers on the table.

'I need the money now,' he said, whispering, but louder than he normally spoke.

'You have to bury her right now?'

'No,' he said. 'Just pay. Look. Why don't you broker the deal? You give me, say, two thousand up front now for the undertakers and I'll pay it back plus a little extra when this money comes through. You can keep the dog as collateral.' He banged the desk in a 'Sold!' manner.

'I don't want a little extra,' I said.

Again he looked at me in that strange way, like someone trying to work out which way round a modern painting went.

He sat back in his chair, he lit another cigarette, he looked at the ceiling, he looked at the floor. He had the air of an expert on *Gardeners' Question Time* trying to come up with a solution to an infestation of spaceships but finding himself at something of a loss.

'Well, if you could just front me the . . . oh, cobblers to it,' he said.

The dog's ears went back as if it was he and not Gilbert who was in the fan draught.

Lucy, I noticed, had gone back to sit at her desk and was peering round her computer at Gilbert like Jerry looking for Tom.

'Cobblers to what?' I said. I don't like rough talk in the office but I was prepared to make an exception because he seemed in such a difficult situation.

'It,' he said with a shrug. 'You don't get it, do you?'

I was going to say 'Get what?' but there seemed limited point.

'Everyone in the world sees the angle,' he said. 'Ten thousand, the guy's offering you ten thousand. I only want two thousand. Even if you're feeling generous, which no one ever is, you tell me he's offering two thousand five hundred at the most and pocket the rest.'

'That would be dishonest,' I said, 'and immoral.'

The dog tilted his head at Gilbert in a 'point proven, over to you' sort of way.

'Well, rink my dink, I've met the last boy scout,' said Gilbert. 'You're an estate agent, how do you ever survive?'

'I don't understand what you're on about,' I said. I looked at the dog and then back round at Lucy. Both wore expressions that said, 'Don't ask me.'

'No, you don't, do you?' He was shaking his head and looking at me in total disbelief. His voice had changed subtly, I'd noticed. Nothing much, just a harder edge, more streetwise.

He laughed. I looked around for the dog. It had gone.

'It's incredible,' he said. 'You're too much of a patsy to be a patsy. It's a con. There is no Sliding Wisehound.'

'It's gone into the staff room,' said Lucy.

'The mutt we just found outside the station is in the staff room,' he said, 'and the buyer, Mr Wilkinson, known to friends as Texas Tim from Epping, is currently waiting unseen with a very good view of this office so that when I emerge with two thousand pounds of your money he gets his cut before I have a chance to dip my paw into it. We saw you coming back in the funeral car, we saw you were an estate agent. Vulnerable and greedy, we couldn't miss. And we missed!'

'But you'd lose out on eight thousand pounds,' I said.

'Hahhaa!' said Gilbert, with a hoot like a locomotive's whistle. 'There is no eight thousand pounds, the Texan's in on it with me. And he's not a Texan. We'd get you to pay us two thousand of your own money, you twonk. The number you've got belongs to a cheap pay-as-you-go mobile which will be thrown into the nearest canal as soon as the deception is complete.'

'Oh!' said Lucy, suddenly putting two and two together while I was still umming and ahing somewhere around the equals sign.

'We saw the money!' I said.

'Forged notes,' he said, laughing and actually slapping his knee, 'and not very good ones at that! Normally people can't believe they've been conned when they've been conned but you can't believe you haven't been conned when you haven't been conned.' The sentence seemed to puzzle him but then I seemed to puzzle him.

'What if I'd taken the money and told the Texan the dog had run away?'

'No one ever does. I don't know why but they don't. Sometimes people try to take the bent cash but then the Texan finds a sudden need to be somewhere else. It's flawless. Apart from the fact that it relies on you being . . .' he pondered, 'not exactly dishonest but mishonest. Something like that.'

'What made you think we had two thousand pounds on the premises?' I said, suddenly wishing him out of my shop.

'The safe,' he said.

'My dad had that put in,' I said. 'I don't know why. It's where we keep the Christmas party decorations.'

He put his head back into his hands.

'For the love of man,' he said. 'I'm going back to old ladies, they're a lot easier.'

'You're a crook!' I said, somewhat behind the game, I'll admit.

'Yes,' he said, nodding slowly as if to an idiot, or to an idiot if you want to be absolutely specific about it. 'Just give me the mutt and I'll stop polluting your air and go and find myself a proper sucker. They used to grow on trees but the country's going to the dogs.'

He drew the last out of his cigarette and stubbed it out on one of the No Smoking signs. He then pulled another fag from his packet, stood, called, 'Here, boy!' and dropped dead.

He hit the floor like something wet. We later found his unlit cigarette, which had flown from his body very much like the soul-bearing eagle used to from the Roman emperors, wedged into the lovely Lucy's Rolodex.

I'd seen someone die suddenly before. My father, who I loved and who – well, no need to go into that. He was killed in a cycling accident that could have killed me. I only say so because it has entered my mind that watching this man die was unusually painful for me, more so than it would have been for a normal person – for whom it would have been painful enough. It's one of the things I use to help me explain what happened afterwards.

Gilbert had fallen forwards very heavily, narrowly missing banging his head on my desk.

I am ashamed, and I know Lucy is ashamed, that we both assumed this was part of some further con. It's amazing how quickly you can go from complete trust in the extra-ordinary to doubting the obvious through the medium of a con man.

'If you're expecting me to pay for a taxi to get you to hospital then I'm afraid that's out of the question,' I said to what I now know was the corpse of Paul Gilbert.

The corpse said nothing.

Lucy and I maintained a dignified silence. After about a minute, the sort of long minute a teacher spends waiting for a class to be quiet, Lucy said, 'He did fall rather heavily.'

I had to concede that he did.

'He's got blood coming out of the side of his mouth,' said Lucy.

'It could be a pellet,' I said, to my lasting shame.

'I'll take his pulse,' said Lucy, who has always struck me as the decisive sort.

'Make sure you haven't anything valuable on you first,' I said. I'm not proud of any of this.

Lucy removed her earrings at some distance and then approached the body. She put her fingers to the side of his neck.

'Well, if it's a con it's a bloody good one,' she said. 'I think we need to call an ambulance.'

'Hold a mirror to his nose,' I said.

'What for?' said Lucy.

'Why do you think, woman, so he can check his eyeliner? To see if he's breathing.'

Lucy let the sarcasm go; I think she was alive to the stress of the situation. 'He's not breathing,' she said. 'He isn't moving at all. You call an ambulance and I'll start heart massage.'

I did as I was bid as Lucy struggled to turn the great fat corpse over. He wouldn't budge.

The rest is a blur. Us trying to move him, him not being moved, the blue lights, the medics' questions, the police taking our numbers for a statement. The Texan was nowhere to be seen.

Then they were gone and Lucy and I were alone again in the shop.

'Do you fancy a drink?' she said, slightly ashen-looking.

I looked at my watch. Seven forty-five. There was a game at Snake Eyes' place but it didn't get going really until around ten, once all the bullshit had been bullshat and latecomers waited for. That's what I meant when I told Lyndsey that I wanted to be alone – that I wanted to play poker. You're never as alone as you are at a poker table, I think I once heard in some Memphis song. Seven forty-five.

I could manage a quick one.

We were both stunned, unable to discuss really what had gone on. My mind was buzzing like a wasp in a jam jar, my dad, my mum, Gilbert hitting the floor, the great raw squelch of his fall.

I went into the back of the shop to turn off the lights and then I realised what we'd forgotten.

Asleep on one of the low chairs was the dog, the curl of his tail wrapped round him like a cloak.

'Oh no,' I said, 'I'd forgotten about you. Lucy, we've forgotten the dog!'

I don't know what it is that makes men shout for women like that when faced with mild crises. I don't think it's far off from calling for your mum. This is particularly strange for someone like me. I regard asking anyone for help as a huge imposition and go out of my way to avoid getting any. Faced with a crisis, though, I call for a woman. Stick that on your couch and analyse it.

My shouting woke the dog and he blinked up at me.

I patted him on the head and looked into his eyes. 'What in the name of God are we going to do with you?' I said.

'Well, if it's not an awful strain,' said the dog, with a pant, 'I could murder a drink of water.'

2

Barking

Where are the lines drawn – between good and evil, between sane and mad?

I don't know exactly. It's difficult to say, isn't it? The celestial umpire isn't like a tennis judge – he knows the ball can be in and out at the same time. One thing on which psychiatrists concur, however, is that if a dog says anything to you outside of the 'woof', 'bark' and occasional growl range, then you are nuttier than a squirrel's larder.

'Biscuits gum the teeth,' said the dog, drawing back his lips in illustration. 'I have humbly begged for a cleansing bone for some time but you've appeared deaf to my entreaties. Think nothing of it, you have had other things on your mind and you are as the moon whereas I am naught but a varlet.'

'We haven't got a bone,' I said, wondering what a varlet was. Actually, this does scant justice to the tumbling cargo of my mind. Some mental momentum tried to propel my thoughts forward on their regular track despite the fact that the lorry of reality in which they were contained had clearly gone round a very sharp bend indeed.

'Another biscuit, then, I know, is the smallest gift your beneficence will allow,' said the dog with a kind of gracious half bow. I didn't even know I had a beneficence, or what one was for that matter.

This was disturbing. I was led to the inescapable conclusion that one of us in the room was barking – and it wasn't the dog.

'Won't another biscuit gum the teeth further?' I said. Well, what do you do when your lid flips? I know that talking to the animal would be seen by my mum as 'encouraging it' but what other course of action was open to me? Go back in to Lucy and say, 'I'm afraid I've been in conversation with a canine. An unacceptably two-way conversation. Kindly alert the men from the funny farm'? No, you ask it if another biscuit might gum the teeth further.

'You might as well get shot for a sheep as a lamb!' said the dog, hooting out the words through a laugh, as if he found the idea immensely funny.

'Don't you mean hung?'

The dog looked puzzled. 'Everyone I've ever heard of's been shot for sheep-worrying. My great-grandfather only just escaped it himself and the only reason he went near the flock was because he was returning something that one of them had dropped. And may I respectfully submit that the proper word is hanged? A person is hanged, a picture is hung.'

I found this disquieting. Not only that the dog was talking to me but that he appeared to be fully up to speed on grammatical rules which of I had no knowledge of. You see what I mean?

'Are you OK back there?' Lucy was shouting from the front of the shop.

'Where are we off to then, boss?' said the dog with some zeal. In a second he'd gone from talking like an Elizabethan courtier to rasping out his words in the manner of a GI on a twelve-hour pass asking the whereabouts of the really hot clubs in town.

I couldn't say anything, I just stood there feeling alone, the only one like me in the world – like I did that time when I'd been looking through the Yellow Pages and realised there were twenty people making a living out of trophy manufacture in my area – more than Chinese restaurants – and yet I had never won one.

Madness was all I needed right then, save for a home, running a business, planning my life without my sick mum. I simply did not have a window for lunacy. 'I'm sorry, Mr Barker cannot come and value your house, I'm afraid he's away with the fairies this afternoon.' Not on, is it?

'My liege and guiding light,' said the dog, 'are we off to the park for something to eat or are we to prevail upon the hospitality of relations in order to obtain cakes and tea?' He got down from the chair and buried his head in the side of my leg. 'I am your puppet, sir,' he said, looking up at me.

'I've got cakes and tea myself if I want them,' I said, still not fully with it.

'Yer what?' said the dog. 'Then let there be no delay! Let's return to our home instantly and begin our work upon them in earnest. I haven't wrapped me barking gear around any food in a week!'

'What?' said Lucy, coming back into the staff room.

'Ah, the leader's mate,' said the dog. 'I shall defer,' and with that he flipped over onto his back and lay looking up at her.

'She's not my mate,' I said.

'What are you on about?' said Lucy. 'Ooh, it's that dog! I forgot about him.'

'My lady of the digestives,' said the dog, nodding graciously towards Lucy despite the awkward angle of his repose.

'Did you hear that?' I said.

'What?' she said, which is as good as a 'no'. I had no previous experience in the matter but I felt sure that those who had just heard a dog speak were unlikely to reply 'What?' to such a question. Swooning, exclaiming 'Egad!' or at the very least phoning major circuses would be the response I was looking for.

'Hear what?'

I was staring at the animal in incredulity, there being very few other acceptable ways to stare in such circumstances.

'Did that dog make a noise?'

'He sort of slapped his chops,' she said. 'What kind of noise?'

'Umpalumpa! Stick it up your jumper!' shouted the dog. 'How's that for a noise?'

'That sort of noise,' I said.

'You mean barking?' said Lucy.

I breathed in. When he'd spoken she'd heard a slap, when he'd shouted a bark. I, however, had heard a children's nonsense rhyme I'd completely forgotten. I am no psychologist but I thought this a fairly significant gulf in our perception of events.

'You're shaking,' said Lucy. 'Are you OK? You haven't looked very well for a while. Why don't you sit down?'

'I'm OK,' I said. 'There's no need to bother yourself.'

'Please,' said Lucy, 'you look awful.' She gestured to the recently vacated seat.

'I will,' I said. 'My knees are like jelly.'

The dog sat upright in an elegant roll and licked at my knees. 'Trouser-flavoured jelly, the rarest gift, brought on camel trains from the lands of Araby,' he said, tapping his tongue against his palate. 'Drainpipe flavour is the best, they taste rather like liquorice. I think plus fours were only popular because of the advertising: "Get More With Plus Fours". Dog advertising is always more successful when it dwells on quantity rather than quality.'

'He likes you,' said Lucy. The dog had rested his head on my leg.

'He also likes water,' said the dog, with a slightly theatrical rasp.

'Oh, the poor thing's coughing, he's probably got kennel

cough. Shall we get him a drink of water? Listen to him, he sounds terribly husky.'

'Actually,' said the dog, 'huskies have Icelandic accents on the whole.' He seemed to find this terribly funny. 'I'm from Basildon, though the nice part. The water is a good idea, though. And perhaps some chocolate cake to go with it. I'm commonly fed on chocolate cake, it's something of a staple diet for hounds of my tooth, that and the very rarest cuts of steak.' He panted extravagantly, a huge scarf of a tongue adding rather too much emphasis to the point.

Lucy scrabbled about inside the cupboards for a container for the dog's water.

'Can I get you anything?' she said.

'Oh, don't worry about me,' I said.

'I am worrying about you,' she said. 'What would you like?'

'I'd like a cup of tea,' I said. I looked at the dog. 'Do you think he was a stray?' Pretty much everything I was saying at that moment was in an open-mouthed, slack-jawed sort of way, rather like an old bloodhound looking out of the top floor window to see next door's cat parading through his dahlias.

'I was a chartered libertine until I met those two gentlemen,' said the dog, lowering his muzzle in what appeared to be a gracious acknowledgement that I was right.

'Which one is your mug?' said Lucy.

'I don't have a particular one,' I said. Why she asked me that I don't know, she'd made tea for me enough times in the past.

'Oh yeah,' she said. 'I forget. Everyone else has these novelty ones.' I knew what she meant: 'I'm not overweight, I'm under tall', 'The Boss!' Garfield illustrations etc. I'd never bothered.

'No mug?' said the dog, sitting upright with his ears as alert as they could manage – pushing forward but bent over at the top. 'A man's got to have his own mug or no one will respect him. It's the three ts of life, mate – territory, territory, territory!'

'Lucy?' I said.

'Yes?'

'This dog, does there seem anything unusual about him? And what's a chartered libertine?'

She looked at me like I'd gone mad which, I was certain, was the appropriate way to look at me.

'He's very bright-looking,' she said, 'and a chartered libertine's a thing from Shakespeare.' Lucy was arty and was doing A-level English at evening class. 'Years ago you couldn't just wander everywhere, you needed a king's charter to move about. That's what a chartered libertine is,' she said, above the sound of the dog slapping down his water. 'Why do you ask?'

'I have such a charter!' said the dog, stretching his nose into the air and looking down at me like a Roman upon a barbarian at the gate. Not a bad achievement, considering he was a good three feet below me as he did it.

'Where's this charter?' I said.

'Can't find it,' said the dog, tucking his nose into his shoulder, and looking extravagantly sneaky.

'What do you mean, where is it?' said Lucy.

She passed me my cup of tea, instructing me to de-bag it myself. Then she sat down on a chair next to me.

'The mistress reclaims her seat, the order is reinforced,' said the dog, with a deep air of satisfaction.

'Why are you on about libertines?' said Lucy with a fairly deep look of concern. 'Aren't they a band?'

'It just popped into my head,' I said.

Lucy's look of concern deepened to that area of concern that's so deep it's only visible through the use of pressure-reinforced cameras and has blind sea beasts wriggling about around it.

'I wonder if someone's missing him,' said Lucy, talking about the dog but looking at me. 'Maybe they stole him from outside a shop.'

Gilbert had said they found him outside the station, although why I was suddenly going to start believing him I didn't know.

'No one is missing me,' said the dog. 'I am not missed.' He said the last part of the sentence in a kind of 'pity the tale of me' sort of way, with an extravagant sob in his voice. At the time I thought he was hamming it up, if you can accuse a dog of overacting (I've since found out that Lassie is considered very wooden, Hooch of *Turner and Hooch* lays it on with a trowel and Scooby Doo is very moving, to dogs). But the dog wasn't faking on this occasion. What I now know is that dogs are immersed fully in the way they feel at any second, they approach the swimming pool of emotions from the top board rather than slipping in quietly at the shallow end like humans. If a dog tells a sad story to its pack, it's not uncommon for the whole lot of them to be weeping like Italians at a Rossini by the end of it and singing as they root through a bin ten seconds later.

'I think we'd better call up the RSPCA or someone,' said Lucy. 'Perhaps he's been reported missing.'

'There has been no report!' said the dog, looking as if he might swoon, like a nineteenth-century lady in the presence of ribaldry. 'Just one more biscuit for a wretch, I beg you.' He put his paw on Lucy's leg and looked up into her eyes.

'I wonder what his name is,' said Lucy, chucking him under the chin.

'Reg,' said the dog, lowering his head. 'A gentleman of the canine persuasion.'

'I think Gilbert said he was called Reg,' I said.

The dog shrank into his shoulders. 'I apologise for my earlier role, sir,' he said, 'but I, like you, was the victim of deception.'

'What do you mean?' I said.

'He said he had a treat in his pocket and I followed him in. I can see it now, of course, giddy fool that I was. I could smell nothing but he seemed so plausible!'

'Do you think he's hungry?' said Lucy, who was looking at me rather oddly.

'The lady will be pleased to hear that I am starving!' said the dog, suddenly dropping the abject act and standing up stiff as if someone had plugged his tail into the mains.

'He looks hungry,' I said.

'Andwhatyouseeiswhatyouget!' said the dog in one hot breath.

Lucy looked untroubled by this. So it was only me who could hear the dog. I was in a minority of one, a tigger, a nut, registered with the kennel club as a two-footed moonhowler.

'I think we should call the RSPCA or the Dog's Trust,' said Lucy, 'although he's lovely. I'd love to keep him, oh, I really would. He's gorgeous, isn't he? Look at him.'

'Act on your desire, madam,' said the dog, with the confidential tone of a counsellor to the Queen. 'That is my strong advice.'

'Fine,' I said. 'I'll call the RSPCA.'

'Don't let them put me back in the cage!' shouted the dog.

I leant down as if to pat him and pressed my mouth to his ear.

'Don't worry,' I whispered, 'you're coming home with me tonight.'

I'd lost it completely, that was certain. I didn't know exactly how I'd lost it but I figured that the dog might help at least work out where I'd last seen it, if not actually find it again.

'Thank you, sir, thank you! That would be my dearest wish! Your munificence is boundless,' said the dog, pumping up and down on his front paws as if playing a spirited ragtime on a piano. He had some difficulty with the word 'munificence', pronouncing it something like 'munifiiffffence'. The thing was, if this was a hallucination, I actually didn't know what a munificence was and, if I had one, where I might keep it. So where was it coming from?

I went out into the office to my phone. It wasn't the RSPCA I wanted to call but an agency charged with the care of humans.

I phoned my doctor. As it was out of hours I was connected to a switchboard. Press one if you're dying, two if it really could wait until your own doctor is available, three if you've got low self-esteem and just want to feel someone cares about you, four if it's a hoax, that sort of thing. When the GP's not on call, it goes through to an agency who refer you to a doctor who's covering for your own.

The switchboard operator took my details then asked me what was wrong with me.

'Well, if I knew that I wouldn't need a doctor, would I?' I said.

'Arsey!' I was sure I heard him say before the phone began ringing again. A woman answered and he told her my name before handing me over.

'Hello, what's the problem?' she said. 'Archie, I'm working, take Gemima into the back room if you must strangle her.'

'I'm hearing voices,' I said as low as I could, 'in my head.'

'You do know you're on the telephone?' said the doctor.

'Yes, not your voice, other voices. Well, a voice, really.'

'I see. When did this come on?'

'My dog just started speaking to me.' So he was my dog, was he?

I looked to see if Lucy was listening to me but I could hear her saying, 'You're gorgeous,' and the dog replying, 'Yes, but I have been cruelly treated, just one more digestive if you please. In half, I have a delicate constitution. Hurry up, woman!'

'What's he said?' said the doctor.

'He's asked for a drink of water.'

'No threats?'

'No.'

'No hinting that you might do harm, to yourself and others?'

'No. He's giving advice, though.'

'What sort of advice is this dog giving?'

'He's telling me to be more forceful and assertive about

territory. I've got to have my own mug at work, and ı go mad if anyone else uses it.'

'Man's got to have his own mug,' mused the doctor

'Ooh, that's where the relief lies,' said the dog from the staff room. 'There's the nub, rub right behind the ear. Careful with those, lady! They're attached to my head!'

'This isn't particularly helping,' I said.

'My Auntie Beryl used to have a budgie that talked,' said the doctor, sounding as if she was trying her best.

'Did it offer advice?'

'It was only a cheap one,' she said.

There was a pause on the phone, sum tum-ti-tumming and a drumming of fingers.

'How old are you, Mr Barker?' said the doctor.

'Thirty-three.'

'Well, you've had a good innings.'

'A good innings? I'm in my prime.'

'Sorry,' she said, 'I've just returned from voluntary service in Somalia. Alters your perspective on things.' I heard her blow out her cheeks. 'Any shocks or disturbances recently, mindful of the fact that this is an emergency service and I am only paid ten minutes per patient?'

'My mum died. I looked after her for ten years. She was terminally ill.'

I didn't mention Gilbert dropping dead in front of me as I didn't think at the time that it had affected me too much.

'I know she was terminally ill,' said the doctor, 'you just said she died.'

'Don't get testy,' I said.

'Sorry.' She apologised a lot for a doctor. She'd have to keep a lid on that if she was going to make it to retirement without being on the receiving end of a major damages award.

'What's your clearest memory of your mother?' she said with a sigh.

'The funny thing is,' I said, 'I have no clear memory of her. I can't see her at all. Even though I saw her every day for the last ten years I can't see her in my mind's eye.'

My own words shocked me slightly. I'd never realised this before. I felt my mum as a presence, an odour of chrysanthemums, a Lenored towel, diffuse and untouchable.

I heard the flipping of some pages and, 'Eenie, meenie, minie mo, halide, halitosis, hallucinations, there we go. Diagnosis, prescription. There we are. Ah!' she said. 'There's the answer. Visit your own doctor in a few days if things don't get any better, that's the gist of it!'

'The tail pit requires attention. Rub it there, ma'am, just on the back,' the dog was saying.

'This is an emergency,' I said

'Well, I can hardly class it as one. I mean, is he saying anything now? Yes, dear. No, not the normal numbers, add a few over thirty, they're less popular so we won't have to share it if we win. Plus your mother's birthday. Oh, hang on.'

'Just that he wants stroking,' I said.

There was a pause. The doctor adopted a hushed tone.

'Hmm, this might be a long shot. He hasn't said anything about lottery numbers, has he?'

'I'll ask,' I said. 'Any ideas for this week's lottery numbers?' I shouted through. I figured Lucy would think I was talking to her.

'I think it's going to be high,' she said, 'a lot in the thirties.'

'It's a waste of money,' shouted the dog, with his mouth full. 'You'd make more on the greyhounds, as well as providing valuable employment for dogs.'

'He says it's a waste of money,' I said to the doctor.

'Hmm.' The doctor seemed to be thinking. 'It doesn't sound anything particularly serious, Mr Barker. You might not be rational but the dog clearly is. If I were you I'd just nip along to your own GP on Monday. Archibald, a noose is entirely inappropriate!'

So much for the medical profession, I thought, putting down the phone.

'What did the RSPCA say?' said Lucy, coming into the office.

'They said there were no reports of a dog like him missing and to take him in tomorrow,' I said.

We sat for a few minutes in silence, just looking at each other. The events of the day had been hard to take in for Lucy, I thought, and she was galloping two events down on the field to me – no mother's funeral and no yacking hound to contend with.

Eventually Lucy broke the silence. 'So we've a guest for the night, have we?' she said, the second inappropriate use of 'we' I'd experienced in the space of a few minutes.

'Actually,' I said, 'where is he?'

We looked around but the dog was nowhere to be seen. Lucy went to the staff room but it was one hound short of containing a dog.

'Reg?' I said.

There was a noise from below my desk, like bog drainage.

I crouched down to see the dog with something in his mouth.

'This is a very strange sausage,' said the dog, without removing whatever it was from his teeth. 'Less flavour than the usual variety but not wholly unpleasant.'

'Just partially unpleasant, then,' I said.

'Oh yes,' said the dog, sucking at what looked more like a pasty. 'That's where the challenge lies.'

'Give that here,' I said.

'The pack leader has demanded, therefore I must yield,' said the dog, 'though might I formally request he leave some of the very tenderest parts for me.' I wondered when I had become pack leader. I have to say, though, thinking of myself in that way did send a ripple of pride up my spine. The other thing that struck me was how normal it felt to have the dog talking. In the space of ten minutes it had come to seem like the most natural thing in the world.

He spat forth the package and I picked it up. It was a purse, shiny as a berry and ripe to bursting with whatever was inside.

'What is it?' said Lucy, approaching from the staff room.

'More forged notes, I guess,' I said, picking up the piece of kitchen roll Lucy had carried the biscuits in and wiping the purse dry.

I put the purse on the desk. It had the motif of a collie dog picked out in gold in its lower left corner and was secured by a brass crossover clasp. I wondered what Gilbert had been doing with a woman's purse.

'It looks a bit high quality for that bloke,' said Lucy. She clicked it open before you could say 'That's police evidence, we'd better not touch it'.

Money burst out as if it had been spring-loaded.

'Look at all this!' said Lucy, picking up a £50 note and holding it up to the light. 'It's a real one!'

'I think we should call the police,' I said. 'The owner of this will want it back.'

Lucy was already into the purse, though, like an anteater at a termite's mound.

'There's ID in here,' she said, 'and keys.'

There was one of those small cardboard address labels inserted into a cheap plastic key ring.

'Mrs Cadwaller-Beaufort,' it said. 'If found, please return to Charterstone BN99 AE9–BN98 DR3.'

Someone whose house covered two postcodes. I'd never known that before.

The note, I thought, was a communication from a different age. To the owner it clearly said, 'Here are my purse and keys. Please be so good as to return them.' To the twenty-first-century finder, however, it said, 'Here is my bottom. Kindly burgle it off.'

There was a further card inside the purse. Eastbourne and District Libraries.

The library card photo was a strange one. At first I took it for a still life of a cabbage patch but then I realised it was a photo of an old lady – one of those you get from the booths – staring from a wall of dogs, utterly endogged in fact. There were so many dogs that it was difficult to tell exactly how many. I counted four collies, a couple of Scotties and a Peke the first time around but when I looked again, a Jack Russell seemed to have appeared from nowhere and a collie was missing.

I noticed myself feeling relieved that Reg wasn't in the picture. I couldn't have formed an attachment to him that quickly, could I?

Lucy brought the area A–Z over.

'Crikey!' she said. 'This place looks like it's visible from space.'

I looked down at the large white blob on the map – Charterstone and grounds. Nothing was marked on it at all, other than the word 'private'.

'Have you ever heard of this place?' said Lucy.

I thought I had, somewhere, years back. It was outside my office's area of operation so I couldn't have come across it through work. Where had I heard of it before?

I looked down at the money. There had to be one thousand pounds there. If I took that to a game that evening, won maybe two thousand, I'd be able to give the money back to its owner and be on the road to recovery myself.

'Come on,' said Lucy.

'What?' I said.

'Let's go and take it back.'

'Retrieval, sir,' said the dog at my side. 'There is no higher calling.'

I looked at my bank statement. Perhaps she was right. One evening in my life, I thought, I can stay out of trouble.

3

Fetch

In my years as an estate agent I'd never come across a property that was marked on a road map before but there it was, the stately home symbol and 'Charterstone' next to it, a clear space the size of your thumbnail, as if someone had taken the corner of an eraser to the tiny roots of B roads which fell from the mighty tuber of the M23 to London.

'What are you doing with your nose up the window?' I said to the dog. The Audi was an estate, so we'd put him in the back of the car. There are questions you can ask of a dog in front of other people and they won't think you strange. This is one of them. I've since discovered that 'What do you think I should do about my troubled relationship?' isn't.

'I'm writing,' said the dog.

'Left here,' said Lucy.

'What?' I said.

'Left here,' said Lucy, who thought I was talking to her.

'A help note,' said the dog, with desperation in his voice. 'We're trapped in a box and the world is sliding by! Get us out!' he said. 'I'm surprised to see you're not doing anything about our predicament, just sitting there playing with that frisbee on your lap.'

'Can you write?' I said.

'What?' said Lucy.

'Not while it keeps swaying around like this,' said the dog, making a large smear across the back window while we turned.

'The world isn't moving, we're moving through it.' I sang this, as if it was some song I knew, so that Lucy wouldn't realise I was talking to the dog.

'Don't be ridiculous,' said the dog. 'Look, I'm sitting perfectly still.' He gave a shiver. 'Not natural,' he said. 'I could try barking endlessly at it to see if it stops zinging on by like this if you like.'

'That won't be necessary,' I said.

Lucy looked at me rather strangely. 'How are you bearing up under everything?' she said.

'He's just fine!' said the dog.

One thing is for sure. If someone's concerned about your mental state, telling them your dog says you're fine is not likely to offer them much reassurance.

In certain English tourist brochures you're invited to 'step back in time'. This isn't always a good thing. On my one visit to Liverpool, for instance, I managed to get lost and ended up stepping back in time to what appeared to be the middle of the Toxteth riots of the 1980s. Likewise, if you ever visit a hospital or use public transport in the UK you'll receive a fascinating insight into the operating standards of the Middle Ages that any theme park would struggle to rival. However, as we left Worthing with its 1980s pre-boom feel and made our way past Brighton – which had a kind of defining moment in the 1960s and never recovered from it – I was pleased to be winding back the clock.

It's amazing how quickly you can go from a twenty-first-century jam on an early seventies motorway to stick and leaf lanes that seem untouched by progress or repair workers.

We bowled through the high hedgerows of dappled sun, ducking in to allow other traffic past on the narrow road. We English are a diligent lot and each 'Passing Place' sign had had its first 'a' replaced with an 'i' by the local youths, reflecting a laudable thoroughness.

The evening light laid a calm upon me and Reg appeared to pick up on it too, curling up on the back seat and dozing as the car made its way through the lanes.

I'm not a good map reader and, as it turned out, neither is Lucy. At first we found it quite difficult to locate Charterstone. It may have been indicated on the map but there were no signs for it on the ground and we soon became lost in a maze of tiny lanes, B roads and unlisted roads – to be roads really – only just wider than my car.

We'd been driving around for forty minutes or more and were trying to locate a turn that was after a bend that was after a crossroads that wasn't after the crossroads I'd just gone over when my phone rang. I glanced at it and I could see it was Lyndsey but I didn't answer it. I don't talk on my mobile when I'm driving – obviously it's illegal and so out of the question but even before they banned it I didn't because, well, I just didn't. Not even the hands-free.

I could have pulled over, of course, but I didn't want to tell her about Reg. Also I didn't want to admit I wasn't at the supermarket. I just didn't feel up to aisle war at that moment.

Lyndsey had just had a new cream carpet fitted that she'd been saving for for the best part of a year and I wasn't sure my acquisition of a dog was what she wanted to hear. Red wine had already been banned, coffee was for the kitchen only, shoes were off at the door and hands were preferably washed before entering the lounge.

Lucy finally saw the problem. A curve in the road – more of a warp than a curve really – an obscured road sign, a turnoff that could have been just a continuation but was in fact next to the real continuation that looked like a turnoff.

A couple of warps, a distension and a brief etiolation of the road that wasn't marked on the map – as so few etiolations are nowadays – and we passed the entrance to a village with its 'Charterstone welcomes careful drivers' sign. That has always struck me as counterproductive. I mean, if you make careless drivers feel unwelcome they're more likely to gas it to get out of there, aren't they?

The strange thing about this entrance to a village, however, was that it didn't appear to have a village attached to it. The road, which at this point was more of a dribble of tarmac, just carried on for about four hundred yards between high banks before coming to a stop. In England the end of any country track is regarded as an appropriate place to dispose of unwanted mattresses, prams, weapons-grade plutonium, that sort of thing, so the dog, Lucy and I found ourselves in a sort of informal rubbish dump.

'This looks exciting,' said the dog, breathing up the window to get a look at some large sheets of asbestos.

I looked at my map. As far as I could see I was no more than five hundred yards from the main road between the coast and London but I might as well have been in Oz. We were right on the border of the Charterstone estate, as far as I could see.

'If I let you out of here without your lead, will you stay by me?' I said to the dog.

'We're getting out of the car, we're getting out of the car, ha ha ha, we're getting out of the car,' said the dog. 'Come on, let's go! Rare delights await us! Our paws shall be swift upon the sod, if the sod doesn't run too fast! Ha ha!'

I took that as a 'no' and tied on the piece of string Lucy had found to use as a lead.

We got out and made our way back down the road, the dog hoovering at the floor with his nose. About a hundred yards on

I glimpsed something in the bushes. It was a sign, obscured by clinging ivy.

Short of clues, I decided to have a closer look at it. I ripped back the ivy with one hand, while trying to keep control of Reg with the other.

'There's a bird in that bush!' he said, straining across the road to get a look at it. 'It could be doing anything! Let me see it! That would be my dearest wish!'

'Well, it's only worth half one in the hand so leave it,' I said.

'I haven't got any hands,' said the dog, pulling harder, 'so it'll do me.'

The ivy was largely dead so it came away easily to reveal the message: 'Concealed Entrance 50 Yards'. I scraped the bottom of the sign clear. 'Danger!' it said.

I looked up the lane. Roughly fifty yards in front of me I could see some muddy markings on the road. I guessed this was where I wanted.

'Come on,' I said to the dog who, to be fair, was already coming on, going on, even, straining down the lane.

Adjacent to the markings was a gap in the high bank next to the road. Looking through it I could see a quite steep walled track, disappearing after about a hundred yards over the brow of a hill. The track was barred by a metal farm gate that was secured with a new-ish padlock.

'Hellooo meets obstacle, hellooo meets obstacle, what's he going to do?' panted the dog, as if it was the most exciting thing in the world.

'What do you mean, hellooo?' I said as Lucy followed behind us.

'You're a hellooo,' said the dog, 'like I'm a dog. Don't you know what you are?'

'I'm a human,' I said.

'We call you hellooos,' said the dog. 'It's what you say every time you meet a dog.'

I suddenly didn't feel up to the mission of returning the purse, or even to finding Charterstone. What I felt was hot and tired and mad in a country lane.

Lucy came up to my side.

'You don't look as if you're up to this,' she said. 'Why don't we go home? We can return this tomorrow.'

What happens, I thought, if you surrender yourself into someone else's care? If you take the love you're offered, what do you lose? Nothing. You gain. In my experience, though, it's them that loses. Everyone who had ever loved me had died and too soon.

'We're here now,' I said. 'Let's get on with it.'

'I think you need a stiff whisky and putting to bed,' said Lucy. She seemed dark and lovely and shiny. I felt very aware of the changing early evening light around her. It was as if all my senses had been heightened to a point where familiar things seemed strange and ungraspable. Lucy seemed to glow in the encroaching dusk as if all the light of the day was draining into her. This isn't the sort of thing that gives you much comfort if you're fearing that you've lost your marbles and have less chance of getting them back than the Parthenon.

'Come on,' I said.

The track up to the top of the hill was barred by a locked gate. It seemed virtually unpassable by car anyway so I picked Reg up and lowered him over, then we climbed over it ourselves. We trudged up the lane, picking our way through the weeds, Reg running up a couple of rooks in front of us. The birds took to the air and climbed the hill, calling out in cracked voices across the empty spaces of the evening, as if announcing our visit.

'Fly, strange harbingers!' cried the dog after them. I didn't think anyone had cried anything since about the 1930s but there was Reg doing it like it was second nature.

'What's a harbinger?' I asked Lucy.

'A messenger,' she said, 'normally of doom.'

'Great,' I said.

At the top of the hill was another locked modern gate but this time with a stile to one side of it. We crossed it and continued up a short rise and were confronted by a third set of gates quite unlike the others. These were your full stately jobs, huge stone pillars enclosing broken-down wrought-iron work.

Reg sniffed at one of the pillars and nodded in a 'very much as I suspected' manner. He ahemmed and began.

'The Charterstone estate. Built in 1820 by the early industrialist Charles Beaufort, one of the first exponents of "responsible capitalism". The estate is noted for its attempts to place factories in a rural setting and to provide decent homes for workers. The Beaufort family reside here to this day, and these gates bear their crest. That's what it sniffs here,' he said.

I went over to him and whispered in his ear, pretending to pat him.

'How do you know all that?'

'Dogs have left information here,' said Reg. He trotted over to one of the pillars. 'I'll just record our visit,' he said, lifting his leg. 'Anything you'd like to add?'

I looked down at my feet. There on the broken gate was a crest consisting of three dogs' heads linked in something of a Viking style. How could the dog have known that? He hadn't seen the crest.

Lucy had already gone through the gates in front of me.

'Come and look at this,' she said. 'It's incredible. It's like Jurassic Park!'

I joined her and saw that we were at the top of a sweeping hill that enclosed a valley in a broad arc. I hadn't been aware that we'd risen this high but we could see miles over a flat weald that lay before us, the lights of towns like pools of fire and the roads like lava flows burning in the long summer dusk.

'What a height!' said the dog. 'We are kings of the earth! Kings of the earth!'

'Wow,' I said, looking into the distance, 'that's Gatwick. It can't be more than ten miles away. Think of the value of the transport links from this place. You couldn't want for better.'

'You old romantic,' said Lucy at my side.

We were on a pale brick road which led away down the side of the hill. A hand-painted sign in front of us said 'The great house', with an arrow helpfully pointing the way.

We followed the road down through a deserted village of old limestone cottages, a boarded-up schoolroom, a sealed well, until in the near distance we saw a cottage apart from the others.

'That place is inhabited,' said Lucy.

'How do you know?' I said.

'There's a satellite dish on the roof,' she said.

The peculiar thing was that as we neared the cottage it didn't seem to near us, if you see what I mean. Or, should I say that it was a lot further away than it first appeared. In fact it was hard to say exactly how far or near it was at all. Something seemed wrong with the perspective.

It was only after fifteen minutes' walk that we understood what it was. The dusk had stolen a dimension from reality. It was only when you actually got near the thing that you realised. It was exactly the same as all the other cottages only massively bigger. It had four huge windows, one huge chimney and a thatched roof the size of a paddock. The door in the centre was a good twenty feet high, so big in fact that it had another regular-sized door cut into it.

We stood in front of it in what had once been a formal rose garden. Most of it was overgrown, with the flowers bursting like faces from among the weeds.

I have to say that I was building up to a most fearful fit of the creeps.

'What do you think we should do?' I said.

'Open the door and continue into the spooky old house,' said the dog. 'Maybe split up for safety once we're in.'

'That's a crazy idea,' I said.

'Not when you find out about the huge sandwiches you get to eat if you do,' he said. 'I've seen a documentary on it.'

'What's a crazy idea?' said Lucy.

'This documentary wasn't in a sort of cartoon form, was it?' I sang, as if to myself.

'That's the feller!' said Reg.

'What documentary?' said Lucy.

'I was talking to myself,' I said.

'About documentaries?'

'Oh yes,' I said. 'I sometimes mull 'em over for weeks.'

'Fine,' said Lucy, with a look that suggested the opposite.

Lucy, someone who I was beginning to realise was a woman of action rather than analysis, gave me that worried look of hers, stepped forward and pressed a bell.

Almost immediately it had finished ringing we heard a strangled cry from within.

'Get back! Get back! Though I have summoned thee, Beelzebub, you will fall to my command. Aahhh! The fiend has me. I have dabbled and now must pay! Horror! Oh horror!'

Reg was wagging his tail.

A hatch slid back in the door and an old woman's face appeared at it, wracked with distress.

'Save yourselves!' she hissed before the hatch snapped shut again.

The dog gave a woof and it opened once more, as quickly as it had closed.

'What do you want?' she said in a rather refined voice, rather like you might imagine a basset hound might speak when warming up to get into full tongue.

'Tell her a bone,' said the dog.

'We—'

'You're not estate agents, are you?' she said, eyeing us up and down.

'Yes,' said Reg.

'We're bringing something back,' said Lucy.

'Are you here to persuade me to sell my estate?' she said.

'No, not at all,' I said. 'We found something I think belongs to you and we're bringing it back.' I waved the purse.

'What's that?' she said, squinting through the slot. 'I can't see very well.'

'It's a purse,' said Lucy.

'With a collie on it?'

'Exactly so,' I said.

'Oh, you've returned it,' she said. 'Do come in.'

The hatch closed and the small door opened. The space inside seemed pitch black, the fragile evening light failing to penetrate it.

'Enter!' said the woman's voice.

Before I could think twice the dog had hopped through and was gone.

Then Lucy disappeared inside. I had to follow, though at the back of my mind I was wondering what exactly had happened to Lord Beelzebub and the demonic hordes.

It was some relief that when I got in, instead of being faced with the dark lord in all his foul glory, I was confronted by a rather musty velvet curtain. I stepped through it and the world swam while my eyes adjusted.

Luckily the hall appeared to the layman to be equally free of infernal manifestations. No Lucifer, no demon. Not so much as an imp.

I looked at my watch. Eight thirty on my shaking hand. There had been no thoughts, just a growing inner trembling, which seemed to get faster and stronger as if approaching some resonant frequency at which I might disintegrate.

We were in a commanding long hall, 40' × 10', with an imposing aspect and scope for development into a bowling alley. You'd have to get all the adjectives out for this one, I thought –

prestigious, imposing, stately. Difficult to heat, my mum would have had it.

It was very dimly lit, painted in a kind of pond-weed green and decked wherever you looked with strange pictures of dogs, not the sentimental sort but long and twisted creatures, as if someone had painted a dog's shadow at sunset but fused it with an anatomical drawing or even a landscape. They appeared as expressions of the contours of the land or of the moving light.

At the edge of my vision, low and to the left, I saw something with a ring of familiarity. A small painting, no more than ten by eight inches, of dogs playing snooker.

Where there were no paintings, deep red curtains hung. No doorways were visible at all and, in the soft electric glow, I was rather reminded of an exhibition I'd been to see that had transported you through the internal organs of a giant human body. 'Here we are,' I almost expected a voice to say, 'in the fleshy chambers of the human heart. You represent a tumbling corpuscle. White blood cells to the left, red to the right, no flash photography.'

'Yes,' I said, 'David Barker and Lucy Miniver, at your service.'

'Reg Barker equally at your service and ready to accept any food,' said the dog.

'You haven't introduced me to the four-foot,' she said.

'This is Reg,' I said.

'Do you know the damp course in this house was one of the very first of its kind and still works to this day?' said Reg, turning his head to get a better angle of sniff up the skirting board.

'A delight!' said Mrs Cad-Beauf. 'I can see by his poise that he is an animal of the first fur.'

'Perception!' said the dog, like sideburned preachers say 'Hallelujah!' 'Bright and fresh as a crystal morn!'

'Oh blinkin' Jesus,' I said under my breath. I've never felt like a sustaining nip of whisky in my life but if I was ever going to feel like one, it would have been then.

'Follow me into the orangery,' said Mrs CB, picking up a

broom. She opened some curtains to my right, pushed back the door they were concealing and stepped inside.

Most orangeries I've come across are quite light places but this was pitch black. I followed her anyway, leaving Lucy and Reg behind me in the hall

'Mr Barker, is that you?' said Mrs Cad-Beauf, like an old-fashioned school ma'am pointing out that if you were going to eat sweets in class you'd better share them with everyone.

'Yes,' I said.

'I regret to inform you that this is the broom cupboard. If you allow me to stow my domestic utensil, I shall lead you to the orangery shortly,' she said. 'Kindly return to the hallway.'

'I do apologise,' I said, fumbling for the curtain.

Mrs Cad-Beauf returned from the cupboard minus the broom. I'd been slightly overawed by the house and hadn't looked closely at her. She was a woman of around eighty, I guessed, wearing a moth-fodder tweed skirt and a white blouse, over which she wore a green cardigan. On the cardigan was a brooch in silver and diamonds representing the head of a collie dog.

She put her hand on my arm. 'I'm sorry about the Lucifer and the legions of Charon speech but we have trouble with trades-men and that sort of thing tends to keep them away.'

'As I imagine it might,' said Lucy.

'Compassion is her smell,' said the dog, 'like crushed hope mingled with the odour of dark berries.'

'I'll give you your purse and be off, then,' I said.

'You and your wife will take tea,' said Mrs Cad-Beauf, as if announcing that the sun would rise tomorrow. 'And this ador-able chap shall have a sausage.'

'You can't argue with that,' said Reg, following Mrs Cad-Beauf back down the hall.

Lucy looked at me and gave me a cheeky giggle. Unlike most things that people give you – socks, underwear, under-sized shirts – I was actually in some need of it.

I smiled back at her and again I could see concern in her eyes.

'Come on,' she said, taking my arm and following Mrs Cad-Beauf.

The orangery at the back of the house was well-maintained, 50' × 20', in good order, boasting a world-class collection of plants, including a charming orange grove, and commanding an enviable position giving a masterful view of the prestigious Sussex Downs and related prestigious countryside prestigiously.

We sat on wrought-iron chairs under the metal and glass of this prestige feature while a dreadlocked young woman of about twenty-two – her name was something like Aia Napa, I believe – served us tea and biscuits. Sausages could be smelled cooking somewhere in the distance.

'I will know all about you, Mr Barker, if you please,' said Mrs Cad-Beauf, patting the purse on the table. She hadn't thanked me for returning it, I couldn't help noticing, but I wondered if this was the aristocratic way, as aristocrat she certainly seemed.

'I'm, er . . .' She hadn't seemed too keen on estate agents, I'd noticed.

'And this wonderful hound is Reg, you said.'

Reg panted up at her in a broad smile.

'Indeed,' said Reg. 'Dog and bon viveur. Specialising in retrieval but qualified in all aspects of general doggery. Partial to cold tea and hot macaroons.'

'I tell all canine visitors that the proper place for beastliness is the rose garden. Kindly indulge yourself only in its confines. That stricture aside, the home is yours.'

'I already have a home,' said Reg, looking at me fondly.

Mrs Cad-Beauf broke off a dead geranium and twirled it in her fingers. I thought of my mum. She'd worn a perfume called Midnight Geranium.

She reminded me of my mum in some essential way. No one aspect of the women could really be said to be similar, it was just that they both seemed at an angle to reality.

'Would you pour the tea, my eyes are not what they were,' said Mrs CB. 'What breed is this magnificent creature?'

'It is my honour to call myself a Sliding Wisehound,' said Reg.

'He's a Sliding Wisehound,' I said.

'He has the coat of a Musclemutt,' said Mrs Cad-Beauf, stroking Reg behind the ear.

'What is a Musclemutt?' I said. I'd thought it was Musclebarker. Or was it Grizzling Blindcur? A Fibrous Shadowsucker? I couldn't be sure.

'Like an Airedale only slightly smoother,' she said.

'Smoother than an Airedale?' said Reg, looking impressed. 'They're among the smoothest hounds there are. I knew one who used to wear a bow tie and could practically mix Martinis.'

The atmosphere in the orangery was airy, too airy. I felt as if the top of my head was lifting off, infused with light, the shiny globules you see when you stand up too quickly dancing at the edge of my vision. It was like I was simultaneously in the scene and watching it from somewhere up in the creepers. I became too aware of detail, like the dust on a bowl of rose leaves which was perched on top of a fine iron stand, Lucy next to me on her chair, close as if for protection, the grip of her hand on mine, the warmth of her body, her smile.

'Your details, Mr Barker,' she said.

'What would you like to know about me?' I said.

'Where did you acquire this fine dog?' she said. Reg had his head on her knee.

'The tension is just on the forehead,' he said. 'There's one great gnarl of it if you can seek it out. Ahhhh, there's the relief.' Mrs Cad-Beauf expertly worked her thumb into the tendons of the dog's head. 'Oh, madam,' said the dog, 'you are a shortfur sorceress. Later we may see how you fare amongst the long.'

I thought she might have asked where I got the purse. As she didn't, I thought I'd tell her.

'It's a bit weird really,' I said. 'The man who stole your purse brought him into my shop and dropped dead. He left the dog and your purse.'

'No one stole my purse,' said Mrs Cad-Beauf, looking puzzled.

'Ah,' I said. Something in Mrs CB's manner made me think I was going to be drawing heavily on my sack of 'ahs' and might even run out and have to go on to the 'oohs' before the day was out.

'You didn't have it stolen?'

'No, far from it. I had just purchased some cakes from Gladdins and Purle when a plainclothes policeman approached me. He explained there had been a series of robberies of elderly folk and, well, I naturally told him I am not elderly, I am old. Fit for the knacker's yard!' she said, as if threatening to gut someone with a sabre.

'We sorted out that misunderstanding and he explained that I was carrying too much cash in my purse and was a target.' I could see what was coming. 'He offered to take the purse and see that it got back home safely. It was only later I found I had left the little door key in it. I assumed you were one of his colleagues bringing it back.'

'No,' I said. 'I'm afraid he was a con man.'

She looked at me with wide eyes. 'And how do I know, Mr Barker, it isn't you who is the con man?'

'I'm returning the money, not taking it,' I said, stating the bleeding obvious.

'And more to the point,' she said, 'you own a dog. This dog has an honest face. It wouldn't associate with a criminal.'

The dog put down his head in a deep bow. 'Honesty, madam, is my motif. My woof is my bond.'

'I'm just a member of the public,' I said, not being sure if that was an appropriate answer to whatever question she'd asked. A member of the public – hey, at least I'd found one club that would have me.

'Was there any money in the purse?' said Mrs Cad-Beauf. She seemed as forgetful as the dog.

'Yes,' I said. 'Over—'

'Keep it!' She raised her arm to command silence. 'I will never hear talk of money and it will serve me right for being so stupid. The careless must carry an extra burden of cares,' she said.

I couldn't let that go. 'It's over—'

She silenced me again.

'My father brought me up to believe that no lady would ever know a bank statement from a slice of the moon and that the only accountant a gentleman knows deals in turf, not tax returns. I will not discuss such things and descend to the level of trade.' Her eyes seemed to bulge on this last word, as if she'd found a Happy Shopper pie in the Fortnum and Mason hamper.

'You must pay tax?' I said. I don't know why I thought I had the right to ask such a personal question.

'Ten per cent, though the government abolished it a couple of years ago,' she said.

'Isn't that betting tax?' said Lucy.

'It was bloody iniquitous, I know that,' said Mrs CB. 'Now where are the sausages?'

'There's a question!' said the dog.

On cue the dreadlocked girl emerged like a modern Medusa from the back of the orangery.

The dog seemed turned to stone, his nose pointing directly at her with only a slight quiver of the body indicating that he was a living thing at all.

'Sausages,' said Aia Napa, who had the sort of voice you more normally associate with being called 'Sophie'.

Mrs Cad-Beauf took the sausages, which were presented neatly on a small silver tray.

'Are they cool?' said Mrs Cad-Beauf.

'They're wicked,' said Aia Napa.

'Cool in the sense of temperature not in that of their fit with current trends,' said Mrs Cad-Beauf with an eye roll that suggested it wasn't the first time she'd encountered this problem.

'Oh, I ran them under the tap,' said Aia Napa with a horsey laugh that takes a minimum of three thousand pounds a term to achieve. I wondered how a sausage could be fashionable. Looking at the dog's face, though, he seemed to find them pretty trendy.

'Timeless appeal,' he said, following the plate with his eyes like a cobra the pipe.

'You have done well,' said Mrs Cad-Beauf, taking a sausage from a plate and cutting it into segments.

She could work a dog, that Mrs Cad-Beauf, I'll say that for her. Reg sat, he gave the paw, he lay, he rolled over, he wagged the tail, extended the tongue and said, 'Ah!' He left and he took and finally he did a little bow to say, 'Thank you.'

'This animal passes every test,' said Mrs Cad-Beauf. 'He can practically talk.'

The dog gave me a conspirational look. 'Our secret is safe,' he seemed to say.

'They can all talk if you have an ear for it,' said Mrs Cad-Beauf. 'They have needs and tastes as we do. You'll notice the curtains in the hall?'

'Yes.'

'I once had a Labrador that complained of draughts.'

Light caught the dust in the high rafters, the tea was delicate on the palate, in the foliage outside the window some bird seemed to chuckle. I was as cuckoo as the contents of a Swiss clock and I knew it.

'This is a remarkable property,' I said, trying to centre myself. I'd heard that the footballer Diego Maradonna used to be able to juggle a ping-pong ball with his feet even when he was smashed. Some things are grained within you and, in my case, that meant talking about houses. I could, and did, talk about it in my sleep sometimes.

'My great-grandfather built it,' said Mrs Cad-Beauf. 'You have, perhaps, heard of the industrialist Artemis Beaufort?'

'I've heard of him, I think,' I said, looking at Reg, who wore the sort of look that said, 'You've already been told all you need to know on this subject, I think you'll find.'

'The house was built in eighteen forty-two,' she said, 'with a damp course that has not needed to be replaced to this day!'

Reg pumped forward a back leg in a motion that I took for, 'I told you so.'

Now she came to mention it I was sure Artemis Beaufort was one of those Victorians you saw in pictures, lounging with a cigar up some ship or bridge they'd just knocked up in a lunch hour.

'This was his project,' said Mrs Cad-Beauf, 'an exercise in benevolent capitalism. The idea was to provide houses and education for the workers in an idyllic rural setting and they would be more productive.'

'As has already been mentioned,' said Reg, as if polishing a medal on his chest.

'And this is where he lived?'

'In a style exactly the same as the workers, only bigger,' she said. 'The orangery was added later. Of course the businesses failed or were sold, Artemis's loins didn't prove as fecund as his mind. He had one child, who had one child, who had one child and so I find myself here, alone.'

'Your husband's . . .?' said Lucy, and I could immediately see that she wished she hadn't. I knew why she'd been so insensitive, though: it was the atmosphere of the place. The only experience people like us have of being in places like this is from guided trips around stately homes with tour guides, who virtually goad you into asking things like, 'Which member of the family suffered the most painful death and can we see a re-creation?'

'Yes, he is dead, but that's the trouble with men, isn't it? High performance, low reliability. Like his old Bugatti. He died thirty years ago.'

'Do you have any children?' I said. These questions would have been intrusive in normal circumstances but they just seemed to pop out. Mrs Cad-Beauf, short on company, I supposed, seemed happy to talk.

'One child. This world wasn't for him, though.'

'I'm sorry,' I said.

'There's nothing to be sorry about,' she said. 'Here, let me fetch a bag for your money.'

'I've said I can't take it.' I said it firmly and directly so she could tell I wasn't refusing as a matter of form.

There is a dance that's normally done in these circumstances, the 'I can't – but you must', where the participants bob back and forth until the weaker party accepts. The weaker party in these cases is always the person refusing the gift.

'Really,' said Lucy, 'it's very kind of you to offer but we didn't come here for a reward. We came here because you'd lost your purse and if we lost something we would hope that someone would return it to us.'

Mrs Cad-Beauf smiled. 'You seek to increase the sum of good in the world, Mr and Mrs Barker. And you have succeeded. There are very few people who do that today.' She looked at me like a woman at a shop window admiring a hat she had no intention of buying. 'Tell me, are you in a caring profession?'

I laughed. 'Quite the reverse, I'm afraid. I'm in an uncaring profession.'

'Don't tell me you're an estate agent!' She was laughing too.

Somewhere in the high beams of the orangery the tendrils of the plants seemed to hold something metal – an ornament of blue and gold like a kingfisher's wing. It seemed to move in the dust beams, answering the sunset, light to light.

I opened my mouth and the words swam out like tadpoles.

'As a matter of fact,' I said, 'I am.'

Mrs Cad-Beauf smiled at me, patted the dog's head and then burst into tears.

* * *

'I tried everything to keep you out,' said Mrs Cad-Beauf, dabbing her eye with the end of her cardigan, 'and you've got through, and in the worst possible way.'

'What way?' I said, figuring it was about time I made for the exit or, if I couldn't find it, went and hid in the broom cupboard.

'With kindness,' she said. 'You are irresistible. You are a tide, an elemental force before whom I can only succumb.' She looked at me fiercely.

'Think twice before you do any succumbing at all,' I said. I was fairly confident I could make it out of the room before she pounced on me but not at all sure where I would go then. I hadn't noticed if the entrance was concealed by a curtain. What if I got lost in the house? I could be there for weeks.

The dog looked at me in accusation. 'She smells very sad,' he said, 'like rain at a fairground, wet candy floss and leaky cagouls.'

I addressed Mrs Cad-Beauf.

'Please accept that we came solely to return your purse. We had no idea who you were or where you lived when we brought it back and we haven't come here to persuade you to sell your home. My agency has no experience of selling this sort of thing anyway, we're more the one-bedroom-flat end of the market.' I found myself talking quickly and realised that I was overdoing things. I had come there completely innocently and I really didn't have any intention of getting her to sell her house.

'You, Mr Barker, are history,' said Mrs Cad-Beauf.

Lucy and I exchanged looks. Mrs CB seemed the sort to give you the blunderbuss treatment if she didn't like you.

She went on, 'You are the proletariat at the gates of the Winter Palace, the motor car, the silicone chip.' She said the last words as if she'd accidentally sprayed some hair lacquer in her mouth and was trying to get rid of the taste.

'Destiny will not be denied,' she said. 'I've known of course for years that this day would come, that I'd have to sell. I'd imagined my assassin would be a little more vulgar than you, though, Mr Barker. Do the Horsemen of the Apocalypse smile as they sow their destruction?'

I'd never actually met them, so I couldn't comment. Probably, I thought, given modern consumer service training.

She certainly seemed to have lost it since I'd told her what I did for a living. I was used to people taking it badly, wheeling out the 'Why are there no old estate agents? Because it is possible to die of shame' line but I'd never quite had Mrs CB's reaction before.

'Hold on,' I said. 'No one's asking you to sell this place. I didn't want your purse so I'm certainly not after your money.'

'No,' said Mrs Cad-Beauf, 'you're not. And that is what makes you so fatal to my fantasies. You are a messenger of fate, offering me the easy way out – the knife in the warm bath rather than the lions in the Coliseum. I must move on, Mr Barker. I've known it for years and you are simply the tool by which that squalid little job must be accomplished.' She poured tea into a cup and her heart into her words.

'We have always been a lucky family and I am lucky to have found you. The honest estate agent, the good Samaritan. I saw it last week. "Destiny wears a blue tie." ' Her eyes seemed to mist over, as if communing with forces unknown.

'You see the future?' I said. Something about her and her house had given me that impression from the moment I'd arrived.

'I read Mystic Meg in the *News of the World*,' she said, 'and I look out of the window. Nine-tenths of this estate is in ruins. I need to do something to save it from the vandals and the weeds.'

'Have you thought of going to the National Trust and opening it up to the public?' I said.

Mrs Cad-Beauf sniffed. 'Have you met the public, Mr Barker?'

I didn't reply. I thought it was obvious enough that I had.

'Well, I don't care for their company. The last thing I want is a bunch of sticky-fingered proles crawling all over my soft furnishings, thank you.'

'There must be some other way,' I said. 'Why not sell some of the land and use that money to live off?'

She stared out of the window, into the informal overgrowth of the formal gardens.

'This place is too big for me,' she said. 'No, what I need is sheltered housing of some sort, in the best modern way. Mr Barker, I want you to sell this place for me and I want you to sell it quickly.'

'I could,' I said, 'but you don't seem particularly convinced you should leave.'

'I'm entirely convinced,' she said, 'just not very happy about it.'

'It would fetch millions,' I said.

Mrs CB looked pained. 'Mr Barker, I will not have such vulgarity in my presence. I will go into sheltered accommodation, you will ensure there is enough money to last me twenty years there, though I doubt I shall see that many months, and the rest shall go to a good cause.'

'What good cause?' I said.

'Dogs' homes, Mr and Mrs Barker. Dogs are my passion, as you can see. I have painted them, I have loved them and now that I can't look after them I have let them go. But when I go, they shall prosper.'

A one-bedroomed flat, the nicest you could buy in East Sussex, would cost maybe half a million if you were trying to throw the money away, one hundred thousand if you weren't. That left, by a quick estimation, bloody millions for dogs.

'You'll need to sign off the figures,' I said.

'You shall do that for me, Mr Barker. I really have no interest,' she said.

'That puts me in a difficult position,' I said. 'There's no one checking to see I'm honest.'

'You are honest, Mr Barker,' said Mrs CB. 'You show it in your actions and your face. I thought the idea of leaving this place was an impossibility. But you are an impossibility, aren't you? An honest estate agent.'

I could see this was going to be hard work. I did suggest that she got someone to help her go through the whole process, to make sure she understood how much money she was intending to give away.

'You do understand,' I said, 'that you're proposing giving away a massive amount of money. Haven't you got any relatives?'

'Dogs have been my relatives,' said Mrs Cad-Beauf, sweeping the room with her hand. 'They are my kith and my kin. I want only to see them and their brothers and sisters happy and well cared for. If I had millions to give away, I should still give it to dogs' homes.'

'You do have millions to give away,' I said.

'Then I shall give them to dogs' homes!' she said, virtually stamping her feet on the floor and gesturing as if she might put her fingers in her ears if I continued waxing on the wonga.

What the hell, I thought, people spend millions on much more stupid things – football teams, yachts. If she wanted to make the dogs happy, who was I to talk her out of it?

'If you're really certain,' I said, 'I could make an appointment to come and value the place.'

I'd need to do some research, that was for sure. I wasn't even certain where estates like this sold and even less clear what its market value would be. I could practically hear developers slavering at the prospect of getting their hands on it, running a road to the A23 and watching the city money pour in. I would also have to establish who exactly she wanted to sell it to, to make sure it went to a buyer who would respect her wishes for the estate.

'Come any afternoon,' said Mrs Cad-Beauf. 'I only ever go

out in the mornings. The afternoons have seemed a struggle for me of late.'

'My commission will be . . .' I was going to say one per cent. Normally it was 1.5 but on a place like this, one was a fortune.

She held up her hand. 'Your business. And it will be fair. You have an honest smell,' she said, taking a long sniff at me.

I didn't think it wise to delve.

'Fine,' I said. The first bars of Bach's Air on a G-String rang out. It was my mobile.

I answered it, as Lucy asked Mrs Cad-Beauf if she could direct her to the loo.

'Hello, twonk,' said the Pieman. 'I'm wadded up and ready for the taking. Are you along tonight? Dark Satanic's along and so is the Singing Detective.'

Dark Satanic's real name was Phil Mills, hence the dark satanic. The Singing Detective was a bookie we played with who'd never quite recovered from a teenage bout of acne of the sort normally reserved for Pharaohs who particularly displeased the Lord.

'I'm coming along,' I said, eyeing Mrs Cad-Beauf's purse on the table.

'Good,' said the Pieman. 'Get ready for a spanking.'

'It is you, Pieman, who should be stuffing the book down his shorts,' I said. 'A visit to Sketchley's beckons.' I hung up.

'May I offer you a biscuit, Mr Barker?' says Mrs Cad-Beauf.

'You may, Mrs Cad-Beauf,' I said.

Mrs Cad-Beauf sat up straight.

'Mr Barker,' she said, 'would you like a biscuit?'

'Actually,' I said, 'about that cash . . .'

'Does that mean the biscuit's going begging?' said the dog.

4

Sliding

I did take the money, true, but I tried to give Mrs Cad-Beauf an IOU. She wouldn't take it so I promised her that I would redeem it against my commission when I sold her house, sooner if I won that night. This was swift work while Lucy was in the loo but I managed it.

It seemed, though, that other obstacles were to be overcome before I could get to the poker game.

No sooner had we pulled back onto the A23 to go home than Lucy announced, in a rather motherly way, that I had had a very hard day, with my mum's funeral, the death of Gilbert and even the delight of being given Mrs Cad-Beauf's house to sell, and should go home to bed to get a good night's sleep.

'You look awful,' she said. 'Let me come in and make you something to eat and a hot toddy then I'll put you to bed.'

She was right, of course, I was knackered in one sense. The proximity of the game, though, gave me an emotional charge that turned my exhaustion into a kind of hyper-wakefulness. I felt like the hospital must feel when the power fails and the emergency generators kick in with a slightly different flavour to their voltage, like a child in a room lit by candles and experiencing for the first time the thrill of the revealing dark.

'I could do with turning in myself,' said the dog. 'All this world rushing by's making me tired. Goodnight.' And with that he curled up in the back of the car and was asleep in a second.

How does the addict think when faced with such a situation? Buy food, 30 minutes; cook, 30 minutes; eat, 10 minutes; goodnight, 10 minutes. Get in car and drive to game, 30 minutes. Nearly two hours out of the game. Oh no, she wants to give me a hot toddy, milk and whisky. I won't be able to drive. That means I'll have to get a cab and will arrive half drunk to be cast to the vipers.

When I say addict, let me say this. If I was an alcoholic I wouldn't be one of those who's found lying in the gutter, who wrecks his relationships with friends and family and dies at forty. No, I'd be the sort who just turns up for work every day with a hangover, who's mildly embarrassing company, red in the face and dies at fifty-five.

I don't know why I couldn't just say, 'Actually, I'm going to a poker game.' Perhaps it was because I was her boss, perhaps because I didn't want her to know that even after such a long day, even when I could feel my hands shaking on the wheel, I didn't want to do what every other sane person would want to do and have a lovely girl cook him tea and then get an early night.

'I haven't actually got any food,' I said.

The dog turned in his sleep, saying something like, 'Nightmare of starvation.'

'We'll buy some,' she said.

'I'm not that hungry.'

Again the dog twitched in his sleep, blowing out air through his cheeks in a high poof. 'I'll have yours then,' he mumbled.

Lucy put her hand on my knee. 'You didn't eat at lunchtime, and I'd guess you didn't eat at breakfast. I've seen the strain you've been under with your mum and for one night you can let someone look after you rather than pretending everything's all right,' she said.

'Please let me go to poker,' I felt like saying. 'Tonight, just once, don't make me be normal and nice.' Instead I gave her a weak smile.

'We can make the dog a bed,' said Lucy. 'We'll get a box from the shop and cut out the front and then we'll put some pillows in for him.'

The appeal was certainly there, making a bed for a new dog with the easy company of Lucy to see me through the night. It was one of those things that you'd remember for the rest of your life, like sleeping in the tent in the garden when you were a kid or the first time you saw the sea.

'I love watching dogs sleep,' said Lucy. 'You can almost feel the cosiness coming off them.'

I could almost feel the cosiness coming off her words but I was faced with a problem, wasn't I? I had more than a grand burning its way through my pocket but no way of getting it to a room full of men I didn't like in order to give it to them without offending a girl I was very fond of who was offering me a lovely night in.

I wanted it but I couldn't have it, my brain simply could not accommodate it, couldn't bear that reality with its complications. What it could accommodate was the endless repetition of the cards, the figuring of odds, the smoke and the harsh light and the company of people with names like Shagger Burns, and trying, if only in miniature, to destroy them. No-brainer inter-action.

'No bed for me, sir,' said the dog, who had stirred on the mention of 'dog'. 'I have known only the turf and the tarmac all my life, such comforts are not for one of my station.' He spoke in something of the tone of the orphan boy offered Christmas at the big house.

We stopped at some lights coming into Worthing and my phone bleeped up a message.

'Oh no!' I said, looking down to see that I could take advantage of three months' free Wap.

'What is it?' said Lucy.

'Lyndsey,' I said. 'She's, oh, I can't believe it. Her trouble's flared up again. Just when we thought we were out of the woods. I'm really sorry, Lucy, I'm going to have to go round there.'

This wasn't strictly a lie. Lyndsey's trouble was condensation on a poorly fitted replacement window. And indeed the condensation was rough in the mornings. I might have implied it was Lyndsey on the phone but I didn't say it so it wasn't a lie. Look, this is poker, OK. It's different.

'Why do you lie?' said the dog.

'Gosh, is she OK?' said Lucy.

'She is,' I said, 'but she needs me there tonight. Look, if I give you the money for a cab, can I drop you at a rank?'

'You're lying,' said the dog. 'Your heart is rattling and you're sweating more heavily. Why do you lie?'

'I don't need any money,' said Lucy.

'Please,' I said, 'take some, you've been very kind to me.'

The 'please take some', 'no, I can't', batted backwards and forwards between us until we reached the cab rank. Eventually I made her take twenty pounds and waved her goodbye.

'Make sure you get to bed!' said Lucy as I gunned away.

Well, I would, eventually.

Night was coming down as we approached Snake Eyes' place. The dog had developed something of a critical streak on the way there.

'I don't like it when you lie to Lucy,' he said. 'She knows you're lying too.'

'I'm not lying,' I said, 'and she doesn't know I am.'

'She did because she went cold slightly and her stomach rumbled,' said Reg. 'She was anxious. It's easy to see when you hellooos are lying.' He was now sitting directly behind me with his head on my shoulder. 'Basically what happens is that you dilate and constrict. Skin perspires, glands excrete.'

'And how does a dog know all this?' I said.

'We are noted for our sensitive noses and ears and are attuned to the emotional world in a way that would be impossible to explain to hellooos, no matter what their power and access to food. I mean, that sums it up, doesn't it? Hellooo.'

'What do you mean by that?'

'You think that's a greeting.'

'It is a greeting,' I said. 'You can't argue with that.'

'This,' said the dog, 'is a greeting!'

'Reg!' I said, turning to see him raise his back leg in a classic Alsatian lamp-post salute.

'The world of smell reveals so much, though,' said the dog. 'From sniffing an information point I can tell how someone's feeling, who their family is, historical facts they've picked up, everything. Slightly more than hellooo.' He said hellooo like a nine-year-old girl saying, 'So there!'

'You can't tell all that from a lamp post,' I said.

'How did I know everything at Charterstone then?'

'Because you're a symptom of me being nuts and overworked and stressed and I must have heard it somewhere before,' I said.

'That's very hurtful,' said the dog. 'How do I know you're not a symptom of my madness? How does anyone know anyone else really exists and it isn't all a dream?'

Now he had a look on his face like that of an old-fashioned housewife being told that the milkman wasn't taking the pint back because it didn't smell off to him.

'I am not sitting here discussing philosophy with a dog,' I said.

'Which speaks volumes for the faults of relying on a subjective reality,' said the dog, 'because anyone would confirm that's exactly what you're doing. Ball retrieved, your throw.'

'Well, if you're so sensitive to emotions then you'll know how I'm feeling now,' I said, glowering at him.

'Crushed bicycles and Diet Coke, which you don't like but buy anyway, a tuna baguette when you really want the BLT. Sliding tyres and the sad flowers,' he said.

Jesus Christ, I was going to the doctor the next day, that was for sure.

'I said how do I feel, not how do I smell.'

'A smell is a feeling, a feeling is a smell,' said the dog, looking puzzled. 'You can't describe one without the other.'

'Crushed bicycles,' I said, 'is not a smell.' I could feel the trembling inside me step up a pitch, almost out of the range in which it could be perceived but taking over every fibre of my body.

'On you it is,' said the dog.

'You should shut up,' I said. The last time I'd been near a crushed bicycle my dad had been under it.

We'd pulled up at Snake Eyes', in a particularly shitty part of a particularly shitty coastal town. I felt that tingle of anticipation that comes just before a game.

'Look,' I said to the dog, 'I have to concentrate when I'm in here, right? So I don't want one word out of you.'

'You dilate and excrete when Lucy is near, but that's a different sort,' said Reg. 'That's because you find her very attractive. That's the sort of dilation and excretion we call love.'

On the word 'love' he looked up from my shoulder into my eyes like a gypsy violinist saying, 'A mey-lo-dee for the lady?'

Love is dilation and excretion. I couldn't really see it on one of the cartoons.

A light came on in the front room. They'd moved through to the games arena.

I clamped my hands over Reg's nose to hold his jaws together.

'Not one word in here!' I said.

'My lips are sealed,' said the dog in a muffled voice from beneath my grip.

'Keep it that way,' I said, releasing him.

'I shall put a sneck before my snout, sir,' he said, running his tongue around to unglue his cheeks from his teeth. I think that meant he was promising to be quiet.

Never, I thought, had a man gone with more enthusiasm to his Golgotha. Like Jesus – there seems to be no good end to a sentence that begins that way – I was skint. But if I was him I'd have tried to join in the game of dice for his clothes at the top of the hill.

The dog hopped out of the car, ran around the front garden and lifted his leg against a tree with a 'Zing ding ding!' as I entered the hovel to be greeted by Snake Eyes' mum.

Snake Eyes' mum was a lovely Scots woman who'd managed to stay cheerful despite the numerous knocks that life had given her – alcoholic husband, emotionally disturbed children, being treated lower than a slave in her own home, hardly able to breathe owing to cigarette consumption, haunted by strange illnesses – the usual drill, nothing to shout about.

Mrs Watt always saw the bright side of everything. One of the players, a painter and decorator – Prudence (so called because he never pays – not without the application of hot irons any way) – had commented that her wallpaper was peeling. 'Oh fuck, no, love,' she said, 'it's just that the walls of these houses are very straight.'

She'd moved to the south coast, she once told me over a fish paste sandwich, because it was convenient for home.

'It's as far away as you can get without leaving the British Isles,' I said.

'That's what I call fucking convenient,' she said. 'Have you met my family?'

She was supportive of Snake Eyes because she was aware that, before poker, he'd had no friends.

'It's good that our Wullie has got some fucking pals now,' she said.

'Yes,' I said, looking at Snake Eyes, who in truth had eyes more like a toad if we're going to stay with reptilian comparisons, like a poorly repaired teddy bear if we're not. One seemed higher than the other, only by half an inch or so but then the positioning of eyes is a science of fractions of millimetres. His brother had the same affliction but the opposite eye was higher. His mum used to photograph them side by side and claim something had gone wrong with the print.

'Everyone has one wonky kid,' she'd say, looking at the pictures, 'but why did I end up with two of the fuckers?'

Snake Eyes' mum let me in through the back door with a, 'Hello, Dave, how the fuck are you? Oh, you've brought a friend!'

'I'm very fucking well, Mrs Watt,' I said. Mrs Watt swore virtually every third word so it seemed impolite not to do the same. The dog blanched slightly at the bad language, if anything covered from head to toe in brown and black fur can blanche. He didn't like swearing of any sort, I found out later, and said people only did it to look big and stupid.

'They're doing it to look big and clever,' I said.

'No,' said the dog, disbelieving. 'Then they must be really stupid.'

I put my fingers to my lips to remind Reg to be quiet.

Mrs Watt patted Reg and said some sort of colloquial stuff full of 'wee' and 'bonny' and 'haway withya, ya shite'.

'He's new, do you think the lads will mind? He has to stay in sight of me, really.'

'They won't fucking mind if I don't fucking mind it's my fucking house,' said Mrs Watt, elongating the dog by rubbing the fur under his chin until he curved up from his tail to his nose in one great tick of canine approval.

I went to the door of the front room and Reg followed me.

'Er, I'm with this dog if that's OK,' I said as Reg came into the room.

'Your private life is your own,' said Snake Eyes. 'Does it want a drink of water? Remembering that's all the change you're going to get out of me this evening, you great nowk.'

'I would, actually,' said Reg, 'and any of the large pile of sandwiches I noticed on the table in the kitchen. I'll try the jam.'

No one commented that the dog had barked, so I guessed that he hadn't. I gave him a quick shush anyway, making a sign with my hand as if it was clamped round his muzzle.

'A drink of water would be good,' I said.

'Mum!' shouted Snake Eyes. 'Bowl of water please!'

Snake Eyes' mum came in with a bowl of water, strangely quickly.

'Can I fucking charge that?' she said. The poker school gave her a fiver each for materials and effort with the sarnies.

'Why not?' I said, sitting down at the table. 'Money's not going to be a problem any more, actually.'

'I can see you're in the money,' said Shagger Burns. 'New bird and everything.' He gestured towards the dog.

'I'm not a bird, I'm a dog,' said Reg.

I never liked Shagger Burns. He seemed to me to be one of those men who should only exist in caricature – the gold jewellery, the cars with the personalised number plates, the extravagant claims of sexual conquest. He'd also once called my mum 'Osama Ben Hur' after he'd bumped into me pushing her in her wheelchair all wrapped up in scarves in the street one day, which I didn't like at all.

Still, I thought, I would take particular pleasure this evening lighting my cigars with his tenners. This was one of Shagger's habits after a particularly big win and I'd been unfortunate enough to witness it twice. If you add to this the fact that he persistently called us 'small fry' and referred to the serious money games he played 'at the big house' on Saturdays, you can see why I didn't relish his company.

Shagger was a member of a group of players who called themselves the Folding Society, folding being demi-criminal slang for money, people for whom the word 'cash' didn't seem tough enough.

Still, it transpired that my losing streak was not yet to end, becoming something rather wider than a streak, a losing blob maybe.

When the card came down I just could not get arrested, even though I'd returned to absolute basics – throw away the rubbish, be aggressive when you do have good cards, patience brings reward.

I ask you, what happens when the first thing that affronts your eyes when you get your cards is a pair of queens, the light glinting off them as if through stained glass?

I've read that the feeling you get in the great churches, that light-headed awe, is known as the numinous. Well, that's what I got looking down at those queens. Numin-bleeding-ous.

A very quick word about poker here. The game we play is dead simple. You get two cards dealt to you that no one else sees and no one else can use to make a hand. There's a round of betting, the details of which are too dull to go into, then three cards that everyone sees and everyone can use come down. This is known as the flop. You look at your cards and see if you can make, or have a chance to make – there are two cards still to come – a good hand of five cards.

If you have what it takes, you stay in and bet again. If you don't, you throw the cards away and lose whatever money you've already shelled out. Better to throw bad cards away and lose a little than stay in and lose a lot. Then comes a fourth card and a fifth so there's a total of seven cards on the table from which you have to make the best hand using five of them. That's basically it. I'll go through the details of the hands as they come up, or maybe I won't. I've tried this on Lyndsey and she always makes a large yawning motion and says, 'Here's a bet for you. I bet you can't shut up.'

So back to my two queens. On these cards you've no choice, have you? You bet big. You know it, I know it, that dog knows it. (In fact that dog knows it better than most.) So, rat-a-tat-tat, you shell out. Shagger bites at his top lip and follows you. The flop comes down and you pick up a queen of diamonds, the very image of lady luck.

Shagger's in up to his neck but you know he's bluffing because the chances of him having anything better are something like a hundred to one and the last time a hundred to one shot came in, Elizabeth Taylor was riding it in *National Velvet*.

'He seems confident, sir,' says the dog, causing me to hold his jaws together with my hand again.

I sink in for £1,000, borrow £300 more and another £100 to see the cards, and the bastard's got a full house, tens and queens, and I haven't got the bus fare home.

'I'm surprised you're bothering to stay for the sandwiches,' said Shagger, as I toothed the cheese and pickle at the break.

'Best hand I've had all night,' I said, holding up a couple of egg mayonnaises in a fan.

'I should imagine that's the last meal you'll be having for a while,' says Shagger.

'You're right,' I said. 'I'm skint, thanks . . .' I can't bring myself to write what I called him but let's just say it's very like the word 'can't'.

He practically purred as I insulted him and I could see my tactics had worked. It's good to look pissed off when you lose, like it really hurts, because it lets the others enjoy beating you all the more. It's my hope that this pleasant and fragrant memory will stick in their minds and cause them to act in rashness in future in an attempt to live it again. Hasn't worked so far.

'Still, it won't be for long, another few weeks and I'll be in the money.'

'Oh?' says virtually everyone, looking like vampires hearing that the blood bank's opening late Thursdays.

I don't know why I told them and I've certainly regretted it since, but tell them I did.

'I reckon the commission alone will be worth the top side of a hundred thousand,' I said. Not only has Shagger drawn me into his coarse world of boasting about money, he has provoked me into exaggeration.

This had the desired effect, though, and everyone looks miserable at the news of my good fortune, even though I know the bastards are thinking they'll have a large slice of it for themselves before long.

'The funny thing was,' I said, 'that the daft old bat's put the whole thing in my hands. She doesn't even want to know how much I'm selling it for. It's very lucky she got me or she could fall into the grip of some right swindlers,' I said.

'You've overbuttered these sandwiches,' said the Singing Detective as Snake Eyes' mum came into the room very much not giving a fuck.

'I quite like that,' said the Pieman, who was eating one of his own pies, partly through gluttony but partly in an attempt to get the sort of steak and kidney breath that could repel a Panzer division. Lots of players do this – stink in various subtle ways to make the others uncomfortable.

But Shagger wasn't listening to them. He was looking at me.

'Actually,' he says, 'I've got some friends who might be very interested in that.'

He wasn't talking about the sandwiches.

5

Cat Calls

Lyndsey shops at Sainsbury's. She didn't allow herself this slight yet significant extravagance lightly or quickly. She transferred from the more character-consistent Kwik Save, eight miles away, when she decided to try to sell the old Clio.

The saving in petrol might only be two pounds a trip, which won't offset shopping at a semi-luxury store, but once you factor in the chance of damaging the car and the associated loss in resale price then the change becomes more palatable.

Still, it never set her in a particularly good mood. Me neither. I guess I knew I needed help with my gambling but there never seemed a right time to tell her. I felt I was betraying her. There she was, investing in a device to cut her own hair and there I was blowing thousands on a regular basis. I'd thought at one time that if I made enough from poker I could give her the things that would make her happy so she could be free of the worry of money.

My own attitude to cash was bizarre. There was almost a bigger thrill in losing it than there was in winning. The second after a big loss you feel peculiarly free, like the man leaping from a plane, thinking, 'What was I worried about? This is fun.' Then you realise, of course that – financially speaking – you have no parachute.

No wonder she'd been reluctant for us to take the next step – moving in together. I think she instinctively sensed that I wasn't at a point where I could be a responsible partner.

My mum, of course, had come between us in the past. Lyndsey was slightly miffed when she'd discovered that I gave part of my income to my mum, even though I'd presented it as an investment, in that we'd get the flat when she died. We hadn't got the flat when she died because the nursing company had already mortgaged its value against her care.

Some people ask me why I stay with Lyndsey and they say she treats me badly. The thing is, I know who the real bastard is in this relationship. If I'd spent my gambling losses on us, we could have had ten Clios. She gives it me in the ear about my losses, even though I knock two or three zeros off the figures.

'I'm surprised at you, losing ten pounds on something so stupid,' she says.

On top of this, she's never going to make me feel uncomfortable by buying me a Walnut Whip out of the blue or asking me how I am and meaning it.

She loves me, I know; she says it all the time. And I love her, even though I don't say it quite so often.

Anyway, that morning I installed the dog at Lucy's – who happened to have a Walnut Whip in her fridge, funnily enough. I stayed for coffee among the self-stripped floorboards, the plants and books until I nearly forgot to meet Lyndsey.

I didn't want Lyndsey to be confronted with the idea of the dog until an opportune moment could be found to announce his presence.

As we drove towards the supermarket I wanted to tell her something about my life – anything really. The deception over my losses was getting to me and I felt I had to confide in her, not about the money but about something.

I shifted uncomfortably on the Clio's polythene seat covers, the same ones it had come in four years before. I didn't know why I hadn't told her about my encounter with Mrs Cad-Beauf but I'd felt an inner reluctance to do so. The same for the dog.

I guessed it was the little gambling demon inside me, marking the money for poker and not wanting her to know about it. This clearly meant I had to force myself to tell her so I didn't just hoon away all the money. Also, I knew the depressing prospect of the weekly shop would be hanging heavy over her. I sympa-thised – you can't get out of a supermarket for under fifty pounds nowadays.

'I had an interesting encounter yesterday,' I said.

'Oh yes?' said Lyndsey,

'Yeah, I've got a big deal coming up, I think. It could be worth a good thirty thousand in commission.'

Why did I find myself underestimating her? Was I setting aside a quick £40,000 or so to gamble? No, let's say it as it is. Was I setting aside £40,000 to give to people I didn't even like?

'Wow! Great!' said Lyndsey.

'I'll chip in to the price of the new car, if you like.'

Lyndsey beamed. 'You are nice to me, Dave,' she said. 'I do love you like crazy.'

'And you're nice to me,' I said. She raised her eyebrows, waiting for our standard reply.

'And I love you like crazy,' I said.

We drove on through the bleak surburbia and I noticed her frowning.

'Are you OK?' I said.

This is very often the kind of thing I say to her when I actually mean, 'Cheer up, you miserable cow.'

'Yeah,' she said, looking far away. This is often the sort of thing she does when she means, 'No, I am being a miserable cow.'

'What's the matter?'

She swallowed. 'I don't know, I was thinking how nice it was of you to offer me the money and then I just thought how daft it was that I was so pleased with five thousand pounds.'

Did I say five thousand? I thought I'd just said I'd chip in.

'That's quite a lot of money,' I said, which it was, even by the standards of my gambling.

'Yeah,' said Lyndsey, sadly, 'it is to us, isn't it?'

'Isn't it to anyone?'

'Not to Paul McCartney,' she said. 'Or Elton John, or Richard Branson or Sting or lots of other superstars.'

'We're not superstars, are we?'

'No,' said Lyndsey, turning into the car park disconsolately, which isn't the safest way to do it, 'we're not.'

The car pulled up. 'We're not free like them,' she said. 'We can't do what we want when we want and we can't be who we want. I don't want to be a chiropodist, David. I want a hacienda on Mustique.'

She stared past the steering wheel at the sportsweared flock of shoppers moving about the car park. A homeless limped across our path shoving a trolley stacked with his possessions, dirty discoloured plastic bags, a blue tarpaulin and newspapers, topped off by a grey plastic crutch. Why wasn't he using the crutch? Why was it on his trolley? He was making something that should have been a support into a burden. This stirred some unreasonable thoughts in me. Use it or lose it, I thought. The scene gave me a shiver. He seemed to me like some undead shopper returning from a phantom superstore with his rotten goods, a man past his die by date.

'It could be worse,' I said. 'Look at him.'

Lyndsey shook her head. 'He's not that different to us. He's poor but so are we. I'm sure he's no more miserable. He wants a house as much as I want a hacienda and he's got about as much chance of getting one. He's homeless, we're second homeless.

We haven't even got anywhere in Dorset. We're not even as free as him with our low-paid jobs. At least he gets to limp around all day. I'm in looking at feet.'

'Lyndsey,' I said, 'we are free because we love each other. Love is freedom and love is free.' I meant it, though I was sure I might have seen Jerry Springer summing up with very similar thoughts.

'It's just cost you five grand,' she said, brightening up.

'Is that worth a kiss?' I said.

'You're not going to turn me into your prostitute, are you?' she said, giving me a saucy eye.

'I might,' I said.

'Good,' she said, leaning over and plunging her tongue into my mouth.

There's one thing I'll say for Lyndsey, when it comes to the sack she says, 'Paint me gold and black and call me *Felix Terribilis.*' One of her favourite games is to pretend to be a call girl and I have to pretend to be a punter, stuffing fivers into her bra and knickers as I tell her what I want her to do. I know this sounds rather typical of her character but I do get the money back. Well, most of it.

So it was that I was lingering by the organic veg section, inspecting a pack of quality chives, while Lyndsey stacked up on spuds when my phone rang.

I didn't recognise the number. I answered it.

'You don't know me,' said a voice, something of a statement of the obvious, I thought, 'but I'm an associate of Philip Burns. Shagger, to you.'

He said the word 'Shagger' as if he was holding it in tongs, and at arm's length at that.

'Oh yes,' I said, wondering what radicchio was.

'My name's Michael Tibbs. I run the Folding Society at the big house. Philip thinks you might be a useful addition to our circle this evening.'

There was something in his voice that made me quite nervous, though not in a bad way. Like when I'd played for the school team and we'd got through to the East Sussex finals. Stepping onto the pitch I was shaking like a leaf, though I was also aware this was the crowning glory of my life. All right, I didn't have much of a life then but that's how it felt, ice cold and hot all at the same time. However, all I'd needed to play football was a pair of boots and an inflated idea of my own ability. Come to think of it, the East Sussex finals probably were the crowning glory of my life. Oh dear.

'Sorry,' I said, 'I wouldn't be a useful addition to a game of shove ha'penny this evening. I'm skint.'

I heard Tibbs breathe in. 'The Folding Society is always quite sure when it selects its members. We would be willing to advance you a sum in order to play,' he said.

I knew what had happened here. Shagger Burns had told these bastards that I was a prime mug and that if they tried they'd have my business, my home and the Ted Baker off my back. I felt anger rising within me that they could treat me with such contempt.

I was on a losing streak for sure, but it had to end eventually. It wasn't as if I was suddenly playing all that badly. If they let me in it was them, not me, who'd be handing over the keys to their cars, houses and timeshares.

'How much can you advance me?' I asked.

'As much as you want,' said Tibbs.

With a credit facility like that, I thought, there was no way a player of my class could lose. The man was clearly deranged, asking for it, a patsy.

'What time and where?' I said, as I noticed Lyndsey waiting for the man with the special offer gun to get to the coriander. 'And, er, can I bring a dog?'

6

Howl To Make Friends and Influence People

Perhaps humans can sense things too sometimes. Something about Tibbs's manner when I suggested taking Reg along made me want to distance myself from him.

'I'm looking after him for a friend,' I said, 'and he tends to chew things up if he gets left on his own. Maybe I could come to a game in a week or so when I can get someone to look after him.' I didn't mean this. I was desperate to go immediately but wanted to sound cool.

'We need you at this game,' said Tibbs, in a way that suggested he wasn't a man of inexhaustible patience. 'You can bring the dog, as long as you keep it under control.'

Michael Tibbs, otherwise known as Michael the Cat, was, I have since discovered, one of the leading property boys in the south, known locally as the Weald-axing maniac for his success in building on the fragile Sussex flatlands.

The big house was, as it suggests, a very large property right on the Seven Sisters cliffs, benefiting from magnificent sea views, a south-facing orchard, three garages, a stable and excellent transport links.

This prestige development comprised I don't know how many bedrooms as I'm pleased to say that I never visited them.

The games room, however, was quite magnificent, a deep red nook, a pocket of cigar smoke and manliness at the corner of the house, 25' × 13', in excellent decorative order.

We were greeted at the door by a butler. When I say a butler I actually mean a man dressed up as a butler. Few graduates of any of the finer butling schools would have answered the door with the word 'Yo!' or standards are not what they were in the young Queen's day.

I have to say that the Cat seemed to run a quality table. Normally I play poker with people who think that by the word 'suit' you're referring to hearts, diamonds, spades and clubs, not the Savile Row variety. Here, though, the boys were dressed and in your top togs. I was glad I'd chosen to dress up, if only in my black Burton number. Wear a cheap suit with a quality shirt and tie and you'll look fine, goes the mantra. It made me wish I'd bought a quality shirt and tie, instead of my auntie's one-size-fits-almost-all special and the standard Next neck gear.

The dog at least looked top drawer as I'd lashed out on a leather collar in a subtle tartan from up town by writing a cheque for it. You've got a guarantee card, the bank can't touch you.

He'd also had a bath, much against his wishes.

'It'll do you good,' I said.

'How will robbing me of my smell, my very identity, do me good?'

'We tend to see that as a good thing,' I said, running the shower attachment across his back.

'At least spare the tail!' he whimpered. 'It is the font of my me-ness, the splendid advertisement of my fame.'

I had no idea what he was on about.

'No can do, I'm afraid,' I said, splashing the lemon-scented Mucky Mutt up his brush.

'Oh, pity me!' he cried as I rinsed him off and towelled him down. 'I'm, I'm, I'm . . .' He stopped for a moment and glanced back at his body. Then he looked at me with dawning delight. 'You know what,' he said, 'I'm only soaking wet! Bonus!' He freed himself from the towel and went shooting around the flat. 'I'm wet, I'm wet, I'm soaking blinking wet,' he said, narrowly avoiding running into a wall.

'Why's that a good thing?' I said.

'Well,' said the dog, shrugging, 'there are dogs out there who are quite dry.'

I didn't press him further. I was discovering that some parts of canine logic are best left unexplored.

So there he was in the Cat's hallway, his fur fluffy and big from the conditioner, looking as scrubbed and cleaned as a boy on his way to his bar mitzvah.

'Welcome,' said the Cat. I think the sight of Reg quite unnerved him, really. Poker is about front and show. Bringing something with you that refers to your gentler life outside isn't quite playing by the rules.

For your own self-esteem you want to think of people by nicknames like the Blond Ayatollah (so called because his name is Muller and that corresponds to Mullah in the poor-spelling world of poker), a man who dealt in knock-off batteries and, it was rumoured, had murdered, one New Year, four Sinatra numbers, back to back. You want him staring in your face and saying, 'I'm going to take you down, Neighbour,' not showing you pictures of his kids on their pony. If you wanted that you could go to work.

'This mutt looks a bit like you, actually,' said the Cat, grinning pleasantly at the dog like a man who was trying grinning pleasantly for the first time and finding he had no great talent for it – uncasual in his casual slacks.

'He's not mine,' I said. I don't know why I wanted to impress that on him but I did.

'It's more a client consultant thing than a contract of owner-ship,' said the dog, nodding.

'They do say dogs come to resemble their owners,' said the Cat, leading me towards a heavily panelled door, 'or is it the other way around?' Again he sounded like someone embarking on module one of a 'Learn Small Talk' course.

'It's actually both,' said the dog, as if pleased to be able to impart an interesting fact, 'due to ion exchange.'

I felt a question rise inside me. The dog obviously felt it too because he went on.

'It's the patting and the stroking. Ions, or charged atoms, from the human hand bond with other atoms in the dog and vice versa. Eventually the human is part dog and the dog part human. It explains the tendency of old ladies with Pekinese to snap at people,' he said.

'I'm going nuts,' I said, accidentally out loud.

'What nuts?' said the Cat. He gave me an odd look. 'You're not gay, are you?'

'Not really,' I said.

The Cat seemed to find this less than reassuring, as did I. I mean, if you can't answer a question like that with confidence, what chance are you going to have with the uncertainty of the cards?

The dog sniffed at the floor. 'Many lonely people have passed through here,' he said, with a long 'lonely'.

The butler had reached the door in front of us and he opened it to reveal a card table surrounded by men drinking and talking.

'Mr Barker and . . .' the butler looked down at Reg who looked up in a wide and expectant grin, 'dog,' said the butler in that dropping tone that the man on Final Score uses to say, 'Queen of the South 3, Hamilton Academical . . . 0.'

We went into the room and the Cat introduced the company, by name and job title, as if he was impressing on me that I was playing with the big boys. It all washed over me, a blur of solicitors, a chief superintendent, someone who I thought might have been a celebrity gangster.

I still hadn't been invited to sit down.

'Is . . .' I couldn't really remember Shagger's first name, 'Mr Burns not joining us?' I said.

'Not this evening,' said the Cat, pleasantly. 'He must be busy, I suppose.'

'Mr Burns isn't a member of the Folding Society,' said a soft-faced fat man in a pink shirt. 'He visits occasionally but he's not,' he waved his hand in the air as if trying to summon the words from the ether, 'a person of quality.' It occurred to me that I had no idea whether this man was a person of quality or not but he was certainly a person of quantity.

'I'm obviously a dog of quality,' said the dog, looking up at me with his top lips pressed down, like Benito Mussolini lapping up the applause for a speech.

The Cat gave an indulgent nod towards the man.

'Stephen here has his views!' he said with a smile, like the parent of a pierced adolescent. The man gave a grunt.

The Cat spoke to me. 'If I could just prevail on you to stand for a second longer, Mr Barker. The Folding Society is a poker school but it is also much more than that and there is a formality we observe before games. I'm afraid non-members can't take part in this but you're welcome to watch. Please, browse the drinks and have Jenkins pour you one.' He extended his hand and I turned to look where he was indicating, behind me.

It was as if light had burst from the ends of his fingers, as I saw the alcove for the first time, a crystal cavern of sparkling whites and deep ambers. It was a drinks cabinet, of a sort, but one you could walk into. It was difficult to guess the dimensions as it was mirrored on the inside and lit in such a way that it was difficult to tell where the drinks ended and their reflections began. A prestige feature, to be sure, a talking point and a centrepiece, though to one side.

I gazed inside and it seemed like all the world was on offer, ancient-looking brandies, modern-looking vodkas, things decanted and bottles untouched, the boundaries between the real and the reflected unguessable.

'I recommend the Remy Martin 1901,' said the Cat with a smile.

'Have you got any lemonade?' I said. I figured I'd better keep a clear head in this company.

'Waaater!' said Reg.

'R. Whites?' said the Cat, widening his eyes in an 'are you one of us?' expression.

'*Naturellement*,' I said, 'and a water for the hound?'

'San Pellegrino?' said the Cat.

'*Bien sûr*,' I said. I hadn't realised I could speak so much French.

The Cat gestured to the butler who rattled around inside the cabinet until he found a fridge.

While this was going on the Cat sat down at the table and waited for the cacophony of his servant's endeavours to subside.

Once I had my lemonade, which had a thumb-print on the glass, and the dog had his silver bowl, the proceedings began. All eight men at the table linked hands and the Cat began to intone a prayer.

'Let us remember at this meeting,' he said, 'those less fortunate than ourselves. Let us remember the starving children, the sick, the unhappy, the endless nations of poor. Let us remember them and know who we are.'

'We remember them and we know who we are,' intoned the men.

'Bunch of twits, if you ask me,' said the dog, scrunching up his nose where the bubbles from the water had got to him.

I shushed him, not with my mouth but with my eyes, rather like my mum used to do to me in company.

'They should howl if they want to express solidarity,' he said, into his collar.

I put out my hand in a 'Stop!' sign to prevent an illustration.

'I'll invite you to sit beside me,' said the Cat, 'or do I just say "down"?'

The room laughed but Reg shook his head.

'Two entirely separate requests!' he said, as if pointing out a schoolboy error.

Sit I did, with the dog wedged in under my feet.

'Let's deal 'em,' said the Cat.

The unspoken rule of poker is that everyone pretends to be hard. This lot, though, looked as though they'd been pretending so long they'd rather convinced themselves of their act.

The butler came over and offered people cigars. I went to take a large Cohiba but had some difficulty freeing it as it was packed against the others so tightly.

The Cat leaned over and did it for me, expertly extracting one with a single finger.

Well, he'd had more practice, hadn't he? The butler cut the end off it and lit it for me. I inhaled, feeling like Joe Dolce must have felt on *Top of the Pops* – enjoy it while you can, you're not coming back.

Then another man in a kind of bellhop uniform came into the room, pushing an elegant wooden trolley on which were stacked arrays of chips. I'd never played with anything but money before and I felt a thrill go through me as I looked at them.

Beautiful colours of reds, blues, purple, gold, the big scary black ones and the friendly striped ones, like sliced seaside rock. They seemed mystical to me, signs that meant more than what they represented – more glamorous than money and more dangerous too.

The chips were invented for two reasons – so that large

cumbersome amounts of cash aren't flying around the table and, more importantly, so that the gambler has a psychological separation from what they really represent – hard, cold, earned cash.

It would be easy to be sentimental and say that a black £100 chip represented saving the sight of fifty children in Africa, or schoolbooks for the underprivileged in our country, but what it really represents, of course, is the sweat of your brow, a hard black drop of condensed effort – a day in the shop, an hour at the solicitor's desk, a mahogany slice of your coffin for which you have mortgaged your youth in exam room, office and study.

In the gambling room, though, it's a magic token, a beautiful bead to be glided across the baize as the Gods of Olympus might have slid ships across the Aegean towards Troy. It's not money, it doesn't feel like money and yet, and yet.

'How many would you like, David?' whispered the Cat.

'Front me two grand,' I said, looking round the table.

The Cat coughed lightly. 'The minimum bet at this table is one hundred pounds,' he said.

'Better make it three then,' I said, 'three large.' For some reason I laughed.

'Make it four,' said the Cat. 'A little welcoming present.'

'Great!' I said.

Now I wasn't, for a second, thinking that the Cat was such a nice guy that he'd decided to give me £4,000 out of the goodness of his heart. I wasn't thinking that I was such an all-round great fellow to be with that these people wanted me with them at any price and I wasn't thinking that the Cat fancied me. No – I just wasn't thinking. I had handed over complete control of my mind to this chap who lives inside it – the gambler. He doesn't think, he just gambles. If anything at all goes on inside his head it's something like, 'Shiny chips! Bright lights! Cards! Oh yeah!'

The dealer dealt and the players played, cautiously in my case. Poker isn't such a vicious game that you can get fleeced in seconds even if you're being careful. Well, you can get fleeced but it takes either tremendous bad luck or a real effort from the other players to do it.

I suppose I should have felt flattered, then, that I was the sole object of their attention that evening. I should have expected it but at the very moment when my guard should have been up, I put it down. It wasn't my money, was it? I couldn't get into trouble, or that's what the gambler was telling me.

The gambler is very much like a dog in a butcher's shop. He is not entirely immersed in the present, his ears will occasionally flatten when he thinks of the butcher returning from the freezer but then his teeth will sink into the meat and he'll be over-whelmed by its taste. 'Oh, the texture, oh, the flavour, the dripping fat and the succulent flesh, the bone on the tooth, oh, oh, oh! Ahhhhh!' as a size nine lands on his rear.

So it was that I saw the looks exchanged across the table, the semaphore of eyebrows communicating their complicity. This isn't cheating. There's nothing in the rules that stops players working together, other than the fact that any sane person will walk out as soon as they realise it and, if the type, may cut up rough about it.

I saw all this but still I went on. Why? Because to the gambler this is just another gamble, one more risk, and risk is what the gambler feeds off, it's what he wants. To steal a quote from my hosts, it's who he is.

I was holding some mediocre cards against two remaining players and considering folding when the Cat said softly in my ear. 'I hear you've picked up some interesting business lately.'

The next hand was being dealt and, waiting for my cards, I felt like a fat lad in the seconds before the jelly is served.

'It's very dark and there is a distinctly menacing atmosphere,' said Reg from beneath my feet.

'I hear,' said the Cat more firmly, 'that you've picked up some interesting business lately.'

The cards slide across the table towards me, blank backs that will turn to reveal swirling vortexes of nothing or jewelled jacks, queens and kings.

Bingo, two tens. Now let's see who wants to play.

The flop and – there is a lord in heaven – ten diamonds roll cold and hard into my hand. Three tens. Is that solid? Put it this way, if Saddam Hussein had had three tens in Baghdad he'd still be there today.

Three fold and five are in. Pay day.

'I'm getting out!' said the dog.

'Sit back down, you bastard!' I said to him, which caused something of a ruffle at the table. I shot them my best obsequious grin.

'I HEAR,' says the Cat, 'that you've taken on the sale of Charterstone.'

Four fold like origami and it's down to me and the Pig.

'Whatever,' I say, hypnotised by this oinker in the pink shirt who's vacillating over what to do. Or pretending to vacillate. I can tell he's no good because good players bluff by what they do, not how they act. No one gives a shit if he's scratching his head and miming 'Don't know, don't know' under his breath. If he had a 'tell', a sign that indicated he had a particularly good or bad hand, it wouldn't be that obvious, just a flicker of an eye, a raised finger on the table. We poker players look for these like we're panning for gold. 'Sod the extravagant expression of worry,' we say, 'give me the shoulder drop, give me the lick of the teeth or the dilating nostril. With these I will weave magic.'

Is this pig ever going to make a decision? I wondered. If he didn't play I'd only win a grand back, but that would be a start.

No, seemed to be the answer. Still, what do I care? I'm sitting pretty as a parade with trip tens – three of them to the rest of you.

The Cat was looking at me directly. 'Perhaps we could have a chat about Charterstone at the break?'

'Sure,' I said. Then I, as in the person who walks around day to day, does my job, eats my meals, sleeps with my girlfriend, suddenly woke up.

'Would you like to buy it?' I said

'Yeah!' says the Pig. 'I would.' He slides his stacks of candy-coloured money beans across the table and it's all I can do to stop myself grabbing them there and then.

I put my remaining wodge against his and, professionally, do and say nothing else.

Normally when a player puts the last of his wonga into the pot it's known as being 'all in' and the cards are turned. I wasn't going to let him off so easily, though.

I was going to borrow more and sizzle his bacon good and proper.

The Pig's eyes widen to the size of a 5p coin. Another two and a half slide across the table. I'm tempted to shout, 'Squeal, like a pig!' but I don't. The chances of him having a better hand than mine are roughly equivalent of his heart lasting past middle age. Zilch.

I gesture to the dealer, who I have decided for some reason necessary to my fantasy life is called Hervé. 'Five,' I say.

The Cat raises an eyebrow. 'I'll cover it,' I say. Even if the worst came to the worst and this miserable lowlife beat my noble tens I could, er, think about that later. It wasn't going to happen though.

'No, please,' says the Cat, 'you're our guest.'

The chips are pushed towards me, the multicoloured pills I need for my addiction.

The Pig comes back at me and I go all in.

There's a year's wages for a middle management job in most parts of the country in the pot right there.

Suddenly I see Lyndsey and the Clio. There are about three new Clios in the pot at this particular moment. The gambler wants to keep going. 'It's not your money!' he says. I, however, who looked after my mum and return purses to old ladies, want to stop. 'It's not my money!' I say.

'I don't like this man, he's laughing at you,' said the dog. I took it he meant the Pig.

The Pig calls me, the horde of chips sliding across the baize to meet my own, to mate with it and create something beautiful.

Like many things that weren't going to happen, it then happened.

He turns over his cards. Two sixes to go with the two on the table. It is a well-known and largely uncontested fact that two and two make four. Four and I'm out the door. Four sixes. The number of the bastard. For the second time in a row I've got done on three-of-a-kind.

I feel as though I am falling down a well. It's not my money but the Cat now owes the Pig £9,000. A whole Clio. The gambler, who has featured so very largely in my mind up until that point, says, 'See ya!' and disappears in a puff. As he does, I see him for what he is. Not the bootlace-tied, sharp-Stetsoned king-slinger I'd taken him to be but a grubby little man in an anorak who'd given up on success and self-esteem in the real world and was seeking it instead in the closed company of numbers.

He'd gone, leaving me, the man who won't park on a double yellow line because it's unfair to other road users, alone in this room of vipers and one dirty pigging pig.

'You want to leave too,' said the dog, sniffing my shoe. 'Can we go now?'

'Refreshments!' said the Cat. Bizarrely, he looked quite pleased, or more pleased than a man who's a Citroen and a bit down on the evening should have been.

I realised then that I should have asked a question that the gambler had been keeping me from asking.

'Why did you invite me here?' I said.

'I have a deal for you,' said the Cat, standing as a pyramid of sandwiches and canapés were wheeled in.

'Actually,' said the dog, 'I've changed my mind. There's no atmosphere so menacing it can't be banished by a ham sandwich.'

'I'm all for deals,' I said, mechanically shovelling in a salmon and cream cheese snap.

'Good,' said the Cat. 'It's very simple, really. It's come to my attention that you have acquired the commission to sell Charterstone.'

'Yes,' I said, relieved. I could see by the careful way he handled a caviar snap that he perhaps intended to buy it. Don't ask me how I could see that, I just could.

'How did you do that?' said the Cat. 'We've been trying to get the old bat to sell for years.'

'The Bat asked me to,' I said. You can go too far with these animal nicknames sometimes. The Cat, the Pig, the Bat. If everyone has different nicknames, newer players would face being called the Wailing Grebe or the Thompson's Gazelle.

Mind you, there's a Tibetan bloke who plays out of Streatham who's called the Llama, so I suppose anything's possible.

'You're a friend?' said the Cat with a look of mild concern, like a real cat hearing of industrial discontent in the Whiskas factory.

'I regard all my clients as friends,' I said. The Cat looked as if he had ingested a fur ball. 'I don't know her,' I said, 'but she lost something and I found it and returned it to her and she asked me to sell the place for her.'

'It was pure luck?' said the Cat.

'Well, yes. Although I'm not sure she really wants to sell. I'm going round next week and making absolutely sure it's in her best interests,' I said. I hoped it was. I'd taken her purse money and was going to write it off against my commission.

The Cat looked at me, placing his top lip over his bottom. The dog looked at the Cat also with his top lip over his bottom but as a matter of genetics rather than attitude.

'In her best interests?' said the Cat.

'Yes,' I said. 'I regard myself as more than an estate agent really. More of a property consultant. It's not all about commission.'

A look of puzzlement crossed his face, like a vicar asking God for an explanation why someone had pissed in the font.

'What is it all about then?' said the Cat.

'Providing a service,' I said. 'Self-respect.'

The Cat smiled, showing a set of immaculately dentised teeth. 'I understand,' he said, 'but this isn't about self-respect. It's about much more than that. It's about money.'

I could see he thought he'd dropped the equivalent of a royal flush onto my low pair.

Of course I'd guessed by now why he'd invited me to the game and fronted me money. He wanted to get first dibs on Charterstone, to get the deal done and dusted for a reasonable price before it went into some bidding war and the price went through the roof. That's why he'd got me in his debt. Unfortunately I was going to have to tell him that my first loyalty was to Mrs Cad-Beauf, nine large or no nine large.

As I thought, he came to the point quickly.

'We'd like to buy it, Mr Barker,' said the Cat.

Other members of the society, I noticed, had been taking a close interest in what we'd been saying. The Pig, for a start, was too close to the back of my neck for my liking.

'And,' said the Pig, hot on my collar, 'we'd like to cut you in.' I glanced back to see him making a motion like someone feeding ham into a slicer.

This was clearly a very embarrassing situation I'd got myself into. I felt sure that if they could just lend me some more money, say five grand, I could win back my losses and leave free from their debt.

'Let me clear one thing up,' I said. 'I'd be delighted to put any offer you wish to make to Mrs Cad-Beauf but I'm afraid we're jumping the gun a little here, I haven't even valued the property yet.'

'Don't worry,' said the Cat, 'we have.'

'Oh?' I said, wanting to point out that whatever his surveyors said was fairly irrelevant, the proper test of its worth being what the market would bear; you could be looking at twenty-five million, you could be looking at sixty. 'And what figure did you come up with?'

'Four hundred thousand pounds,' said the Cat. 'Another R. Whites?'

7

Putting the Cat Out

'Are you aware that what you are proposing is completely and utterly illegal?' I looked at him in such a way that, had I worn a monocle, I would have lost it.

The Cat looked slightly puzzled.

'Well, yes,' he said, 'but don't worry, we've done our research and it's very difficult to prosecute. Beyond that it's an almost undetectable crime.' He licked a little bit of cream cheese from the end of his finger.

'Not to me it's bloody not, mate!' I said.

'Not mate!' said the dog, for emphasis. He was standing beside me in a gesture of solidarity. 'What are we on about?' he said. 'What is the exact nature of this unpleasantness, which is certainly most unpleasant if a little difficult to pin down?'

I was halfway through a miniature samosa at the time the Cat dropped his proposal into the conversation, like a three-bar fire into a jacuzzi, and I felt like putting it back. It felt mildly compromising to be accepting his hospitality. However, I quickly remembered that a samosa wasn't the extent of my debt to him.

'Now you really are all dilations and constrictions,' said the dog, 'And he's being very hostile, we must immediately . . .' he paused, briefly hypnotised by the samosa, '. . . and if you're not going to eat that may I humbly submit a request that you drop it to the floor where I might try it upon my tooth?'

'Well, you presumably wouldn't tell anyone,' said the Cat, looking at me like my old teacher Sarky Banthorpe used to look at the special needs pupils. 'You call it learning difficulties, I call it sloth,' I recall was his motto. He was particularly popular with the brighter pupils for his ability to show the slow boys enough to know they were being humiliated but little enough to obscure exactly how.

'No one here's going to tell anyone and I suppose your charming canine friend isn't going to tell anyone, so what is there to lose?'

'I'll tell every dog in the neighbourhood,' said Reg. 'I'll lay it up every post! What am I meant to be telling them?' He was quite frustrated at this point, although no one seemed to notice him speaking.

The Cat turned to the room as if they would back up his words.

'We're talking about an estate worth around twenty-five million in its present condition, perhaps more,' said the Cat. 'We figure that after development we'd be looking at a resale value, as a prestige gated community, of around forty million. Redevelopment costs are about six million, including Mrs Cad-Beauf's four hundred thousand. You're looking at a straight profit,' the word profit seemed to make his lips wet, 'of thirty-three million pounds. Your taste would be five hundred thousand, plus the six thousand from the commission on the sale on behalf of Mrs Cad-Beauf. You will dip your beak for five hundred and six thousand pounds.'

A murmur rumbled through the room. Approval, awe, something. It was like the pupils of Plato hearing the great man make a conclusive point. I noticed I had replaced the half-eaten samosa on the tray. This fact was not lost on the dog, who wore a look of considerable hurt.

'It's not on behalf of Mrs Cad-Beauf, is it?' I said. 'It's the reverse of on her behalf.' As far as I could see it was like saying they'd dropped the atomic bomb on behalf of the people of Nagasaki and Hiroshima. Actually, I think they do say something like that, don't they?

The Cat laughed, and it occurred to me that this was a sight few people ever saw. He went around with a permanent half-smile on his chops but I didn't get the impression that he was the sort given to laughing.

'You drive a hard bargain, Mr Barker.'

'No, I don't,' I said. I wasn't driving a bargain. I wasn't even in the passenger seat of a bargain. If anything, it looked as if I'd been bound and gagged and stuffed into a bargain's boot.

'You have us at a disadvantage,' said the Cat. 'You are the key to this deal. Name your price but be careful. You're not dealing with mugs.'

'He doesn't have his own mug,' said the dog. 'I told him no good would come of it.'

I couldn't believe what I was hearing. To suggest I'd defraud an old lady, no matter what the inducement, was ridiculous.

'One million pounds,' said the Cat. 'There are eight of us here and that's a sixth of the profit due to even the highest investors. It's absolutely our ceiling.'

'One million hounds?' said the dog, who had clearly misheard. 'That is an army, sir. The world would be yours, though the logistics of feeding them all would be astounding! A single tin-opener just wouldn't be up to it.'

One million pounds is roughly 125 Clios, even if you take the full extras package. I'm talking about CD, electric windows, the lot. The thing is, that thought would have stopped me even if I had been unscrupulous. Looked at in that way it's not actually very much. I mean, how many Clios can you have?

Money's very helpful, it can't be denied, but the things that made me happy – the dog, Lyndsey's love, knowing I at least tried to be a decent and pleasant human being (I'm running a little bare here) – had nothing to do with money.

So why did I find gambling so attractive? I don't know but, oddly, most real gamblers value money very little. When I say 'real' what I mean is addicted, even if only mildly. What they like is gambling, not necessarily cash. Money becomes slightly unreal to gamblers. One million pounds is simply the key to two million pounds, which is the key to four which is the key to nothing and beginning again. A million pounds is a lifetime playing whist in a pub or one spin of the roulette wheel. Money isn't real. Gambling is.

'You can announce the good news to Mrs Cad-Beauf tomorrow,' said the Cat. 'Mr Wilkes here will arrange the conveyancing at a preferential rate and I believe we may be in a position to exchange contracts with all haste,' he said.

'I won't do it,' I said.

The Cat nodded, graciously. 'You won't because you have no guarantee you will ever receive the money,' he said. 'However, I offer you two guarantees. The first is the criminality of the exercise. We would be culpable if you went to the law. Not as culpable as you but culpable. The second is that I am willing to offer you membership of the Folding Society.'

He stroked his fine whiskers and a hush fell on the room.

'That means,' he said into the dry silence, 'that you will receive our support in all matters of local business. Any property sales we make come through you. If we advise clients we advise them to deal through you and to trust you. We allow you to manage our rental properties. In short, you become a player – a rich man benefiting from the company and favours of rich men.'

'Well, that all sounds very nice,' I said, 'but I'm afraid it's out of the question. I simply won't defraud Mrs Cad-Beauf. I like her and even if I didn't like her I still wouldn't defraud her. It's not what I do.'

The Cat frowned. 'Attempt to be serious, David. We are serious men.'

'Attempt to be serious!' said the dog, nudging me with his shoulder. 'He's a bit of a nasty piece of work, this one.'

The other members of the society shuffled their feet in what I suppose they took for a serious way. They didn't make a bad job of it, really.

'I am serious,' I said. 'I'm sorry, I'm not dishonest.' I thought I'd put it in language he could understand. 'I know who I am,' I said with a shrug.

The air seemed alive, vibrant, teeming with some biological energy that flowed through the Cat to form his words.

'In that case,' said the Cat, 'I'd like my money back please. Now.' His anger was boiling beneath the surface, like a one-man mob.

When I said money wasn't real to gamblers I didn't quite get it right. The presence of money isn't real. Its absence is as real as rain.

I tapped my pockets, finding myself a little short at that moment.

'You'll get it back,' I said, not exactly sure how. Then an idea struck me. 'Actually,' I said, 'if you front me another five thousand I'm sure I could win it back.'

The Cat smiled, biting his bottom lip so he looked a bit like one of those Samurai war masks.

'Credit facilities are withdrawn,' he said. 'I want my money.'

I looked down at the polished floor. It seemed like the surface of some strange lake, inviting me to dive in and disappear from that harsh scrutiny.

'I'm a little short at the moment,' I said.

'In that case we'll operate the normal rate of interest,' said the Cat.

'Which is?'

'One hundred per cent a week,' he said. 'Nine thousand pounds plus two lemonades at one pound fifty each (club prices) and three pounds for bar snacks. In seven weeks you'll owe me a million and then you'll sell me the house anyway but you'll do it for free.'

'I'm afraid I don't accept the terms,' I said.

'We've had people who haven't accepted the terms before, haven't we, Harry?' said the Cat to the man he'd introduced as a 'senior policeman'. 'What happened to them?'

'I don't know,' said the policeman. 'They haven't been seen for a while.'

'Are you threatening me?' I said.

'He's definitely threatening you,' said the dog. 'He's sweating up for a fight! Let me growl at him and if that doesn't do it, can we scarper?'

'I knew I'd forgotten something,' said the Cat. 'Do as we say, or else. There you go, I've remembered now.'

'I'd like to leave please,' I said.

'Grrrr!' said Reg, rather unconvincingly.

'Do,' said the Cat, 'and think about what's good for you. Mr Wilkes will contact you in the morning. He'll give you the details of the solicitor you're to use for the old lady. And now get this stupid stinking dog out of my house.'

'Hark at Lord Muck!' said the dog. 'If you will allow me, sir, I might show him my teeth. I think that might improve his attitude markedly.'

'No, Reg,' I said, although I did notice the dog was curling a lip.

The butler came and showed us out, Reg growling ever more fiercely until he closed the door behind us. 'I'll have the lot of you!' shouted the dog to its blank face.

It was unfortunate, really, that when I reached the car park the car wouldn't start and I had to call the RAC.

As I sat in the Cat's car park watching the bankers and the solicitors and the accountants pull away in their Lexi, Mercedes and Jags, it occurred to me that life was passing me by, that, as Lyndsey had said, I wasn't free.

'Your main bearing's gone, I think,' said the RAC man, after several attempts to start my car.

'Well, I've been under a lot of pressure lately,' I said.

8

Woof Is a Four-
Letter Word

I'd felt mightily threatened by Michael the Cat but I wondered
if I was being paranoid in writing it all down on a sheet of
paper. I imagined that, if I went missing, no one would have
any idea what had happened to me if I didn't make some sort
of record.

I sat at the table, looking out of the window and watching a
cheery red-faced man in a gas board cap disconnecting my
supply. The bowl of Cheerios I was intending to eat seemed to
sum up my prospects at that point, a flotsam of zeros suspended
there in front of me.

'Ah,' said Reg, stretching into what yogists call a downward dog and eyeing the bowl of food I had put down for him.
'Extend the limbs to purge the foul accretions of the night!'

I hadn't a clue what he was on about.

There was a sheet of A4 next to the bowl on which I'd written,
'Avowal of D. Barker'. That sounded grandiose and unpleasantly
as if I was already dead, so I crossed it out and wrote, 'Suggestion
of criminal enterprise by M. Tibbs to D. Barker'. Then I detailed
the whole scheme, penny for penny, as well as I could remember

it, showing the bribe he'd offered me and the illegal profit he intended to take for himself.

I'd hand that in to my solicitors to be attached to my will, I thought. That way, should I get the chop, Tibbs would be implicated. I'd let him know what I'd done and it might put him off acting against me.

Look on the bright side, I thought, staring down into the Cheerios. Not zeros but little life rings, tiny circles of hope.

Reg came out of his downward dog and stepped forward to quark down his food. A quark is a subatomic particle that is said to cease to exist before it actually exists. So it was with the dog, the borderline between being about to eat, eating and having eaten invisible, and detectable probably only at some strange Swiss laboratory.

I didn't manage to finish my cereal. I gave it to the dog as he assured me it was very good for the coat.

'The food here isn't as good as at Lucy's,' he said, with crushing dog honesty.

'What happens at Lucy's?' I said.

'Steak, chicken, ham and the odd sausage roll,' said Reg, with the air of a boy racer confiding that 'She'll top 140. In fourth.'

'Anything else?'

'Not really. Jim gives me the odd biscuit and bit off his plate,' he said.

'Who's Jim?' I said. 'I haven't heard of a Jim, why has Jim never been mentioned before, who the hell is Jim?'

'Hark at you!' said the dog. 'He's this rugged sort in a lumberjack shirt. Smells strongly of aftershave and moustache.'

'What's he doing at Lucy's?' I said.

'Acting quite the coquette,' said Reg, in a confidential tone. 'He normally holds the slice of chicken so it's just out of reach. Then, as I go up into human position on my hind legs, he holds it up further still. A hop secures the meat.'

I looked to the heavens. 'What's his relationship like with Lucy?'

'She gives him food,' said the dog, with a gracious bow of the head.

'Anything else?' I said, not wanting to be too obvious.

'Drink,' said the dog, with an air of self-satisfaction, like he was getting all the questions right.

The thing is with dogs, you actually can't be too obvious.

'Are they having a relationship?' I said.

'Free food and drink!' said the dog. 'I'd call that a relationship, wouldn't you, by jingo? Ai Karumba!'

'Do they kiss?' I said.

'Regularly,' said the dog.

I felt my heart sink. It would be better if she was going out with him, I thought. Even asking the questions felt like a betrayal of Lyndsey.

'Does she love this Jim?' I said.

'Oh yes,' said the dog, 'but not like I love you. Do you love me?'

I lifted one of his ears and lightly scrunched it. 'I love you very much,' I said. How quickly that had happened.

I felt very warm inside. I had the dog who loved me and Lyndsey who always told me she loved me like crazy, sometimes when looking into my eyes. OK, the dog had looked into my knee, but there you go. The distance to my eyes was a lot longer for him and he had to risk straining his neck.

Lyndsey and I rarely said 'I love you', the ringing 'Love you like crazy' – like off that film where you don't think the posh bloke's going to get the girl and then he does – being our more common expression of feeling for each other but that was my fault as much as anyone's.

The 'I love you' words had never come particularly easy to me, though I had said them to her – the first time after a year and three months when the bells had chimed for

New Year's Day and Bono had loudly informed us that all was quiet.

It seemed I could only say these things on the big occasions, though, when the passions of the world sweep a man up and to do anything else you would have to swim against their tide. New Year's Eve, weddings – I'm doing that list-straining thing again – any time when emotions are raised and alcohol is sunk.

With Reg, though, I didn't need the wind behind me, I could say it with the wind in front of me. His wind, even.

There was a clack at the front door. I went into the hall and there was an expensive-looking envelope. It was addressed to me but whoever had filled it in had the address wrong.

I opened it. Inside was one of the Cat's chips – a £500 one. I turned it over in my fingers, I flicked it and stroked it. It seemed as magnetic to my eyes as a sausage to the dog. Life is a slot machine, I thought. Go on, stick it in. Then I looked inside the envelope. There was a note. In a scrawled hand it said, 'The carrot.' What came next? Obviously the stick. I trousered the chip and dogged up Reg into his collar and lead. Sod worrying, I thought, it's a beautiful day.

What was it, I wondered as we strolled to meet Lyndsey through the bright blue afternoon on the seafront, that could make you love something so quickly?

I suppose he brought out some fatherly quality in me but I was sure I didn't love him just because he was dependent on me. It occurred to me to ask the dog for his take on this.

'You say you love me,' I said, as we approached an ice-cream stall. They were doing pistachio, which is my favourite. The dog was skipping along by my side, looking up at me.

'Oh yes,' said the dog.

'Why?'

'You are so very kind,' said the dog, bowing his head slightly. 'Excuse me,' he said. 'I am slightly weak from hunger.'

'You had your breakfast,' I said.

'When was that?' said the dog.

'This morning.'

'If you say it is so,' said the dog, glum as Monday.

'You did. And you finished off my Cheerios,' I said.

'That's not suitable food for a dog,' said the dog. 'It's full of little holes and those holes go into the stomach and collect together and make one large hole. No wonder I'm starving.'

'You had half a can of dog food as well,' I said.

'Meagre recompense for my labours on your behalf,' said the dog.

'Well, it's exactly the amount the manufacturers recommend,' I said.

'And are these manufacturers dogs?' said the dog. 'Because if they were, I'd venture they'd recommend a whole lot more.' The dog was looking at the ice-cream stall, drooling while simultaneously pretending to be suffering from low blood sugar – not incompatible conditions, I supposed.

'Would you like an ice cream?' I said. I didn't see how one would hurt before I took him to the vet and established a proper diet for him.

'I could probably manage a couple of the very smallest Magnums,' said the dog.

'Magnums are only one size,' I said. That size, as I recalled, could be adequately described by the word 'large'.

'Then if that's all they have, I shall make do,' said the dog. 'I find the double chocolate the least demanding on my constitution.' Although he said the words in a delicate, almost fragile, manner he had a look on his face as if swallowing a cannonball fresh from the gun wouldn't have done him much harm.

The ice creams were bought and we sat on the front, watching the seagulls wheel and listening to their sad cries which seemed, even halfway through an ephemeral and transient confection like a Magnum, like echoes of eternity.

It was perhaps not the ideal time to tell Lyndsey about Reg, I reflected. Her carpet was a problem but, beyond that and even more seriously, as she was the person closest to me I didn't really see how I was going to conceal from her the fact, or fiction, that he was talking to me.

I ate my chocolatey delight while the dog watched me. He'd chomped through his quicker than you can say 'Two pounds thirty each, try to make it last.'

Two pounds thirty. About one four thousandth of my debt to Tibbs.

The dog swayed before me, hypnotised by the motion of my hand between its resting position and my mouth.

I sucked the last of the chocolate away and sat tapping the stick on the bench.

'You haven't eaten your stick!' said the dog.

'You don't eat the sticks,' I said.

'That's the best bit,' said Reg. 'That's why they hide it in the chocolate, so you leave it till last.'

I threw it down to him and he chomped it in. The stick, the Cat had implied, was coming next. Not one with a lolly on it. I imagined the Cat trying to beat me with one of those old lolly sticks that used to have the jokes on them. He still looked quite menacing.

'Aren't you afraid of splinters?' I said to the dog, who was crunching away.

'Gives it an edge,' he said, with the face of someone enjoying a slightly hotter curry than they were used to. 'On the subject of loving you,' he went on, 'I'd love you even more if you bought me a packet of chips.'

'I think we should take things slowly,' I said. The dog glummed down his chops before charging off after a passing roller-blader.

'Wheels on the feet. 'Tis not natural!' he shouted.

Taking heart from the pleasant weather, I phoned Lyndsey, telling her I had a surprise.

'What surprise?' she said.

'Wait and see.'

'Not that big red sex toy from Ann Summers?' she said.

'Lynds, that was the fire extinguisher,' I said. It was an old joke between us, but we both enjoyed it.

We always met at the same open-air café, with the plastic tables and polystyrene cups like it didn't want to get above itself, the hand-painted sign and charming boards of green and white like something from a fifties childhood, suggesting maybe that it had somehow finished up below itself. I knew where she'd try to park, just over the road, so I kept a lookout for the Clio, and when I saw it coming I told Reg to hide round the corner.

'In the café?' he said, pulling back his lips over his teeth like he was getting them ready just in case they should be called on to do any munching.

'Just behind it,' I said.

When Lyndsey appeared, I remembered why I loved her.

She had a grace to her, a poise which I knew she'd perfected as a girl by walking with books on her head. She was slim, blonde, fake tanned and pretty.

To me there seemed something of the light of the morning to her and by that I mean a radiance but also a reality. She centred me, for want of a better word, made me see the world as it was and could be, not how I let it be. The smoke of poker rooms seemed a long way off when I was with her.

'Hi!' I said, standing to greet her.

'Hi,' said Lyndsey with a peck on my cheek.

'And helloooooo!' said the dog, who had come shooting from behind the café to greet us. He interposed himself between us in a kind of high-tempo bottom wiggle, looking up at Lyndsey and panting.

'Ooh, hello,' said Lyndsey, looking down at the dog but not patting him. 'He seems friendly enough.'

'I am friendly enough,' said the dog, wagging his tail. 'What you see is what you get, what you get is what you see,' he said, panting hotly.

'This is the surprise I was telling you about,' I said.

Lyndsey tipped down her sunglasses.

'You haven't bought me a dog? I can't afford to keep a dog. Dave, I've only just got a new carpet. This is ridiculous.'

'No,' I said, 'this is Reg, and I'm, er, looking after him.' A slightly more ambiguous statement than I am capable of feeling proud of.

'Very well too!' said the dog.

'For who?' said Lyndsey.

'For me,' I said. I thought I owed it to her and to Reg to come clean. 'We found him in unusual circumstances.'

'We?'

'Me and the staff.' I always avoided Lucy's name when I was with Lyndsey.

'What unusual circumstances?'

I told her and then she asked me why I hadn't told her before.

'I didn't want to complicate things. I wasn't sure how you'd take it. I know you're not that fond of dogs.'

Lyndsey fondled the dog's ear like a three-star chef inspecting some no-star pastry.

'Why can't your staff have him?'

The dog looked between Lyndsey and me in mild panic.

'I want him,' I said.

Lyndsey shrugged. 'Fine.' She smiled. 'If he comes to my house, can he stay in the garden?'

'In the garden, all the time?' said the dog. 'That is too kind, to play and run and bark at the stars for days, that would be my dearest wish.' I was beginning to notice the dog had quite a few dearest wishes.

'Yes,' I said. I was confident Reg could soften her attitude given time. I didn't think he'd ever make it onto the sofa but I thought he might be allowed in the house as long as I got him some of those dog boots they put on fire-sniffing dogs to stop them damaging their feet. It'd be just like wearing a pair of slippers indoors.

Lyndsey quite liked Reg already, I thought, as she knelt and began scrunching his ears. Reg took a sniff at her and then went a little stiff.

'What's the matter?' I mouthed at him from behind her back.

'I don't think she's a hundred per cent pleased to see me,' said the dog.

'She'll come round in time,' I mouthed again.

We took tea, ignoring the dog's recommendation that the flapjacks were particularly good at this time of year and his advice that if we didn't like flapjacks then crisps were in season and that the scones smelled mighty fine.

The outside of the café was a little crowded, so we went and sat on a bench towards the back of the promenade, looking at the sea.

It was a warm day and I regretted bringing my coat, which is the sort of thing the dog claims sums humans up. Sun, sea, a beautiful woman, an exemplary dog of the sort upon whom the empire was built. Ooh, this coat's a burden. Actually I think that sums up the English rather than humans as a whole, but the dog's experience, as far as I knew, only extended to the English.

So everything was great, perfect really.

I looked at Lyndsey who, as comfortable in my company as in her own skin, had picked up a paper and started reading it. For a second, even though I knew she was beset by worries and cares, she looked carefree; sunglasses and cigarette, the light tan which I could never be certain if it was fake or real. She had fake tan, for sure, but the bottle never seemed to go down. I'd teased her that she only had it because it was fashionable and that her fake tan was real and therefore fake.

'Gets dull in that office, does it?' she said, implying I had nothing better to think about.

'Oh, show me a home where the buffalo roam and I'll show you a very messy carpet!' sang the dog in the background.

He made me laugh, that hound. I felt close to him and I felt close to Lyndsey.

'Lyndsey,' I said.

'Mmmmm?'

'I love you.'

Her eyes looked up from the paper and she smiled.

'Good,' she said. 'I love you too.'

Then I go and spoil the moment by saying something stupid like, 'Ya! Ripper flipper, how's your fat dipper?' sang the dog. I wondered where he got these songs from.

'Horoscope?' I said. This was one of our rituals.

Lyndsey turned the pages. 'You will shortly be coming into some money,' she said. 'About time.' She read some other stuff about avoiding motor racing champions and how a subscription to pay-per-view TV would yield gold.

'How about mine?' said the dog, pulling up alongside us.

'Try his, he's a Gemini,' I said.

'How do you know?'

I shrugged. 'We got together in June so that's where I'm putting his birthday.'

Lyndsey read: 'Today is a day for letting your hair down.'

The dog took on a look of slight puzzlement. 'We'll call it fur,' he said.

'You are not what could be described as a pack animal,' said Lyndsey.

The dog opened his mouth and looked up at her with an expression of great trouble.

'I think in fairness I could,' he said.

Tea, unfortunately, goes right through me and before long I needed the loo. Lyndsey said she'd look after Reg.

The sun and the company had steamed the worry from my mind so I wandered along the front untroubled except for the mild anxiety that always attends a visit to a public convenience on the south coast, which is that it might be full of men having sex with each other.

Luckily there was no need to ask anyone to get off their knees to allow me in and I strolled back without a care in the world. Until I saw Lyndsey with a sheet of A4 in her hand.

I knew immediately what it was. I'd brought what I'd written about Tibbs with me and left it in my coat pocket. She must have moved my coat for some reason, and it had fallen out.

However she came to see it, the fact was that she had seen it and was now reading the document with a big grin on her face.

'Clucking ducks, David, you didn't tell me!'

'Tell you what?'

'This deal with Michael Tibbs. Is that Michael Tibbs the property developer? Wow! You are on your way up! Good grief! Dave, that's excellent news, well done. Come on, let me buy you a drink to celebrate.' She gestured towards the tea urn.

The dog was on the other side of the promenade turning fast, broad circles as he quartered the ground.

'It's not that clear-cut,' I said.

Lyndsey looked at me sideways, much in the way the dog had in the morning when I'd been squeaking my teeth. Don't ask.

'It seems clear-cut,' she said.

I looked out down the promenade, the sea a field of sparkles in the sunlight.

'Tum ti tum ti tum ti tum, tara lala, sheabungo!' The dog was motoring past us on the sniff, humming a tune to himself.

'There's a problem with it,' I said.

'What problem?'

'It's a bent scheme. It's dishonest.'

'Nyyyyeeeeeow!' The dog was coming back at speed, aeroplane style. 'This is the sort of precision flying that makes these boys the envy of the world,' he said, clipping my trouser leg as he passed.

'How's that?' She looked genuinely concerned. I know Lyndsey well and there's no way she'd want to get involved in crime. She's more willing to bend the rules than I am but I knew she wouldn't defraud an old lady.

So I told her, the lot. Well, I left out the bit about betting thousands of pounds of money that could convert any number of kitchens, but the rest I left in, including the invitation to join the Folding Society, which I explained honestly as a kind of self-interest group. 'So you see why I can't go through with this,' I said. 'There's no chance of being caught – the police who'd have to investigate are members of the Folding Society and the crime would never come to light anyway but we'd be doing the dogs' home charities out of millions of quid.'

'Watch who's turf your marking, flatnose!' shouted Reg at a passing boxer.

'A dogs' home?' said Lyndsey as if she'd never heard of the idea.

'Not just one dogs' home,' I said. 'The League for Canine Advancement at Patcham first and then other local homes, and whatever money is left over to go to national dog charities.'

'National dog charities?' she said, moon-faced, like she'd been lashed with a wet kipper.

'It'll do a lot of good,' I said.

I then saw a look on Lyndsey's face that I'd never seen before, which is unusual, because I've seen most of them. Utter, total, abject disgust I think about covers it. I expected her to explode but instead she just said, in a quiet voice, 'Not to us, it won't.'

'Help!' screamed Reg, who was being chased by the boxer.

I put my hand softly on her knee. 'It won't do us any good to get involved in this. Bad things come from bad things, good things from good. I've met these people and they're different to us, we're not like them.'

'No,' said Lyndsey, tears coming to her eyes, 'we're not. We don't live in big houses, we don't take holidays when we want, we're not even sure if we'll ever be able to pay off our credit card debts. We've never even been to Mustique. Our lives and our loves are tied down and we will never break those ties unless we grasp our opportunities. That's how those people are different, they exploit opportunities when they see them. You have to take what's offered you, Dave, or you're a fool.' She put her hand on top of mine in a kindly way.

'He's chasing me!' shouted the dog, tearing past in a tumble of legs and ears. 'Save me, he means to have my bones!' The boxer, I noticed, was happily trotting off after its owner in the opposite direction.

'I can't do this, Lynds,' I said. 'It's against who I am.'

Lyndsey looked as unhappy as I've ever seen her, worse even than when we got stuck in traffic going up to the first day of the Moben January sale – sixty per cent off for the first ten customers. We were number fifteen.

She drew in a breath. 'Why?'

'There is no why. It's just not me. I don't do that sort of thing. It's wrong.'

Lyndsey looked at the dog, who was approaching a tiny Yorkshire terrier.

'Oy, short arse, hop it!' he shouted. 'This is my territory, get your nose up that information point. Can't you smell?'

'How is it wrong?' said Lyndsey. Her voice was without anger. She was more like someone who had just received a particularly shocking piece of news. 'This is the sort of thing that gets decency a bad name.'

'It's not our money. It's Mrs Cad-Beauf's to do with as she sees fit.'

Lyndsey couldn't look at me. She gazed out to sea, into the shimmering heart of the light. A sleek yacht slid past. It wasn't the most opportune moment for a symbol of ostentatious wealth to appear.

'I thought wrong was if people got hurt,' she said.

'Well, yes.'

'So the old lady gets her flat. The dogs get two hundred thousand pounds or more, which must be the largest single donation they've ever received, and we get...' She put her other hand on mine and looked into my eyes. 'Freedom, or at least its beginnings. I'm struggling to see who suffers here.'

'No need to be like that!' said Reg, as the Yorkshire terrier yapped at him. 'I'm only pointing out I was here first.'

I didn't know how to answer her. I could see what she was arguing but if you can't do those things, you can't do those things. You can't expect an elephant to fly, no matter how much encouragement you give him.

A man was walking down the front with a box of fried chicken. Reg followed him at a low-slung lope, intoning, 'Drop the box, drop the box, drop the box, the bin's too far, just drop the box.'

'Can we just leave this?' I said.

'I'd like to leave this,' she said, sweeping her arm across the seafront, 'this shithole.'

'Hey,' I said, 'you're talking about a shithole I love.' She wouldn't be deflected.

'You'd get five hundred thousand up front, maybe a million if he sticks to his second offer, and who knows what deals to follow?' said Lyndsey. 'What do you want to be? A loser or someone who can offer others something, someone someone might want to be with,' she said, 'perhaps forever.'

I thought this was a low blow. I'd wanted us to get married, particularly since I knew it would please my mum, but Lyndsey said she wasn't ready.

'Lyndsey,' I said, 'if you want to be with the sort of person that can do this then you don't want to be with me.'

That sounded more like an ultimatum than I'd intended.

'Oh, the bone men of Burundi sing bring back Jason Cundy!' sang the dog, wheeling across the promenade. He was clearly enjoying getting the air in his fur.

'How much did you charge for that car?' I'd sold the old Civic about two years before.

'That is hardly the point, Lyndsey.'

'How much did you charge?'

'Two thousand five hundred.'

'And what did *What Car?* say it was worth?'

'Two thousand three hundred and fifty.' She knew this had haunted me.

'So you charged one hundred and fifty more than it was worth.'

'I put it in at that price to bargain down. He just didn't bargain down.' I couldn't believe it. He'd just walked in, looked at it, stumped up the price in readies and driven off. It had later been found in London with two Kalashnikovs and half a pound of Semtex in the back and there had been some considerable unpleasantness with the police about the matter when they'd checked the numberplate and found my address.

'It's exactly the same. She's not going to bargain up. She doesn't want to know about money. Just give her the four hundred grand and let her die happy in her sheltered flats. If she wants to go to someone else she can. It's her laziness not your deception that's costing the dogs' home.'

I breathed in. 'She's coming to me because she trusts me. She's chosen me because she thinks I'm honest. I can't throw that back in her face.'

'Ahh, mounds and mounds of Pedigree Chum becoming mounds and mounds of shit. You'd rather buy dog shit than a decent life for us.'

'I'm not going to buy anything. It's not my money, end of story.'

She looked down with an expression of great sadness. 'Sit here and listen for a second, Dave. What do you hear?'

'Traffic,' I said. 'The sea?'

'Oh, there's a lot more than that,' said the dog, who'd loped up again. I shot him a look to silence him.

'No,' said Lyndsey. 'It's the sound of people lying. Parents lie to children, children to parents, we even lie to ourselves that one day this whole thing isn't going to end coughing our guts up in some nursing home. Everybody lies. All the time and to everyone. The world is a lie. Reality is a lie we tell ourselves to get us through the day-to-day.'

I shrugged. I had nothing more to add.

'What would you say if I came back with a hairstyle you hated?'

'That's hardly the point. There's a difference between sparing someone's feelings and depriving someone of millions of pounds.'

'Depriving *dogs*!' she said.

Reg's jaw dropped in shock, as if it was the most outrageous suggestion he'd ever heard.

'That's irrelevant.' It was but I could see how to some people it might not be.

Lyndsey looked at me directly. 'I think I'd better go home and consider what I do want then,' she said quietly. 'And I suggest you do the same. Call me when you've made up your mind. If I were you I'd do it sooner rather than later. And go to the doctor and get something for your nerves. You look awful and you're talking like a madman.'

'It's not about my depression,' I said.

'I never said it was. So you're depressed, are you? I thought so. And you think that you have the right to go making stupid decisions that will wreck our lives. I could have you sectioned for this.' She was pointing her finger at me.

'Lyndsey, please,' I said.

'I'm not going to sit here if you're going to be like this, David. I'll see you again when you've decided to do something with your life and sort yourself out. I don't like losers, I'm afraid.'

'Aren't we going to the cinema tonight?'

'Why would I want to go and sit in the dark gazing up at some amazing fantasy world I'll never be part of?' she said. 'No thank you. I'll just stay in and read about over-pronation caused by cheap trainer design.'

She stood and walked off towards the bright traffic.

'Lynds, don't be like this!' I shouted after her. I let her go. This silent treatment was her style. She'd come round in the end.

'Chicken!' she shouted over her shoulder as she walked away.

'Is there a piece for me!' howled the dog, flattening me back into the bench.

I watched Lyndsey get into her car and hammer out of the parking space.

'Was it something I said?' asked the dog panting at my feet. I looked down. He'd thoughtfully brought me an old plastic bottle from the beach. 'Have a chew on that,' he said. 'That'll make you feel better.'

9

Lucky Dog

When in debt, when in extreme debt, when money is the central concern of your waking hours, their taste, their smell, when it is the theme that defines your life like the vein does the blue cheese or the ball the game, then a few hands of cards for big cash against expert players is just what you need.

I'd had a brainwave that day. I had twenty cheques left in my book. Hoon along to a bureau de change, write yourself out a £50 cheque with your guarantee card and one minute and ten per cent commission later you're £45 to the good while the bank looks impotently on. Genius, eh?

I left Reg at Lucy's and spent the afternoon visiting various bureaux.

When I returned to collect the dog, Jim was there, clean-cut, ruggedly handsome but with a rather strange over-tight T-shirt on.

'He's been a little sweetie!' said Jim.

'Won't you stay for a while?' said Lucy.

'No,' I said. 'I don't want to intrude.'

'I quite like a bit of intrusion,' said Jim.

'You're welcome to stay,' said Lucy. 'We've made a nut bake.'

'Nut bake,' said the dog, as if trying the words for the first time and finding he liked them.

'I need to go,' I said.

The word 'need' was a good one. Where did I need to go? To Snake Eyes' and poker, need like the schoolchild needs the loo an hour after the weak orange squash and twenty minutes before the coach is due to stop.

At Snake Eyes' that night I got the usual cheery stream of fucking enquiries as to my shiteing health from his mum and assured her that both the dog and I were very well. Top bollock, in fact.

The game didn't begin at all positively. This wasn't just because Mrs Watt had supplied us with only Panda Cola to drink, still with a sticker on – 25p for 5. The gift of a Panda Cola says one of two things: either the person hates you or they think your teeth are too yellow. Either way, it isn't good.

The first hand told me my luck was out, my second seemed to say it wasn't coming back any time soon, my third that it had emigrated and wasn't very good at keeping in touch. Hand four was a personal message from God that he hated me and hand five indicated the Devil felt very much the same way.

'Who dealt this filth?' I said, folding again. This is an expression card players use when they've dealt themselves a bad hand. I seem to come out with more of these when I'm losing than when I'm winning, like I'm trying to convince myself that I'm good at cards by my familiarity with the lingo rather than my familiarity with the cards.

Throughout this period I could hear the dog grumbling away in the background.

'This isn't a very nice place, you know, it's full of smoke. It's horrible and no one here respects you. You need to impose yourself on this pack, sir, or trouble will ensue. I can mark the carpet for you if you wish.'

'Not necessary!' I said, rather loudly. I think the others thought this was some comment on the cards.

'That one with the funny eyes has a funny smell to him too,' said the dog. 'He's full of false pride. Prick him and he'll burst. Just stand up to him and he'll disappear. Sorry for speaking, sir, but I feel I must defend you.'

It seemed to me that the dog was taking Snake Eyes a bit too seriously. Or maybe he'd got him spot on. Poker was the one realm in his life where he'd had any success at all. I know he erected fences for a living and seemed to put up a fair few privately as well. He'd held down the job well but poker was the arena for his dreams and the engine of his self-esteem. It took his disability – one eye looking to the heavens, the other to the depths, a kind of balance I suppose – and made it glamorous. It also gave him an excuse to wear sunglasses indoors, which I think was the game's original appeal.

The table was a reasonably good one, six of us – Moron George, me, Snake Eyes, Fast Eddie, the Pieman, Charlie Attwood the builder and his mate Archie Mander, a plump plumber who – God is bountiful – liked to drink. He wasn't a bad player until about his eighth can and then he'd start adopting the cunning strategy of saying, 'Oh, these cards are shite,' when they were good and saying, 'Yes!' and pumping the air with his fist when they were bad. Now me and the lads may never grace the top tables at Vegas but we'll be into a mug like that quicker than Horlicks. We called him the Leak, owing to his job and his regular toilet breaks.

Hand six was better, a cowboy and a deuce with another gunslinger and a swan in the rest of the cards. That's two kings and two twos to you; not bad at all.

Still I was nervous. 'You're nervous!' shouted the dog, some-what unnecessarily. It's like telling someone they're going bald – really? I hadn't noticed. I shushed him out of the corner of my mouth.

I'd got skinned on trip tens at Michael the Cat's and, though it's two pair and I haven't a care, I actually had a care. The next card up, though, and I was breathing easy as a black swan swam into view to join its two cousins in my hand. I was in business.

As luck wouldn't have it, it was Snake Eyes I ended up facing when the chaff fell away and the wheat grew strong.

There's no use trying to guess what Snake Eyes is thinking by looking for tells, the little ticks that reveal whether a player is confident or bluffing. Snake Eyes came to poker with a number of highly pronounced facial tics. These were largely caused by the fact that the other boys at school used to run away from him shouting, 'Unclean, unclean!' I seem to recall there was an attempt to try him for witchcraft one lunchtime which finished with him being tied up and 'floated' in the school pool. I'm surprised the games teacher went along with it but, there again, Snake Eyes wasn't very good at sport so he only had himself to blame. And as the teacher said, Snake Eyes may actually have been a witch. Better safe than sorry.

In the interests of the game, though, Snake Eyes had developed even more facial tics, to conceal his original ones. The effect was that he looked rather like an astronaut undergoing re-entry, one of those guys who's picked for his brains rather than his looks – though no one would have picked Snake Eyes for his brains.

He might not have been clever but he had a kind of low cunning and, having had to come to terms with so many insecurities himself, was very alive to them in others. He could smell my weakness like a Great White can a soggy Elastoplast.

'Raise,' said Snake Eyes. He's a serious player and never bothers himself really with trying to fake any reaction to his cards.

I was nervous. He was very confident and most times when players like the Snake (see, I've made him sound more threatening in my mind) are confident it's because they have something to be confident about. Do I lose the money I have in or do I sink in for more and risk losing even more?

I raised him. If he wanted to put me down he wasn't going to put me down cheap. He immediately raised again, a thumping wodge that would require the last of my meagre funds to call. Here we are in the nightmare scenario. I'm faced with the same decision as last time but now it's amplified. Should I just take a moderate hit or should I call with all that remains of my money and face the long walk into the night or the fireworks of a big win.

'I don't like that man you're looking at,' said the dog, who was wandering about behind Snake Eyes.

'Shhh!' I said.

'I cannot be silent, sir.' He took a deep sniff of the air. 'Mind you,' said the dog, 'he's just got a lovely sweat on. Ooh, fear brings out the bully in you, doesn't it?'

'Fear?' I said, turning to Reg with very much the expression he turns to me with when I say, 'Walk.'

'He smells of customs officials and tax men, street gangs and credit card bills,' said the dog.

'Is that dog growling at me?' said Snake Eyes.

'Reg!' I said, though Snake Eyes had seemed to bring out the bully in many people for most of his life.

'He sweats from his arms and not his face,' said the dog. 'Ha, ha, ha!' It was the first time I'd heard Reg laugh, cackle even, as opposed to his normal chortle.

'What do you mean by this?' I said, out loud. Snake Eyes thought I was talking about the cards, trying to unsettle him in any way I could. He said nothing.

'He's preparing to run,' said the dog. 'He's scared. The funny thing is,' he took a big sniff, 'I don't think even he knows it. Half of his body is relaxed and the other half is trembling.'

I was tempted to observe that this might be more to do with unkind genetics than anything immediate – there was no reason to suspect that Snake Eyes' nervous system had been any better put together than his face – but I thought the dog might have something.

My mind began to wander from the cards. I felt angry at myself anyway for missing a night with Lucy. Even if Jim was going to be there it didn't matter. I'd so wanted to talk to her, to take joy in the dog together, and instead I was here, in an over-lit room with a bunch of sniping misfits. Get it over with, I thought. Finish this hand and turn it in forever.

'Urine!' said the dog.

'Not now,' I said.

Snake Eyes thought I was talking to him again and ignored me harder, if such a thing is possible.

'He has emitted a small but significant quantity of urine,' said the dog. 'He is a coward and all his fears are seeming to crowd upon him.'

'He's only in for five hundred pounds,' I said to the dog. This wasn't a lot of money to Snake Eyes, not at that moment anyway. There were times in his life, and there would be again, when it was a fortune. If he was scared on £500, how did he handle some of the hands he'd played which occasionally must have got near to the value of his mum's house, or a bloody good extension anyway? A second question I'd never asked myself before popped into my head. Why, when Snake Eyes was sitting there folding a good £5,000 worth of paper, did he live with his mum? I was beginning to see a different side to him.

Snake Eyes gave his first response. 'You getting messages from beyond the grave, twonkhead?'

'You'll be able to send me one after this hand,' I said.

'Very good!' said the dog, with a refined chuckle. 'He's shaking.' For some reason Reg was whispering like a spiv from an overcoat. I looked but I couldn't see.

'How do you know?' I said.

'I just know,' said Snake Eyes, who thought I was talking to him.

'We dogs smell fear, we have an instinct for it.'

'He's afraid?' I said.

'His body is a mass of dilations and constrictions,' said the dog. 'If he could, he would run.'

'Yeah, terrified,' said Snake Eyes. 'I think I shall soil my lingerie.'

Everyone looked rather ill at this point, including Reg.

'Don't you mean boxers?' said Shagger.

'I know what I mean,' said Snake Eyes. He was clearly trying to put me off.

I decided to go with the dog.

'That's done my nuts,' I said, 'all in. I wish I had more, Snakey, but five hundred's my limit.'

Snake Eyes smiled and put down his cards. 'I know it's not the form,' he said, 'but this shite Cola's going right through me. I need to go away to the bog.'

Snake Eyes stomped upstairs and we heard him through the wallpaper and prayer-thick partitions of his house loudly relieving himself.

'He hasn't washed his hands,' said the dog as Snake Eyes returned. He took a long sniff. 'There's fear all over them too.'

'By fear,' I said out of the corner of my mouth, 'are we talking piss?'

'In this context, yes,' said the dog.

It was my turn to deal next and I found this rather unsettling.

'What are you on about?' says Snake Eyes.

I said nothing.

'Fucking surrealist,' says Snake Eyes. 'Salvador Dali here trying to do ma heid in.' Even though he was born in Worthing, Snake Eyes becomes slightly Scots when he's rattled. It's the influence of his mum.

He looked at my pile of money. 'You want to raise me properly, big man?'

I don't shrug, which he took for a shrug.

'See, I've got another three thousand out back there. And I fancy your car. So if you put your car in I'll give you a crack at this pot. If you have the knob for it, of course.'

'Oh, don't, sir,' said the dog. 'You have just done your nuts, as he must know.'

The dog, I remembered, didn't have any of those. 'I am not a neuter,' he'd said to Lyndsey. 'I prefer to say that I'm a one-off.'

'Let's see the money then,' I said.

I wanted to see how Snake Eyes would react.

He went into the kitchen and emerged a second later with a good £3,000 of the crinkly stuff.

'All right, Timothy,' he said, as if being Timothy wasn't a very good thing to be. Daft, I know; I simply record what he said, don't expect me to explain it. 'Raise!'

He threw it onto the table like Detective Clint Eastwood confronting a murderer with the one piece of evidence that puts him in the frame.

'Over to you, little piggy,' he said.

The 'little piggy' gave an unpleasant insight into the workings of his unconscious, I thought. Here was a man who had heard of the three little pigs and identified with the wolf.

'He's really scared now!' said the dog. 'Absolutely terrified.' I couldn't quite believe that the dog was getting into poker, which is strange because I was getting quite used to the idea that he spoke. The idea of having him painted holding a fan of cards, running off four thousand prints and clearing up in the catering trade lavatory decoration business briefly occurred to me.

'Bet me!' said the dog.

'You're not worth three thousand pounds,' I said.

'No, you're not, shitehawk,' said Snake Eyes, who again thought I was talking to him.

'That's very hurtful,' said the dog. 'I'm worth a lot more than that.'

'To them,' I said. 'To me you're worth a lot more.' I hadn't known that before.

'Salvador,' said Snake Eyes, regarding my conversation.

I picked up my car keys.

What it is to put yourself into the hands of others. What it is to put yourself into their paws, which are theoretically safer as there are two more of them.

I didn't make the bet because I was angry with myself. I didn't make it because I needed the money. I did it because I trusted the dog.

Snake Eyes grinned as he watched the keys dangling on the end of my fingers. He started humming the theme tune to *The Muppets*, implying with brilliant association that I was a Kermit.

'Let me tell you,' he said, 'they don't let dogs on the buses round here.'

I looked at the dog.

'Still scared?' I say.

'It is a mask, sir, a mask!' said the dog, wagging his tail. 'He struts like a crow in the gutter but inside it is all puffery'.

I flipped in my car keys. 'Call.'

Snake Eyes drummed his fingers on the table and the dog panted, as if accompanying him in some natural rhythm experiment.

'There you go,' said Snake Eyes with a broad smile.

Four aces were, in truth, the last thing I expected. Luckily the twonk had two pair, which is good enough but not when I had a house full of dodgy builders and deuces. He'd been bluffing, he'd seen I was weak and gone in for the kill. He'd also, very gratifyingly, played like a complete idiot. He'd seen my losing streak and thought he couldn't lose. So he lost.

Nearly £5,000 at one play. Oh yeah! I went to high five the dog but he only had a paw so we made do with a high four.

Snake Eyes leant back in his chair as if it didn't bother him, a sure sign that it bothered him.

I looked down at the dog. Like Lucy at Mrs CB's, he seemed to have taken all the light in the room into himself and to be glowing as if he'd just descended from heaven. Do angels take the form of dogs? I wondered. Probably not while appearing to shepherds if they don't want some sling stones up their heavenly bottoms, I thought.

Why had I told this animal to be quiet before? If I was in any doubt about my madness, there was the proof. A goldmine, a canine oracle at my feet, a bank of super senses at my disposal. I couldn't lose and I wouldn't again.

'Well, fuck me sideways,' I said.

'I hardly know you,' said Shagger. 'I think we should start with a date, a trip to the cinema maybe. See how it goes, you know.'

As a result of Snake Eyes chasing his losses, the Leak's drunken bravado and, crucially, the dog's insights, I walked away from the table £9,000 the richer.

Life was looking up. Even the dorks on the table could see it.

'Maybe you've finally shat out your bad luck,' said Fast Eddie slowly, causing a couple of players to replace sandwiches. Fast Eddie was a rather studious boy at school and brings enthusiasm but no great talent to street slang. He knows you have to be vulgar but doesn't have any command of pitch like the best swearers do.

Another way of looking at this, of course, is to observe that people generally swear for emphasis. Since Fast Eddie lived his whole life under a condition of sort of reverse emphasis – I emphasise the slowness of the movement, I emphasise the badness of the breath, I emphasise the meanness of the brain etc. – there was hardly one aspect of his existence that you could report without using an upside down exclamation mark. A disappointment mark, a failure mark, something like that.

I looked hard at him and I knew, there with my dog, my canine goldmine, that I was leaving him and his kind. I was moving up in the world.

What's more, I had enough money to pay back the Cat.

10

In Arcadia

The next day I'd picked Lucy up from her house because she wanted to walk the dog and we trod the woods with a skip and a hey, which is the way God made woods to be trod.

The insane worlds of dog and poker were going swimmingly all of a sudden, especially when you consider I'd already fixed myself up with a game at the Buddhist's house that evening. The Buddhist was a rich actor with spiritual pretensions but that wasn't why he was called the Buddhist. He got the name because when he'd first started he'd been murdered every time but he kept coming back for more. Now he was a skilful player but it wouldn't do him any good. It would transpire in the weeks to come that he had an over-active adrenal gland. He may as well have had a sign on his head saying 'bluffing now'.

I'd rung up the number the Cat had given me.

'Yep!' said the butler, causing me to reflect that you really cannot get the staff nowadays.

'Would you tell Mr Tibbs that this is Mr Barker. I have his money if he would like me to deliver it to him.'

'Hold on,' said the butler. 'I'll get a pen.' There was some scrabbling in the background. 'Marie, have you got a fucking pen? Marie! Marie, where are you? Ah, this'll do. Yes, now what time is this delivery?'

I arranged to go to the Cat's the next night. It wasn't a visit I was particularly relishing.

With Reg and Lucy in the woods, though, my problems seemed diminished, the buzzing green of the bright summer filling up my head and irradiating the worry from my mind.

The dog chased a squirrel. 'Come back here, goofy, I'll yark your arse for you!' he shouted as he ran towards a tree.

'I thought you didn't like bad language,' I said.

'Arse is descriptive,' said the dog like the winner of a cake-making competition sliding a Marks and Spencer's box under under the table with his foot. 'It's not rude.'

'Why do you chase those squirrels anyway?' I said.

'Do you hear what they're saying about you?' he said, a vortex of fur circling the bottom of its tree. I didn't enquire further with Lucy there.

The dog told me so much about animals. Ducks, apparently, are generally polite, swans a little haughty but thick, ravens rather obsessed with their role of symbols of mortality (Edgar Allan Poe went to their heads apparently) and horses simply do not give a shit, if only in the metaphorical sense. Cats, well. I won't go into what Reg said other than to record that prejudice is a stain on even the most pleasant characters.

'You never talk much about your girlfriend,' said Lucy.

'Well, you know, I've tried to keep my private life private,' I said.

'Sorry,' said Lucy.

'But, you know, that's changed since Reg.' Why was I suddenly 'you know-ing'?

'So,' she said, linking my arm. 'She seems very glamorous whenever I've seen her.'

'Well, she is,' I said.

'You must love her very much,' she said.

A squirrel looked down at me from a branch. I wondered what he was saying.

'She knows how to bring out the best in me.'

'The best in you's already out,' said Lucy. 'You're kind, straightforward, you give a lot to other people. Perhaps too much. Maybe you need someone to bring out the worst in you.' She gave me a cheeky nudge.

'I'm not sure I like the idea of needing someone,' I said, 'or someone needing me, really.'

'A truffle!' shouted the dog, rooting beneath a tree. 'Oh no, it's just a bit of wood.'

'Doesn't everyone need to need someone?' said Lucy.

'Well, there's need and there's need, isn't there? There's need need and there's needy need. Everyone needs need but no one needs needy.'

'Ah,' said Lucy, 'the deflecting power of humour.'

'Something of a stock in trade in my family,' I said. 'Have I told you the one about—'

She squeezed my arm to stop me. 'Wit is like playing the piano,' she said. 'It's a fine skill but not appropriate to *every* situation.'

I was uncomfortable with this desire for seriousness. Lucy was normally such a light presence in my life, a smoother of the way, a furnisher of Walnut Whips and suggester of advertising captions.

'I find that highly inappropriate,' I said, pulling my mouth open with my fingers in the approved schoolboy wide-mouthed frog style.

Lucy gave me another nudge. 'Seriously,' she said, 'I'm interested. How did you end up in this self-reliant world?' The way she stressed the words 'self-reliant world' seemed to say that she didn't see it as a particularly good place to be.

'I'm not self-reliant,' I said, 'entirely. I don't know. It's just the idea of being so central to someone's life. It's a bit . . .' I didn't feel I could finish the sentence. I wanted to say 'pretentious' but that's not quite what I meant. Dangerous maybe, but not that either. The words at my disposal seemed like a photo of a view – representative of the reality but wholly inadequate to it.

'Wahey!' said the dog, running through my legs.

'Aren't you central to Lyndsey's life?' said Lucy.

'Lyndsey needs me,' I said, 'and of course I need her but . . .'

'But what?'

'I don't know,' I said. 'I suppose I don't feel smothered by her. She's her and I'm me.'

'And never the twain shall meet?' said Lucy.

'That's about it,' said the dog who had bowled up at our side, an ear cocked to the conversation. 'I met a twain once. Great tall thing.'

I didn't know what to tell her really. I've never felt too easy talking about myself in this way.

'I love her,' I said, 'not maybe how I expected to love someone but in a way that suits me.'

'But are you happy?'

The dog dropped a stick at my feet and I threw it for him.

'I'm not unhappy,' I said. 'It seems to me that the vast majority of the misery in the world is caused by the pursuit of happiness.'

'And some of the happiness,' said Lucy.

'Can we talk about something else?' I said.

'I'm sorry. I've said too much.' It wasn't her presumption but her concern that made me feel uncomfortable.

'Say what you like, I'm not touchy about it. I can't explain it,' I said. 'It's not what I expected from . . . you know.' I left the standard love-shaped hole in the middle of the sentence. 'But she gives me what I want.'

Lucy squeezed my arm again. 'I've never been a great believer in the illuminating power of cliché, but do you get what you need?'

The illuminating power of cliché. Sometimes Lucy reminded me of the dog, the way she used these long words that fairly buckled the brim of my hat on their way into my head.

'The stick tried to escape but I've captured it,' said Reg, dropping it at my feet.

'How about you? Do you get what you need?' I said. 'I mean, you're a very bright woman, don't you have any ambitions beyond doing my filing?' I'd been going to ask her about Jim but it seemed too personal. She made me uncomfortable talking about Lyndsey, I didn't really think I could do the same to her.

Lucy laughed. 'I suppose that's what my A levels are about. I don't know, though. I'm comfortable where I am really.'

'You don't feel it necessary to pursue perfection?' I said. Now it was my turn to give her a cheeky nudge. I somehow felt unfaithful to Lyndsey doing it. I mean, it wasn't anything, we were just nudging each other cheekily. A cheeky nudge is a cheeky nudge, right? Complete and entire unto itself. There's no resonance in a nudge. Not like a bonk.

'Why didn't you do your exams while you were at school?' I threw the stick for the dog again.

'Oh, I don't know, I . . .' she seemed to get lost inside herself, hypnotised by the arc of my throw.

I knew how she felt.

It was great to see the stick's high parabola connect with the dog's pumping straight line, compromise and return. Reg took me into the moment and lost me there, like a molecule in the surf, as if I was no more than an expression of the rhythms of nature – a means to the flight of the stick, the dog a means to its return.

Then the rhythm broke. The stick, which had been harmlessly end over ending when the dog didn't succeed in snatching it from the air, suddenly stuck, protruding from the ground at a forty-five degree angle, like a miniature anti-cavalry device.

The dog, his tongue a crazy banner, was on it in a blink. At his age dogs can turn as quickly as any cat, though they don't shout about it in the same way. So Reg dodged but his awful momentum still carried him forwards. He'd got his front paws past the stick but a trailing leg betrayed him. The spike dug into him on the inside of his leg, about halfway down the bulge, barrel-rolling him over, his whole being trapped inside an awful squeal.

We started running even as he was hit. He was lying cowed on the ground, shaking in a fearful way.

'I shall surely die!' he was yelping. 'No one can bear a pain like this, it will never end, never ever end!'

'Roll over and let me look at it,' said Lucy.

'It's a wound, it needs to be hidden!' said the dog, shying away from me.

'Humans look at them,' I said. 'Trust me.'

Meekly the dog flipped onto his back. I was relieved to see it was only a graze, though a nasty one.

'It's going to be all right, I think,' said Lucy.

'Bury me in the collar you bought me!' said Reg.

'You won't need burying,' I said.

He put his paw on my arm. 'Think of me whenever you hear the wind in the trees,' he said, his eyes seeming to mist over. 'I'm fading now.'

I picked up the stick. 'Bloody thing!' I said, hurling it away.

'I'll get it!' shouted Reg, corkscrewing onto his front and hammering off after it.

'I thought you were meant to be hurt,' I said as he returned.

'It didn't mean it,' said Reg, 'but I shan't be happy if it does it again.'

'Don't ham it up in future!' I said.

'The ham's up?' said the dog, nearly knocking me off my feet. 'Where is it? I'll wolf it down!'

That was the end of the deep and meaningfuls between me and Lucy for the day. For the rest of the afternoon we just walked in the woods and talked about nothings – ghastly people on the TV, ghastly politicians, ghastly customers in the shop.

In the evening we stopped for a couple of hours in a pub by the river.

I flicked the dog a crisp from the bench while Lucy stood down by the water watching some ducks.

'You want to savour your food,' I said as he downed it. 'That hardly touched the sides.'

'I am savouring it,' he said. 'That crisp goes beautifully with the ginger pudding.'

'You haven't had a ginger pudding,' I said.

'You gave me a piece last Thursday!' said the dog as if I'd gone mad.

'That was a week ago!'

'Oh yes, and I've been enjoying it every day since,' said the dog. 'It's still in the air by the bin and I can smell it on the sweat of my paws. More than that there's the idea of the pudding, its soul. Once you've eaten a piece, it's with you eternally.'

'So you're still enjoying the pudding six days after you had a bit?' I'd only given him a tiny slice.

'Yes,' said the dog, tilting his head to one side like he does when things puzzle him. 'Aren't you?'

'No. I eat it and that's that.'

'Ooh,' said the dog shaking his head. 'You want to savour your food.'

The veils of evening were falling over the river, the long trees throwing their branches skyward in supplication to the dying day. This was something I'd never noticed before. Mostly I'd just seen it get dark – and a lot of the time I didn't even notice that.

'Put your arm round me please,' said Reg as we sat finishing our drinks.

I did and he leaned into it. Lucy was on the other side. I wanted to touch her too. I knew, though, that I couldn't. From inside a complex relationship a new one is bound to seem easy and relaxed. But these relationships only seem uncomplicated because they haven't been given the time to develop complications. A year or two, I thought, and we'd work the tiny differences between us into something to be unhappy about.

'This is lovely,' I said, gazing at the river. 'The light-enchanted water.' You can get away with that sort of thing with a dog.

Humans are a different matter, though. Lucy looked at me. 'Do you like poetry?' she said.

'Yes,' I said, 'and I also like saying things like "the light-enchanted water".'

'Have you ever read Ted Hughes's "Pike"?' said Lucy.

'Only the first bit,' I said.

'Awful, isn't it?' she said.

'Yes,' I said, gazing into her eyes. 'Truly vile.' A late summer's day, the long sun in the trees and a beautiful girl discussing poetry. Of course I was happy.

I realise I had fallen in love, with the dog, maybe with Lucy, perhaps even with the situation. To love someone is to alter and transcend your former self, like oxygen and hydrogen combine to become water. I really felt, there with Reg and Lucy, that I was someone new, in some odd way that was only just within the grasp of my understanding.

'Will you be seeing Lyndsey tonight?' said the dog as we waited for Lucy to finish returning the plates to the pub.

'I don't think so. I'm not flavour of the month at the moment,' I said.

The dog looked relieved. Then a look of curiosity came over him. 'What is flavour of the month?' he asked. 'I'll give it a taste.'

'It's an expression,' I said. 'It means she's not happy with me.'

The dog wore his puzzled look again, as if his forehead had suddenly become a size too big for him.

'What's a month?' he said.

'A time of year,' I said.

'The flavour I first remember is rain-soaked ice cream,' he said, 'and I remember all the children were nervous.'

'Why were they nervous?' I said.

'I don't know,' said the dog, 'but they were, and the sun shone sometimes.'

That, I figured, would be summer. The children would be nervous because of the June exams and the sun would have been shining from time to time.

I'd tried pressing Reg on his past but he seemed genuinely blank about it. How old he was I couldn't guess. The vet had said about four. He'd been well fed for a stray, which is what his recollections seemed to indicate he'd been.

'What's the flavour of this month?' I said. It was August.

'Sweat and sun lotion, wasp in a sandwich and thin newspapers. The taste of leather on willow,' he said.

'Don't you mean the sound of leather on willow?'

'I once found myself by mistake in a cricket storeroom,' said the dog, slinking at the memory. I guessed someone had caught him and given him a thick edge with a bat.

Still, this month might have the flavour of resolution.

Only the Cat needed to be dealt with, Charterstone sold, and we would be in the clear. Ready for our future together. As I walked back with Lucy to the car, life seemed more simple.

It was then that I realised I'd managed to leave the keys inside the car. It was the one the garage had given me while they fixed mine – a complimentary car but something of a begrudging one. Needless to say it didn't have central locking.

'I'll have to call the RAC,' I said.

'Oh, I don't know,' said Lucy.

She bent down to the ground and picked up a long piece of wire that someone had thought appropriate to leave in the car park of an area of outstanding natural beauty.

'Here,' said Lucy. She slid the wire between the rubber and the glass of the window and the door opened with a pop.

'Where did you learn to do that?' I said.

'Not on my A levels for sure,' she said. 'Shall we go?'

11

Cat Scratch Fever

So I was still zippety do da-ing as I parked at the Cat's cradle later that evening.

I'd left Reg with Lucy for the night. As I'd gone through the door I could hear him saying, 'Actually he's been cruelly starving me ever since I've been with him, all I ask for happiness is a bowl of chicken breast.' Luckily I knew she couldn't hear him.

The Cat's car park had quite a few cars in it, some of which I recognised from my previous visit. I'm not a car nut or anything, it's just that when you're stuck there waiting for the RAC to turn up you don't have much else to look at.

There was the usual array of Porsches and Mercs you find wherever rich people gather. It occurred to me that we weren't that much different from animals ourselves – our wants and needs were simple, a bone, a walk, a Merc, a yacht.

I have to say, I was a little bit scared. The Cat had hinted at the possibility of rough stuff, so I'd decided to tell him that I'd informed a number of people about the possibility of him doing something nasty to me and that I'd deposited the letter with my solicitor.

I hadn't actually informed anyone, other than the dog and Lyndsey.

'Oh, don't worry,' said the dog, casually, 'that's just barking.'

'What do you mean, just barking?'

'A display, a front, they're all full of it. When you bite someone you don't bark first, it lets them know you're coming. The first they know of it is when they've got your teeth in their leg.'

This bucked me up a bit. If people really intend to kill you they don't threaten you first. Lee Harvey Oswald didn't give JFK a death threat. And anyway, if the Cat killed me, he'd never get the sale.

I'm aware this is what might be called circumstantial comfort but it was comfort nonetheless.

I made my way up the steps to the pointed arch of the Cat's front door and I rang the bell. He answered it himself, which surprised me.

'Hope I didn't frighten you, Mr Barker,' he said, making an unconscious scary gesture with his hands, like children do when they spook you.

'You mildly disconcerted me, it has to be admitted,' I said.

'Do you have my money?'

I held up the briefcase and he put forward his hand to take it.

'Half-time, son,' I said. 'These briefcases don't grow on trees. Ninety-nine pounds it set me back. Bring your own bag.'

The Cat held his hand to his forehead with the strong implication that he was dealing with lightweights, which he was.

'Jenkins, bring a bag!' he shouted back into the hall.

He stepped out onto the porch. He was a bit like a cat, I noticed, with slow, controlled movements that suggested he might burst into a blur at any minute.

'Have you thought any more about our conversation?' he said.

'Yes,' I said.

'And?'

'My position remains as before,' I said, altering my position to stop him getting too close.

'Cigar?' He produced a silver container from his pocket.

'Go on then,' I said. I'd heard the CIA once tried to kill Castro with an exploding cigar, until they'd decided it was a silly idea and that they should wait for him to die of lung cancer.

I took one, he lit it and I puffed away. Somehow I felt the dog's disapproval wafting over the rooftops from Lucy's ten miles away. I knew I should be minimising my contact with the Cat, but there I was, if not maximising it, certainly extending it.

'There's a game on inside if you fancy it,' he said.

I took his chip out of my pocket. 'No thanks,' I said. 'You may as well have this back.'

Even as the words came out of my mouth they felt strange. My legs certainly thought so as I could feel them preparing to trot through his door. It wasn't that I didn't feel like it, I did, I always feel like it. It was just that I didn't feel confident that without the dog I wouldn't get myself back into the same mess I'd been in before.

I didn't realise it at the time, but that represented a massive step forward in my thinking. I don't think I'd been able to envisage bad outcomes from gambling for ten years before that. When I say envisage them, I knew they existed, but never at the time I was about to gamble. Then I could only smell the milk and honey of the promised land.

The Cat sneered at me. 'I wasn't entirely serious. This is a big money game.'

I'd noticed in the car park that one of the cars was a McLaren F1 – over two hundred thousand quid to you for cash, guaranteed to get scratched if left unattended.

'If you want to count the money then I'll be off,' I said. I didn't like the Cat. He seemed to have his priorities all wrong.

He took the chip and studied it.

'Funny,' he said, 'in there it's worth five hundred pounds.

Out here, nothing. Shows things are only what people choose them to be.'

He was losing me slightly on that one. I took it he wasn't really used to this evil tempter role and was having to wing it rather. His normal mode of operation, I supposed, was to cast his pearls before his swine and watch them munch.

'Eh, yer what?' I said, which wasn't quite how I'd meant to put it but covered the broad sweep of what I meant.

'I know you're a man who likes to do the right thing,' he said.

'Yes,' I said, hoping that the 'right thing' wasn't some sort of modern dance craze and that he was proposing we throw some shapes around the car park.

'Well, the right thing isn't always obvious, is it? Terrorists think they're doing the right thing, for instance.'

'I don't think you can equate me with a terrorist.'

The Cat gave me a look that implied he might like to.

'In this case you're defending the old bat when she doesn't require defending,' said the Cat. 'She's massively rich in her own right, the dogs will get a handsome sum anyway and you and your partner will have a golden future. Where is the problem?'

This was the tack Lyndsey had taken.

'She wants the dogs to have the money, it's her money so the dogs get the money.'

'And the trustees of the charity get new cars and trips to see dogs' homes in the south of France, new offices, higher salaries. Who knows where it will stop? Dogs carted about in Rolls-Royces with the staff driving them at weekends? Or mansions in the country?'

'Why does that bother me?'

'Because,' said the Cat, 'if you don't spend her money on yourself, someone else will on themself.' He looked left and right, as if someone might overhear. 'If you don't get her cash, some other bent bastard will.'

'What do you mean, "other bent bastard"? I'm not a bent bastard.'

'So it satisfies you that you're going to be sitting in that shitty office of yours like Johnny Twonk,' I wondered who Johnny Twonk was, 'while some dogs' home wonk sets themselves up for the rest of their lives on money you could have had if you'd had the balls to take it. You're a one-off, Mr Barker.'

I thought of Reg. He'd called himself a 'one-off', meaning he'd been neutered. I felt pretty much the same about crime as he did about sex, I was sure. The idea didn't occur to me. I could see a vague appeal, had some residual stirrings when watching cool gangster movies but I knew in my heart that I didn't have the equipment for it myself.

'I can't be honest for the rest of the world,' I said, 'I can only be honest for myself. I'd rather be an honest pauper than a rich liar,' I said, paraphrasing my dad.

The Cat looked at me with some curiosity, like a real cat might look at a strange ball of fluff, trying to work out what it was.

The butler butled out with a plastic bag. The Cat waited until he'd gone back inside and then opened my case and began counting the money.

'Changing the subject, how is the lovely Lyndsey anyway?' said the Cat. 'Still slicing off the athlete's foot?'

'How do you know about Lyndsey?' I said.

'I've made it my business to,' said the Cat. His face was expressionless but in my line you get used to reading things into expressionless faces.

'Am I to take this as a threat?' I said.

'You take it how you like,' said the Cat, dropping the chip into the pocket of my shirt. 'Now if you'll excuse me I've got a couple of very rich mugs to fleece.'

12

Canine Rhymes

I love Lyndsey for so many reasons.

We met when I sold her a flat. I'd thought she seemed more interested in me than the properties I was showing her from the first. That was four years ago and during a new time. When I say new time, I mean it's like with the dog. For the weeks leading up to meeting him everything seemed to be about dogs.

In the weeks around when I met Lyndsey, everything seemed new. The Audi was new and I was enjoying the strange feeling of modern motoring. My previous car had been an aged Peugeot 205. Because I'm not a car person I'd thought it was fine until it broke down one day and the mechanic referred to 'what you expect with a car of this age'.

You're curiously connected to the road in an old car like that, but not in a good way, more like you might be connected to the mains, rumbling up an A road, creaking down a B, thundering on the motorway with the radio scarcely audible

In the Audi, though, I seemed to glide, cut off from all reality. In that silent bubble I felt untouchable. For weeks I drove about saying things like, 'Engage warp drive, Mr Sulu,' and 'Make it so,' when on the way to Kwik Save. I'd bought a new car, despite the fact that I could almost see my dad covering his head as if about to be struck. 'That's five grand you've lost by driving out of the showroom!' he'd have trembled.

The spending fever had caught and I'd lashed out on a couple of new suits, some trendy clothes from a shop in Brighton. I'd had my hair cut in a different way. That is, they still used scissors but a different style, closer in parts, longer in others. I can't really remember it now. My mum got a new wheelchair too.

It was Easter. You see what I mean by new.

This is when Lyndsey walked into my life.

I'd noticed her straightaway, as soon as she came into the office. It would have been impossible not to. She was beautiful.

Woof, woof! I thought, as soon as I saw her. She had long straight henna-dyed hair at the time, with beautiful green eyes, snow-white skin and a wicked witch glint in her eye, with a light, relaxed way of speaking. She was expensively dressed, or so I thought, in the trendy gear of the time – the pony skin boots, suede skirt and hippy-chic top.

So I was surprised when she told me she was only looking for a one-bedroom flat. These were the days when chiropodists could afford one-bedroom flats, by the way.

I think I recognised a bit of myself in Lyndsey. She was someone who'd always imagined she'd be doing something different to what she was. She came from a very poor family – her dad was unemployed and her mum was a cleaner – and from this background becoming a chiropodist had seemed a key to untold wealth. Her education, however, had broadened her horizons enough to make her realise how narrow they were.

She wanted more and I'd wanted to help her get it.

Unfortunately, given the fact she'd overstretched herself slightly in buying her flat, she was always running to stand still, doing long hours and having to watch the pennies. Her aim of getting an Open University degree and moving into marketing

– an area she imagined, probably rightly, to be much more lucrative than chiropody – seemed almost impossible to attain. She just didn't have the time.

We hit it off from the first. I knew that I liked her because I was talking shit. I was nervous and I know now that she recognised it, treating it as a compliment. We were going to see a flat near the seafront, which I thought she could afford if she pressed her bank and I pressed her case to the owners – a company who wanted it off their books quickly.

'The parking round here isn't good if you haven't got a resident's, though,' I said, 'and people are always just throwing their cars anywhere.' I shouldn't have been telling her that, as an estate agent, but I wanted to be absolutely honest with her and, at a subconscious level, I think I wanted to establish some sort of sympathy between us, to feel that we were connecting, even over something as trivial as parking.

We'd pulled up outside the flat – her flat as it now is – but there wasn't a space to be had within three streets. Normally I would have parked three streets away, because parking restrictions are there for a reason and I don't mind walking, but I wanted Lyndsey to see me as a bit more of a devil-may-care sort when in fact I was more of a 'devil-may-care, might he? Ooh, do you think we shouldn't do it then?' sort.

'Sorry it's taking so long to find a space,' I said.

'Don't worry about it,' she said. 'I like being in such a nice car.'

I ummed and ahhed about what I should do. In the end I was fairly sure that I didn't want to look like a ditherer so I double-parked outside the flat.

'Here I go,' I said, 'throwing my car anywhere. Bit of a hypocrite.' I think I must have worn a look of deep guilt.

'I shouldn't worry about it,' said Lyndsey. 'Hypocrisy's at least half a high standard. It's better to apply your morals only to other people than not apply them at all.'

'Quite,' I said. She had a laidback, smiling, slightly detached way to her that, to be frank – and it must be understood that I would never act on this with a client in any way – made me want to rip her clothes off there and then.

I showed her round the empty flat, all the time wanting to ask her out for a drink. Professionalism, though, prevented me.

'I like it,' she said.

'There's a sea view if you look past those houses,' I said, peering out of the window.

'Great!' she said, joining me at the window, uncomfortably comfortably close.

It was a phenomenon I later came to associate very strongly with Lyndsey, that of being intensely aware of the naked woman beneath the clothes.

'I like it, but have you got a furnished flat you could show me?'

'Yes,' I said. 'It's good to get an idea of what these places look like with furniture in. The next one we're seeing's in the same style.'

'Does it have a bed?' she said.

And that was the start of our romance, a tumble of passion and lots of passionate tumbling.

I became obsessed with her for a time, to the extent that I'd personally take on any houses near her surgery so we could meet at lunchtime, madly coupling in other people's homes, like burglars of love.

We got on so well, and Lyndsey seemed to genuinely delight in my company. I certainly did in hers. She was always so sexy and, on the surface at least, had a hard outlook on life that I found an amazing and funny contrast to my own.

She started me smoking, for which I'm incredibly grateful. If I didn't smoke, the average poker room would be like torture to me. As it is, I can contribute to making it torture for others.

The first time we got it together was on someone else's bed. Just after we'd got it together, she lay naked on the bed, with me nearly having kittens that we'd made some noticeable derangement of the sheets.

The house belonged to a David Rice, a metaphor therapist.

Lyndsey leaned down over the bed to get her bag, her lithe and muscular body raising the suggestion in my mind that the sheets weren't going to get any more disturbed after one go than they were after two.

'What are you doing?' I said.

'Looking for my bag,' she said. She turned back over, having retrieved it. She'd also got hold of a folder.

She opened the folder and began to read it, lying on her front. With the other hand she opened her bag and took out some cigarettes, which made every fibre in my body want to take them off her. What were the chances that David Rice, with his large Tibetan tabla on the walls and his t'ai chi sword lying on top of the rush-weave laundry basket, smoked in his room?

'Metaphor therapy,' said Lyndsey, opening the file, 'what is that like? Ooh, I think I know the chap who this file is about. Cigarette?'

'I don't,' I said.

'Why not?'

I picked up the packet. 'Smoking Kills!' I read, giving the warning the appropriate dramatic emphasis.

Lyndsey propped herself up on her elbow and lit the cigarette.

'Health and fitness are the concerns of the fuckless,' she said.

'Well, in that case,' I said, moving to open the window and feeling her eyes on me, 'I might try one.'

So Lyndsey and I started in passion. And continued there, largely. Whatever else has been wrong with our relationship, this has always been right. It's the rock, or the wood in current parlance, on which everything else is built.

The love came slowly. At first it was a feeling of togetherness, two school kids bunking off the days, the stolen hours spent in childish enthusiasm for adult pleasures, even if sometimes she did go too far.

'It's great, this,' she said one day as she looked beneath the bed of a doctor whose house I was selling.

'I know,' I said.

'More than just the sex, though,' she said, as dreamily as one can when rooting beneath a bed from on top of it. 'We can be whoever we want. This house is ours and this life is ours. Today, we're Dr King and her naughty nurse,' she said. 'We can choose. Aha!' She emerged with a large, pink, multispeed vibrator.

'What are you going to do with that?' I said, slightly alarmed.

'Put it somewhere her mum might find it when she visits,' said Lyndsey.

I was about as comfortable with this idea as if she'd inserted it in me.

As it happened, she slipped it into the bread bin before she went but I returned in the afternoon and replaced it beneath the bed.

Lyndsey got her flat and moved in and I suppose it was the bonding of building her home together that cemented our relationship.

She changed, of course, as everyone does. I think for the first two years of any relationship you're sort of on your best behaviour, hiding your more ugly selves. I hid my goodie-goodie, unadventurous nature and she hid, well, what would you call it? Something like depression. I think that when we first started seeing each other she was buoyed up by the excitement of going out with someone who had a new car (which he wouldn't replace until it fell to bits, though she wasn't to know that), who had some money to spend (if largely on cards, though she wasn't to know that either). It made her feel like she was going somewhere.

But eventually the novelty wears off and you begin to see that life on an estate agent's income is not much freer than life on a chiropodist's, that for most people happiness is like a horizon, you can see it, you can walk towards it but you can't touch it.

But still, our love grew, in supermarket visits, in Pizza Express and Ask, in a weekend in Paris and two in the Lakes. I always had the mild impression that for her it was a just-enough love, not a Kwik Save love or even a Safeway but nowhere near a Marks and Spencer's and certainly not a Harrods. Maybe somewhere between Sainsbury's and Waitrose.

The dog couldn't see this, unfortunately, and a certain distance had developed between him and Lyndsey.

'Permission to speak freely, sir?' he said, one night as I came out of the shower following a big game.

My winnings were on the difficult chair. I call it the difficult chair because it used to be the easy chair but now the stuffing's gone and it isn't very comfortable any more.

I nodded at him, towelling myself down. I could tell he was suppressing a smirk. He thought it hilarious that I had showers. 'Every time you go in that room it rains and you never learn, do you?' he said.

'Speak,' I said.

'Thank you, sir. She wants so to be pack leader. She acts as if she's in control when you're there, you defer to her all the time. Would it not be better if she were allowed to go and form her own pack. Then you could form a pack with nice Lucy and me. Perhaps Lyndsey could form a pack with this Michael Tibbs.'

I hadn't told the dog that Tibbs was called the Cat as I didn't want to prejudice him in his judgements.

'It doesn't work like that,' I said.

'That's exactly how it works!' said Reg. 'Tibbs gets what he perceives to be a high-value female, you get a higher value female, one that is kind and nice and distributes biscuits,' he said.

'This isn't all about food, is it?' I said. I'd noticed a change in Reg's manner to Lyndsey when she hadn't given him the end of her ice cream on the beach.

The dog's ears went flat. This isn't always a sign he's guilty, it's just a sign he feels accused. It's like that stiff-legged walk you get going through customs. You know you've nothing to declare but they don't, do they, behind the glass, so the situation demands guilt and you end up walking like they've already got a hand up your bum.

'I just ask that you think about it, that's all,' said Reg. 'I don't think she's one hundred per cent on me, your Lyndsey.'

'Does she have to be one hundred per cent on you?' I said.

'If I'm to . . . If you're to . . . Yes!' he said.

'Well, I'm not sure she's one hundred per cent on me, if it's any consolation,' I said.

The dog looked hurt, as if a lack of enthusiasm towards me was an insult to him.

'We've been together a long time,' I explained. 'Things can't always be like they are in the first flush of it all. You come down to a sort of functional level of love.'

Reg's jaw dropped, trembling slightly.

'And will this happen to us?' he said. 'You and me? I had no idea the universe was so cruel.'

I tapped the bed for him to climb up beside me.

'Ooh! Special privileges!' said the dog, forgetting what he'd just been talking about. He sat on the bed upright and proud, as if he was modelling to be struck on a coin.

I remembered what he'd said, though.

'No,' I said, 'it won't happen to us.'

He picked up the thread of the conversation. 'Why not?'

'Because our love is different,' I said, putting my arm round him.

'I thought so,' said the dog, snuggling in to me.

In seconds he was dozing, as dogs have the capability to do, lightly barking out of the side of his mouth as he chased some phantom squirrel.

I'll say this about dogs, you can forget your air ioniser or your scented candle; for pure relaxation you can't whack a hound. It was as if his tiredness was too big for his body and a radius of sleep gently pulsed from him. A wide and inclusive recumbence, a calming glow. The rhythm of his breathing was slow and time seemed to slow with it.

He puffed the cheeks, blowing as he slept and saying under his breath, 'Now that's what I call retrieval,' his paws trotting out in some imaginary gallop.

Then he seemed to hold his breath for a second, as if diving into some deeper trance.

'Don't leave me here,' he said. 'It must be my fault you're going. Oh, what have I done?'

I put my hand on his forehead.

'Don't dream tonight, Reggie,' I said, and he was quiet.

13

An Inspector Calls

Looking back on it, I'd have expected them to act more quickly than they eventually did.

A month had gone by between my last meeting with Tibbs and him launching his first move against me. Not very much had happened on the Charterstone front in that time. It was early August which was a write-off because all the big buyers would be at their gîtes in the south of France or wherever they go nowadays. I didn't fancy nipping round and doing the valuation right then. There was, I thought, plenty of time for that.

I'd decided to launch the sales campaign towards the end of September. British people, even the top entrepreneurs, don't actually realise they're back at work until some time in October when they look in the mirror, notice that their tan is fading and put two and two together, so I thought that a small delay wouldn't hurt us.

In that time my poker had gone from strength to strength. I was winning enough to spend a fair bit of money on the flat and I hoped that, once my mum's inheritance was paid back, I might be in a position to ask Lyndsey to marry me again.

My success had meant I had to move away from Snake Eyes' game for the most part, to plough more lucrative fields. I still dropped in from time to time though, occasionally bringing with me a couple of fat lads – our term for big spenders – so they could win back some of the money I was taking from them.

Of course, I didn't always win, that would have made me too unpopular but I had refitted my flat on the proceeds of my gaming and Lyndsey was as Clioed as woman was ever Clioed, as I'd bought her a new Renault with more extras than *Ben Hur*.

This success alone would have bonded a more shallow man than me to the dog but I didn't love him for his money. I think his enthusiasm was his most endearing quality. The dog's basic state was that everything was fantastic. It was quite difficult to find something Reg wasn't enthusiastic about.

'Something in a bag!' he'd pant, as I came home with a couple of CDs.

'I don't think you'd like these,' I said. 'The Carpenters aren't your style.'

'If they're in a bag they must be good,' said Reg. 'If there's one thing certain in the world, it's that.' And he snuffled up to it.

'Washing!' he'd shout, as I emptied my laundry basket. 'Watch it whirr and change the smells. It's like magic.'

'I thought you liked dirty smells,' I said. 'I shouldn't have thought Persil was up your street.'

'I do like *interesting* smells,' he said with heavy emphasis.

'But this machine simplifies the smell.'

'But it goes whirr first!' said Reg, as if delivering a conclusive point.

It was around this time that I began to dream. Banal stuff, really. I was in a corridor full of doors, rather like the one in *The Matrix Reloaded*, it has to be said. I could hear Reg barking, which was unusual because I'd concluded that I didn't really hear him bark, I just heard him speak. I knew it was him and no other dog. I had that baseless certainty you have in dreams that he was behind one of the doors and yet I didn't bother to open any of them. It was as if I had all the choice in the world but a total inability to make it and I didn't know why.

Then things got a little more difficult to interpret. I knew there were wheels there, for instance, though none of my conventional senses registered them and the number M345667 came up, followed by some letters that weren't letters and numbers that weren't numbers.

I'd woken one night to see Reg next to me on the bed, staring intently at me.

'Are you all right?' he said.

'Yes,' I said.

'You were talking in your sleep.'

'I was dreaming,' I said. 'What was I saying?'

'Lyndsey,' said the dog. 'Over and over again.'

'Strange. She wasn't in the dream at all.'

'Like a dog, he hunts in dreams,' said Reg. 'Tennyson. He was a Staffordshire bull terrier actually. All the Lake poets were dogs, they went there for the walks.' A look of puzzlement came onto his face. 'I dream,' he said.

'What of?'

'I'm running down a beach chasing a ball,' said the dog.

'Yes?'

'That's it. What do you think it means?'

Like a dog, I left it.

It was ten o'clock on an overcast Monday morning and I was finalising the ads for Charterstone when she called – in tears.

Reg was in the office with me, and Lucy and the others had been making a fuss of him. I'd been sitting back in a slight reverie, dreaming of poker winnings, past, present and to come. Threats inevitably recede with time. You start to feel cocky and go from running from the cover of one lamp post to another to swaggering around saying, 'Come on, do your worst,' once you're fairly sure they're not going to do their worst. The phone rang.

It was Lyndsey, booing her eyes out.

I'd seen Lyndsey fill up with tears before – at my mum's funeral, for instance – but I'd never heard her bawl, largely because I'd never given her reason to bawl.

'Dave,' she said, 'it's terrible! I've been threatened.'

'How?' I said.

'I was treating a patient this morning and he just loomed at me over a corn,' she said.

Lyndsey had been relatively quiet on the subject of the Tibbs deal, particularly since I'd bought her the full works package on the Clio, causing her to let out a grateful 'Papa!' at the moment of bliss.

I had noticed something in her, though, ever since she'd found out about it. Anyone who didn't know her so well would have assumed she'd got a new lease of life.

We'd been up to London more times in the six weeks since Tibbs's offer than we had in the previous four years. We'd been to restaurants and plays and bars and art viewings, which was great, particularly as I'd bought a video recorder I could understand and managed to tape *Big Brother*.

We'd had tea at the Ritz which made even me, with my card player's unreal attitude to money, have a real attitude to money. We'd seen card master Job Phillips – called Job because of his legendary patience – there. OK, he was working as a bellboy, but I knew he'd be back, he was just biding his time. He knew no other way.

We'd taken a room, which was roughly the price of my last four holidays combined, and made love using some very expensive antiques as support.

'Wouldn't it be great to do this all the time?' said Lyndsey.

'They wouldn't let the dog in,' I said.

'You and your dog,' she said. She'd become a bit angry when

she'd found I had a picture of him in my wallet. I had a picture of her too, I don't know what she was complaining about. Admittedly it had been a bit over the top to buy him a network rail card but we'd had a bet that the man wouldn't notice he was filling it out for a dog.

He'd stamped the photo without a word and then said, 'Day return to Barking, is it?' which had given us all a laugh.

During our London excursions Reg stayed with Lucy, which he regarded as a treat. They'd stay in together watching old movies while she asked him if he'd like another sausage and he assured her he could fit in a small one if she coated it in mayonnaise to help it slip down.

These thoughts, though, were far from my mind as Lyndsey related the story of how she'd been on her own with a new client, having just snicked off a troublesome corn, when he menaced her.

'What did he say?'

'He said that my boyfriend was annoying some very influential people.'

'That's not a threat,' I said.

'He said that he'd kill me if you didn't do as they said, in a horrible way.'

'That's a threat,' I conceded. 'Did he put a time frame on this?'

'I didn't ask him for a bollocking business plan, David.'

I could see I was being unreasonable.

'Let me come round and see you,' I said.

'Would you?' said Lyndsey. 'And could you stay at mine tonight, it'd make me feel safer.'

'Of course,' I said, wondering if Lucy would take the dog. Lyndsey's white carpet, of course, was incompatible with a dog, she said. I said it was incompatible with being on the floor, but there you go. Lyndsey wouldn't stay at my house because she needed her creature comforts by her, though not, it seemed, my comforting creature.

'What are you going to do, Dave?' said Lyndsey. I could hear the stress in her voice.

'I think I'd better go round and talk to Tibbs again,' I said.

'Oh, thank God!' she said.

'Don't worry, love, I'll tell him he can't push us about like this.'

There was a silence at the end of the phone before Lyndsey let out a great wail.

'He can push us about like this though, can't he? What are you going to do? Set your stupid dog on him?'

'Oh, so he's a stupid dog now, is he?' I said, feeling myself prickle. The dog, who was upside down on his back so that he could be fed chicken tikka from Lucy's baguette, looked round with alarm as he heard the 'stupid dog', like Prince Philip hearing that the pot had finally got to Harry and he was going on a hunt protest.

'Dave, can you take this seriously? Someone has threatened to kill me and it's in your power to stop them. So why don't you stop them?'

'What are you proposing, that we give in to them?' I hissed down the phone, the first time I think I'd ever done so.

'What other course of action is there, David?'

'Well, we can't just let them walk all over us.'

Lyndsey sounded near hysterical. 'They're going to walk all over us whether we let them or not!'

'Look, don't worry,' I said, 'I'll sort this out.'

'Well, there's got to be a first time for everything!' said Lyndsey and slammed down the phone.

I wanted to call her back but I thought I'd better give her some time to calm down. I realise now that this is pretty much the strategy Chamberlain employed with Hitler but there you go.

Reg had come over to me so I kneaded his ears and tried to concentrate.

'What's the problem?' said the dog.

'Tibbs has threatened Lyndsey,' I said.

'Great,' said the dog, 'that must be exciting for her.'

'No,' I said, 'it's a bad thing.'

'Oh,' said the dog, who I've already noted was accustomed to seeing the bright side of just about anything.

I told Lucy to institute a diary mix-up – that is, to tell my next appointment that there had been an error and I was away on another call – and went out to the car.

Reg wanted to come, even though I told him he'd have to sit in the car and wait.

'To be appointed a guard would be a great honour, sir,' said Reg. 'It's one of the highest callings a dog can aspire to.'

I was glad to take him because the car's one of the few places where I can speak freely to him during the day. At work we get by in whispers or stolen comments behind desks and in the staff area.

'Open the door, oh, esteemed conveyance,' said the dog. He'd finally got the idea that the car was moving and not the land around it.

'It can't hear you,' I said.

'Is it deaf?' said Reg. Reg seemed to treat the car with a lot of deference. 'It's so strong and fast,' he said once, 'and that fat man who really annoys you but who you always watch said on your television the other night that cars need to be treated with respect.'

'That was *a* car, a Porsche,' I said, wishing I'd never allowed him to watch *Top Gear*. I'd hoped it might educate him in road use but all we'd got for a few days was him going around talking like Jeremy Clarkson. This is maddening enough in Jeremy Clarkson; in a dog it's unbearable. There you go, he's got me at it now.

Peculiarly, Reg had the same attitude to cars as my dad used to have. I remember once travelling to the shops with him in the old Lada. 'They're cheap and that makes me cheerful,' he said.

'So you're planning to get rid of this, are you?' I said.

He practically lost control of the wheel, instinctively putting his hands back to the ten-to-two position, as if attempting to cover the car's ears. 'Don't let it hear you say that!' he said.

'Why not?'

'Because,' he whispered, 'if it knows you're going to . . .' he could only mouth the next words, 'let it go,' he glanced about him, 'it'll go wrong. You'll never get rid of it.'

'Load of shite,' I said, as the big end went.

We drove quickly towards Lyndsey's work, Reg with his head out of the window in the classic dog style.

'Why do you do that?' I asked as he leaned into the wind, cheeks billowing, his tongue like a pink vapour trail.

He came back into the car, a manic look in his eyes. 'Because I can!' he said, wild as the wolds, before plunging his head back into the onrushing air.

There was a certain coldness between Reg and Lyndsey. He went very tight-lipped whenever I mentioned her. I realised he didn't like her very much because it is quite difficult for a dog to go tight-lipped.

'You don't like her, do you?' I once asked him.

'I do like her if you like her,' he said, his ears going flat as if I'd just caught him with his head in the biscuit tin. 'She is a pack member and I will remain loyal until she ceases to be so.' He'd sounded offended. Still, he didn't seem to be taking the threat to Lyndsey very seriously.

I really didn't know what to do about the Cat. I knew property developers weren't all boy scouts but I'd never imagined anything like this went on, or that I would become involved in it.

I pulled up in the car park outside Lyndsey's surgery. She's attached to a kind of treatment clinic which houses GPs, chiropodists, physios and other sorts of therapists.

The dog asked if he could come in, seemingly forgetting that he'd promised to guard the car.

'What happened to it being the noblest calling a dog can aspire to?' I said.

'If you are determined that species should prove a bar to progress,' he said.

'For the next ten minutes I am.'

'OK then,' said the dog, settling down on the back seat. 'I'll just kip here.' I couldn't help thinking that the world would be a better place if we all went about our affairs like that.

Lyndsey was in the surgery reception area, still crying. The receptionist was comforting her and trying to persuade her to call the police.

'Lynds!' I said.

She stood up and threw her arms round me, not even bothering to check my suit for dog hair. I knew things were bad.

'She's been in a terrible state,' said the receptionist.

'Not as bad as my feet!' said an old lady in the waiting area, who I presumed was having to wait while Lyndsey composed herself.

'What did he look like?' I said. I don't know why I asked her that, it just seemed relevant at the time.

'He's on the CCTV,' said the receptionist. 'Shall we have another look at it?' She showed a little more relish for this than I thought strictly proper.

Lyndsey was still crying on my shoulder.

'I think that might be a little traumatic,' I said.

Lyndsey looked up at me, her face raw with tears. 'No,' she said. 'I think it would help.'

'I'll get the tea on and then we can all have a look!' gayed a man I recognised as one of her colleagues, a physio I'd met on a Christmas drink once.

'I'll be with you in five minutes for your orange badge, Mrs Prentice,' said another woman, who I think was a nurse. 'We've just got some staff business to attend to. Does anyone know how it rewinds?'

'You'll get two hundred and fifty pounds if you send the video in to *Crimewatch*!' said Mrs Prentice, coming forward more speedily than you would think a disabled parking permit applicant would be wise to do.

'That's *You've Been Framed*,' said the nurse.

'Can I see?' said Mrs Prentice.

'Oh, OK,' said the nurse.

Someone did know how to rewind it and we all sat in a back office as the strained black and white, which announces the world over that someone has given it to someone who didn't want it, began to roll.

Lyndsey's surgery itself wasn't covered by CCTV, so all we had was an image of the man checking in.

'That's a great picture of him,' said the receptionist. 'You could go to the police with that.'

I knew, however, that going to the police was out of the question.

To anyone else he wouldn't have looked that menacing. He wasn't a tall man, he wasn't a broad man but he was a policeman. He was the man I'd played poker with at Tibbs's. I recognised the bald dome, the 'why in God's name does anyone wear them?' moustache, the head that turned like a searchlight scanning the surgery. We couldn't go to the police because the police had come to us.

I put my head into my hands. Now, I thought, we are in trouble.

14

Running Dog

As I left the surgery, a great part of me wanted to confront Tibbs there and then, to tell him I'd written letters to journalists, that my solicitor had received instructions with allegations that would be put to the proper authorities if anything happened to me or anyone I loved.

The dog stuck his head over the back seat like a neighbour across a fence.

'You are scared, sir,' he said, 'and so I must be too.' He gave a shiver.

Lyndsey had told the other staff at the surgery that the man had just become angry and threatened her for inventing verrucas. The staff at the centre had been insistent she at least logged the offence, though there was nothing they could do to make her go to the police.

Part of me, though, was out of its depth. Lyndsey had made me promise to at least think about giving in to Tibbs's demands, and so I did.

It was, obviously, the best way out. There was no reason to suppose that he might not still be willing to cut me in for a deal and I could probably get an enforceable contract drawn up with him.

I also got the feeling with the Cat that, should I join his Folding Society, he'd turn out to be a person of his word. People like him need others to work through and there was no reason to expect that he would cheat someone who was useful to him.

If I was in uncharted territory on this one, Lyndsey was in outer space. She was so upset that I'd do almost anything to put things right for her.

I asked the dog for his advice.

'What are we going to do about the Cat?'

'Which cat?'

'Tibbs.'

'He's a cat?'

'It's his nickname.'

His eyes narrowed. 'Only one way to deal with cats,' he said. 'What?'

Reg said nothing, he just pulled back his lips from his fangs.

He was right, I had to trust my first instinct and stand up to Tibbs. However, trusting my first instinct is not my first instinct.

Back at the office I looked up the Cat's company – New World Developments. Lucy was in alone at her desk, the lads being out with clients. I wanted to tell her – everything – but it wouldn't come, I couldn't get it out. But just her presence seemed to make me feel calmer, like the dog when he was asleep, she seemed to radiate a feeling that things were OK with the world.

Things, however, definitely were not.

I picked up the phone, ready to confront the Cat, if at a safe distance.

The dog looked on expectantly. He hadn't quite got the idea of telephones, believing when I'd first met him that the person on the other end was in some way shrunk and inside it. I'd explained that people talk down tubes, and he'd seemed to kind of get the idea of that.

A secretary told me Tibbs wasn't in and asked me if I'd like to leave a message.

'Tell him this is David Barker,' I said, 'and . . .' I was doing that thing with the lists again, overstretching them.

'Ah, Mr Barker,' said the secretary. 'I may be able to put you through to Mr Tibbs after all.'

There was a short delay, during which I was played some light classical music of the sort I'd come to suspect the Cat would choose for his hold theme. There was something very unrefined about his attempts at refinement, I had decided.

'Mr Barker!' said Tibbs.

'Now you listen to me, you feline fuck!' I said. The dog nodded his approval. Lucy looked up in surprise.

It occurred to me that the Cat might have thought I was being friendly, in a pokerly way, so I decided to clear things up. 'You go anywhere near my girlfriend again and I'll be round your house with a baseball bat,' I said.

'That is David Barker, the estate agent of Son and Barker?' said Tibbs.

'This is me,' I said.

'How do I know it's you?' said the Cat.

'What do you mean, how do you know it's me?'

'What's your mother's maiden name?' he said.

'Cornhill,' I said, for some reason answering him, 'and it's me that should be asking the questions, matey boy.'

'What did you say you were going to do to me?'

'Come round your house with a baseball bat,' I said. 'Have you been paying attention?'

'And what will you do with this baseball bat?' said the Cat.

'Stick it up your arse!' I said.

'Metaphorically or literally?' said the Cat, who wasn't proving much cop at being threatened.

'Literally!'

'So you are very clearly threatening to harm me?' said the Cat.

'I'll do more than harm you, you bastard, I'll kill you,' I said.

'That's the way, that's the way!' said the dog, spinning around in front of me.

There was a snort. 'I think that should be enough for the tape,' said the Cat. 'If any harm comes to me now, Mr Barker, people will know where to look, I warn you. Furthermore, I may decide to pass this on to the police.'

That was supposed to have been my script. The dog was wagging his tail, confidently awaiting my response.

'I can't believe you threatened Lyndsey,' I said.

The dog laughed under his breath. 'That told him,' he said. 'You are masterful, sir, masterful.'

'Despite the evidence,' said the Cat with a little purr in his voice. I could tell he thought he had me.

'You won't change my mind,' I said. 'I've taken steps to make sure this all comes out if you do anything to us.'

'Pow, pow, pow,' said the dog, doing a very poor impression of boxing by rolling his shoulders.

'So did the last chap,' said the Cat, 'and very little came of that.'

The dog looked at me expectantly but I couldn't think of anything to say. Instead, I just heard the words come out of my mouth.

'Please don't hurt her,' I said. 'She means the world to me.'

'Oh, Christmas crackers no,' said the dog, pushing his head into his collar. 'Mmm, Christmas crackers, turkey. Nice. Where's the turkey?'

'There is no turkey,' I mouthed.

'Then why did I mention it?' said the dog.

'Let me tell you how it's going to be,' said the Cat, making me wonder if he was going to suggest I gave my love to him, à la Mick Jagger. 'You are going to take the money we're offering you. The five hundred thousand. You can join our society and life will be good for you.'

'And if I refuse?'

'Then until the end of the week it's a bit more stick, with the carrots still on the table. After that it's only stick,' he said. 'Oh, and can I apologise for not instituting this chain of events earlier. There was a question over our own finance for a while but now that is going to be resolved.'

The dog was looking at me in horror.

'You're going to give in to him!' he said.

I just put down the phone.

'Sorry,' I said, as Reg stood gaping.

'Sorry for what?' said the dog, coming over to me and nuzzling into my leg. 'You'll have to forgive my short-term memory, it's very . . . oh.'

'Bad?' I said.

'That's it,' said the dog.

I've said before that sometimes events seem to hover in the air, half formed, for weeks before they actually happen.

So it is, it seems to me, with human contact. How many times have you heard from an old friend just as you were thinking of contacting them? I'd no sooner put the phone down on the Cat than Lucy was gesturing at me from the other side of the office.

'It's Mrs Cad-Beauf,' she said. 'She wants to speak to you urgently.'

The urgent matter on the mind of Mrs Cad-Beauf, as it turned out, was that I had omitted to send her a seller's contract.

'You have left yourself exposed, Mr Barker,' she said. 'I will see you shortly.' She put down the phone.

The call also reminded me that I hadn't valued the place. Why was I putting that off? Or perhaps I hadn't. If I didn't sell the property then the whole pressure would be off me. I could say I'd been sacked by Mrs Cad-Beauf.

I appreciate this is the coward's way out but, there again, cowards are experts at finding ways out and sometimes it pays to follow their example.

Mrs Cad-Beauf, I was sure, wouldn't sell if I didn't represent her and then perhaps I could advise her on using some of her wealth to make her surroundings more suitable for a woman of her age. I could advise her on getting a nurse, I could help her with wheelchair access. If she wanted company I could tell her how to develop some flats and get some posh grannies in of her own.

The prospect nearly made me skip for joy. So what if I'd be £100,000 in commission the poorer? I'd be free of worry, completely.

'Reg,' I said, 'our problems are at an end.'

'What problems?' said the dog.

'The Cat, all that sort of thing.'

'I was trying not to mention those,' said Reg. 'I thought you meant Lyndsey. I know you would feel lonely without her but might I suggest you form a larger pack, perhaps taking in some of her friends and then exclude her?'

I held his nose. 'I don't want one more word out of you about Lyndsey,' I said. 'She's a very nice woman and all she needs is a little understanding. Do you hear? Not one more word.'

'Mmmmmm,' said the dog.

'What did you say?' I slackened my grip around his nose.

'I shall stubble my whids,' said the dog, by which I supposed he meant he'd shut his trap.

I let him go and he went to the back of the shop where Lucy was making coffee.

I mulled and mawed in my seat, turning things over in my mind.

Lucy came in with my coffee in a large mug marked 'David's mug'.

'Oh, whose is this?' I said.

'Yours,' she said. 'I thought you'd like it.'

'Thanks,' I said, feeling myself colouring slightly. Why did I have such difficulty accepting this sort of thing? It's nice, isn't it? People like people being nice to them. That's why it's known as being nice to them, for God's sake.

'Some trouble earlier?' said Lucy.

'No,' I said, 'not at all.'

'That bad?' said Lucy.

'I'm afraid so,' I said.

'A problem shared often provides the other person with a good laugh,' she said, gesturing to indicate that she was ready to listen.

'Maybe not this one,' I said.

Somehow her just being there gave me the strength to do what I needed to do, though.

Lucy went into the back of the shop, with the dog singing a song about custard creams, while I called Lyndsey to tell her that I was going to sort everything out.

'You're going to go through with it?' she said, with relief in her voice.

'Just leave it to me,' I said.

Lyndsey didn't seem very happy about leaving anything to me. She'd decided it was too dangerous for her to stay at her flat and was going to her mum's for the evening. I thought this was a good idea. For one it would be safer, even the tentacles of the Cat, if a cat can have tentacles, couldn't stretch to finding out where her mum lived. For two, there was a big game at the Pieman's that evening and I, under my new nickname of Big Dog, poker slang for the underdog and also a clear reference to Reg, had been invited. My luck was ready to die, or so they thought, and they were practically circling above my head, waiting for the moment I dropped. But I wasn't going to drop, was I? Not me. Not Big Dog.

I kicked back in my chair, feeling better than I'd felt since I'd agreed to sell Mrs Cad-Beauf's home for her. Finally I had a way forward that satisfied me. I looked at my watch. Five thirty, no evening appointments, time to go home.

15

Yesterday's Man

It's only once in a while that you truly look at yourself, as I did that evening.

In fact I didn't so much look at myself as look at the fridge. Quiz me on nutrition and you will find me bang up to date on various proportions of carbohydrate, protein and fat in the diet. In a youth of competition cycling, one picks these things up. Quiz me on a dog's requirements and you will find me even more at ease.

Look inside my Smeg, however, and you will see a different story. Five litres of full fat Coke, four packs of Mars Bars, three of Snickers and a pack of Marks and Spencer's herb salad, approaching the anniversary of its stay in my flat.

Also in this fridge are a pack of six organic dried pig's ears, eight packs of 'good boy' balanced nutritional chews, ten cold organic sausages, dog gravy to liven up remaining biscuits and a large box of what look like canine Cheerios.

It became clear to me that I was taking better care of the dog than I was of myself. It isn't so unusual for card players to fall into such habits and I'd at least avoided the hard liquor, taking only the occasional nip of whisky to steady my nerves.

Since my mum died this bad eating had been something of the way of it. I often used to eat my meals with her, cooking on Fridays when she didn't have meals on wheels. Because I shopped for my mum I also shopped for myself. A tinned steak and kidney pudding may be revolting but, served with mash and veg, it's a more nutritious meal than a Mars Bar, fun size or no.

I served Reg some dinner and we had a chat about whether I should call Lyndsey or not. Reg was firm that even in times of stress the dominant animal does not make the first move.

I was very uncomfortable with this, but there was nothing I could do about the coolness between Reg and Lyndsey and I wasn't up to having an argument with him about it, particularly if it was to be followed by an argument with her about what we were going to do with Mrs Cad-Beauf.

Instead, Reg tucked up in his new basket, I left the house and called her on the mobile.

At first she didn't answer and I had a sudden fit that they'd got at her.

Then she did answer. 'Yes?' Her voice was curt.

'I just want to see you're all right.'

'No thanks to you.'

'Lyndsey, please.'

I could hear her voice cracking as she said, 'Why don't you call me when you've decided what's more important in your life, me or a load of old dogs.' She put down the phone and I just didn't have the energy to call her back.

As I've already noted, some weeks seem to have a theme. That week, it seemed, the theme was stress.

I was patrolling the own-brand section of Insanesbury's, noting the 19p a can beans and speculating that twenty cans would cost less than £4 and come in very useful in case of chemical or biological attack when my attention was taken by the back of a man's peppery bouffant, which was floating towards me past Dishes of the Orient.

I didn't know at the time why I registered it, lost in general anxiety about terrorists and specific anxiety about strong-arm property developers, but I did.

The beans looked inedible to me and I concluded that anthrax might be a more appealing way to die than being bored to death by bland food. I was about to turn right into organic when I suddenly went cold.

The bouffant had tucked a sleek mobile between his ear and his shoulder and was talking on it as he manoeuvred his trolley past an obstruction caused by shelf reloading.

'Yeah, I see what you're saying,' he was saying, 'but what exactly are you saying?'

His voice was different from how I remembered it, but I still remembered it.

'Say!' said the bouffant. 'Say I say, say around £10k, what do you say?'

I was now alongside the trolley and I could see the face. The hair was an old man's but the face, though golf-weathered and Costa-fried, was discourteously young and unlined. No one had the right to a young face after what he'd been through. If everyone has the face they deserve at forty, he should have had a skull.

Suddenly the bouffant said, 'Ah, Loyd Grossman!' and turned hard right towards the pasta sauces, colliding with my trolley.

'Sorry!' he said. 'Yacking on the mobile, didn't see you there!'

He looked at me only briefly and he didn't recognise me. But I recognised him. It was Darren Swain, making a deal on a mobile phone, just like he had been when he killed my father.

I sat, purchaseless, in the car.

It had been inevitable, I suppose, that in a town the size of Worthing I would bump into him again one day but I'd been spared that for over ten years.

At first, of course, I'd looked for him, in that young man way of imagining what I'd do if I got hold of him.

This doesn't mean that I'd sought out his house, which I could have done because I knew where he lived from the inquest, and it doesn't mean that I carried a knife or a bat but I did look for him. When I was out about the town or going to work, I'd see a BMW and think, is that him? Is he going about his business while my dad is dead?

And then I tried not to look for him, which is the same as looking for him more.

I'd see a man in a suit across the street and I'd imagine it to be him. Then I'd have to follow him to check, not resting until I saw that the hair was the wrong colour, the man was too old or too young.

I don't know what I would have done if I'd found him. Pretty much what I'd just done in the supermarket, I suppose, stand gaping like I'd just been won at a fair and then watch him disappear.

My father, it appeared, was almost wholly unremembered by Darren Swain. Surely, even after ten years, he should have recalled me, especially as he'd just run into me while talking on a mobile. It seemed not. Strangely, it was me that felt guilty.

My dad was fading. The prints that he'd made on life were disappearing. Even the spectacular manner of his death was only held in one mind now – mine – and, to be honest, the details were sketchy.

I can still feel the bang, and recall the terrible awareness of the relatedness of things that an accident brings. 'That is there, that is there, that is moving towards that.' It's something you feel in the slo-mo, rather than think or see. In the seconds of collision, older senses seem to awaken and you escape yourself, utterly participating and utterly removed.

There in the car park, tumblers of my brain clicked into place, the miniature planets of neurones and atoms inside my head lined up, the conclusive red piece slid into the Connect 4 board and the memories came into my mind like a rave onto a village green – unexpected, unwanted, unpleasant and unignorable.

It was my first summer home from collage after my degree. I say collage because that's what we used to call it, owing to the vile hotchpotch of architectural styles that made up the campus.

One hot Thursday we'd cancelled the afternoon's appointments and gone out cycling – a hobby we shared.

If we hadn't, I wouldn't be an estate agent now. What would I have been? It's too long ago to remember the passage I didn't take, the door I never opened, the sweet I never sucked.

On our way back home we'd stopped at the Dog and Duck overlooking the river. (I've since found out that dogs quite like ducks and, when the birds are shot, they think they're carrying them back to hospital.)

I knew my dad had something serious on his mind because he offered to get the drinks in an uncharacteristic lapse in a lifetime of frugality. 'A pint of Guinness, please,' I said, containing my surprise.

'If anything should happen to me, son,' he said, returning from the bar and handing me my half, 'then I want you to promise me that you will look after your mother.'

My mother. When the doctors told us she was going to die I'd thought they were making a medical point, not a philosophical one. I mean, we're all going to die, aren't we? Ten years of decline it took.

I remember when the illness first hit her and we'd yet to have the ramp installed at the front door.

'Most blokes only have to do this once,' said my dad, lifting her out of the wheelchair and across the threshold.

'I'd never considered the romantic possibilities of major nerve disease,' said my mum.

This is why my dad had come the maudlin 'should anything happen to me' line at the pub.

'Don't be daft, Dad,' I said, leaning on the Children 'Welcome' sign. My dad had loved those quotation marks.

'Really,' he said. 'I want you to promise me. You and I are all she's got. If I go, she'll rely on you. I want to know you won't let her down.'

The firmest promises we make are those we think we won't have to keep. My dad was one of the healthiest pensioners I knew, still capable of showing the fitter forty-year-olds a thing or two in the cycling club time trials – especially when it came to getting his excuses in first. I didn't hesitate.

'I won't let her down. How could I? Dad, I want you to know. You've been like a father to me sometimes.'

'Ha ha ha,' he said. 'If you do let her down, you bastard, I'll be back to haunt you.'

'You won't have to,' I said. 'For one you won't die and for two I, well . . .' the word 'love' wasn't used in our family, though it was felt. 'I really like Mum.'

'Good lad,' he said, pretending to adjust his gear cable tension to avoid facing up to the emotion. 'Now mine's a pint of Brew XI. Oh, and a Scotch egg.'

It was unfortunate for both of us, then, that on our journey home, we encountered Mr Swain, a sales rep too giddy with the novelty of talking on his suitcase-sized mobile to look where he was directing his BMW 3 series.

My dad was killed outright in front of me, just next to the layby flower stall. We left tributes by the side of the road but you couldn't really tell what was in memoriam from what was on sale, a confusion I believe the flower man encouraged. 'How can we know the dancer from the dance?' asked W.B. Yeats. I feel this is a similar point, only more depressing.

It was my fault too. I was slightly bored by his company and wanted to get back to get ready to meet a girl I'd been seeing and walk her home from work. When I say I was bored, not exactly that. Just that I'd had his company for so long, was sure that I was going to have it for much longer. It was me who suggested taking the dual carriageway back instead of the winding B roads. Because he could see I was nervous to be ready for a date and because he loved me he indulged my haste and he died.

In the end, I suppose, it's the way Dad would have wanted to go. He'd seen a few people using mobile phones when driving and warned no good would come of it. So he went combining his two favourite hobbies – cycling and being right. He would have been pleased that, however late in life, he'd been proved totally and unarguably correct. My mum wanted 'He Told Us So' on his gravestone, which the vicar – after some initial misgivings – agreed to.

Friends said we were resorting to humour to cover our grief. 'That's what it's for,' my mum said.

I can still recall the transition, of things going one way to things going another – people, atoms, forces of kinesis, lives. Then my dad was dead, lying there in that terrible Day-Glo pink cycling top my mum had ordered from the catalogue. He'd hated that top but he'd worn it to please her. 'Once', said the sponsorship. I still have a picture of him standing next to a sign saying 'Take the train', the N making up Nonce. We used to have a laugh.

The tiny details of the accident are not there any more. I can remember standing at the side of the road with Swain babbling – somewhere between apology and accusation – and looking at the back of my hands and being surprised that I could still do something so mundane.

Then the feeling came over me, as if my head was projecting into space by stages, like a child's address – Dave Barker, the layby, the Downs Road, West Sussex, England, Britain, Europe, The World, The Solar System, The Milky Way, The Universe. I don't think it ever came back, I don't think I ever felt like me again.

'Life goes on,' the vicar said to my mum.

'Not for George, it doesn't,' said my mum.

The vicar, pissed at the party after the funeral, told me that my mum was one of his more challenging parishioners. I guess he meant she listened to what he said, which was never going to be a comfortable experience for a man like that.

Life was going on though, and with coarse haste, even there in that layby with the ambulance taking my dad away. Though the sun seemed like a strip light and the veins on my hands seemed to glow, I thought, is this how it is? So normal? So . . .

'Come away from the road,' said a copper. 'You're in danger there.'

That's not what I heard, though. I heard, 'We're not sure that God has finished with you yet, he may not have had enough.'

I sat for a while in Sainsbury's car park, waiting for Swain to come out. The sign in front of me said that the car park was for customers only. I felt stupidly guilty that I wasn't technically a customer and then anger at my guilt. Who feels guilty about something like that? Was it worse than guilt, though? A feeling that if I didn't play by the rules I'd get punished? Was it cowardice, a real bone-deep cowardice?

Still I wanted to nip back in and buy even a Twirl that I could show if challenged.

That went beyond cowardice – that was virtually superstition. Who was going to challenge me? One of the acne-ripe collectors of trolleys, or the grey-haired litter pickers? Actually, I thought, you know what old blokes are like about rules.

Eventually Swain came out, pushing a well-loaded trolley and chatting away to a pastel-blighted woman, probably his wife. Then he got into his car – a BMW 7 series, he was obviously doing well – and drove off. That was it.

If you don't see a meaning in life, if you don't hold that in some way what we do matters, that there are consequences, where does that leave you? Sitting in a large house overlooking the sea, making fortunes by defrauding old ladies. Happy.

I drove back numbly and I didn't think any more about it. The thing about working with the public for so long is that you evolve a public face. You don't carry a row into a client meeting, not if you want to keep the client. Depression, anxiety, fears and negativity are left at the door. I'd carried this over and now had a public face for myself, where I was the public.

I opened the door to see Reg wagging his tail in front of me.

'Are you OK, boy?' I said, asking a question of the dog that I could quite easily have been asking of myself.

'There's a brick in the front room,' said Reg. 'It belongs to someone who works in a smoky environment and who often visits his nan.'

16

Window Pain

'OK,' I said, taking off my coat and hanging it on the trendy hat stand I'd bought with one of the store cards as soon as I'd discovered Reg's poker abilities.

'And it's really draughty in there,' he said, casually scratching his ear.

'Why's that?'

'You know I'm not good on "why" in the world of things.'

This was true enough.

'OK, anything else?'

'Yes,' he said excitedly, pleased to be able to help. 'The window's broken.'

I looked down at him. 'Was there a large noise at any point today?'

'Come to think of it there was. Just before I noticed the brick.'

I wasn't too worried about the glass. I was planning to have the windows replaced anyway with the proceeds of my future wins, so it was no loss. And the immediate threat was useful in a way, it snapped me out of my Swain-based reverie. Like the dog says, you can find something positive in anything – even baths.

'Is there anything attached to this brick?'

'A piece of paper that has been used to wrap sandwiches. It's got some stuff on it like you have in your pens.'

'Ink,' I said.

'That's the fellow!' said Reg, wagging his tail.

There were two messages on the answerphone.

The first was from Lucy. Reg nodded towards the answerphone in a meaningful way as he heard her voice. I felt sure he only liked Lucy more than Lyndsey because she came round to walk him and Lyndsey never did. I wondered if he'd ever be convinced that Lucy's interest in me was purely platonic, or whatever platonic would be if it meant 'solely interested in someone's dog'. Caninic, maybe.

'Grrrrrr, woof!' said Lucy, though she is not a dog, in any sense. 'Hope to see you both later. If that's OK with you.'

The second was a call of a different timbre.

'Get the message?' it asked, in a voice straight out of ITV drama's 'threatening criminal' genre. 'Get the message?' Now it doesn't take a degree in philosophy to see the problem with that, although I do actually have a degree in philosophy. Either I've got the message – in which case he knows the answer – or I haven't – in which case he's wasting his breath.

I'd got the message, though, and so had Reg.

'Fight or flight?' he said, running up and down the hall as if there was a fire in the house. 'Fight or flight? Fight! He's only little! Get the swine!' He leaped towards the answerphone, growling

'He's not here, Reg,' I said, grabbing hold of him by the collar.

'I heard him!' said Reg, smelling the air with a look of puzzlement troubling his chops. 'He came in when Lucy left.'

There was a bang on the ceiling from the flat above. Mrs Craybourne complaining about the dog barking again.

'Have you been barking in the day today?' I asked him. Even though Reg is an unusually intelligent dog he still has difficulty holding more than one thought in his head at a time. This threw him off the scent of the recorded threat, if you'll pardon the pun.

He bridled slightly, as if composing his fur. 'I've been singing, to pass the time, if that's what you mean.'

'Oh dear,' I said. Mrs Craybourne who lives above had threatened to call the council, as well she might. I tell him and I tell him and I tell him not to make a noise and then I tell him again and then he forgets. It's not his fault. As dogs have gifts, so they must have handicaps.

I went into the front room and there, sure enough, on the floor was a brick like a Victory Vee on the end of a tongue of glass. It had missed the tastefully understand rug that I'd just bought on the store cards by an inch and had taken an unsightly gouge out of my floorboards. It had a note round it which was in a rather sorry, soggy condition, as if someone had chewed it.

The first part of the note was illegible. The second part, however, was quite clear.

'Do this or die,' it said, in something of a scrawl.

'Did you chew this note?' I said to the dog.

'Don't know,' said Reg, his ears going flat and his shoulders hunching. He might have been telling the truth. I mean, in that he didn't know. He did chew it, definitely, but dogs have very good memories for some things but relatively poor ones for others. There's a physical memory, though; his body knew he'd done it, that's why it was giving me the submission code.

'And if I did chew it, who could blame me?' he said. 'I get very bored when you're out.' I noticed the edge of the sofa had taken a bit of a hammering too.

It had taken ages to convince him the sofa wasn't just a big sausage.

'It's got a skin, it's got stuffing, what am I not getting here?' he'd said.

'Do this or die.' I tried to make out what I was meant to do but it was completely illegible.

I couldn't be bothered to clear up the mess immediately. No one had burgled the place all day because of it, so there was no reason to suspect they would at night. Anyway, I felt too mentally drained to think about it even if they did. Until Reg had started giving me advice on poker, all a burglar would have got at my house was practice. Now, though, I'd got rid of all the old stuff and put in the top drawer Habitat. I'd even thrown out the old sofa, the one I'd had at college and where I'd first got it together with the luscious Pauline Priestfield. I had no real attachment to anything I'd bought simply because, with Reg as my ace in the hole, I thought I could replace it at any time. Strangely, my sudden good fortune had made my life less meaningful.

I put down the blinds, turned on the Corbusier lamp on its long arm and tapped the sofa for Reg to get up next to me.

A dog is a marvellous thinking tool and kneading his ears and massaging his shoulders I began to wonder how seriously I should take this communication from Tibbs.

Then I noticed the time. Seven forty-five. I'd have to be off for the game.

I exchanged Reg's day collar for a more formal night job, leaded him up and set out into the early evening.

On the way across my landing I saw Martin from the flat next door searching his pockets for his keys.

'Geeza!' said Martin, in his military haircut. I think he used to be in the Marines but was thrown out for being too rough. Flicked a towel at a colleague in the showers and broke his leg, something like that. He's a friendly enough sort, though, as long as you stay on the right side of him. This is another way of saying he's not a friendly enough sort – friendly enough sorts do not require staying on the right side of.

'Geeza,' I said, to prove I can mix it with these hard sorts.

'He went to see his nan earlier today,' said the dog out of the side of his mouth as he sniffed at Martin. I ignored the implication. If it was Martin who threw the brick through my window, I didn't want him following it up with one to any of my more valuable structures – like my skull.

'You noticed that brick in your front room?' he said.

'Yes, sort of,' I said.

'I've got a good clue,' said the dog. 'He smells of fighting, this one, all metal and clashes.'

This doesn't surprise me. Martin is a bouncer by trade. That is, he works in a smoky environment.

'Any idea who sent it?'

'Not exactly,' I said.

'Well, when you find out, let me know, would you?'

'Why's that, Martin?' I didn't really know him, why would he be interested?

He inclined his head in a 'good question' sort of way and said, 'Well, this afternoon, about four, I'm in the back room giving the missus one when there's this crash at the front window. Naturally my curiosity is piqued. So I finish the job in hand quickly and have a shufty in my front room. What I see doesn't please me. It's only a brick with a note on it. Worse still, it's come straight through my glasswork.' His lips were pursed and he was nodding as if he expected me to share his outrage, which I thought it wise to do. For a second I was troubled by the image of him 'giving his missus one'. His wife, who I call Martina the Marionette, is about four foot eleven and a woman of slender build.

'Naturally, I can see this is amateur work, and it's obviously a bunch of *muppets* who've decided to start playing silly bastards. If I give someone a visit they get a brick in the head, not through the window,' he said as if relating that a good way of keeping slugs off your lettuce is to set it on a south-facing slope.

He gave a little smile and mimed bricking someone in the head, just in case I'd missed the point. I hadn't. Reg watched Martin's hand rise and fall, cringing slightly, as did I. Reg didn't like violence of any sort. I can't say I'm that keen myself, particularly when its focus is yours truly.

'Of course, when I read the note I can see it's all been a misunderstanding. It's obviously got some stuff on it that appertains not to me at all but to you. I nip round to give it to you but you're not there. I can see the message is important, as is its context, i.e. the method of delivery. So I nip it through your window for you.' He gave me a neighbourly wink.

'Thanks?' I said.

'No problem. But keep the brick and if you do find out who did my window I'll ram it up his arse for you,' he said, all bonhomie.

'Oh, too much,' I said, not wishing to bother him.

'He will do it,' said the dog, 'he's not lying.' I kind of didn't have to be told that. Martin opened the door to his flat. 'Drop the money round for the repairs whenever you like,' he said.

'You can have it now,' I said. I took out the roll I'd got for poker, about £2,000 in fifties.

'How much?'

'A hundred should cover it.' His eyes lit up when he saw the cash.

'Have two hundred, for the bother. It's only paper,' I said, using an expression I've been looking to use in anger since I was a kid. You can't say it without rolling your shoulders and, to tell the truth, I wouldn't have wanted to stop myself, so I went for it. 'Roll,' I went. It felt great.

Martin smiled broadly. 'You're a dark horse, Davey boy, a dark horse.'

I think he quite likes to live next door to a dark horse.

'You can't remember what the note said, can you?' I said.

'Something about your dog,' he said. 'I didn't know the League for Canine Advancement had a paramilitary wing.' He seemed to find this mightily amusing as he disappeared through his door . . .

I glanced down at Reg. His ears were so flat he looked as if he'd had a bucket of water thrown over him.

'What in the name of God would they want with you?' I said.

Poker seemed to go in a flicker. On the dog's advice I'd quadrupled my stake, although my heart didn't seem to be in it. It occurred to me that I wasn't even a particularly effective addict. Perhaps I was getting bored with the game.

Reg and I walked back through the mock Tudor avenues of leaf and replacement window, taking in the smells of the late summer night. I needed the rhythm of a walk just to settle myself.

Reg seemed to enjoy it too, pulling after every sniff.

'Can you not do that?' I said.

'No,' he said, 'I must.'

'Why?'

'Because a sight invites but a smell compels,' said the dog, slavering at a discarded KFC wrapper.

'Whatever,' I said, letting him pull.

As the front of the flats loomed, though, I felt my fears returning, or rather a fear. Tibbs, yes, and the criminal act he threatened to force upon me, but something else as well, like a big ball of something stuck in my throat that I could neither swallow nor cough out.

I turned the key in my door gingerly. In the bedroom of my flat I could see the light was on.

For the evening I'd been away from it all, hiding in a poker game – a kind of mezzanine floor between the levels of existence. Reality, meaning unpleasantness, was about to begin again. There was someone in there.

17

A Way Back In

The person in the room bothered me, as uninvited people in your bedroom at two in the morning are wont to do. I felt myself shaking. Down on the lead the dog was straining forward with his hackles up.

It did occur to me to go and fetch Martin but I had the feeling that this wasn't the sort of thing that dark horses did.

The appearance of Swain had me rattled too, though not the operating, poker-playing wise-cracking me who had handed out two hundred quid to replace Martin the Marine's windows. It had rattled me internally. It was as if my inner structure had disintegrated and it would only take one tap to see the whole thing collapse.

It somehow reminded me of when I was at school. I'd been a bit of a sensitive lad, a member of the theatre group. I remember being stopped on the way home one night by a gang of kids from the estate. I knew them. 'What the fuck is this?' said one of them. He took my copy of Love's Labour Lost from my hand. Unwisely I'd been reading it and rehearsing as I went along.

I can remember the kid who took it, his big, vital face, his earrings and the hardness of the tendons of his neck emphasised by the softness of his soul boy sweater. He knew me, I didn't know him.

'Everything about you is arse, isn't it, Barker?' he said. 'It's all shite, isn't it?' He didn't hit me, he didn't have to. I felt his scorn and I felt he was right. He saw realities that I didn't; I had a head full of stupid ideas, a fancy lad that the world would devour.

That's how I felt as I saw the light on in my room, that I was ready for a long overdue dose of reality, that I was going to get what I'd had coming to me for so very long.

Life felt ready to crack. I heard the movement in the room. Reg lunged forwards saying, 'I'll rrrrrrrip you to bits, I'll grrrrind your bones with my teeth, I'll tearrrrrrrr your flesh!'

I unhooked him from the lead and, as I did so, he stopped pulling. He looked round at me. 'Well, go on then,' he said. 'See who it is.'

I looked about for a weapon. Weapons seemed to be something I'd forgotten to get from Habitat on my spending spree. There was, however, the heavy reading lamp next to the sofa. I tore off the shade and inverted it to make a club. I seemed to be building myself up to an act of violence, saying to myself, 'If that's what I can do to a lampshade, *a lampshade I like*, what could I do to a burglar?'

The dog was still uttering threats but, as he later explained to me, he was allowing me, the pack leader, to have first go at the assailant. Protocol insisted, he said, that he went and hid behind the sofa.

I decided that I had to take the initiative from whoever was in the room.

'I know you're in there!' I said, 'and I'm calling the police!' The two exclamation marks in one sentence show, I think, how serious I was. As I said the words I knew that I'd missed the most obvious course of action and looked about for the phone.

A day before, I wouldn't have had to look for the phone because I would have known where it was. Unfortunately I'd bought a cordless job and hadn't quite got the knack of putting it back on the base station.

There was a clump and a thump and the door opened.

'Is that you, Dave?' said Lyndsey. She was wearing one of my T-shirts and her hair was disordered. This was the first time she'd stayed at my flat in over a year, largely because she'd termed it a 'pit'.

Her being there was certainly surprising, though not as surprising as the livid bruise which covered the side of her face.

'If you're going to hit me with that lamp,' said Lyndsey, 'I suggest you unplug it first.'

The dog, perhaps wisely, remained where he was behind the sofa.

It seemed the thugs had come for Lyndsey as she'd stopped at traffic lights on the way to her mum's. Ironically, one of the doctors who worked at her health centre had driven with her to her flat to pick up a change of clothes and had seen her into her car on the way to her mother's. I felt very guilty at this part of the story. I should have insisted that I went home with her. Something had stopped me though, I don't know what. At a deep level I don't suppose I took Tibbs's threats seriously. I did now.

It had been a hot evening and despite the new air-conditioned Clio, habit had meant Lyndsey was driving with her window down.

A man in a crash helmet had hopped off a scooter and belted her in the face. He'd then hopped back on and driven off before she could get his number.

She'd been trying to call me on my mobile but I hadn't heard the phone ring, I'd had it turned off.

'I'm sorry,' I said. 'I'm so sorry.' I held her, feeling like an idiot. I'd been living in my head while the real world had been falling down about me.

'I'm so scared, Dave,' said Lyndsey, trembling in my arms.

I heard a noise of discomfort from the dog behind the sofa.

'This can't go on,' said Lyndsey. 'They'll end up killing me. Look at your window.'

Again the dog grunted, like an old man having difficulty lifting himself out of bed. I looked down at the glass on the floor, the brick on the table where I'd been trying to decipher the message.

Then I looked at her bruise. I had ignored her needs and buried them beneath my own. Guilt seeped through me and I bowed my head, in the manner of a contrite canine.

What kind of people were we dealing with? I couldn't imagine how anyone could manage to inflict such a hard blow through the window of a car. Surely the person wouldn't have been able to get much power into it from that angle. We were clearly dealing with some pretty heavy people.

'Have you had that checked?' I said.

'I went to casualty. It's OK, there's nothing broken.'

The dog came out from behind the sofa.

'Lyndsey,' he said with a nod of acknowledgement, like the Pope saying hello to the Archbishop of Canterbury while making an un-Christian sign under his cassock.

'He's barking at me again,' said Lyndsey. She was understandably upset after what had happened to her so I didn't blame her for not trying harder with the dog.

'He's only saying hello,' I said.

The dog smiled briefly, as if to confirm it.

'He's showing his teeth now,' said Lyndsey.

'He's just got an itch,' I said. 'Reg, go in the bedroom for a moment, would you?'

'With pleasure,' said Reg. As he went past he gave Lyndsey one of those looks that policemen give seventeen-year-old drivers of brand new BMWs.

I got Lyndsey a glass of wine and held her in my arms on the sofa, cuddled in against the savage world.

'You've made a big difference to this place,' she said, looking at how I'd Ideal Homed the living room. 'I might even come and see you a bit more often now. If you get something in the fridge.'

This is one of the things I loved about Lyndsey – her resilience. The world can throw what it will at her and she will throw it back.

'It was about time,' I said.

She looked around us. 'You've put a lot of value into the flat,' she said. 'It's much more attractive to buyers now.'

'I know,' I said. 'I'm an estate agent, remember? Do you think I should sell it then?'

I couldn't tell if she was suggesting I moved in with her.

'There's not a lot of point thinking about anything until all this is over, is there?' she said.

'No.'

I couldn't think straight. I was sure my plan of withdrawing from the Charterstone sale would work but I wasn't sure Lyndsey would be in the mood to hear anything other than that I intended to give in.

'Are you going to do as they say?' said Lyndsey, looking at me from beneath her bruise. I couldn't refuse her but I couldn't say yes either.

'I can't see any other way at the moment,' I said. I realised I'd lied to her but it didn't feel as bad as the lie I was thinking of telling, that is to say that I was going to capitulate when I had no intention of doing so.

'Good,' she said, with a smile. She kissed me. 'Let's go to bed.'

I helped her to her feet and we went hand in hand towards the bedroom. Then I laid her on the bed with a kiss and went to clean my teeth.

The lower molars were up to buff and I was beginning on the incisors when Lyndsey let out a scream as if she'd been thumped again.

'What's the matter?' I shouted in a spray of Colgate.

'It's your dog,' she said. 'He's attacking my clothes!'

And there he was, Reg, looking over his shoulder at me, his eyes defiant, his nose sloping guiltily down, his muzzle completely covered in the fluff of what had once been Lyndsey's cashmere sweater.

18

Property and Values

I had, of course, gone ballistic at Reg and the next day, as we set out for Mrs Cad-Beauf's, he and I weren't on speaking terms.

The car rumbled through the lanes while the dog sat with a firm jaw, not looking at me but remaining aloof, frozen in his composure apart from the occasional lapse when he saw a rabbit and would bound up at the window shouting, 'Long-eared slacker!'

I intended to end my association with Mrs Cad-Beauf that day but I'd brought a seller's contract with me just in case.

Just in case what? I don't know but it was there anyway. There was no way I was going to sell the place for her but maybe I was in some way allowing for the possibility I'd be persuaded without knowing that's what I was doing. It's enough to make you believe in the subconscious. That and the fact I'd been waking screaming in the night.

When I say the dog and I weren't on speaking terms, what I mean is that, like most people who aren't on speaking terms and who are sharing the same space, we were actually saying quite a lot to each other.

'You could see how upset she was and that she'd been beaten up and yet you go and do a thing like that, you bad dog,' I was saying, as Reg found something of interest out of the car window and looked hard at it.

'Why did you do it?'

Still silence, the nose taking in the air as if his mind were on loftier concerns.

'I won't allow you to have a biscuit at Mrs Cad-Beauf's,' I said, 'nor any biscuit until you tell me why you did such a thing when you could see she was upset and hurt.'

'I can live without biscuits,' said the dog, trembling at the idea like a forty-a-day man saying he could quit any time he liked.

'You're very bad,' I said, 'and you know the stress she's under.'

'What about the stress I'm under?' said the dog.

'What?'

'Nothing!' he said. I could see he was eyeing the brown paper bag of breakfast muffin that I'd left in the footwell.

'Take your eyes off that as well,' I said.

The dog did. 'Do I get a biscuit?' he said.

'I told you, no biscuits until you explain yourself.'

Reg leaned down over the back of the front seat, sniffing at the muffin bag.

'I told you to leave that alone,' I said.

'I'm a simple fellow,' said Reg. 'I work on a task and reward basis. If you don't wish me to look at the muffin, I'm afraid you're going to have to compensate me with a biscuit.'

'I'll compensate you with a bloody thick ear in a minute,' I said.

'I should have thought you would have had enough of violence in the last couple of days,' said the dog with a haughty sniff.

We were approaching the gates of Mrs Cad-Beauf's house so I left it, despite the fact that I was in serious danger of having my muffin drooled on.

We stopped at the bottom of the lane and got out. I told the dog that, despite our differences, I expected him to display a professional attitude while on a client's premises.

'I would never allow a personal disagreement to come between us and our work,' said Reg.

Our work, it was now.

'And if I might proffer a word of advice,' said the dog, 'tidy yourself up a bit before we go in to see her. Her eyes might not be good but it's the effect that being well-groomed has on himself, rather than the client, that the professional seeks.'

'You are not an estate agent,' I said to the dog.

He looked at me, stunned. 'Then why am I here? Are you telling me there's some sort of glass ceiling in operation for dogs? It's OK for us to be guards and retrievers, finders and keepers but not to do any more challenging work? There are opportunities, I know. My uncle said he rose from police dog to judge.'

'All right,' I said, without the energy to argue any further, 'you're an estate agent. OK?'

'Good,' said the dog, 'although we haven't discussed the issue of my remuneration.'

'How about a can of dog food a day?' I said.

'Done!' cried the dog. 'And a biscuit or equivalent for every successful sale.'

'Does this mean I can fine you for the cost of a new cashmere pullover?' I said.

Lyndsey wanted a new sweater and had suggested I cut the dog's food supply in half until I'd saved enough money to pay for it. At 25p a day that would be half rations for a year. 'He has to learn,' Lyndsey said.

To be honest I didn't really care that much, about the clothes, that is. I cared that Lyndsey had had to suffer another upset on a day of upsets but it was only a cashmere sweater, wasn't it?

I'd managed to stop her giving the dog a boot but only just. She'd wanted to tie him up outside on the landing of the flats but I wasn't having that so into the kitchen he went. I'd snuck his basket in to him after she'd fallen asleep and seen the discs of his eyes shining in the light of the doorway. I'd patted his head and asked him why he'd done it but he was as mute as a normal dog.

'You're not deaf,' I said. 'In fact I happen to know you've got superior hearing to anyone I've ever spoken to.'

Only when I went to leave the kitchen did he speak.

'Fool,' he said. Or it could have been 'Food'. Either way, I ignored him.

As we approached the houses at Charterstone it occurred to me that the Cat and I had undervalued this place, it exuded so much charm, the little cottages either side of a narrow, winding track of pale yellow brick. It must have been put there in the last forty years, I thought – the colour a conscious reference to the film, but it was subtle enough and weed-cracked enough to avoid looking twee.

And then I realised what the problem was going to be. Charm doesn't have space for parking. Take any modern estate. It looks like shite but the one thing you can do is park your car.

In the village of Charterstone the lanes off the main drag were scarcely wide enough to take a shopping trolley. On top of that, restoration costs a fortune compared to building from new. The Folding Society weren't going to restore the villages of Charterstone, they were going to knock them down and, in the unlikely event of their being unable to get around any triviality like the buildings being listed, they'd simply build something next to them, wait for someone to be hurt when messing around in them and then declare them a menace.

If I didn't defend this place, if I didn't make sure it was sold with caveats and safeguards to a sympathetic developer, this was all going to go.

In one way I shouldn't have minded. I mean, it was just some old broken-down buildings, the remains of some egomaniac's dream. Importantly, though, they were old broken-down buildings that I liked and I knew I didn't like modern housing estates, though I'd sold enough houses on them.

As we stopped at the house I could see the little door in the big door was open and Mrs Cad-Beauf was waiting for us.

Reg, true to his word, was quite the professional dog, approaching her excitedly and gambolling in front of her, singing, 'Greetings to a welcome friend, hail, great soul, traveller through the coruscating infinities of the night, now show us yer biscuits!'

'Oh,' said Mrs Cad-Beauf, 'hello, Reg. Oh, you good boy, I've missed you. Hello Mr, er . . .'

'Barker,' I said, extending my hand.

'Of course,' she said.

'His eyes are remarkable,' said Mrs Cad-Beauf, patting the dog. 'Really like our old Priscilla's.'

'What breed was Priscilla?' I said.

'Priscilla was the maid,' said Mrs Cad-Beauf, slightly shocked.

I suddenly imagined the dog in a bonnet, for some reason. He'd gone through the door and was rooting about in the internal corridor.

'It's been years since we've had a dog in this place, I can't look after them properly now myself,' she said.

'Why don't you have a dog and pay someone to walk it and look after it?' I said. 'You'll have plenty of money.'

'You can't have a dog and then send it away!' she said in her fruitiest upper-class voice. 'They are not children!' She clapped her hands sharply twice. 'Mr Barker, your carriage awaits.'

From round the corner, stately but dreadlocked like Boadicea on her chariot, came Aia Napa on a golf buggy.

'Actually I need to have a word about all this,' I said.

'Over tea!' said Mrs Cad-Beauf, closing the door on us.

Oh well, I didn't suppose it could do any harm to give her a valuation, just so she'd have a rough price.

We toured the grounds by buggy and I valued the place at around £25 million, roughly, having already done my homework on similar properties before I got there.

Aia Napa then took us into the house but instead of turning left into the orangery, we turned right through a green baize door behind a curtain. We were in a huge, dusty billiard room – a large table, its feet carved into Art Deco Dobermanns, was in the centre, complete with ancient balls, the white only just distinguishable from the yellow, and cues lying on the table as if someone had been interrupted halfway through a game.

'We can conclude our business on the card table,' said Mrs Cad-Beauf, gesturing to a fold-away table positioned between a chaise longue and a wicker chair.

There's something about a card table, isn't there? Makes the heart skip a little. The virgin baize, the feeling of destinies won or lost. Or matchsticks exchanged. Mrs Cad-Beauf went for the chaise longue and I helped her to sit by moving the table forward slightly. There was something about her, not the grand manner but something in what Reg had said – the great soul – that made me want to observe old-fashioned pleasantries for her, to make sure she was comfortable, to wait until asked to sit.

Mrs CB rang for tea.

'Well, the valuation of the property is—'

'Vulgar!' said Mrs Cad-Beauf, holding up her hand to silence me.

'You really do need someone to take care of the money for you,' I said. 'You can't just trust it all to me.'

'You are my representative, Mr Barker,' she said. 'I know you will look after my interests.'

'Well, I've been meaning to speak to you about that.'

'Ah yes, my wider financial affairs,' she said. 'I have them here.' From behind her she hauled a large battered briefcase.

I stood to help her.

'Open it,' she said. 'All my bank statements are in there. There's a box in the orangery with the rest of Daddy's affairs in it.'

I have to say I was more than a little curious.

I opened the case to find it neatly compartmentalised by cardboard dividers, one a year, going back about thirty years. Inside each file were twelve bank statements in date order. She hadn't opened any of them. Not one.

'Do you mind if I . . .?'

'Go ahead,' she said, looking up to the ceiling like a Tory MP confronting breast-feeding in the House. 'I've never bothered looking at them since a clerk was rude to me. I've no intention of doing so if all they're going to contain is abuse. I'll open the chequebooks but nothing more.'

I opened the latest.

'It's only pin money in there anyway,' she said.

Her current account stood at two million nine hundred and eighty-four thousand pounds twenty-five pence. Her no-interest current account.

In the orangery, 'Daddy's affairs' – stocks and bonds – added about another £20 million to her wealth. That was in the stuff I could see at a glance.

She should have been paying a fortune in tax on the earnings on those but bureaucracy is like a bully. Ignore it hard enough and it will go away. Or at least that seemed to be the case with Mrs Cad-Beauf.

'Who pays the electricity on this place?' I said, as she rang the tea bell again, harder. Aia Napa was normally a lot quicker than this.

'That was all taken care of by a man in a cap,' she said.

I took it she meant direct debit.

'Do you have a will?' I said.

'There should be a solicitor's card in the top of the briefcase,' she said.

'Is all this going to dogs' homes too?' I said.

'Heavens no!' said Mrs Cad-Beauf. 'The donkey sanctuary in Cornwall will benefit too!'

That at least gave me a clear conscience. Mrs Cad-Beauf had money to burn and no wish to spend it on anything other than animals. Her ignorance in financial affairs was in some ways her protection. She assumed she had very little and so spent relatively little. It meant she would easily have enough to see her through the rest of her days.

'Look,' I said, 'would you like me to get these affairs in order?' I thought it wouldn't take me more than a day or two. She could forget about the money she'd loaned me – formally forget that is, she had in fact already forgotten – and I'd get everything straight for her at the bank and the sheltered flat.

If I put her affairs in order in the next couple of days, there would be less messing about when she died and her solicitors would be able to detect if any sharp-clawed Folding Society type had been fleecing her, I thought. She needed a decent accountant, a decent solicitor and a decent financial adviser. It might be possible, I thought, to manage the first two but the third was a clear impossibility. Lyndsey, though, was very hot on the *Which? Money* stakes. I was sure she'd be able to help. I knew that she wasn't a fundamentally dishonest person and that, given time to reflect, she'd see that it was wrong to take Mrs Cad-Beauf's money – even if she was going to lavish more on canine accommodation than is commonly lavished.

I have to say, self-congratulatory as it is, it gave me a bit of a glow to be helping the old lady. I'd helped my mum for years just because I didn't really have any choice. It appeared, however, that I had a talent for caring and, more to the point, enjoyed it. I'd seen that in just my short time with Reg. I could set her up

with some proper advice and then bunker down until the whole
Cat thing blew over.

I sat down next to her with the great bundle of papers at my
feet as Reg snapped at a fly that buzzed his ears. I was parched.

'You look parched, Mr Barker,' said Mrs Cad-Beauf. 'I will
call again for refreshment.' She rang her handbell again deli-
cately, not with force but with emphasis. 'Since you last called,
Mr Barker, I have decided that a little more help than Aia Napa
can provide is in order in the short term. As luck would have it
a butlers agency representative called just after your last visit.
Although I can't say this one is up to the standards of my father's
man.'

A bell answered down the hall and Mrs Cad-Beauf smiled to
herself like a dog who knows *exactly* where he has buried his
bone.

After ten minutes there was a thump and the door opened. A
silver tea tray appeared through the doorway followed by a
'Jesus' and a large rattle. There, fully togged up in butling gear,
was the Cat's Jenkins.

'Your tea, missus,' he said.

'Ma'am,' said Mrs Cad-Beauf, as if it wasn't the first time
she'd had cause to remind him.

'Whatever,' said the butler, coming across the floor like Jeeves
on temazepam.

All the stress that had been draining out of me during this
visit to Charterstone came flooding back in.

They couldn't, surely, be attempting to kill Mrs Cad-Beauf.
The money would go to the dogs' homes as set out in her will.
Then I saw the plan: ingratiate themselves, get the will altered,
have the whole estate for nothing.

The only flaw in this was that Jenkins seemed incapable of
ingratiating himself with a Jehovah's Witness.

The tea was poured – or rather thrown into the cups – while
Reg looked at Jenkins very much like he looks at squirrels when

he's on the lead. That is to say, he gave the impression of having been flash frozen, going mightily stiff and upright, his ears high and his eyes wide.

'What's this bloke's game?' said Reg.

Jenkins eyed the dog. 'I don't like the look of him!' he said.

'Since you are the butler and he the guest, that opinion is highly irrelevant,' said Mrs Cad-Beauf, covering the dog's ears.

I felt as though I was falling down a well, the dark closing in around me. As an aside, I've always wondered if people who have near-death experiences when they're injured falling down a well see a bright light going away from them and then one coming towards them. When they're rescued I wonder if they're a bit wary of being carried into the light. I mean, how could you be sure?

'Whatever,' said the butler, taking a sugar lump from the chinaware and popping it into his mouth. He gave me a wink, turned on his heel, tripped over the carpet and made his way out.

'He's going to have to go,' said Mrs Cad-Beauf.

'You can say that again,' said the dog and I, as one.

Mrs Cad-Beauf gestured for my contract.

'How long has he been with you, Mrs Cad-Beauf?' I said.

'Oh, about a week,' she said.

'You are keeping your valuables locked up, aren't you?' I said.

Mrs Cad-Beauf raised her eyebrows. 'Mr Barker, my family have had staff this past two hundred years. I am well aware of the necessary precautions.'

'I don't trust him,' I said.

'And neither do I,' said Mrs Cad-Beauf, 'but he will do until I can find someone more suitable. Please, to business.'

I've never found public speaking easy and this felt as though I was addressing an audience. I hemmed and hawed for a moment and finally got it out.

'Mrs Cad-Beauf,' I said, 'I don't actually feel I can represent you in the sale of your house. I think you would be unwise to move.'

She looked at me with her head at an angle in pique and like a Peke.

'Have I missed some event, Mr Barker?'

'What do you mean?'

'Are you collecting for charity, "staff vents its opinions day", a pound coin, whatever one of those is, per go?'

'I feel you would be ill-advised to leave,' I said. 'You've lived here all your life.'

'Aren't I allowed a bloody change?' she said, with some force.

'Of course,' I said, 'but I think you could effect that change here.'

'Where I choose to *effect* the change is my own business,' she said.

'Yes, but if you would just examine some plans,' I said, pulling out an ideas sheet I'd drafted.

Mrs Cad-Beauf raised a hand. 'If you are going to show me something on an overhead projector,' she said the words as if she had caught just such a projector the week before, fouling her shrubbery, 'I'm afraid I am immune. My mind is made up, Mr Barker, and you nor hell's legions shall divert me from this resolution.'

'And if I refuse to represent you?'

'Then I shall get someone else. I have started on this course and I shall not be deflected from it. I've had letters, you know. Do you know a Messrs Tuckley, Perry and Gibbs?'

I did. They were the local big boys, a firm that had done several very lucrative deals with the likes of Tibbs.

There seemed no way out, I was going to have to go through with it. It would mean moving Lyndsey out of Worthing for a while, probably myself as well. Tibbs had threatened about Reg too so perhaps it would be best to move him to Lucy's as a place of safety.

'Do you intend to represent me, yes or no?' said Mrs Cad-Beauf.

The dog sat wagging his tail at her on the chaise longue, not for any particular reason, just because he liked her and liked everything unless he was given a direct reason to dislike it.

I didn't mean to say the words but at that moment it seemed I no longer had control over myself, as if I was just some conduit for things bigger and more powerful than myself. Something like fate, without wishing to lay it on with a trowel.

'Yes, OK,' I said.

I drew breath. For a minute the pressure of the last few weeks seemed heavy on me. A talking dog, an ambitious girlfriend, falling out with an unpleasant gangster, the meeting with Darren Swain, it all seemed like a ball of tension trapped within my throat. I thought of Lyndsey's poor face.

I took out the seller's contract, which was largely filled in. The space for the sum of the sale seemed intensely white and strangely large, like a field of snow waiting for me to fall upon it and make my angel. Or to follow the canine recipe for yellow snow.

My pen felt like a snake wriggling between my fingers.

The Cat had threatened Reg in the note on the brick, hadn't he?

And then something spoke. I'd like to say it was the tension, growing a little mouth and piping from inside me, I'd like to say it was the madness that had seen me arguing with a dog about the best way to approach a client, but it wasn't. It was me.

'Nothing matters,' it said, 'nothing matters.' For some reason it sounded like Darren Swain.

'Four hundred thousand,' I wrote and for a second the weight wasn't there any more.

Mrs CB stretched forward her hand to take the document, like Adam reaching out for God's lightning bolt on the start of *The South Bank Show*.

I passed it to her. She took out a pair of half-moon glasses and squinted at the paper.

'I'm afraid I'm rather short-sighted,' said Mrs CB. 'Can you show me where to sign?'

'Let me, ma'am,' said Jenkins from over my shoulder. For once, he had entered the room quietly. 'And if you like I can file it for you afterwards.'

19

Welcome to the Fold

'I think we clinched that deal admirably,' said Reg, in between bouts of cheek-kiting with his head out of the window of the car on the way back. 'Thank you for stepping in and backing me up. I thought we might be about to lose it when I was sitting there on the sofa but to tell the truth it was becoming a bit tiring constantly wagging my tail.'

He said this in a goofy, excited way like he'd never had so much fun in his life.

Dogs have little nose for money, kind of the down side of having a big nose for everything else, I suppose, and Reg seemed pleased that I was now talking to him. He didn't mention what I'd done to Mrs Cad-Beauf at all.

'Welcome to the world of commerce,' I said to him as we wheeled through a Land Rovered village and narrowly avoided a man in a pink shirt who was scrubbing mud off the road in front of his house.

'Do you think I should get a lead like yours if we're going to be in business together?' said Reg.

'I don't wear a lead,' I said.

Reg snorted out a laugh. 'So what do you call that thing round your neck then?'

'It's a tie,' I said. 'No one's holding it.'

'Every time you put it on you end up going somewhere you don't want to,' he said. 'That's what I call a lead. I can't have a soft cloth one like yours so perhaps you might consider one like mine, in leather. Corporate identity.'

The last word was said with vibrating cheeks as his head went out of the window into the wind.

'Dog logic,' I said, 'and I'm not having a leather tie because I'm not a blues musician or a Glaswegian bouncer.'

'Nyeeeeooow!' said the dog, as we rounded a corner. 'How about renaming the business Barker and Dog? Or Dog and Barker?'

My phone rang and I answered it, driving on one-handed.

'Well done.' It was the Cat. 'I'm glad we can stop all this unpleasantness, it really isn't the way I choose to operate.'

He continued. 'I knew you'd come round eventually. Life is like a game of cards, it always goes to the one with the most patience.'

'Will you stop gloating and just nonk off?' I said.

The dog looked hurt. He didn't always understand when I was talking on the phone.

'Yes, rather super-villain of me, wasn't it?' said the Cat. 'I suggest you announce to the Bat tomorrow that a sale has been secured and we can move from there.'

'Great,' I said. 'Now there's just my major guilt to deal with.'

'There's no need to feel guilty,' said the Cat. 'The old bag has untold wealth. Her lifestyle won't change one bit, in fact it'll probably improve. The details of the transaction will be on your desk tomorrow. Congratulate yourself, you're half a million the richer and your girlfriend has taken her last beating.'

I felt a deep anger inside me. That bastard had beaten Lyndsey up and I was determined to make sure he paid.

'Oh, the woods are deep and the streams they flow, that is where I'll dip my toe!' sang the dog at the top of his voice, as if that toe had just been shut in a door.

I clicked off my phone and suddenly realised something. For the first time ever I'd been talking on a mobile while driving my car. And I'd nearly hit that yuppie who'd been scrubbing his road to try to make the countryside more like the city. I wondered if he was going to trample kebabs into it when he'd finished.

I pulled the car to the side of the road, underneath a railway bridge. A sign announced the Sussex Heritage Trail, following the disused Brighton to London railway.

My hands were shaking. The dog put his head on my shoulder.

'I knew you'd take the hint,' he said but I was just staring blankly ahead into the trees, the greens and the browns losing their loyalty to the shapes of nature and floating before my eyes as mere colours, a green pool waiting to receive me.

'I knew you'd take the hint,' said the dog again, more firmly and with a really uncalled for lick of my ear.

Still I stared into the swimming green. Darren Swain had learned nothing from the death of my father, he bore no scars, he didn't twitch, he didn't tremble as he held his phone. And now neither did I.

'That is where I dip my toe!' said the dog, gesturing with his head towards the trail. 'If you could hurry up, mate, to be honest it's more than my toe I need to dip.'

It was very clear, I thought, that I wasn't the person I had taken myself to be.

'The peasants are at the gates and the guards cannot hold them!' said the dog, loudly in my ear. 'Rich Tea, they go straight through you!'

'What?' I heard his words but I couldn't concentrate on what they meant.

'There's gonna be a borstal breakout!' said the dog.

'Oh.' For some reason he didn't seem as attuned to my mood as he normally was. I guessed it was because he was so pleased with himself for having helped secure a deal, as he saw it.

I opened the door and out he hopped with a big 'Vuuuung!' The dog often illustrated his movements by making noises like this, like kids do when they're pretending to be in fast cars or transforming into the Incredible Hulk.

I always keep a change of clothes in the boot of the car just in case I decide to hop off into the woods with the dog at lunchtime or after work and I nipped into the cords, waxed jacket and stout shoes. Look, if you can't wear these things with a dog in the country, where can you?

Reg was already quartering the ground, eyes down, saying, 'Leaf, stick, leaf, stick, leaf, stick, leaf, stick,' as if taking an inventory. There had been no sign of the 'borstal breakout' he'd threatened, only a couple of gestures at lifting the leg.

It occurred to me that I might be corrupting him, that I was turning him into a liar. He'd mentioned deceitfully wagging his tail at Mrs Cad-Beauf and there he was pretending to want to have a squat in order to get a walk.

Whatever, he'd read my thoughts and had got me to do something I wanted to do anyway.

We followed the railway trail through the downs, meeting no one. What had made me do it? Pressure? Or was it just that the dog's view was right and that humans see causality when there is none.

He'd told me a story once about a walk in the woods.

A human might say that we went in the car to the woods, I put on my wellingtons and we set off into the trees. In the trees we saw some squirrels and some other dogs and then we came back to the car, I took off my wellingtons, put on my shoes and we drove home.

This is what the dog said. 'The doors to our dwelling place finally opened and we found ourselves in the car. Oddly, trees appeared. Marvellous. I say oddly because last time we got into the car the beach appeared and sometimes our house appears when the beach disappears but this time it was trees. His feet transformed! Also marvellous. Small and old and smelly, they became big and large and new and smelling of oils and extraction processes (don't ask). We went into the woods (dogs get the idea of going somewhere if they actually walk themselves) and the feet brought out squirrels and soft ground. Especially marvellous. Then we followed the feet back to the car. I tried warning him not to get in but he did and I had to follow. As I feared, the woods disappeared and we found ourselves at home again. Super marvellous, dinner appeared.'

Perhaps the dog was right. Things just are.

'Everything is wonderful!' said the dog, bombing back and forth between the bushes on either side of the track.

'How's that, Reggie?' I said.

'Mrs Cad-Beauf seems happy, you seem happier, I'm happy, the birds in the trees are happy. Lyndsey's miserable. Life couldn't be better!'

How could he not smell the guilt on me?

'I told you not to bring Lyndsey up,' I said.

'Sorry,' said the dog. 'Look, a magpie!'

The black and white bird was bobbing across our path, the very symbol of bad luck.

I'd read somewhere that to deflect the bad influence you have to spit and bow to the magpie and say, 'Hello, Mr Magpie!'

This I did but it didn't seem to impress the bird.

'Up you go!' said Reg, running gently towards it in a low lope.

The bird flew up into a tree.

'Whhhaaaay! I love it when they do that!' said Reg.

I looked up at the magpie. Would it bring me bad luck? I couldn't be sure, but it seemed to be smirking at me.

20

Double Your Money

I'd agreed to meet Lyndsey at her flat that evening.

The dog was in the dog house with her, which ironically isn't a very good place for a dog to be, and so I dropped him off at Lucy's, who seemed to be having some sort of dinner party.

Lucy's flat was an old place she rented near the station in Worthing. She'd done a lot to make it her own, throws over the old sofas, large black and white prints she'd taken of the seafront and, just above the fireplace, a framed picture the size of an old-fashioned portrait, of Reg in flight, snatching a ball from my hand on the command 'Spring!' I remembered it had been a wild windy day and my hair was blown up into a mad fuzz, like a Druid who'd been sent back from the sacred grove to smarten himself up a bit for the pagan gods.

'Big air!' the dog had said as he'd left, a regrettable result of me allowing him to stay up to watch late-night *Motocross* on Channel 5. And we had plenty of high fours with his paw after the more spectacular catches.

'That's a great photo,' I said to Lucy.

'It's easy taking good photos of the stars,' said Lucy, giving Reg a head-rub.

'Damn right!' said the dog. 'What's a photo?'

I'd tried explaining this to him but I'd given up halfway through an argument about whether it was possible for him to be in a little box when he knew perfectly well he was standing in front of me.

I was introduced briefly to a couple called Dave and Petra. Jim was there too. People at a table illuminated by fellow feeling and the glow of a candle. This was a world that I should have been part of, I thought.

Lucy saw me to the door. 'We can have him tomorrow if you like,' she said.

'We' fell from her mouth like a bowling ball from a shelf. I knew I had no right to want her to stay single because I had no intentions towards her myself. It was just that . . . There was no just that, really, but it was just that.

'I'll give you a call,' I said.

'Do,' she said. 'You'll have to come over for dinner yourself one day.'

'I'd like that,' I said. 'Perhaps you could invite your friends.'

'Or not,' she said, raising her eyebrows. As I went she gave my hand a little squeeze. I felt something brush against my leg and looked down to see Reg.

'You'd do a whole lot better with her, you know,' he said, before turning to the room with a loud, 'Now who can praise me best? This evening let us be extravagant, ladies and gentlemen, for I find myself open to flattery.'

'Bye,' I said, pecking Lucy on the cheek and heading off to my car.

Half an hour later Lyndsey's door loomed before me. I knew she would be immensely relieved by my news but something inside me didn't want to tell her. I'd turned off my mobile after the Cat's call had left me so shaken and I hadn't been able to bring myself to turn it back on again.

The night was warm and I hadn't bothered with a coat, my shirt being enough. I rang the door and noticed that the honeysuckle around her window was in flower, its scent sweet on my gentle senses, making me feel that things might just about be all right if I could get through this difficult time. Above her porch I noticed a bird was nesting, and further up another.

Lyndsey wouldn't have moved these for the world, even if they did make a bit of a mess, because I knew she was kind and she loved animals. It was just a misunderstanding that had grown up between her and the dog. It would all come right with time.

'Baby, thank God, I've been so worried, how are you?' She was wearing her nightgown, though her face was made up to hide her bruise. She'd done a good job and you couldn't really see the swelling at all.

I put my arms round her and we kissed.

'I have done the deed,' I said. 'It's going to be all right. It's over. I've given in to them. We're going to be rich and some dogs are going to be rich but not quite as rich as they might have been.'

Lyndsey seemed to quite forget her bruise as she gave me a big squeeze. 'I'm so happy!' she said. 'Oh, this is fantastic, come in, come in!'

I went inside and saw that she'd been distracting herself with some *Interior Design* magazines.

'We're in the money!' she sang out, spinning round as if she'd just won the lottery, which I suppose in a manner of speaking she had.

'Have I got something for you!' she said, still ecstatic, and I could see that she had because under the nightgown she wore the full clichéd but it isn't a cliché because it works bonking kit of stockings and suspenders and sexy bra.

She returned from the kitchen with two champagne flutes and a bottle of Veuve Cliquot.

'Don't stand there with a face like a slapped arse,' she said. 'You've done it now, so you might as well enjoy it.'

I knew she was right. Things were as they were and life had to be lived.

'Take off all your clothes,' she said, with a growl in her voice.

'I thought that was your job,' I said.

'In this case it'll serve the dual purpose of letting me get at what I want to get at quicker and ensuring that your trousers, which are covered in dog hair, don't ruin my sofa,' she said.

I did as I was bid and on the sofa and on the floor and rather uncomfortably near to the bamboo in the glass vase our stress and relief and desire blended and bubbled, seared and soared.

We finished in what, pre-dating the appearance of Reg, had become our favourite position, her examining the carpet, me examining the sweep of her back.

When it was over I poured us another glass of wine and we lay together on the sheepskin rug I'd bought her with my first big poker win. I'd known it was tacky but a little bit of superstition inside me said that if I bought something tasteful with a poker win the goddess of the cards would consider I wasn't spending my money properly.

For some reason I recalled my dream of the doors and the dog's dream too.

'What do you dream about, Lynds?' I said, staring deep into a radiator.

'You know,' she said, kissing me softly on the back.

'What?'

'What we have now. Escape. Living without fear of the next bill,' she said.

'I mean real dreams,' I said. 'The ones you have when you're asleep at night.'

'I don't know. I'm chasing something, maybe a balloon.'

So, like the dog she hunted in dreams.

She went on, 'I think it was that French film they always used to show on the telly when we were kids. It's always somewhere nicer than I grew up, like one of those French towns anyway.'

It did occur to me that the average refugee camp had slightly more charm than where Lyndsey grew up but I didn't say so – hot and cold running pensioners and a local shop where packets of fags were served through a grille. Come to think of it, packets of fags were served through a grille at my local off-licence. However, there was no comparison to where Lyndsey had spent her childhood. The pub that her dad lived in tried to offer dry roast peanuts once and lost its clientele because it had gone 'gastro'. When I say lived in it, I don't mean he had a room, just that he was in the bar more than the landlord was.

I often thought that if Lyndsey had come from a more middle-class home she'd have been running the country.

'Or there are endless lines of dragons or sea serpents or something coming past me, beneath me at an angle, and there's this roaring noise.'

'What do you think it means?'

'I don't know,' she said. 'Nothing, I suppose. I always thought dreams were like the test card.'

'What do you mean?'

'They're what your mind shows you while essential works are being carried out. They're a sort of screensaver that comes up when your head's doing its filing work. They don't mean anything.'

I wanted to tell her about the dog's dreams of being abandoned but I guessed he was still persona – or canina – non grata with her.

'Do you ever dream about me or your mum or anything?' I didn't mention her dad. Her father had given them nothing but trouble their entire lives. If she dreamed about him then I thought it was up to her to tell me, not me to ask.

'I don't dream about anyone,' she said, 'except myself.'

Sometimes I felt so sorry for her. She'd been forced back on herself. She was the only person she'd ever had to rely on. I thought then, as I'd thought since I first knew her, really, that I would be the one to change that.

She looked into my eyes and I felt I understood why I loved her. By nature I'm someone who cares for people. This isn't a selfless thing at all; it's how I understand myself in relation to others, as calling the shots in a way. When you're giving something, you're in control, aren't you, no matter how well-meant it is? Lyndsey was someone who had never been given anything her whole life. Whatever she'd had she'd had to work for. So I felt drawn to her, to fulfil her need for nurture and mine for nurturing.

Neither of our positions is necessarily that of good people. There are plenty of bullies who do nothing but care, care people down to the bone, and there are plenty of people who give a lot for the support they receive. I think, though, that Lyndsey and I are good people, or at least tending to the good, though we have our faults like anyone.

Even with Lyndsey's apparent emphasis on becoming rich. It wasn't that she loved money, she just hated being poor. I know that sounds very much like a Klansman saying, 'We don't hate black people, we just love white people,' but it's true. She wasn't mean, she was just careful.

The rug we were lying on, for instance, was a case in point. I'd wanted to buy it for her the second I'd got my big win but she'd made me wait for the sales. She was as concerned about me spending my money wisely as she was about doing so herself.

It was strange, I thought, how two flawed but compatible people should have found each other.

As she looked at me I had the idea that she was wanting me to ask her to marry me, to buy her a ring and complete our happiness.

'We should plan how we should spend the money,' said Lyndsey. 'It's not every day you get a million quid coming your way.'

'It's five hundred thousand,' I said.

Lyndsey took on the look that Reg does every time you say the word 'steak' – slightly incredulous, fully alert.

'It's a million,' said Lyndsey. 'You said when you first met him at that card game that you bargained him up to a million.'

'I didn't bargain him anywhere,' I said. 'I told him to sod off.'

'Whatever, he said a million.'

'Well, now he says five hundred thousand.'

Lyndsey smiled. 'Let me talk to him,' she said.

'I don't think that's a good idea.'

'Considering I'm sporting the mother of all black eyes and you're in exactly the position you'd have been in if you'd just said "Whippy do da, sign me up!" as soon as Tibbs made you the offer, then I think what you think's a good idea and what you think's a bad idea isn't such a reliable guide to what is and is not a good and bad idea, don't you agree, David?' She didn't seem angry, in fact she clinked my glass in a 'aren't we quite a pair!' way.

'You might make him decide to offer us nothing,' I said. I didn't like myself for saying that. In fact, I realised, as the drink made me glow, that I should perhaps give whatever money the Cat did hand over to one of Mrs Cad-Beauf's dogs' homes.

'Let me handle this Cat!' said Lyndsey, slightly tipsy and teasing me.

I looked at her. She was giggling away – she never could handle champagne. I didn't think she'd take very kindly to me suggesting we should turn the £500,000 into dog treats.

'Just leave it, Lynds,' I said.

'OK,' she said, swaying like a dog entranced by a sausage.

I went out to the loo and looked at myself in the mirror. I had that big birthday feeling, the 18, 21, the 30, the 40, the 60, I should imagine, where you expect everything to be different but it appears that nothing is.

I am not the reflective sort, though there is no better place than in front of a mirror to be reflective.

In the bathroom light every line in my face seemed apparent. I remembered when I'd got my first wrinkle, a furrow from my eyebrow to the first line on my forehead, which doesn't count because everyone has them, even some kids.

I'd denied it was there, convincing myself that it was a trick of the light. But the fact that it appeared to be a trick of any light you shone upon it, including a desk lamp on an extension lead run to the bathroom mirror and shone Gestapo-like at the face to interrogate the crevasse, rather pointed to the fact that it was there. The fact that Lyndsey could see it too was no good sign. So I'd accepted the wrinkle, learned to live with it, welcomed it as my own, a defining part of my face, a foreign guest on the virgin territory of my brow.

Unfortunately the wrinkle seemed to want company and, after about another year, a second had appeared beside it, rising up in a V from the other side of my nose, leaving me with a triangle of unmarked flesh between, like some religious mark, so the signs of my old age made me look like some priest of the new.

Even then I accommodated it and gave in. 'OK, that's it,' I said. 'Two's fine, I can live with two,' as if this policy of appeasement would be enough to stop the relentless armies of time leaving their tracks across my face.

Now, in my drunken state in the lemon-bright bathroom, it looked to me as if my skin had suffered some retreat from Moscow, under heavy fire.

How old was I? Thirty-three, which somehow felt like youth's last stand. How old did I look? I don't know.

From inside the bathroom I heard a strange sound and I saw that my face was moving.

'What's so funny?' said Lyndsey, who was standing behind me with a towel wrapped round her.

'I don't know,' I said.

'Well, you were laughing at something.'

I shrugged.

'A million quid?' she said, smiling to see that I'd come round to her way of feeling, having come round to her way of thinking earlier in the day.

'It's five hundred thousand,' I said.

She gave a big grin. 'It's a million!' she said, and from behind her back she produced my mobile phone. 'Never get a man to do a woman's job,' she said. 'You're too soft.'

She pressed a button on the phone and threw it to me. 'Last number – M. Tibbs aka the Cat,' it said. I'd been bored when I put the aka in.

'You better start looking for a nice place for us,' she said, putting her arms round me. 'And this time, try to get a decent deal. We'll need the money left over for when we get married.'

21

Bye Bye Baby

I am not an experienced liar and I had sort of assumed that a lie enters your life, prowls around a bit, raises its cap and makes for the door.

Not so. A lie is your child and, like a child, requires nurture. It cries out as you sleep, demanding to be fed with the milk of midnight speculation, it shakes you from your chosen tasks to remove the shite that it has created – you must dress it and soothe it and watch it grow. Ignore it and it will die, leaving you with some very stiff questions from the powers that be.

My brain, which had hitherto represented itself to me as a 'one thing at a time' sort of fellow, started showing a talent for multi-tasking, at least when coming up with horrific worries.

Number one worry was that if Lucy did find out about the Charterstone deal there was the outside chance she'd go to the authorities. It would be bad enough if that meant I was exposed but what if the police turned out to be in league with the Cat? They could harm her.

You'll see here why I'm not suited to the life of a criminal. My mind is full of 'powers that be', 'authorities', 'forces of law and order', that sort of thing. I doubt if your natural-born tea leaf ever has these ideas in his head until the rossers snap the cuffs on him.

So it was for Lucy's protection that I told her that we had dropped the Charterstone project. Since we weren't going to advertise it or do any more real work on the project, hiding the truth from her was fairly straightforward. She still saw the dog but I kept much more of a professional distance between us.

This, however, became rather difficult the day Lyndsey came into the new offices – all green and modern and near the high street, the offices, that is. It was the day before we were due to complete on Charterstone and though I hadn't begun to breathe easy I'd become somewhat accustomed to the discomfort.

About a week after I'd agreed the deal with Mrs Cad-Beauf, Lyndsey, intoxicated by an edition of *Property Ladder* on Channel 4, had decided to jack in her job and begin life as a property developer. Some people would enter property development by buying themselves a new BMW, a secretary and a lot of sharp clothes. Lynds was still in the Clio, still in the clothes she normally wore, writing her own letters and doing her own research. She'd decided what she wanted to buy with the £500,000 we'd have left over from the new house – more money. She said that by investing in studio flats we could make a massive return on our investment in rent or sales once we'd done them up. It was hard to argue, I probably should have done it myself years before.

Anyway, in she came, hot with the energy of a new idea, waving a couple of pieces of paper, the bling from her new engagement ring threatening to have the eye out of the unwary.

'Look,' she said, 'look what Tibbs has just faxed me through.'

The dog was asleep on the floor next to me and, at the sound of Lyndsey's voice, his ears ruffled as if beneath a troublesome draught. Lucy, who'd been changing some stuff in the window at the time, looked pretty much the same way.

This association with Tibbs was a strange one to me. First she'd bargained him up to a million, now she was getting faxes from him. It was a strange way to proceed, I thought, considering their relationship had started with him having her menaced and beaten.

I took the paper and examined it as I'd examined thousands like them before.

It was a description of houses.

'Live a peace (sic) of history,' said the title. 'Situated in 98 acres of stunning Sussex countryside The Charterstone gated community is the most prestijious (sic) Development in the south-east for Years. Comprising of 40 Self Contained luxury-Homes and 20 Executive flats the Community offers Everything for the most demanding and discerning of Clients.'

The list went on to describe how the £750,000 homes were built in the Florida style, swimming pool, communal tennis courts, supervised play areas and crèche facilities.

I couldn't say anything.

'It's a draft of the brochure,' said Lyndsey, 'and – get this – Tibbs will offer us one for six hundred thousand against what he owes us.'

I hushed her in case they heard.

'That's very generous of him,' I said.

'Not really,' said Lyndsey, still in a high state of excitement though lower. 'They're only costing him three hundred thousand apiece to put up so he's saving three hundred thousand in commission he would have paid to you. We get a seven hundred and fifty thousand pound house, he saves money, everyone's happy. I'm so happy, so happy!' She spun round on her chair and came to an abrupt stop in front of me, her ringed fist an inch from my face. 'Look at that for a hot rock!' she said.

The dog made a moaning noise from the floor. The new seats we'd got were too low to the ground for him to lie under but it didn't stop him trying.

From her desk Lucy tried to look as if she wasn't listening. Everyone was happy, said Lyndsey. I was struck by the number of times in dealings with Tibbs that everyone could be happy. Financial Prozac, he appeared to be.

I found myself sweating slightly.

'How's he going to get planning permission on this?' I said. 'Isn't it listed?'

'He got planning permission years ago. The village is going to be left undeveloped as a feature attraction. You don't need to own somewhere to have plans on it considered,' said Lyndsey. 'He's had these for a year or more now.'

'It's a bit . . .' I looked left and right but everyone was busy. Lucy was typing something so she couldn't have heard. 'It's a bit tasteless, Lynds.'

Lyndsey looked puzzled. 'Not at all,' she said, gazing at me over the stone of the ring. 'It's being built by the same people who do all the footballers' houses in the north.'

'Not the design of them,' I said. 'You know, all that with Mrs Cad-Beauf and then actually going to live there. I'm not comfortable with it.' I'd hoped that I might be able to put the whole thing behind me and forget about it.

Lyndsey shook her head. 'It's a seven hundred and fifty thousand pound house for six hundred thousand, David.' She sat with her hands open, like a woman checking to see if it was raining.

'But it's not worth anything to me if it makes me uncomfortable,' I said. 'It sounds stupid but it's meant to be a home as well and I can't feel at home when I'm forced to confront something I'm ashamed of every day.' I said this quietly so the other members of staff wouldn't hear me. The dog heard and removed himself to Lucy's side.

Lyndsey laughed. 'I think the time for tender feelings was before you did something to make you uncomfortable,' she said. 'If you can't stand the guilt, don't stain the quilt.'

I just sat looking at her while the dog, who had woken up, told Lucy to rub him as only she knew how and Lucy determinedly typed on.

'I wasn't happy with that, I'm still not happy with it,' I said.

She looked alarmed for a second, stroking her ring as if expecting a genie to appear. 'You're not thinking of pulling out of this, are you?'

I patted her hand. 'Of course not,' I whispered. In fact I'd been doing nothing but thinking of pulling out of it, I just couldn't see a way of doing it without losing Lyndsey, either by her walking through the door or by the Cat chopping her up.

The decision seemed to have a momentum. The more I thought I could walk away from it, the harder it seemed to do so. I'd felt for years that I was swimming against the flow by always trying to do the right thing; having turned the other way, I was amazed at how easy the going can be with the current behind you.

. 'Then if you're going to do it, do it, and do it quickly,' said Lyndsey. 'You can't do this and still pretend that you're the sort of person who doesn't. You are. Get used to it.'

I smiled. 'Hypocrisy's at least half a high standard,' I said, reminding her of one of her own bon mots from years before.

'And guilt is just a dream,' she whispered, looking over towards Lucy. 'It's a message from an imaginary you, someone who didn't do what you did. See who you are, David. I do and it's not such a bad person. All we've done is bent the rules a bit.'

I couldn't help wondering if a high court judge would take the same view. Then again, he'd probably turn out to be a member of the Folding Society himself.

'I'll tell the Cat we want the house,' she said – he was the Cat now, was he?

'There's a name for women who talk to cats!' said the dog loudly from the other side of the office. I wasn't too worried about this. He had sensitive hearing so could clock on to things that Lucy wouldn't be able to.

'Look, Lynds,' I said.

'Burn the witch!' said the dog. I couldn't believe he got all this information from lamp posts.

'You'll get used to it,' she said. 'It won't even cross your mind after a couple of months. If we act now we'll be in the first house to be finished. We could be inside before Christmas.'

'Can we talk about this later?' I said.

'There's no point,' said Lyndsey. 'I'll leave the plans with you. And try to put on a smile. We're meant to be enjoying this! I'm enjoying this, aren't you? Come on, Dave! We're so lucky.' She waved the ring in front of my face like a small boy might a model aeroplane. I was pleased to see she was so happy to be engaged and I wanted to make her happier.

Lucy came over to my desk. She passed me an envelope. Then she leaned forward towards Lyndsey, rather like detective sergeants lean down at bang-to-rights suspects.

'The great thing about self-congratulation is that at least you know it's sincere,' she said. 'Well done, by the way.'

Then she was out of the shop, slamming the door behind her.

'You want to get yourself some labels, love,' said Lyndsey to Lucy's back. 'You can't be buying your clothes from the classified ads forever.'

I smiled weakly at her and opened the envelope. It was Lucy's resignation.

A note was attached to it.

'Require no reference so will work no notice. Supatemps are a good agency.'

Speechless, I put it into my desk.

'Pshhw, pshhw,' said Lyndsey, flashing her diamond at me, as if it was some super-heroine call sign. 'Where are you taking me tonight?'

22

Dog House

Lucy was not at her house that evening and she wouldn't answer her mobile or phone.

I wasn't sure what I would have said to her anyway. Not why, I knew the answer to that.

It was plain what had happened. She'd overheard Lyndsey and decided she could no longer work with me now that I was revealed as a low snake.

Something needed to be said, though. The nearest I could get to it was that it wouldn't be the same with a temp. I decided that, if that was the nearest I could get to it, then it might be better if I cut my losses and stayed far away from it.

I felt like something needed saying, though I wasn't sure what and to who. The dog didn't understand the first thing about dishonesty so I'd have to spend irritating hours with him just to get the basic concept over to him, at the end of which he'd probably say something like, 'I should just be nice to everyone, if I were you. It always works for me.'

Lyndsey – how would I explain? I knew her dreams were too near now for her to step back from them. And how could we?

The contracts had been exchanged. Any withdrawal now would be incredibly messy and risk blowing the whole thing. I was in bent paperwork so far steeped that to go back would have been more wearisome than to go on. I knew what Lyndsey would say anyway. Lucy had left me the name of a temp agency. Hardly the action of someone who was thinking of dobbing you in to the peelers.

The next morning, still weary from the 4 a.m. poker, I looked down at my desk. The last Walnut Whip Lucy had bought for me sat there in its squat glory, the lambent cellophane enticing the eye to the dark promise within. I picked it up and fondled it. A chocolate tit.

What have I done? I thought. Not in the 'what have I done?' way of someone who has put the house on 16 red seeing the ball land on 17 black but in the 'what have I done?' way of someone arriving at Asda with not the faintest memory of what he was meant to be buying.

Something seemed missing. OK, I know it was Lucy but something else too.

'You smell sad,' Reg had said after our normal pot-busting excursion at cards, 'like the diary of an ancestor discovered in a drawer.' He put his head on my knee and looked up into my eyes through the lamplight.

'I'm OK, Reggie,' I said.

'You should take a flea, sir,' said the dog. 'It is a well-known canine cure for melancholia.'

'How's that?' I said.

'Because there's nothing like an itch in the pits for putting your other problems into perspective. And when it is gone, the lack of it will make the world seem bright.'

Cheaper than psychotherapy, I thought.

That afternoon I made my way out to Charterstone to be with Mrs Cad-Beauf when the deal was completed.

This isn't, I have to say, normal estate agent practice; sitting back and watching the bank account grow being the more normal state of affairs. I was certainly doing the latter, however. Poker games in a bigger league were the order of the day and the dog kept coming up trumps, if you can come up trumps at poker. My overdraft was gone and I was well on the way to making my first £50,000.

I'd arranged a removals van for her things and a taxi for Mrs Cad-Beauf. At the last minute I changed my mind, had the car valeted and went to pick her up myself.

I'll give Tibbs this, he doesn't mess around. The deal, if it went through without a hitch – which it would since the solicitors on both sides were in his pocket – would complete at three. It was two thirty and already three lorries full of temporary security fencing were waiting at the gates, along with a couple of dog vans.

By the time I got to the main hall – by car this time as the gates had been opened – the removal men had come and gone.

Aia Napa let me in and I went through to the orangery, Reg running before me to greet Mrs Cad-Beauf. She gave him a big welcome and he rolled over for her to tickle his tummy.

Mrs Cad-Beauf was with two stout country ladies, the sort you'd think twice about trying to knock off a pole with a quarterstaff.

'Here he is,' said one of the ladies, eyeing me, 'the destructor.'

I felt reptilian beneath their gaze.

'Don't be unpleasant to Mr . . . thing,' said Mrs Cad-Beauf. 'This is my doing. One cannot avoid change and the place needs sprucing up.'

'It's going to be a lot more than a sprucing up, Edith, I keep telling you,' said the woman.

'I'm sure you're exaggerating,' said Mrs Cad-Beauf.

'Am I exaggerating?' she asked me directly, with the sort of look reserved for a gorillagram at a wake.

'This is the way of things,' I heard myself say. 'It's how things are and you can't avoid it.'

'You can't avoid it if you don't try,' said the woman. 'In my view you have hoodwinked this poor lady into parting with all she holds dear in the pursuit of profit and into the bargain you have wrecked a way of life.'

'Say sorry,' said the dog.

'There's no need for sorry,' said Mrs Cad-Beauf.

She went to the edge of the orangery and looked out through the glass, her face to the light.

'This is the last time I shall look upon this view,' she said, in a strong voice. 'The lazy dahlias, stirring only for the breeze or the hoot of an early owl. The deep lanes, dark in the afternoon.' She coughed, to stifle the emotion. 'In the summer's midnight you can hear guitars and whistles and strange music across the wood. You can hear the living.'

The dog turned to her with the look of a Roman senator hearing Caesar announcing triumphs in the east.

'Broken dreams are not like broken biscuits,' he said, 'they lose their sweetness.'

Mrs Cad Beauf went on. 'I have seen houses rise and fall here, Mr Barker, and now it is my turn to fall, to be replaced by a bypass. This end was written in its beginning. The estate was born of the industrial age and the forces of history that built it will see it go like a sandbank given and taken by the tide. Not to pass but to become.'

'It needn't be this way,' said one of the ladies but Mrs Cad-Beauf seemed to be in a trance.

'The light moves on the fields, and the wind wrinkles the sea and what does it matter if I am here or elsewhere as they do?'

'But you have history here,' I said, 'all your memories are here.' Why was I suddenly trying to talk her out of it? Cowardice. I still couldn't accept that I was one of the bad guys. That made me one of the worse guys. If she suddenly changed her mind, there was precisely sod all I could do about it. I suppose I just couldn't face up to what I was doing.

'Deep age changes the past, Mr Barker. It no longer seems like a series of events but like . . .' she moved her hand across the dust beams, 'like one thing among other things. Like a word in a chamber of echoes. We saw but we did not understand. "We have hoped for the wrong things and dreaded the wrong things," someone once said.'

'That's very bleak,' I said. 'So what is—'

'The meaning of life? Mr Barker,' she said, fixing me hard with her left eye, 'I'm buggered if I know.' She gave a shrug and stroked the dog's ears. 'Love, probably. And loss. Two sides of the same coin.'

My phone buzzed in my pocket. I knew it would be Lyndsey, telling me the money was in or wasn't in. Whatever, that the deal had been completed. It was three o'clock and nothing could be changed.

'Sorry,' I said, as in the distance we heard the lorries start their engines.

'You've nothing to be sorry for, Mr Barker,' said Mrs Cad-Beauf. 'The world isn't the way we would like it to be. That's not your fault.'

I helped her into my car while the women watched us. I half expected the Cat to pull up in his Jag and tell us all to get off his land. That wasn't his style, though. Like a real pro, he'd won and the winning was enough.

It wasn't good grace that kept him away. It was simply that he had more profitable ways to spend his time.

As I went round to let Reg into the back, a magpie settled on one of the twisted birches of the rose garden and cawed down at us.

'It says you're for it,' said Reg, looking unusually glum.

'I know I am,' I said.

23

Love Me, Don't Love Your Dog

Mrs Cad-Beauf went into the sheltered housing and the Cat moved in, digging a road round the listed village and fencing it off to prevent the entrance of children followed by lawsuits. There were no local children anyway.

I let Lyndsey handle the buying of the house. I sold my flat and hers, obviously, but beyond that I didn't get involved, even on an emotional level really. I just went along with things.

We took a trip to the Midlands to visit Britain's biggest pet shop, where I put in an order for a heated kennel. It was designed to be plumbed in to the central heating, which would be run outside the house. It was quite a large thing, about six feet high, and on a variety of levels so the dog could choose where he slept.

We'd tried booking it through the internet but that's no good for dogs as pictures don't mean much to them. Reg was happy for me to describe it to him but I thought he'd better see it in the wood.

He'd been quite excited at the idea and had gone inside to try it out.

'I like the top level,' he said, invisible inside the roof. 'It feels very safe when people can't see you.'

'I knew you'd like it,' I said. 'Do you think that's where you'll sleep?'

'Oh no,' said Reg, 'there wouldn't be room for you up here. We'll have to take the ground floor.'

'Right,' I said, realising we had some difficult conversations ahead.

'Do you think we could get one with a big chimney like Mrs Cad-Beauf's?' he said. 'I could stick my head out of it to keep guard.'

In the end I made him forget about the chimney by getting him a new ball on a string and, after some unpleasantness when a hamster goaded him from a cage, we placed the order and returned home.

We went to the dogs' home with Mrs Cad-Beauf to arrange the donation – what it would be spent on, how to ensure the greatest benefit to the dogs and if she could have a plaque to her and the memory of her dogs. For £250,000, which was the size of the donation, they said they'd name the charity after her. Naturally the sum wasn't mentioned. *Noblesse oblige*, as does villainesse, though that may not be Latin.

'You don't need a plaque to your memory,' I said. 'You're still being experienced, people don't need to remember you.'

It made me feel better to see how pleased the dogs' home was with her donation, not least the fundraising manager who mentioned more than once how good this would look on her CV. If she'd got £24 million odd I guessed she would have died of shock.

'I won't outlive these puppies,' said Mrs Cad-Beauf as we passed the cages. 'I'm ready for a rest now, Mr Barker.' I'd noticed that dogs were given to melodramatic statements and it appeared that Mrs Cad-Beauf, a lifelong dog fan, had picked up the trait.

'The long day closes,' said Reg, 'a lovely sleep beckons. The eternal question of the unconscious hours looms. What . . .' his eyes looked distant and an air of deep reflection settled over him, 'is for breakfast?'

However, it appears that life sometimes is melodramatic in itself. Six weeks after Mrs Cad-Beauf moved into her sheltered housing my eyes strayed from the property section of the local paper to the sport and, making sure none of the staff was looking, on to the paper as a whole.

It was the afternoon and, Walnut Whip-free, my desk looked bare, poignant even, which is a difficult way for a desk to look. I could have bought my own Walnut Whips, I suppose. I'd found it embarrassing when Lucy bought them for me but now that I had the opportunity to buy my own without fuss, it seemed I didn't want to. Odd.

The newspaper's familiar stories of minor thuggery and jumble sales were impinging on my retina without making the leap to the brain when I saw a familiar picture – the head of Mrs Cadwaller-Beaufort, like a noble cauliflower, protruding from a patch of dogs.

'Dog gone – mutt lady slips the leash of life' said the headline, confirming my view that standards were not what they were under the previous editor.

I felt a tremble go through me as I read. Reg came to my side. 'You aren't all right,' he said. There's no need for an empathetic creature like a dog to ask if you're OK. Normally he will tell you how you are and, though you might not believe him, he will be right.

'Not really,' I said. 'Mrs Cad-Beauf's dead.'

The dog looked puzzled. 'Dead?' he said. 'I'm not exactly sure what you mean.'

I read the first paragraph of the piece aloud. 'Dog-loving blue blood Mrs Cadwaller-Beaufort, the well-known Sussex bene-factor, died yesterday aged 93.'

'So what does this mean for our relationship?' said the dog.

'Well, we won't be seeing as much of her, that's for sure,' I said.

The dog was still puzzled. 'I thought only people you didn't know died,' he said.

'What do you mean?'

'Well, I met a dead fox the other day in a bush and I didn't know him but I didn't know it happened to friends.'

'What did you think happened to them?'

The dog slapped his chops. I could see he was miserable.

'I've never really thought about it,' he said. 'That's a very tough one.'

I read on. 'The heiress lived in her family's seat of Charterstone near Duckfield until last month when she moved into sheltered accommodation, selling the estate to New World Enterprises to be developed into luxury housing.'

'Will you die?' asked the dog.

'Well, yes,' I said, 'one day.'

He took on the look my dad had when he'd found a hole in a new sock. 'But they're M and S,' he'd said, over and over again, like a scientist unable to explain a new reading on an old experiment.

'Then what will I do?' the dog said, panicking. 'You won't be able to open a can for my dinner if you're all cold and mouldy like that fox.'

The temp looked over from behind her word processor.

'What's up with the dog?' she said.

'I don't know,' I said. 'It won't be for a long time and who knows what will have happened by then,' I whispered in his ear. 'One way or another I'll always look after you.'

'What is death?' said the dog. 'Do things just choose to stop moving?'

I looked at the story of Mrs Cad-Beauf in the paper.

'I don't know,' I said. 'I think sometimes they probably do.'

There are junctures in one's dealings with animals when, try as one might, it is impossible to decline from sentimentality. This was such a juncture. The dog looked up at me and I coughed harshly to avoid him seeing the tear in my eye.

'It is a mystery,' said Reg. 'How could you surrender this?' He seemed to go into something of a trance. 'A ball falls from the light across a dark field. Desire and fulfilment conspire to joy. The sun ignites the tumbling clouds, the tumult of the blood, no future, no past, just a consuming instant, as fur, muscle and bone sing with the impulse of delight.'

He sat down and raised a paw, in thought perhaps.

'And yet even the sparkle on the ocean is a movement and a movement is a passing. Life does not change, life is change. It's an awful thing, to be the one constant in a cosmos of relentless alteration.'

'Would you like a custard cream?' said the temp, who had fitted quite well into Lucy's role.

'Not 'arf,' said the dog, wagging his tail.

I read the rest of the story as the temp led him away. Mrs Cad-Beauf had a long association with the Sussex Kennel Club and until the late 1980s had been a successful breeder of Border collies, though she was noted for her work establishing dog shows for mongrels too. In later years failing health had prevented her from keeping dogs but she was a regular judge at local dog shows right up until she died.

There were some quotes from local dog potentates and that was it. The phone rang and I thought I'd finished the story. I know now, of course, that I hadn't bothered to read the last paragraph. Given what happened afterwards I don't know if I wish I had or wish I hadn't.

I picked up the phone. It was Lyndsey.

Despite the fact that there had been some struggle about us moving into Charterhouse, which was officially a 'dry marina' project – that is, modelled on a marina but with no boats – we'd been getting on famously.

When we completed in October we were moving in as the first people on the site, into a home that was to be ready before all the rest to show what was available. The Cat had knocked another £25,000 off if we agreed to let the place be used as a show home for the first year and Lyndsey had ripped his arm off, particularly as a car dealer member of the Folding Society had sold her an ex-demonstration Land Rover Discovery at a knockdown price, so the relatively unmade roads wouldn't be too much of a problem. She said she'd give me a lift to the main gates and my old Audi, though I thought I'd invest in a new pair of wellingtons and walk with the dog.

I tried to reconcile Lyndsey and Reg. I'd even bought her a dog guard for the Discovery.

'Thanks!' she said, genuinely pleased. 'I'll put it in right away. It looks very classy, doesn't it, like I've got Labradors or something.' Then her face darkened. 'If you think this means he's coming in the car you've got another think coming,' she said.

Still, I felt more accepted and loved by her than at any previous time in our relationship, the golden first months aside.

She'd bought me a beautiful Mont Blanc pen and had it inscribed 'For future deals', and we were planning to go abroad on holiday for the first time ever. Previously Lyndsey had always been too busy saving to go anywhere but now we were going to Greece for a week in November, on which she'd secured a great off-peak deal.

We also came closer together through her new interest in property. She was genuinely fascinated by what I had to say about investments, where I thought was up and coming, where down and going. She even suggested a few things for the business – wider advertising, targeted flyers through people's doors in areas where we thought we might make a quick return, tying ourselves in to mortgage brokers and financial advisers. She'd been a waste to the foot trade, really, because she had such a natural business brain.

So I got a little warm glow when I heard her voice on the other end of the phone.

'I've got a date,' she said. 'We can be in in three weeks, or as soon as they lay down some sort of road surface to our house.'

'Great,' I said. 'Do we know exactly what the address is because I need to get some stuff delivered. What's the number?'

'It doesn't have a number!' said Lyndsey, and I could hear the pride in her voice down the phone. 'It's got to have a name and we can choose it!'

'Well, how do I get something delivered in the meantime?' I said. I'd paid for the outdoor kennel and I thought I might as well nip down there, bung an onsite plumber a monkey and get it fitted to save mess when we arrived.

'Can't you get it delivered to your flat?' she said. 'I don't think we're really meant to have anything there before we complete.'

'This is a new and welcome respect for the rules,' I said, teasing her, 'but it's too big.'

'What's so big you can't have it at your flat?' she said. She sounded excited. 'Is it a moving-in present?' She was teasing me now. I know I might have portrayed her as slightly grasping but she wasn't that bad.

'It's Reg's kennel,' I said. 'It's a bit of doggy palace, I'm afraid.'

The phone went quiet, the kind of silence that tells you something is coming, like that between the ticks of a clock.

'What's the matter?' I said.

'Didn't you read the stuff from the solicitor?'

'No.'

'I sent it to you.'

'You might have sent it to me but I didn't read it. What's the matter?'

'The estate,' she said, 'it's child-friendly. I thought that was why we were moving in.'

This was true. One of the brightest things that had happened was that Lyndsey and I had discussed trying for children. We hadn't actually been trying but we hadn't been not trying either, she having come off the pill and no alternative method of contraception being selected in its place.

'So?'

'Dogs aren't allowed on it,' she said.

I looked over to the staff area where Reg was being patted by a fat client who looked as if the exercise was a bit of an effort.

'Oh no,' I said, 'that can't be right.'

I left Reg at the office and tore round to meet Lyndsey. As it was a nice day she'd suggested we meet on the promenade and I stood in a whirlwind of agitation in front of the metalled sea.

A group of teenagers sat littering on the grass near me, discussing the twin obsessions of English youth – getting off their tits and getting on to someone else's. To my left a man was eating with his mouth open on a bench, to my right a woman belted her child because, she said, it had been asking for it. Everything seemed to annoy me and I knew I was brewing for an almighty row.

Lyndsey finally appeared – fifteen minutes late. I knew that the main thing she'd discovered in the Discovery was how much harder to park it was than the Clio and she was now quite used to having to drive around looking for suitably large spaces. One way of looking at it was that she got longer in its air-conditioned luxury, I suppose.

She was dressed in the tracksuit pants and Duffer top she often wore when working at home and came towards me with the air of an athlete approaching an erring official.

Because I could feel the anger building inside me I made an effort to keep cool.

'This is all bleedin' convenient, isn't it?' I said, which was about as cool as I could manage.

Lyndsey looked at me hard. 'If you've come here to abuse me I'm going back right now.'

'It's you that's . . . abused me,' I said, pruning a bad word out of my sentence.

'In what way?'

'By sneaking the fact that I'm going to have to get rid of my best friend in the entire world into the property contract.'

'I thought that was me,' she said quietly.

This is what they do to you, these women. They annoy you incredibly, unbelievably, and then they turn it round so it's you who's in the wrong. I'm sure it's what these men do to you as well but I wasn't dealing with one of those, was I?

'It is you,' I said. 'You know what I mean.'

'I don't,' she said, looking at me with some kindness. 'I knew the dog meant a lot to you but I thought you'd weighed that against what we stood to gain and come to the decision that it was worth it. I even marked the part on the contract in high-lighter so you'd see it. You can't accuse me of deceit, Dave.'

'I haven't read the contract, have I? I'm so full up with guilt about moving in in the first place that I can't even think about it. You should have told me.'

She put her hand on my arm, which made me want to pull away from her with violence. I didn't, obviously.

'I didn't want it to seem like it was coming from me,' she said. 'I put it in front of you and left it up to you to object. I can't say fairer than that.'

'I love that dog,' I said. I felt the tears come up in me.

'Oh baby, I know you do,' she said. 'Come on, give me a hug.'

She put her arms round me.

'The thing is,' she said, 'this is about the rest of our lives, how we're going to live. The dog might be two, he might be seven or older for all you know. He might get hit by a car tomorrow. Whatever, one thing's certain, you're going to spend most of your life without him. You can't let it wreck your future. What if everything went well and we got enough money to move to St Kitt's? We couldn't take him there.'

St Kitt's now. We'd moved on from Mustique.

I saw the boxer who had chased Reg ambling down the seafront like the king of the landing in a prison.

'I don't see how missing out on living at Charterstone would have wrecked my future,' I said. 'I don't want to live there anyway. I'd have been happy in a smaller, more expensive place.'

Lyndsey shook her head. 'But you've made me very very happy, doesn't that count for anything? It's not like you have to get rid of Reg anyway. Lucy will be glad to have him, I'm sure. You're always saying how much she likes him. And you'll see him every day in the shop.'

I hadn't even told Lyndsey Lucy had gone, I realised.

'Lucy left work ages ago,' I said. 'I haven't seen her since.'

'I still bet she'd take the dog. She likes that sort of thing,' said Lyndsey, as if it was a weakness.

I realised that my love for the dog wasn't anything to do with what he said, though I often found his views interesting or amusing; it was about who he was and it would be very difficult to share him any more than I did already. The idea of only seeing him occasionally, of the odd walk even if Lucy would agree to it, was hardly thinkable. I wouldn't be sharing him, he would be someone else's dog. Lucy would be the first call on his loyalty, the number one, the pack leader.

I turned out to the sea, to the shifting floors of light on the summer water. What was it the dog had said? 'Life doesn't change, life is change.'

'This is done now,' said Lyndsey. 'We can't go back on it.'

'We could sell it, probably for a profit, and move somewhere nicer,' I said.

'I can't think of anywhere nicer,' said Lyndsey. 'We've got a swimming pool, access to tennis courts, supervised play areas for the kids. It's what I've always wanted, David, short of moving to Florida or—'

I held up my hand to prevent her from saying 'Mustique'.

Can giving in become a habit? I suppose so, though I did genuinely want to make Lyndsey happy.

'I couldn't make a bigger sacrifice for anyone,' I said, with the sort of certainty in the future that tempts God to think, 'Oh yeah? Try this then.' My brain couldn't get into gear. Had I said something that implied I'd go along with giving Reg away? From her reaction it seemed I had.

Lyndsey leaned forward and kissed me on the cheek.

'You'll be OK,' she said. 'Come on, let me buy you an ice cream. You can probably get the money back on the kennel anyway.'

24

Pills and Bellyaches

The next day I picked up a prescription from the doctor and went to the chemist's. Reg had to wait outside, which I thought was ungrateful of the pharmaceutical industry, considering how dogs have suffered for its cause.

There seemed no peak to the summer, every day hotter than the last, the sun an angry eye searing down on my deceits and frailties.

'What's this prescription for?' I asked the woman at the counter.

'What's Salbarbymyl for?' she shouted to the chemist at the back of the shop.

'Auditory hallucinations,' boomed the chemist.

'Auditory hallucinations,' said the woman.

'Not so loud,' I said, glancing at the queue.

'I didn't say anything,' she said, raising her eyebrows in an 'over to you', way.

I drew in breath. 'Are there any side effects?'

She looked at the packaging. 'Visual hallucinations,' she said.

'What sort of hallucinations?'

She shrugged. 'I don't know, a foul ghoul maybe.'

'So I choose my form of madness, do I?'

'Life's a bitch,' she said.

'Then it wouldn't be allowed in here,' I said.

Before I left the store I swallowed a pill so the dog wouldn't see me and ask what they were. I'd just put it into my mouth and was marbling it around wishing I'd bought a drink to go with it when my phone rang.

It was Lucy. There had been so much stress going on that I'd failed to notice how much I missed her until I saw her number flash up on my mobile.

I felt a skip in my stomach and nearly didn't answer it. Bollocks to it, I thought. When things are bollocksed already there's no real harm in saying bollocks to them. It doesn't make much difference.

This is fate, I thought. I hadn't been able to ring her to ask her about Reg and now she was ringing me.

'Hello,' I said.

'Hiya.' Her voice was shaking as she tried to force out a jaunty manner.

'Yes?'

'David . . .' That was strange. As I am neither posh nor gay, no one has ever called me David, not even my parents. Even in business I'm Dave as I don't like to be thought of as the sort of person who is too good for a monosyllable. It felt for an instant as if she was talking about someone else, that she was about to announce some bad news about him. But it was me.

'David, I need to talk to you.'

'About Charterstone?' I said.

'That's part of it,' she said. She sounded very upset, not like she was about to tell me she'd reported me to the police. Mind you, I suppose it would have upset her to report me to the police.

'I need to talk to you too,' I said. 'I need to ask you something.'
I could see Reg poking his head round the corner on his lead,
making the automatic doors open and close while saying something about 'sesame'. 'When can we meet?' I said.

'As soon as you like,' said Lucy. 'Will you bring Reg?'

'I think this is better alone,' I said.

The pills had no immediate effect. If anything, the dog became
more talkative on the way home.

The one thing you could certainly say about Reg is that he
was interested in life. Keen, is how you'd describe him, often
without any particular focus, just generally all round keen.

While he'd been waiting outside the chemist's he'd put two
and two together and come up with the reason he hadn't been
let in.

'I'm beginning to think the relationship between us and
humans isn't as two-way as I'd been given to understand,' he
said with a look of deep trouble.

'Why did you think dogs got left there, then?' I said.

'I thought the humans were buying them a surprise,' he said,
his enquiring nose pointing up at the bag containing my drugs.

'They don't so much look down on them as think they carry
disease,' I said.

'Never,' said the dog, 'have I heard anything so offensive in
all my life.'

'We do prize dogs for their loyalty and courage,' I said.

'Wholly patronising,' said the dog. 'We are victims of object-
ification and commodification in an over-reaching system of
humanarchy.'

I did need the pills, it seemed. The dog's language was
becoming ever more complicated.

'Have you swallowed a dictionary?' I said as we made our
way to the car.

'I only gave it a nibble in a bored moment,' said the dog,
looking downcast.

When we returned home I looked around for my Concise Oxford. There it was, on the floor, its cover chewed, announcing itself as 'The foremost authrty on ct Eng', owing to some canine editing.

Lucy and I had arranged to meet at a cheap bar – the Upside Down on the main drag. She'd suggested the café on the seafront but I'd had enough of the shifting floors of light, the metalled sea etc. etc. as a backdrop to emotionally difficult events so I decided to try potato wedges, motorway service station decor and 'the curry club – Chicken Boona plus 2 pints and a poppadom £6.23' instead.

I left the dog in the flat, much to his annoyance.

'What exactly am I going to do while you're away?' he said, pushing his brow forward so his fur stood on end. It's fairly easy to tell when you've ruffled a dog's fur because – well, it's obvious really, isn't it?

'Sleep?' I said.

'Sleep!' said the dog. 'Can it be true I am to be so honoured? Oh sir, your largesse is as a light unto me.' Then, from the corner of his mouth and with a sideways eye, 'Sofa OK?'

'Since you've nearly eaten it you may as well cover it in fur as well,' I said. There wasn't any hope for him and Lyndsey.

Lucy was seated by the window, the light at her back, when I arrived.

I hadn't seen her in a couple of months and already she seemed to be changing subtly, wearing earrings I'd never seen, drinking spritzer when I'd had her down as a dry white wine, tiny signs that she was slipping towards becoming a stranger. I'd never considered us close until we parted.

She seemed beautiful to me, both sparkly and dark, if such a thing can be imagined. Kindness seemed to radiate from her. I, a vile serpent of the grass, felt unworthy to be in her company.

I smiled and put a gift bag down on the table.

'You left without giving us a chance to give you a send-off,' I said.

It was her leaving present – a CD, some perfume, chocolates and a card signed by me and the boys. Rather sentimentally I'd put a paw print from Reg on it too, even though I'd had to endure a debate about why, when I'd drummed into him the necessity of having clean paws, I was now blacking them on an ink pad.

She seemed touched.

'I'm sorry, I was only thinking of myself,' she said, touching the bag but not opening it. 'I rather forgot the form. Say thanks to the boys for me.'

I shrugged and looked into her eyes.

'I know why you went,' I said.

She glanced down at her drink. 'I'm sorry.'

'It's me who should be sorry,' I said. 'The dishonesty is hard to live with. It's just the way things went, you know. Life isn't always about what we'd choose for ourselves.'

'Not always, but sometimes,' she said. 'If you want something you have to ask.'

Someone put a record on the jukebox, some rapper saying how proud he was to be selfish. Vice is now virtue, the ugly beautiful, wicked means excellent.

'I feel I've done something very bad.'

'It's never too late to go back,' she said.

'Sometimes it is. I feel I've crossed a line.'

'Well, you haven't killed anyone,' she said.

'I'm not too sure about that,' I was going to say, but I didn't.

'I do need to ask you something,' I said. I was choking up a bit and pretended that my drink had gone down the wrong pipe to disguise it.

'Whatever it is, I'll say yes,' she said.

'You don't know what it is yet.'

'You wouldn't ask me something I wouldn't want to yes to,' she said. 'I know you wouldn't.'

'This requires you and me to be linked in a serious way,' I said, 'and for a long time. I don't know if you're comfortable with that.' Who would want to associate with a criminal? Half the country, if the lyrics to the rap song were to be believed, but not a pretend criminal of bling and boo yakka, diamonds and guns to you, a real, tiny, dismal criminal who does his work not with the pimps and the gangstas but with the trusting old ladies in the smell of their decay.

'Ask,' she said, like a frozen shopper willing the appearance of a bus that was an hour late.

'I need you to take care of Reg,' I said, 'permanently.'

I could see that my words had shocked her. First I'd turned my back on my principles, now on my dog. So what? I was on a losing run and a losing run is a losing run, right? There's nothing you can do about it, just get on with losing.

'Of course,' she said, after she'd recovered her composure. 'You know I'd do anything for you.'

I had to turn away, feeling the heat rise inside me, as if I'd been bought a thousand Walnut Whips at once.

My phone rang. It was Lyndsey. I answered it.

'Hello, hero!' she said. 'Today's tasks are!' There was a long list, including something with echinacea in it. I was to get some fish but not go until later in the day when it would be on special offer.

'Love you like crazy!' she said.

'Love you like crazy,' I said, clamming shut the phone.

'What was it you wanted to talk to me about?' I said to Lucy.

'I don't know,' she said. 'It's not important now.'

25

The Hard Goodbye

Even though I tried to put it from my mind, D-Day, D meaning dog, came ever closer.

The days rolled on and kitchens were looked at, sofas chosen, work surface materials decided upon. I knew the moment when Reg would have to be told was approaching.

A week before we were due to move in I decided it was time.

Breaking the information was never going to be easy but I thought I'd do it in an environment where he'd feel most comfortable.

I'd tried to offer Lucy some money to get a bigger flat with a garden but she wouldn't hear of it. She was starting a full-time course at the University of Sussex and since full-time at university means four hours a week, the dog would have someone with him almost always. Besides, she said, she liked her flat and didn't want a bigger one.

I also feared she might say something to him. 'You're coming to live with me, you big handsome brown fool!' for instance, which would inevitably fire off questions in the canine mind.

On top of this . . . On top of this nothing. It's just Lucy seemed part of a world that was moving towards the light and I part of one that was going in the other direction.

'Where would you like to go today?' I said to Reg on the Saturday I had appointed to tell him. 'Choose anywhere you like, the Downs, a forest, anywhere.'

'Anywhere?' said the dog.

'Anywhere,' I said.

'Anywhere?'

'Yes, anywhere.'

'Anywhere?'

'Why do you keep repeating yourself.'

'I was just trying to see how many times I could make you say that word,' he said.

'What, anywhere?' I said, pretending to be fooled.

'Four!' he said. 'The highest number ever and a record in repetition, even for you.'

Dogs count on their right paw and never get to five, which they might have, given a thumb. I'd once asked Reg what was the first thing he'd do if he had a thumb.

'Get a can opener!' he said, slavering at the thought.

'Where would you like to go?' I think I managed to keep the stress out of my voice, even though he'd repeatedly told me something was wrong with me in the last week.

'There is one place,' he said.

'Where?'

'That big place we pass on the way to Waterfield Ponds,' he said.

I couldn't think of where he meant. It was largely dual carriageway up to the ponds.

'Where the cars go round and round,' he said, imitating their action by spinning about.

'Where's that?'

'Just before the ponds!' he said, like I was thick.

'You're not talking about Windham Island, are you, the circular thing with the flower bed in the middle?'

'That's the one,' said Reg. 'It looks fascinating, quite surrounded by whirring metal. I saw some pigeons on it the other day and they seemed to be having a heck of a time.'

'It might be a bit difficult getting on,' I said.

'You said anywhere!' said the dog, drumming his back foot in expectation.

'Well, as long as you're careful,' I said. 'You know you mustn't run into the road.'

'I won't damage any cars,' he said in that teenage 'you can trust me, Dad, you know' way of his.

He'd kind of absorbed my lessons on traffic but hadn't quite got the reason yet.

'You're standing on the kerb of a busy road and you desperately want to get to the other side,' I said when we first met. 'What do you do?'

'Just go!' he said with a blade-keen nod.

I'd at least got through to him on that front.

Pulling onto the island caused a bit of surprise among other motorists – us going straight on when the road went left along with sense, reason and the rest of the traffic.

'What do you think you're doing?' shouted a red-faced man in a new car.

'He's just jealous because he hasn't got time to come too,' said the dog.

He leapt from the car and stood looking around him, very much as I guess Columbus must have done on landing in the new world.

'Wahey!' he said, which is, I believe, exactly what Columbus said when he got off his boat.

Reg ran round the circumference of the island chasing the traffic, ever faster until it seemed I was surrounded by one big blur of dog.

'He's coming on the island, he's going off the island, he's coming off the island, he's going on the island,' he said, commentating on the progress of the cars.

How do you tell someone something like this? In my pocket was a book, *You're Going To Live With Your Auntie – Kids, Divorce and Bereavement*. It advised stressing the positives of the situation, that it was being done because the parent loved the child, that the new carer couldn't wait to begin the relationship, that though it looked as if life was about to get worse it was in fact about to become better.

This didn't feel like divorce or bereavement, though, it felt like having your kids snatched by social services because they'd decided you fed them too many e numbers.

I'd imagined this scene would take place on a beach, at the setting of the sun with the eternal rhythms of the cool ocean mocking our passing miseries, human and canine. Or perhaps on some killing ground, some disused lot or car park where the murderers go about their work.

I threw a stick for the dog, one he'd left in the back of the car. He chased it and caught it, chewed it slightly and then returned it.

Slowly circulating the island I could see a police car, the policeman pointing at me and gesturing. I didn't know what he was saying. It occurred to me that in our casual gestures deaf people might often find offence. If someone's waving their hands about, who knows what foul words they might be making. Or poetry, I suppose.

Maybe the policeman was signalling, 'Like as the waves make towards the pebbled shore so do our minutes hasten to their end.'

I doubted it, though; that sort of thing was more common with policemen in the north of England.

The dog returned the stick and I threw it again, as the patrol car, all lights flashing, drew up at the island.

'What are you doing?' said the policeman, getting out with a 'why are you bothering me, you muppet' walk.

'Exercising my dog.'

He nodded. The dog returned the stick.

'Is he likely to run in the road?'

'No, he's well-trained.'

He nodded again. The patrol car was now causing more of an obstruction than we ever had.

'You can't do it here, this is . . .' All of a sudden a glazed look came into his eye. 'You know,' he said, 'when I came into the force I wanted to catch criminals.' He put his notebook away. 'I've actually got better things to do with my time. Try not to stay for too long.'

He got back into his car and pulled off.

I took the pills out of my pocket and looked at them. That was definitely a hallucination, I concluded.

The dog was chewing on the stick.

'Why do you do that?' I said.

'What?'

'Every time before you return the stick you chew it,' I said. 'Why's that?'

'I'm punishing it for escaping from your hand,' he said.

I laughed. 'It's not escaping, I'm throwing it.'

The dog looked at me, his eyes suddenly cold. 'You think the world revolves round you, don't you?' he said.

'You do,' I said, 'at least on this island.'

It was then I knew – he knew. Not in the human way of knowing but at some canine intuitive level he had realised what I was about to say.

'I have some good news,' I said.

His eyes narrowed. 'It looks like bad news to me.' Then he began to tremble. 'It's worse than bad news, it's the worst news. You're leaving me, aren't you? Here on this island, to trust myself to fate again!'

'No,' I said. 'I'm not leaving you.'

'Yes you are,' said the dog. 'I can tell, it's how it went last time. You're going away. You're going to do something horrible like make me stay at Lucy's.'

This came as a shock. The dog had always enjoyed staying at Lucy's, lying on his back being fed beef jerky like a Roman emperor with a bunch of grapes.

'I thought you liked Lucy. Steak, chicken and the occasional sausage roll.' I reminded him of what he'd told me went on there.

'I like her but she's not you,' he said, pushing his head into my leg. 'I want to stay with you. I like you more than I like steak and chicken.' He involuntarily licked his lips as he named the meat.

I knelt down to touch him, rubbing his fur under his chin the way I knew he liked it.

'And I want to stay with you too,' I said, 'but I can't. It's . . .' I couldn't say it, but he could.

'It's Lyndsey, isn't it? She doesn't want me.'

You can't lie to a dog. Well, you can but there's no point.

'Yes, it's Lyndsey,' I said. I was going to say it was the Charterstone rules but he and I knew that wasn't true. It was Lyndsey who had shoved him out, her ambition, her cost-cutting, her basic dislike of dogs really.

The dog looked down at the ground.

'You love her more than you love me?'

I didn't have the words to say what I wanted to say.

'No. I don't.'

'Then why be with her instead of me? We could be happy together in your flat instead of joining her pack.'

'She's given me a choice,' I said. 'I . . .' I wanted to say that I had to choose between her and him but I couldn't get the words out. If we could have been together forever the choice would have been different. Dogs, though, don't live forever.

'It's not Lyndsey!' said the dog, clearly shocked.

'Then who is it?' I said.

'You,' he said, weakly. 'It's you who doesn't want me. Oh no! Oh no! It's like in my dream.'

'Oh Reggie,' I said, patting his head. Even in his rejection he sought physical comfort from me. 'It's not like we'll never see each other. Lucy will bring you in to work and I'll be able to walk you and . . .'

The dog shook his head. Perhaps the tablets were causing more effects than I'd thought – maybe they were pills with only side effects and no main therapeutic purpose, issued by doctors and pharmacists to particularly annoying patients.

'I am your dog or no one's,' he said.

'Reggie, you like Lucy,' I said.

'I do like her,' he said, 'but I won't be shunted around like a chattel. I have my pride and I have my dignity. What I don't have if you are rejecting me is my faith. I'm sick of humans. I want to go into the home. I will say goodbye to the hellooos.'

'Don't be ridiculous,' I said.

'I'm not being ridiculous,' said the dog. 'I'm doing what's good for me. How do I know that in a few months or a year I won't become inconvenient to Lucy?'

'Lucy won't ever leave you,' I said.

The dog looked at me and I could feel the desolation seeping off him.

'That's what you said,' he said. 'I wish I could be like that cold fox in the bush.' And then he shut his mouth and said not another word. The pills, it seemed, had worked.

26

Dog Gone

Lucy had staged a welcome party for Reg. All her friends were there, including Jim who was linking arms with her and giving her cheeky nudges in what I had to observe was a fairly resonant way. There was a banner, a cake made from a 1979 Blue Peter Album recipe for treats for pets and a drink for she and me.

I didn't stay for it. I said I had to get back to Lyndsey. Instead I went round to Snake Eyes' and lost a couple of Clios worth of cash.

Lucy's hospitality came to nothing on his first day there when she left him alone in her flat while she went out for a pint of milk.

When she returned, the damage – well. The insurance put it at £3,000. I wouldn't let her claim, of course, and paid it myself.

A vase full of water had been knocked onto the TV, the sofa stuffing was all over the carpet or would have been had there been anything left of the carpet, plants were overturned, rugs destroyed, curtains wrecked.

On top of this, Reg wouldn't even let her into the room to

inspect the wreckage, just growling madly at her and snapping at the door every time she went to open it.

She called me, of course, and I came straightaway. She was in tears, saying he'd wrecked everything she'd ever worked for and that she was frightened of him.

I went into the room. I knew him so well, he was only doing an impression of a fierce dog and he even looked guilty as he saw me.

'Does it have to be like this?' I said.

He didn't say anything to me, just stared at me through his deep brown eyes. He didn't need to speak. I knew he was asking me the same question.

The fact was that it did need to be like is. Lyndsey was right – how long does a dog live? Not long. And our happiness, her happiness, was exclusive to the dog being there. I was committed to her, so in a straight choice between her being miserable and me being miserable I chose myself. And Reg.

'It will be the home and a concrete floor if you don't behave,' I said.

Reg simply ripped what was left of a cushion to pieces.

Like I've said before, betrayal is a process not an act. We move towards bearing the unbearable in half-steps. I thought that if Reg spent a night in the dogs' home he might come to his senses and realise that he had it pretty cushy really.

I emerged from the room. Lucy was still crying and I put my arms round her. It was the first time I'd ever touched her like that and I was struck by how soft she seemed compared to Lyndsey's sharp angles.

'It's going to be OK,' I said. 'Everything will be fine. I'll write you a cheque.'

'The money's not important,' she said, 'it was mostly old stuff anyway. But what's happened to Reg? I've left him before and he's never done that.'

'I don't know,' I said. 'I'll take him to the vet to see if anything's wrong with him.'

I knew I was lying, there would be no trip to the vet. There was one place Reg was going and that was the League for Canine Advancement to begin his stir.

If you hold your breath there is, for a moment, a point at which you think, I don't see what all the fuss is about with this breathing, it's perfectly easy to do without it.

It seemed in those hours like I had held my breath in the realm of feeling. I was simply acting and the actions had no consequences that I could understand.

I put the dog into the car and began to drive.

'You know where we're going, don't you?' I said.

Reg said nothing, just drew a smear across the window with his nose as he looked out at the sky.

'We're going to the dogs' home, which is horrible. I can leave you there for a week and then you belong to them. I can't come and get you back if I try.'

This wasn't true. I knew that after a week they'd start to offer him to other people but I was fairly sure that in his mood he wouldn't be going off with anyone new.

'I wish you'd see sense,' I said. 'I could tell it upset you doing that to poor Lucy's flat.'

The dog turned away, looking out of the back of the car. He was trembling again.

The dogs' home loomed and I could see they'd begun some work on the main building, the scout hut outhouse look being replaced by standard issue twenty-first century no-brainer architecture in glass and steel. Another bold statement just like all the other bold statements. I guessed Mrs Cad-Beauf's legacy couldn't have come through yet but they were splashing out in anticipation of its arrival.

I took the dog into the foyer. When I'd visited it with Mrs Cad-Beauf it had seemed a welcoming place but now it smelled harshly of old dog and disinfectant. I approached the desk with Reg following along meekly by my side.

The woman behind it recognised me from my visit with Mrs Cad-Beauf.

'Hello!' she said. 'So sorry to hear about the old lady.'

She was in a new uniform, so I doubted if she was that sorry but there you go.

'Yes,' I said.

'Are you seeing Julie?' she said. Julie was the manager who had shown me around.

'No,' I said. 'I'm here for myself, actually.'

She looked at me and then down at the shaking dog. 'Yes?'

How do you say, 'I've been having some problems with this dog and I think a short sharp shock in a dogs' home might do him good. Could I leave him here and pick him up next week?'

'What are your rules on taking in dogs?' I said. 'Is it possible to get them back once they've been put in?'

The woman frowned. 'Not really,' she said. 'You have a week's grace to change your mind and then they go out for re-homing. If you wanted him back you'd have to apply and be assessed. What's wrong with him?'

'He's, er . . .' I couldn't say. I couldn't dob my own dog in.

Reg gave a snarl, the like of which I'd never heard from his lips.

'Oh, he's aggressive, is he?' said the woman.

The dog obliged with a further growl and she started back.

'So you want to get rid of him?'

'I want to see if he comes to his senses,' I said.

'I'm sorry?'

'I thought maybe a spell inside might do him good,' I said, speaking as honestly as I could.

She looked at me as if I'd gone mad, which I concluded I had.

'This isn't a young offenders institute,' she said. 'He's either in or he's out.'

Reg looked up at me, his lips pulled back over his teeth.

'I don't know,' I said. 'I don't know.'

'Why don't you go home and think about it?' she said. 'It's obviously upsetting you. Look at you.'

I realised that tears were rolling down my cheeks.

I knew she was right. I had to find some way to accommodate him, even if it meant moving house. I'd insist Lyndsey and I moved house. My insisting hadn't done much good in the past but insist I would. How could I feel so bonded to an animal in so short a time, I thought, when the same emotions seemed so complex with humans?

'Come on,' I said, 'let's . . . Hell's Bells! He's got me,' as the dog sank his fangs into my leg, ripping my trousers away from my leg at the knee and sending a pain up my leg that exited somewhere near my teeth.

This came as something of a shock and I lost my balance, falling to the ground in a series of momentary compromises: 'Oh, if I can't stand up I'll rest my arm on the desk; oh, if that won't keep me up I'll throw my hands out behind me; Jesus, my backside's come down first, that jolt went right through me; ahh, I've collapsed and now I'm laid out like a kipper on a slab.'

'Oh my word!' said the woman, running round the desk and pulling Reg off. She'd pressed a button and a couple of other women came running from a back office.

As Reg stood snarling above me, with the desk lady restraining him, one of the others expertly threw a muzzle over his face and tightened it.

All the dog could do was seethe underneath it.

'Your leg looks terrible,' said the woman. I looked down to see my trouser leg had been shredded and blood was pouring from a rather nasty wound.

'Don't judge him on that,' I said. 'He's not like that really.'

'Oh, don't cover up for him, you poor man,' said one of the

women who had come to my aid. She'd already got out a first-aid box and was dabbing antiseptic onto a cotton pad.

The other one had fixed a lead to Reg's collar and was dragging him away.

'You won't kill him, will you?' I said.

The woman with the pad smiled. 'Not if we can help it. The behaviour unit can work wonders nowadays,' she said.

I was going to stop them, I was going to take him back, but I didn't. This was the turning point, the step through the door of the aircraft, the ignition sequence on the lift-off. Right up to that second I could have gone back. Then, somehow, I couldn't.

I thought of Lyndsey and of the future. My relationship with the dog hadn't been undermined by lack of love, it had been undermined by lack of time. I had other, longer lasting ties to consider. The dog would be sacrificed to the hereafter.

'Just relax,' said the woman, descending on me with the pad. 'This may hurt a bit.'

From behind her I could see Reg being led through a green metal door.

'Goodbye, Reg,' I said.

The door closed and Reg was gone.

27

Home Sour Home

Life was shiny in our new home. Everything seemed bright and clear, like a picture on a TV set where the contrast is on the blink.

The kennel, despite my protestations, was delivered and lay like a tombstone in its flat pack against a wall in the back garden, waiting for Lyndsey to finish the legal wrangle with the shop to get our money back.

Investments were made and the long evenings of late summer became the shorter evenings of early autumn. I walked alone in the woods and on the Downs.

Of course I tried to visit Reg to reason him out of his self-imposed exile, but he was having none of it.

I'd go into the home every day and visit his cage but he wouldn't come to the front of the pen. I could hardly see him, even, as my view was obscured by a rather needy spaniel who wouldn't take the hint and piss off.

'There's no need to be like this,' I said, taking some chicken from a Tupperware box I'd brought. 'Come on, have a bit. Go away.' The spaniel was trying to eat it and the smell had caused a lot of clamour down the hall. Reg was immovable.

It was such a depressing place to be, long rows of dogs in cages, in two decks. Reg was in a cage on the top level, which meant he was virtually at my head height. I could see him towards the back of the cage, his face turned away and unresponsive.

'I can't believe you like it here,' I said. 'Come on, Lucy's got some steak waiting.'

I saw an ear twitch, no more. He wouldn't reply and so I told him of my walks in the woods that he could be on, of how Lucy had arranged to go on holiday to Cornwall rather than Spain so she'd be able to take him, how lovely the autumn evenings smelled.

The dog was unbudging.

Eventually the people in the home began to give me strange looks when I came in. Julie the manager took me into her office and suggested I didn't visit so often.

'Is it upsetting the dogs?' I said.

'No,' she said, 'it's upsetting you. Can I ask, Mr Barker – I'm more at home with canine nutrition really, but are you eating well?'

'Fine,' I said.

'Do you think you'd benefit from seeing a doctor?'

'No. Do you?'

'Well, when I said do you think you'd benefit, I rather meant that I was sure that the rest of us would,' she said. 'Are you aware that you talk to yourself?'

'Sort of,' I said, making a fifty fifty sign. This didn't seem to offer her the reassurance I'd hoped it might.

There was rather a long pause. No clock ticked but it felt as though one did.

'You need help, Mr Barker,' she said. 'Look.' She took a compact mirror out of her bag and held it up to my face.

There I was, overshaved and red raw, tie done up like a suicide attempt, hair plastered down under a weight of gel.

'I think it's disturbing you, coming here. Perhaps you should give yourself a break,' she said with the air of a woman who wanted a break.

I looked around the office. I guessed I was no more than fifty yards from Reg but I might as well have been a hundred miles.

Perhaps I should surrender, I thought, being something of the surrender expert.

What was it Lyndsey had said when I'd talked about giving up smoking? 'You should find it easy, I always had you down as one of life's great quitters.'

She was right.

Time went wobbly, really, that's the only way I can describe it. The next thing I knew there were two different women shaking me and saying, 'Mr Barker! Mr Barker!' I seemed to be lying down.

'Will you tell me if there's any change in Reg,' I said.

'Dog M20984,' said Julie, tapping a file from behind her desk. 'I certainly will.'

'You've got my number?'

'We've got your number, Mr Barker,' said Julie, 'you can be sure of that.'

'Can I have one last look at him?'

'Of course.'

She led me down to the pens and I made my way to Reg's. It was empty and, for a second, so was every blood vessel in my body.

Julie saw my panic. 'They're cleaning the pens,' she said. 'He'll be round the back. Follow me.'

I couldn't. Whatever inside me had been resisting the full foulness of the reality I was living collapsed and the outside of me wasn't far behind me.

'Mr Barker,' said Julie, taking hold of my trembling arm, as for the second time I found myself on the floor of the dogs' home, 'we'll call you a cab.'

* * *

The weather, which had begun to totter through October, finally fell to bits around November and by December we had sleet, which is like snow but without any of its redemptive aesthetic qualities.

Houses sprang up around us on the estate and I took comfort in Lyndsey's happiness. There was a great deal of difficulty in cutting the road to the A23, however, because Aia Napa and her friends had got wind of it and lashed themselves into the trees in a rather well-constructed network of houses. I got in trouble with Lyndsey for taking them some cakes.

The swimming pool was dug, though, and the tennis courts would have been usable had it not been for a wind of the sort that causes polar bears to look at each other and say, 'Ooh, it goes right through you.'

Our potential neighbours could be seen coming into this modern ark against the twenty-first-century tide of crime and poverty. Four-by-four, they came – Jeep and Land Rover, BMW and Toyota, all streaming through the booth and barrier that had been put up while the gates were being refurbished.

When the dog left I'd inspected the bank account in which I kept my poker winnings. In the final weeks with Reg I'd been moving up to bigger games, mostly in London, a couple in the north. I'd been invited as a big player. Universally they said I couldn't bring the dog, universally they said I could when I wouldn't come without him.

One shaven-headed lunatic of a minder had spent the best part of half an hour searching the dog for hidden cameras before saying, 'Do you know his skin's slightly dry? What do you feed him on? Cod liver oil works for my Staffs.'

My memory pixelated and rearranged itself. Into view came the dark book that Lyndsey didn't know about and never would, repository of my lies and deceptions, now nestling in the safe at work.

The account stood at £400,000 on the day Reg left. By early December, it was £20,000 and diminishing. A week before Christmas I took out a loan on the business to allow myself to go to a game with some ex pats from Split in Croatia, in Dudley. Playing with these Dalmatians, I got bitten. A week later I lost a wodge to a Bavarian whose family had made their money in wool. God was trying to tell me something. My mind just wasn't on the games but I couldn't not go.

Throwing away large sums of money somehow made me feel better, perhaps because I was no longer in debt to the dog, or to show myself that I could sustain bigger, more shocking losses, or even to test if there were more shocking losses available in the world. I know there are but at the time it seemed unimaginable to me.

Mrs Cad-Beauf had been buried very quickly after she died but, I noticed while not scanning the property section of the local paper again, she was to have a memorial service held for her on 24 December at a little church near where she had lived.

Apparently it had been her custom to open up Charterstone over Christmas to help the local dog charities with the overspill of puppies. The dog people had wanted to thank her but, as the vicars get rather busy over the main God-bothering period, they'd booked a free slot early on the 24th at ten in the morning, well before the once-a-year crew would be in pissed for midnight Mass.

I'd just put down the paper and was thinking to myself how much Reg would have wanted to go when the phone rang.

Andy was putting someone through and mouthed at me from the other side of the room that it was urgent.

I picked up the receiver, noticing that I had a bit of egg mayonnaise on my tie. This was slightly worrying because the last time I'd had egg mayonnaise for lunch was two weeks before. I wondered if that had anything to do with the younger staff's suggestion that I take on an 'overseeing role' – which means never getting to see the whites of a client's eyes and just spending my time making a nuisance of myself with filing.

'David Barker of Son and Barker!' I said, loudly. For some reason my voice sounded cheery but as if I didn't quite have a grip on the volume control. I didn't feel cheery but I'd rather got into the habit of grinning like a twonk as my life simultaneously came together and fell apart.

'Mr Barker,' said a man's voice. It sounded strangely familiar, something in the tone, the stress on the syllables, although I knew I couldn't have known who it was because I didn't know any Australians and this voice definitely had that twang, though with overtones of posh English.

'At your service,' I said.

'You don't know me but I'm making some enquiries into the estate of the late Mrs Cadwaller-Beaufort,' he said.

I went cold, like a dog in the spotlight halfway from the larder with a leg of ham in its mouth.

'Oh yes?' I said.

'You were quite bound up in the whole thing, more than an estate agent normally is, I understand.'

'I tried to help her put her affairs in order,' I said.

'That's what it's about really,' said the voice. 'I'm just running over her books for the sake of a little i dotting and t crossing and I thought you might be able to help me.'

'I'd be delighted,' I said. 'Can I ask who I'm speaking to?'

'Oh, silly me,' said the voice. 'This is her son, Miles Cadwaller-Beaufort.'

That feeling you get when you've stood up too quickly came upon me – largely, I noticed, because I'd stood up rather quickly. I dropped back into my seat like a sweating jack-in-the-box.

'This world wasn't for him,' she'd said. I thought she meant he was dead, not manning the barbi on Bondi.

'Oh,' I said, with the studied casualness that ten years of poker playing teaches. 'You're over for the memorial service.'

'Exactly,' said Miles. 'They put the old girl down so quickly that I didn't have a chance to come over for the funeral and, besides, I was in the middle of a huge case and couldn't get away.'

'Case?' I said, in a register normally only audible to the likes of Reg. He heard it though.

'Indigenous peoples vs Whitehaven mining,' said Miles. 'I do a lot of my work in that neck of the woods nowadays.'

'What sort of work?' I said, as innocently as I could. The last panic like this I'd experienced was when I awoke in a white funk one morning after dreaming I'd forgotten to pay my TV licence. This, I need hardly say, was much worse.

'You're blinking dead, mate,' he said, although a tape recorder wouldn't have heard that. It would have heard the words, 'International property law.'

'Luckily my financial position allows me to do my work for free so I pick and choose good causes. For the last five or so years I've been in South-East Asia and Australasia,' he said. 'I kind of like working from the beach.' This was followed by a warm chuckle of the chillingly manly, never deflected from its purpose sort.

'Worthing has a beach,' was all I could say. He gave me the details of his hotel – the Hotel Hotel at Brighton – and arranged to meet me at the service.

'So that's that then,' I said, scribbling down the address with an automatic hand. 'Can I ask, what happened in your case in Australia?'

'Oh, we won, Mr Barker, we won. We always win. Someone doing something for the love of it will always beat someone doing it for money.'

'Right, see you Friday,' I said, placing down the phone.

'Are you OK, Dave?' said Andy.

'Sort of!' I said with a smile, reaching for my bottle of pills.

28

Who's Sorry Now?

A property lawyer – the words sank in bitterly, like red wine into the new carpet of a man who had refused the Scotchguard option.

For those of you who have never had the fundamental fabric of your existence ripped asunder, let me assure you it is an experience best avoided.

I'd already nearly popped my eyeballs with stress over the previous months after committing a crime – something that had come as naturally to me as unpowered flight – and now I was about to be found out.

I'd kept the newspaper containing the news of Mrs Cad-Beauf's death and now read the last paragraph of the story. 'She leaves one son, the internationally feared property lawyer Miles Cadwaller-Beaufort.' Fear! Fear! Respect wasn't good enough for this guy, he wanted fear.

Taking a long hard look at myself, I realised I had made a number of rather poor decisions based on the original crime, decisions that I would not have been in a position to make had I not committed it, either financially or emotionally.

Number one on the list was getting rid of the dog, as was number two, three and four. An amazing companion and a goldmine too. What had I been thinking of?

The crime itself, I decided, was bound to be discovered. If there was one thing that Miles Cad-Beauf had exuded on the phone it was competence. He had a bit of the Des Lynam 'you're in good hands here' to him, unflappable, intelligent, wise, cool, patient and deadly. I had no problem getting past two on that list.

Action of some sort was imperative, although I couldn't think what.

'I can't tell you over the phone,' I said to Lyndsey, bursting with discomfort, as I strode towards the car park.

I'd skipped the preliminaries and was already on to worrying about the difficulties of explaining to my cell mates that, though I was in for defrauding an old lady, I was basically a good egg who had been terribly misused.

'No one got hurt!' I'd be saying.

'Beg to differ,' would say Mr Big, greasing something unpleasant in the showers.

'You sound awful,' said Lyndsey. 'Are you all right?'

'No,' I said, 'and neither are you or any of us.'

'This isn't some wild stress thing, is it?'

'What do you mean, wild stress thing?'

'Well, you haven't been acting very normally recently, Dave,' said Lyndsey. 'To be frank, if you weren't already on pills I'd recommend you get some pills.'

'The only pills that are going to do me any good are bleeding cyanide!' I said, hissing more than I am commonly wont.

'OK,' said Lyndsey, 'I'll meet you. Where do you suggest?'

'Waterford Woods,' I said. 'The car park.' Already I had conceived the idea that someone might be following me and I wanted to make sure we were out of range of any listening devices.

Lyndsey chuckled. 'You're not going to kill me, are you, Dave?'

'This is serious,' I said. When people say that on the TV they say it in a manly, direct voice. I, however, said it rather like a teenage boy bursting for the loo and begging his sister to stop painting her face and let him in.

Lyndsey was late so I had to wait a good half an hour. For some reason I flattened myself down in the car, as if I didn't want to be seen.

I had as yet no plan and I was hoping Lyndsey would come up with one. The absolutely certain thing was that we would have to repay the money. We'd done him out of millions even if you ruled out the profit on the new estate. Lyndsey and I were personally in it for a million. He was going to take us to the cleaners.

In swept the Discovery, gliding over the pot-holed car park like a hovercraft.

Lyndsey backed in next to me, wound down her window and leaned out.

'What is it?' she said.

'Aren't you going to get out of the car?'

'I'm busy,' she said.

'No you're not,' I said, 'you're not too busy for this.' I got out of the car and went over to her. 'Come on,' I said, 'we're going for a walk.'

'I can't, I've only got these shoes on,' she said.

'You can't fool me,' I said. 'I know there are wellingtons in the back.'

She let out a sigh, exasperated. 'OK, OK. I hope this is going to be worth it.'

'I think it will be worth putting on a pair of wellingtons, yes,' I said.

We headed off into the woods. The hollow at the entrance was a dell of leaves. I remembered watching Reg run across it, his russet and black blending with the floor perfectly as he moved across it like a warp in the light.

'Why do we have to go in here?' said Lyndsey.

On reflection I never intended to kill her – and obviously I didn't. But I think I subconsciously had the idea that the news would drop her to the ground and wanted somewhere convenient to bury her to avoid any nasty explanations.

Woods are where things get buried, aren't they? Or dug up again, if you're a dog.

Whatever, death of some sort was in my mind, if only my own.

We stopped by the pond where Reg used to swim. I remembered the first time he'd been in it. He'd always been afraid of the water, sniffing at its edge as if it was something that had landed from outer space and needed exhaustive tests running on it before any more intimate exploration could be chanced.

Moss often settled on the pond, edging it in a smooth green baize. Dogs have superior senses to humans in almost every way but are easily fooled. He'd stepped tentatively onto the moss, reasoning that green things had always held his weight in the past, why shouldn't they again. As it was, as soon as he'd put a paw on it, the paw sank, barrel-rolling him into the pond with a great cry of, 'I am undone!' This was followed by a lot of splooshing about and a sudden declaration that he was the world's best swimmer. After that you couldn't keep him out of the water.

'Why are we going this far in?' said Lyndsey.

'Because I don't want anyone to overhear us or bug us,' I said.

'Bug us?' said Lyndsey. 'Are you paranoid?'

'Yes,' I said. I was delusional so I didn't see why paranoia should be too far behind.

Lyndsey put her hand on my arm and said, in her kind way, 'Dave, please, what is it?'

I drew in breath. The woods felt cold and desolate. I noticed the trees for the first time, nude of leaves, branches stretched to the heavens like pagan dancers.

'They know,' I said.

'Who knows?' said Lyndsey.

'Mrs Cad-Beauf has a son. He's about to find out about what we did. We're all completely and utterly banjaxed. He's a flipping lawyer. A top dog!'

Lyndsey nodded and blew, her breath a plume. A squirrel looked down at me from a tree. Whatever it was saying to me wasn't as bad as what I was saying to myself.

Lydnsey looked into my eyes, in a way she hadn't in years.

'Well, it's all over, isn't it?' she said. 'We're dead. Everything we've worked for's gone.'

'We've still got each other,' I said, hugging her.

I could feel her vulnerability like a vibration between us, which gave me strength. I had someone to be strong for, and for Lyndsey, if not for me, I needed to face down this crisis.

I saw immediately what needed to be done.

Lyndsey had never signed anything, she'd never deceived anyone, she was blameless. All we had to do was transfer the house to her name only, sign over all the money in the joint bank account to her, transfer the name of the business and the car and everything, and bingo. I might do three years, time off at weekends in an open prison, but we'd have something to build from. With my direction and without my gambling the business overdraft might be handled. Playing for cigarettes inside might be the best place for me, it might actually be the foundation of a feasible life together.

The agency would have to undergo a change of name, I probably wouldn't be allowed to be personally involved in it, but I would have salvaged something.

Lyndsey, of course, didn't want to be in such a position but I made her see the logic of it. I didn't think it wise to spell out the level of the debt she'd be taking on immediately. I knew that I could work it through and leave her financially secure in a couple of years and I didn't want to frighten her at a time when she was so shaken.

'It's going to be OK,' said Lyndsey, holding my hand as we left George's office. George is a solicitor I use all the time for conveyancing and he'd promised me he could get the whole transfer done within a day. She seemed to have taken strength from my trust in her.

'It's good to have this contingency in place,' she said as we withdrew the money from Barker and placed it into Swift, 'but we might be able to talk him out of it. She gave the money to dogs' homes so why does he care if it's ten p. or ten million? He probably just wants a taste and then it's Michael the Cat's problem.'

This was Lyndsey all over. After the sudden shock she'd rallied and was already thinking of the future.

'And you know how Michael deals with problems,' said Lyndsey.

'Can I expressly say I'd rather go to jail than have him murdered,' I said as I filled out a form to transfer all the standing orders and direct debits.

Lyndsey sniffed. 'I'm sure it won't come to that,' she said as she watched me fill out the forms. She kissed me on the cheek. 'Love you like crazy,' she said.

'Love you like crazy,' I said.

29

Funeral Wrongs

The Church of St. Nicholas at Faresham Down was built by the Normans, in rather a more substantial way than Tibbs was building our luxury homes, it has to be said.

To see an English church on a clear winter's day can almost make you believe in God. It doesn't lead you to thoughts of the ethereal, though, like a cathedral's stained glass hanging in the vesper smoke, but to thoughts of the rooted and the fixed, a very palpable manifestation of the eternal in buttress and arch, tower and spire. It was here yesterday, it is here today, and it will be here tomorrow, an unmoving island in the living stream.

Of course, only two old ladies and a Peke ever go outside of the main festivals, weddings and funerals, but that, too, is reassuring.

It's as if religion has found its place, discreetly hovering at the side of our lives without really ever being mentioned. The Church of England knows its station and it knows religion belongs to the periphery. Look at the Archbishop of Canterbury – he hardly ever mentions it.

The proper place for religion is of course America. This is where we shipped the religious lunatics all those years ago and where they have prospered. It was in fact part of the deal for independence that they had to keep them. 'You get the vast resources of land, minerals and labour, you get the destiny of the modern age, but you agree to take the religious nutters. You do? Crikey, deal done, strike up the sail, bo'sun, before they change their minds.'

So the church doesn't bother the people and the people don't bother the church. Occasionally the odd parish priest comes along who will keep going on about God but then the parishioners complain in an 'if we're going to suffer this then what was the point of the *Mayflower*?' kind of way and he's told to hold his tongue and concentrate on judging jam at fêtes.

The Church of England wasn't going to fall to its own ambitions, it wasn't going to over-reach itself in fraudulent miracles, it wasn't going to get talked into betraying its principles by a bunch of dodgy poker players and its girlfriend.

I was surprised to see quite a turnout for the memorial. I'd been under the impression that Mrs Cad-Beauf had few friends but there were around thirty people waiting outside the church, along with about six dogs.

I was not surprised, though, to clap eyes on the two women I'd encountered at Charterstone when I'd helped move Mrs Cad-Beauf. I recognised them instantly, despite their smart black.

Even seeing them made me slink. I didn't know how I was going to face Miles Cad-Beauf.

The church stood in its own grounds opposite a pub, which was lucky because I managed to fortify myself with a swift whisky before the service.

I left the pub at the last possible minute, ten twenty-eight, giving me two minutes to make it to the church. I'd said I'd see Miles Cad-Beauf after the service and I didn't want to risk seeing him before.

As I crossed the narrow lane between pub and church and was making my way up the path, I saw him greeting people at the door.

I knew it was him straightaway because the family resemblance was absolute; it was as if his mother had lost thirty pounds, got a suntan and donned a dark suit.

Poker teaches you to keep cool when things are hot. Poker, however, is not the real world. It's a smoke-filled pod floating through reality, a zone where, for the bitten gambler at least, nothing means anything outside of it. Things only begin to mean something when you step outside that pod and then they mean hard. Marriages dissolve, cars are repossessed, mortgages fail.

Poker players, poker players like me, don't know how to act in the world of real meaning. That's why we play poker.

It's much more comforting than the blurred edges of the reality, where you don't deal with people as competitors but as friends, and where you have to deal with them not just with better cards or pretend better cards but with wit, compassion, empathy, intelligence and care for their welfare. All the hard stuff of kindness.

And even if you get that hard stuff right, maybe you still won't get to feel good about yourself. Which is why we find the unwashed, the unwanted, the ugly and the afraid, the hollow men and the stuffed men meeting across card tables from Sydney to Scarborough. Men like poker for the same reason they like war – or the idea of war: 'Oh, I have to shoot him, do I? Well, that's one social situation I can understand.'

So I was shaking. I tried to imagine myself with three kings – even in my fantasies I can't get as unrealistic as four aces – trying to bluff a man I was sure had only a pair. Still my hands wouldn't stop shaking.

I made my way down the path and was about to take a sharp right, skip the service and meet him afterwards when he came towards me.

'Mr Barker?' he said.

'Yes,' I said, now truly trembling.

'I thought it would be you,' he said. 'You have quite the air of the estate agent about you.'

This chilled me slightly because no one has ever said that to me before. People often assume I'm a social worker or a nurse if they meet me out of my suit, a teacher if they meet me in it. I'd never had someone spot me for what I am before.

'Thanks,' I said, noting that he looked more affable than I'd have expected for an avenging angel.

'Come on in,' he said, 'the service's about to begin.' Where his mother had been vague, always giving the impression of searching for the right words, her conversation carving abrupt turns of direction, her son conveyed clarity and precision of thought. Which was not what I'd wanted at all. I felt like I was in the dock when I was in the open air with him. How would I feel when I was in the dock?

I went into the church and sat down at the back. I could see the dogs had been positioned at the front, each provided with a bowl of water.

The vicar stood up and said a few words about how he'd known Mrs Cad-Beauf for nearly thirty years and then said a few more which made it sound like he hadn't. I suppose habits stick and the practice of eulogising people he didn't know had come to inform his style when eulogising people he did.

'She was a worker,' he said, 'and a tireless campaigner for the rights of animals.'

A couple of dogs nodded assent. The pills were at it again.

'She had a kind word for everyone and a fierce streak of independence that saw her live on her own until it became impossible.'

I looked about the congregation. There were indeed people of every stripe – dog ladies who even in funeral black had something of the fur-stuck tweed about them, Aia Napa and her boyfriend who'd literally just come down from the trees, a couple of old folks in wheelchairs, Julie from the dogs' home who was lowering herself in her seat to avoid my seeing her.

'That she was persuaded to leave her beloved Charterstone at the last will be the cause of regret to some and it is the opinion of many who knew her that this contributed to her death. That is not for me to speculate,' he said, as many people do, having speculated.

I felt as embarrassed as a cuckoo hearing its host sparrows trying to work out which one of them it most resembled. I felt my leg tapping, as it often does when I don't want to be somewhere – preparing to leave even though my brain is telling it to stay. Whatever, I wished the vicar had stuck to his off-the-peg memorial service speech: kind and compassionate once you dug beneath the surface, a great watcher of television, a lover of the good things in life – crisps, nuts and beer – not afraid to make their opinions known even when their opinions were already known, that sort of thing. I was thinking about my dad's mate Phil – he who had been dead in front of the test match for hours before his wife noticed. Cold as a kipper when they found him.

The vicar sat down, a hymn was mouthed and the old woman I'd seen at the house stood up.

I expected it right in the ear at that point but she just stood composing herself for a second before saying a few words about how she'd known the Cad-Beaufs as a family since she was a girl and how kind they'd been to her over the years.

Then we were on – par for the course – to 'The Lord Is My Shepherd'. For some reason this made me wonder what subsidies the Lord was getting from the European Union. The stress was causing my mind to wander.

She then read out a poem, which had been written by the fourteen-year-old Miles Cad-Beauf about how much their dog

Flavius liked chasing squirrels. It was, said the woman, a particular favourite of Mrs Cad-Beauf's.

> We'd have squirrel pie for tea
> If a dog could climb a tree
> We'd be wearing squirrel fur
> If we possessed an arboreal cur
> But luckily our hound
> Is rooted to the ground
> So the squirrels, though molested,
> Go wholly undigested.

That's a public school education for you – trotting out words like arboreal at roughly the age we comprehensive pupils were still struggling with joined-up writing.

I looked glumly about the church. There were shields on the walls, each with the name of local dignitaries on them going back to thirteen hundred and something or other. Had these people been men of honour? I wondered. Or had they been like me and Tibbs – breakers of rules, suiters of selves?

The woman said something more about a life well-lived, complained about the desolation being wreaked on the Charterstone estate and sat down. A prayer was said.

We were then on, with grim inevitability, to 'All Things Bright And Beautiful'. After we'd avowed, with generous lip movement and little noise, for the umpteenth time that the lord God made them all, Miles Cad-Beauf stood up, bright but ugly.

He smiled.

'Things pass,' he said, 'this much is certain. Regret and grief are the foundations upon which the hope and love of new generations must build, as trees sprout from the leaf mould.'

Obviously the poetic inclination had not left him, even if the poetry had.

'So in the death of my mother and the passing of her way of

life I can still find joy. Joy that she lived to see her grandchildren and be close to them.'

Oh God, there were grandchildren. I'd shafted them as well, had I?

'Joy that she was able to bring so much happiness to those around her and so much relief to the animals that she and I love. Joy even that the old estate is to provide homes for as many people as my great-grandfather intended, if not the sort he intended it for, and will be where children will grow to know themselves, to love and be loved.

'My mother's life was not a success in the modern understanding of the term. She made no greater fortune from the fortune that she had, she didn't influence the course of events of history, she made no mark on politics.

'However, it seems to me that, as she often said, we can learn a lot from the dogs. They achieve nothing in the public sphere, they do not speculate or accumulate, they have no ambitions beyond a meal and walk.

'And yet what do we love more than we love a dog? It may be because we can read our own thoughts and emotions onto the blank canvas of their furry faces.'

I saw what he meant, although how something could be canvas and fur simultaneously eluded me. I was concentrating on his words, rather than on what he was saying, in the hope that their meaning would somehow pass me by, fail to penetrate.

'But more, it is because the dog realises a fundamental truth of our existence on this planet – that our strength is not in ourselves but in others, in our friends; that there is no greater thing than love returned.'

I saw Reg's face in my mind, his twisting leaps for a bad bounce on a ball, remembered his enthusiasm bursting from him as the car approached the woods. And I remembered him calling me a fool too.

Miles Cad-Beauf was still speaking, words that made me conclude Reg was right, I was a fool.

'So, like her dogs, my mother loved and was loved and that seems to me to be the definition of a meaningful life. Everything else, who you are, where you live, what you do, is just detail.'

He was choking up a little at this stage and, I have to say, so was I. Ironically I'd felt protective towards Mrs Cad-Beauf, yet I was the person she had most needed protecting from.

Miles put his notes down.

'I just wanted to say, I love you, Mum, and I'm sorry I wasn't here for you when you needed me. But I'm here now and I promise that I'll make sure that the work you started and the gifts you wanted to make do all the good you intended.'

I felt a tear loop from my eye, I have to say, but there was something of a hard edge to his voice in the last sentence that I didn't like. Also unpleasant was the fact that he seemed to be looking directly at me.

The service finished with a mezzo singing in Italian a song entitled, somewhat unambiguously for English tastes, 'Death'. One of the Alsatians in the front row went funny, taking on the appearance of being stuffed, as the high notes were reached.

We filed out of the church and into the grounds.

I stood like a spare sadness at a funeral towards the edge of the group, looking up at the sky of the clear blue day and wondering if death brought understanding, if the dead became part of God, omniscient and repaired. Had Mrs Cad-Beauf's confusion over cash disappeared with her passing over, I wondered, and was her angry ghost now looking down at me with a full grasp of the figures?

I looked around to see if anyone else was smoking. Luckily they were and I lit up respectfully, drawing myself to the cold shadows at the side of the church.

This is where he found me, fuming in the penumbra like a Next-clad Mephistopheles.

'Mr Barker,' said Miles Cad-Beauf. This was his mother's common form of address. 'Thank you for waiting until the service was over, it must have been quite a trial.' I think he might have been talking about my cigarette.

'Not at all,' I said. 'I liked your mother and I'd have come even if you hadn't specifically asked me to.'

He pursed his lips and gave a curt nod. 'I've been too long away to remember English niceties,' he said.

'Oh dear,' I said, which gave away more of my true feelings than I usually like to.

'Oh dear indeed,' he said. 'I'll come to the point.'

'That wasn't the point?' I felt like saying. It had seemed pretty pointy to me.

'There were clearly some irregularities in the sale of my mother's property.'

'Irregularities,' I said, nodding.

'Flipping great ones,' he said, raising his eyebrows to emphasise what was already a fairly emphatic statement.

'Flipping great ones,' I said.

'In short, the property was sold for a fraction of its true value. As you were the agent in charge of its sale, you are largely culpable for that.'

'Culpable for that,' I said. I felt as if my whole body was made of something at once solid and pliable, like a ruler twanged upon a desk, and was just bouncing back his words as he threw them at me.

'I suspect you were not alone in this enterprise and so it's my intention to bring down you and your whole gang.'

'My whole gang,' I said. I'm not a criminal by nature, only by deed. Anyone observing me at that moment could have seen this because, what with the service and Reg and everything, I began to cry. Not just the odd repressed tear but swollen great sobs.

This was clearly not what he'd expected. Perhaps he'd thought me a brazen crook who would stand there and damn him to do his worst. He didn't expect the guilty nine-year-old act and, to tell the truth, neither had I.

'Are you OK?' said Miles, looking closely at me.

'Pretty obviously not,' I said. 'I didn't mean to get involved in any of this. I'm not a crook.' I know that's a pathetic thing to say but there again at least I was being consistent. I'd been pathetic when I'd agreed to defraud Mrs Cad-Beauf, I'd been pathetic when I'd got rid of the dog, I was being pathetic in my reaction to my exposure.

'What we mean doesn't count,' said Miles. 'It's what we do. You've acted like a crook so you are a crook. And you'll go to gaol like a crook. Now if you'll excuse me I've got decent people to attend to.'

'I'll help you in whatever way I can,' I said as he went back into the throng, but I'm not sure he heard.

30

Party's Over

'Come on, baby,' said Lyndsey, 'we need to be strong in this together.' Since becoming a developer she'd had more chance to watch morning TV and this, I think, was colouring her way of speaking. 'He's not going to the police. If he was he'd have gone already and he wouldn't have warned you. He wants a slice, that's all, and he's manoeuvring you into a position where you'll give him a big one.' She gave me a little peck on the forehead.

'There might be another explanation,' I said. I was drinking from the big mug with no handle that I'd brought from the office when we moved.

'What's that?' said Lyndsey, fiddling with the cooker. We'd got one of those new stainless steel ones and neither of us could work out the timer. As far as I could see it wasn't linked to any of the buttons on the fascia, more to will. If you wanted it to come on it wouldn't come on and if you didn't, it would. You could come down in the middle of the night for a drink of water to see it cooking nothing, or some phantom pie. The idea was that Lyndsey would put an M&S lasagne in in the morning, it would begin cooking at six and it would be ready when we came in at six thirty.

'He might have wanted to see me in the flesh because he's used to dealing with big tough corporations and being completely nerveless no matter who he confronts. He might want to rattle us and make it personal right from the start. He might want to get the measure of his opponent, to smell his fear on him.'

'Ah ha!' said Lyndsey as the cooker's light came on. 'I'd go for the first explanation if I was a betting woman.' She let out a sigh of exasperation as the light in the cooker went off again. 'Don't worry about it,' she said. 'Where's he staying?'

'The Hotel Hotel in Brighton,' I said.

'Right.' She smiled cheerfully. 'I'll go and sort things out for us. I'll meet him.'

'Phone me straightaway to tell me what he says,' I said. In truth I'd given up. I didn't want Lyndsey to sort anything out. I wanted him to go to the police and for me to be punished and, through taking my punishment, to be redeemed. However, at these times you are capable of thinking of escape and surrender simultaneously. I watched Lyndsey get into the Land Rover and head off for the hotel as an estate agent brushed past me with a couple of his clients. We still had three months to go on the show home deal.

It was Christmas Eve and the sleet was promising to turn to snow. At that time of year even the midday carries hints of evening and lights were on across the remains of the building site and in the big house.

I looked at my watch. Twelve thirty. In half an hour I was due at the office annual piss-up. I felt as unlike an annual piss-up as one possibly can this side of major liver disease. I couldn't face drinking and I was afraid that once I'd had a couple I wouldn't be able to face anything else. I called a cab anyway, just in case I decided to neck the obligatory skinful.

The cab cut out through the Downs towards Worthing and my thoughts turned to Reg. I know it's sentimental to picture a dog all alone in a dogs' home on Christmas Eve but a dog all alone in a dogs' home on Christmas Eve is sentimental, for God's sake.

He should have been at home with me, or waiting for me to come back, excited by the smells from the presents, pushing his nose towards the top of a cupboard where his wrapped bone lay.

And, in defence of sentimentality, a hard heart hadn't got me very far, had it? If, when I'd met Mrs Cad-Beauf, I'd managed to hold on to the thought, 'Boo hoo, she's only a poor old lady, living on her own with no one looking after her in the whole wide world,' then I wouldn't have discovered that she did have someone to look after her, in fact someone capable of looking after almost anyone, and be facing a ten stretch as a result.

I couldn't go and see Reg, though, I couldn't do that to myself or to him. I would soon be inside, I could almost taste it, no matter what Lyndsey said. I couldn't look after him now if I wanted to.

The cab pulled up at Worthing outside Red Al's Blue Nacho Palace, a new and cavernous Mexican joint on the seafront. The Christmas parties were in full swing, kazoos were being blown, margaritas consumed, the odd pair of tits exposed, fun had. I looked at my watch. One thirty. I was late.

I looked through the decorations and the banners to find our table. There it was – the grown team, a sight to make any boss swell with pride. There was Andy and Drew and Andrew, the three agents, both in regulation paper hat and ties askew. There was Maisy, the work experience girl who, by the look of Drew's body language, would by the end of the evening have the work experience of shitting on her own doorstep.

There were both the cleaners, attempting to drink their considerable weight. I felt their care like a load upon me. Once again it was a strain to pay the wages. We'd recruited in times of boom, or oodles of poker cash, and now we were having to pay in times of bust, poker debt.

There also, to my surprise, was Lucy.

A cheer went up as I stepped past a couple of fat suits who were dancing like tormented bears and made my way to the table.

'Here he is, the boss!' said Andy.

'Sit down, mate, let's get you a drink as you're paying,' said Drew. They were good lads really, harmless profit-focused sharks who would prosper in the business.

'Hello, stranger!' I said to Lucy.

'Thought I'd drop by,' she said. I hadn't seen her after Reg had gone away. It would have been a bit too painful.

'Are you OK?' said Lucy.

'If I had a quid for everyone who asks me that question nowadays I could give up this game,' I said, as Drew poured me a margarita, his attention totally on Maisy.

Lucy spoke quietly. 'And if I had a quid for every time you've answered it I'd still be skint,' she said.

I smiled at her, putting on my paper crown LIKE A FUCKING KING! Sorry. I guess I was carrying a bit more tension there than I'd thought.

'I'm OK,' I said.

'Good. It's just that you haven't seemed the same since. You know.'

'I know,' I said. She and I had never spoken of Reg's departure. What would have been the point? Nothing could change, it was like prodding a bruise and saying, 'Yes, still bad as ever, that really hurts.'

Three men at separate parts of Big Al's were doing Monty Python sketches. Two Spanish Inquisitions and one 'A nod's as good as a wink to a blind bat'. I wondered how many there would be by the end of the evening. I felt somehow parochial. In slicker towns they'd be doing *The Office* or *Phoenix Nights*.

'What do you think came over him?' said Lucy.

'I think he had his heart broken,' I said. In truth I'd only had a couple of sips of my drink and didn't have an excuse for such schmaltz, but that's what I thought. It's still what I think.

'I miss him, don't you?' said Lucy.

'Yes,' I said, looking into the depths of my drink. 'I miss him.'

I finished the margarita and ordered another couple of buckets of it. The great thing about Big Al's appeared to be that there was an absolute guarantee of getting drunk. These weren't your tiny designer buckets either. They were the sort of thing that could see many years' service on a working farm.

'Today, Lucy,' I said, 'I intend to get slaughtered.'

I wanted to tell her everything, about how Reg had spoken to me, about how I'd conned myself into defrauding Mrs Cad-Beauf, about the Cat and the fact that I just couldn't seem to sleep in the new house.

I am no experienced pot walloper and I actually realised how powerful a bucket of margarita can be. Had I known, I think I might have stopped after just the one.

All I can remember of the meal is Lucy's disembodied voice saying to me, 'Where do you think he is now?' and me not being able to reply.

At four o'clock my phone rang and I answered it. It was Lyndsey.

'We need to talk,' she said.

'I need to be able to talk,' I said, somewhat drunkenly into the mouthpiece. Lucy seemed to have disappeared, as had two or three of the other staff. Only the cleaners were still polishing off the margaritas.

'Love you like crazy, Lynds!' I said rather too loudly. One of the cleaners said, 'Ahh!' as cleaners are wont to do.

'We still need to talk,' she said.

'We're all at Big Al's,' I said. 'Come on down and have a drink with us.'

'I know where you are, you told me this morning,' she said. 'I'm outside now.'

'Well, come on in then!'

'I think you'd better come out,' she said.

The cold air hit me like a rain of mackerel, leaving me feeling greasy inside my skin.

There's something about transferring from inside to outside when you're drunk that scrambles the senses. My mum always used to maintain it was the air. At Christmas she'd warn guests not to drink too much because 'you might be all right in here, but you wait until that air hits you'.

I don't think it's just the air, although I agree there's an effect. I think it's all about context. Drunks aren't very good at seeing themselves in any context other than the one they're in – 'I am full of righteous anger', for instance, being more understandable to them than 'I am full of Guinness'. So any change of context at all is as difficult to cope with as the biggest you could imagine. When the drunk finds himself out of the bar and on the street, his difficulty in coping will be no different to what it would have been had he found himself deposited naked on the start-finish straight at the Monaco Grand Prix just after the five big lights had gone out, or fixing a pipeline twenty metres down in the North Sea underneath a force niner.

I stood on the pavement, the world whirring in the bright lamplight, my legs slightly bent not so much with the alcoholic effect of the margarita but with its weight.

Lyndsey wasn't drunk. This isn't normally a cause for comment. I'm not normally drunk so the fact that Lyndsey isn't doesn't matter. At that moment, however, I was drunk and so it mattered a lot.

You don't have to be disapproving, you don't have to be angry, all you need is not to be drunk for the drunk to start apologising to you.

'I'm terribly sorry,' I said.

'No,' said Lyndsey, 'it's me who should be sorry.'

We stood looking at each other. I couldn't quite form the exact words I needed. Even in my margarita mullahed state I could see that her eyes were filling up.

'It's worse than I feared,' said Lyndsey. 'It's worse than I could have even imagined.'

'What worst?' I said. I was possessed of an overpowering urge to giggle.

'He's launching a civil case first,' she said. 'That way he gets his money back quicker. When that's done and the money's obtained, he's going to go for criminal convictions. Dave, I'm so sorry.'

'It's OK,' I said. I came forward and I held myself in her arms. 'Isn't the Cat going to do anything?' I mean, I obviously hoped he wouldn't but I thought it only fair to warn Miles Cad-Beauf if there was a murdering moggie on the prowl.

'You can't play by those rules with people like him,' she said. 'He went to school with half the judges in England. He's friends with the Home Secretary. It's not like he won't be missed.'

Threats tend to sober you up rather quickly. I've always thought this is because while the higher, human, brain parties, the older, reptilian, brain keeps itself straight, just in case it has to scarper pretty quickly. When someone has drunk enough to begin to overwhelm even this ancient structure, it just shuts the whole thing down and gets the body to lie on the floor with the hope it won't draw attention to itself.

'What are we going to do, Lynds?' I said.

I sensed it before I even saw it in her face.

'You're bailing out, aren't you?'

Lyndsey gulped. I could see this wasn't easy for her.

'It's just that I have to look after myself, Dave,' she said, with tenderness, her hand on my shoulder. 'I don't want it to be like this but it has to be. It was finishing between us anyway.'

'How was it finishing?' I said. 'I've done everything for you, I've put your happiness in front of mine time and again.' The accusation was clumsy but I felt clumsy, physically and mentally. I didn't know why I hadn't seen this coming.

'Perhaps you shouldn't have,' she said. Her voice was understanding and soft. 'We have to face it, Dave, we're not alike.'

'So why did you go out with me? Why did you move in with me and make me get rid of my dog?'

'Because I thought it might work. Because I thought we might love each other fully, but we can't, can we? You loved that dog more than you ever loved me.'

'Well, I loved him an awful lot,' I said. 'I mean that left me room to love you one under an awful lot.' I could see this wasn't helping.

'It's over, Dave. I don't want a man who can't open his heart to me.'

'Or his wallet,' I said.

'There's no need to be bitter,' said Lyndsey.

'But you're leaving me with a house that's about to be sequestered, a bank account that's going to be grabbed . . .'

'I'm not leaving you with anything,' she said. 'All that stuff is mine now.' She sounded rather proud of the fact.

'So what do I get? Nothing?'

She shrugged. I could see I'd hurt her and I guessed she'd want some payback.

'Well, to be honest, you haven't got any use for anything for the next few years, have you? You'll be going to prison and that's that.' She smiled, looking sadly at me. 'I'm not abandoning you. Who knows, in five or ten years or whatever it is, I may have made my fortune. Look me up and I'll help you out, I'll give you a start. I promise.'

'You're taking my business off me?' I said.

'Before you take it off yourself. Oh Dave, I wish you could see yourself. You've been letting yourself go so badly and – I don't know if I should say this.' She looked into the air, waiting for the permission she knew I couldn't refuse to give.

'Go on.'

'I chanced upon your building society book the other day.' That one at least was in credit, having no facility to be otherwise.

'You chanced upon it in my safe,' I said.

She shrugged. 'You left it open. It was as if you wanted to be caught. You've lied to me, David, you've spent thousands when I've been scrimping. How much of a couple does that make us?'

'I was . . .' But the words wouldn't come.

She was right, I supposed. Looked at from one way she was a rat fleeing a sinking ship. Looked at from another, she was a rat on a desert island, seeing the plume of a steamer on the horizon and thinking, 'After three long years I'm rescued!' I mean, I'd treated her badly, hadn't I?

I'd loved her after my way, I'd tried to indulge her but there had always been an unmeltable core of me that I had kept back from her – the gambling. I don't know why that was.

'I was . . .' What was I doing, locked in poker rooms throwing away thousands while the things that mattered were left to rot?

'Do you love me?' I said.

'Yes,' said Lyndsey.

'Like crazy?'

'I wouldn't go that far,' said Lyndsey. She sniffed. 'You're very kind and I know a lot of men wouldn't put up with me the way I am and I'm grateful for that. But there comes a time when no matter how much you love someone you have to walk away. I can't lie to you and say I'll wait, Dave. It's back to how it's always been really – Lyndsey against the world. And for that I need all the ammunition I can get. How much money have you got in your pockets?'

'Two hundred quid,' I said. I'd been thinking of dropping in on Snake Eyes' game.

'I don't feel too bad then,' she said.

Time seemed to bubble again. The next thing I remember she'd got into the Discovery and was gone.

A seaside town in the rain is a terrible thing. The pleasure palaces, the vacant ice-cream stands, the dismal beach – all reminders of the fun that you are not having. It's all here, it seems to say, but not for you. It's here for some luckier soul on some sunnier day.

Lucy was at my arm. 'There you are,' she said. 'Come and dance! You'll catch your death out here. Come in and dance.'

Suddenly the years behind seemed to evaporate, those in front seemed a waste of breath. There was only one thing that mattered in the world. I took my pills out of my pocket and threw them into the road.

'Reg,' I said, 'I'm coming to get you.'

31

Down Boy

Lucy who, in common with the rest of humanity, had not drunk as much as me that evening, sounded a practical note.

'Taking the bus is too slow,' she said. 'Let's hit the cab rank.'

It was four thirty, dark, with a wet wind coming in off the English Channel. Somewhere in France, I thought, there are people from the olive groves of the Mediterranean trying to sneak into this country. A mad world.

We tore round to the rank. This being Christmas, a large sign had been erected at its front: 'If you are sick in a cab the cleaning charge is £80.'

'League for Canine Advancement, Patcham!' I shouted at the first cabbie.

He looked up from his paper. 'Are you going to be sick in my cab?' he said.

'No,' I said. I felt fine, suddenly more sober, though not sober.

Even though it was Christmas Eve, business looked slow. He glanced down the rank. Patcham was £20 away and he clearly wanted the money.

'OK,' he said, 'but would you hold this newspaper on your lap.'

I did as I was bid and we sped along the amber avenues to our furry goal.

'Is everything OK between you and Lyndsey?' said Lucy.

'Never better,' I said.

'You always say that,' said Lucy.

'Well, for once I mean it,' I said. 'I've dumped the cow.'

This wasn't strictly true of course but it's how it felt. Ever since she'd given me the 'it's not you, it's me' line I'd felt a rare electricity coursing through my veins. I know she hadn't actually given me exactly that line – in fact it was nearer to the 'it's not me, it's you' school of finishing – but I wasn't thinking that clearly.

The sleet had begun again but this time it had made an effort and was trying to do a reasonable impression of snow. Every year I say that it doesn't feel like Christmas. Suddenly it did, a large wave of Yule breaking over me from the brightly decorated car showroom to my left to the 'every year we go madder' illuminated sled on the roof of a house to my right. Despite my impending doom I was starting to feel happy.

What could be better, I thought, here in this pod of festive glee known as a cab, with the lovely Lucy, going to rescue my best mate from a day of cold dog food and the conversation of pit bulls.

Actually Reg had told me that pit bulls are nice dogs whose chief aim is working for racial harmony. They only turn on their owners when they get sick of the bullshit they're spouting.

What could be better? A future could have been better, I suppose, but I didn't feel like thinking of the future. I felt as inseparable from the instant as the chill from the breeze.

We squelched up outside the LCA and I leapt from the cab. 'Twenty pounds!' said the cabbie, like a man who had had his faith in humanity vindicated.

They were still open, or at least not closed, as they were having their Christmas party in-house – the sounds of 'Rockin' Around The Christmas Tree' blaring out into the night.

I held Lucy's hand as we burst across the threshold.

'I've come for my dog!' I announced to the room.

This was somewhat unfortunate as the room consisted of the manager Julie and a boy I recognised as one of the student volunteers. Everyone else had gone home, it appeared, without bothering to clear up the party, and the student, who I was to learn was a nice chap called Dan who did English Literature at Sussex University, had taken the opportunity to satisfy his curiosity about the exact appearance of Julie's tits.

From where I was standing he wouldn't have been disappointed. However, the fact that I was standing there meant that he was going to be disappointed, at least temporarily.

'Ah,' I said. 'I've come to take Reg back, I've changed my mind.'

Julie placed her breasts back inside her jumper without fuss, like an aunt might close a diary upon being disturbed.

'Mr Barker, we are closed,' she said, 'as you can doubtless see.'

'The gaffe's shut man,' said Dan, who was clearly trying some Martian just in case we hadn't understood it in English.

'I'm aware of that,' I said, 'but this is an emergency. I need to reclaim my dog before Christmas morning.'

'Have you been in some sort of fight?' said Julie.

'He's been under a lot of stress recently,' said Lucy.

'And not afraid to share it!' said Julie, standing up.

'My dog, madam, and no flim-flammery!' I said.

'You are aware that he was considered a very dangerous dog, Mr Barker?'

'He bustin' it!' said Dan, who had clearly not noticed my lack of antennae or ray gun.

'I'm aware of that,' I said, 'but—'

Lucy put her hand on my arm heavily. I turned to see her open-mouthed.

'You said "was",' she said. 'You haven't . . .'

Julie shrugged. I felt a jolt in the motion of the earth, like that feeling you get when you think your train has been pulling out of the station and suddenly the train opposite disappears and you find you've been standing still all along.

'Well, what did you expect?' she said.

'He went this morning,' said Dan and for the first time I thought I understood him perfectly

'We have to consider every management option possible in difficult cases,' said Julie. 'We really had no alternative.'

It was as if all the drunkenness in my body had distilled like sediment into my legs, leaving my head clear but my knees heavy.

'But he was so young,' said Lucy.

'Well, that was part of the attraction,' said Julie.

'What do you mean, you monster?' I said.

Julie rearranged her jumper again. Tits are pretty much in or out of a jumper, there's not much of a half measure, but it was as if she wanted to make sure.

'It wasn't me that got rid of him in the first place, Mr Barker. Speaking honestly, if it were not for your association with Mrs Cad-Beauf and her bequest we wouldn't have extended to you the hospitality that we did. A dog is disposed of or not. Visiting rights do not enter into the equation.' She had the tone of a woman who was unused to being called a monster but who might be prepared to let it go this once.

'When did it happen?' I said.

'Just this morning,' said Julie. 'We normally have an absolute embargo on that sort of thing at Christmas but since Reg was such a difficult dog we thought we should strike while the iron was hot.'

'You got rid of him at Christmas?' I said.

'Well, I'm not proud of that,' she said, 'but needs must occasionally.'

'Needs must?' I said.

'Well, he was costing us rather a lot in Pedigree Chum,' said Julie, who I could see had come to the end of her tether with me.

'And he's gone to a very nice family,' said Dan, suddenly lucid. 'They're psychiatrists and willing to work with him.'

'You mean he's still alive!' I said.

'Yes,' said Julie. 'We don't put dogs down here, although we are very loath to authorise placements leading up to Christmas. A dog is for life, after all.'

'I take back the monster,' I said, even though she'd given me a slightly sharp 'dog is for life'.

'Consider it forgotten,' said Julie, with a gracious half-bow.

'Well, if you'll just give me the address of the people who've got him I'll go round and explain the misunderstanding.'

'Misunderstanding?' said Julie. 'There hasn't been a misunderstanding, Mr Barker. Quite the reverse. There is an understanding between our home and the new family that their details remain confidential.'

'Yes, but he's my dog,' I said, trying to make the situation as plain as I could.

'Not any more, I'm afraid,' said Julie with a conversation-closing tone that indicated she was keen to get back to having her breasts fondled by a man half her age.

'Just hand over the details,' I said, 'or I'll spill the beans.'

'What beans?'

'On you and him and your breasts.'

'There are no beans to be spilled on my breasts,' said Julie with dignity. 'I am the manager and I can be here with who I like for as long as I like.'

'Not for rumpy pumpy,' I said, tightly. 'Now the address, if you please.'

Julie looked deep in thought for a second. Then, as if coming to a conclusion that she knew she'd put her finger on eventually, she said politely, 'Piss off.'

'Look,' I said, trying grovelling, 'I've made a mistake. I've thrown away something I was meant to keep and now I need it back, if there's to be any hope for me at all in this world. I've been striving for the wrong stuff for too long. I need him back.'

Julie was a kind woman and could see, I think, that I hadn't meant to offend her, that I was just desperate.

'There's absolutely nothing I can do,' she said, 'even if I wanted to. The Data Protection Act.'

Lucy spoke. 'What does the Data Protection Act say about love?'

'Nothing,' said Julie. 'Look, if I could help, I would, but I can't. I'd like to but sorry.'

I would myself have been prepared to sit it out, to wait there until she gave in which, looking at the sort of woman Julie appeared to be, might have been an extremely long time.

As it was, Lucy said, 'Come on, Dave. There's more than one way of skinning a cat. Get back in the car.'

We went back out into the car park, to the world in white. The sleet had given up being miserable, had had a couple too many, got into the Christmas spirit and turned to snow.

Snow on Christmas Eve, someone you'd always cared for at your side, the cold bringing out your inner warmth, everything as it was meant to be, everything except the thing that mattered most in the world.

I then realised something else was wrong.

'We don't have a car,' I said.

'No,' said Lucy, 'we don't, do we? Follow me.'

She ducked round the side of the building and into the shadow of a large tree.

I realised how cold I was, in my thin suit. When you live your life in a car you have little need for a coat.

The snow fell in extravagant flakes.

'Do you mind if I warm up to you?' said Lucy.

'I'd be grateful,' I said.

I put my arms round her and held her tight. She snuggled into my chest.

Then, it seemed an involuntary gesture, I put my hand on her head.

She looked up at me.

'You look an awful mess,' she said and kissed me on the lips.

I returned her kiss and, as the lights in the main block were dimmed, the night burst out in a choir of barking. The low moon shone fat and yellow, like a shiny brass button on the greatcoat of the night.

'I didn't expect that,' I said, meaning the kiss rather than the moon doing the button thing.

Lucy laughed, a suppressed chuckle I'd never heard from her before, like someone opening a funny email as the boss walked past.

'You were the only one who didn't,' she said. 'I think that dog had worked it out by the end.'

'Actually . . .' I said.

She kissed me again, warm lips and cold nose. This would be taken for a sign of health in a dog, I'm glad to say that I didn't think that at the time.

'Can I ask you a question?' said Lucy.

'Yes.'

'How did you stay with that bitch for so long?'

'I don't know,' I said. 'She was kind to me sometimes.'

'Don't you deserve someone who's kind to you all the time?'

I couldn't answer her, or rather I could. Some relationships are like skin-tight jeans. It's only when you've been out of them for a while that you can wonder what you were ever doing in them. They seem so logical at the time, despite what your friends say.

When had my relationship with Lyndsey finished? It had

never begun. We'd always been two individuals, separate and self-sufficient. Which is what I thought I'd wanted, all I thought I could manage really, until I'd met the dog.

I held Lucy tight. 'I can't believe you can forgive me for the whole Charterstone thing,' I said.

'You only bought a house,' she said.

'I mean the fraud.'

'What fraud?' said Lucy.

'Selling it to developers for the price of a packet of fags,' I said. 'I thought that's why you left work.'

'I left because I saw Lyndsey's ring,' she said. 'I could see you were engaged so I thought there was no hope for me. What's this fraud?'

So I told her. Everything.

'Good grief,' she said, which didn't seem quite adequate to the revelation she was facing. 'You're a crap criminal aren't you?'

'I can't see a way out of it,' I said.

'Get the dog, then go on the run,' said Lucy. 'Assume a different identity and start somewhere else anew. I'll help you.'

'You've got your course,' I said.

'English literature?' she said. 'I'm getting a bit sick of learning fancy conversation. I'd rather be with you and the dog. We're going to get him back.'

'What do you plan to do?' I said.

'Break in, obviously,' she said, 'as soon as they've finished bonking.'

'How will you do that?'

'Don't worry,' she said. 'I used to do that sort of thing all the time when I was young.'

'What sort of thing?'

'Break into people's houses. Me and my brother used to do it. Don't worry, we only used to eat the biscuits and bounce on the beds.'

I was beginning to see a few things in a different light that evening.

We waited for the office frolics to stop. When I was nineteen my average sex act was about two minutes long. You couldn't really even call it an act, more of a scene really, a beat. Nowadays, of course, especially after a couple of glasses of wine, it can go on for hours before the desired result is attained – a sex play, a sex epic even. By old age I'm given to understand you get up to the sex trilogy. Dan, however, appeared to be the exception that proved the rule and seemed capable of going at it for hours.

We stood and we froze, we froze and we stood. My shoes, which are quite good really, began to feel cheap and plastic, like something grey from the eighties. I saw this plastic moccasin in a shop once in about 1986. It was known as a Stallone, giving it a power to depress way in excess of its appearance. That's how my feet felt, as if I was wearing Stallones. Eventually I lost feeling in them.

All the time, Lucy held on to me, radiating animal warmth.

'We'll find him,' she said, 'don't worry, we'll find him.'

I'd never shared my secret with anyone before but there, freezing in the car park, with the life I had known seeming further away than even Reg, I decided she should know.

'The dog talks to me, you know,' I said.

She smiled. 'I've seen you talking to him.'

'He replies,' I said, 'literally. I'm not making this up. I'm nuts. I actually think that the dog speaks to me.'

'What does he say about when he stays with me?' she said. I could see she thought I was joking in some way.

'He says he likes it,' I said. 'He likes you very much, that's why I thought he'd agree to stay with you if I couldn't have him.'

'And why wouldn't he?'

'He said if he couldn't stay with me then he didn't trust humans, and he didn't want to stay with anyone,' I said.

Lucy looked at me like Reg had when I'd told him I could make the car go where I wanted. 'No you can't,' he said, like a kid hearing one of his mates say that he could score one hundred million goals at football.

'Yes I can,' I said, as we drove along. 'Watch. We'll turn right at this roundabout.'

We did and the dog looked to the heavens as if I thought he was an idiot.

'You're just guessing where it's going to go,' he said.

'No I'm not, I influence it,' I said.

'In that case why do you go into town with it?' said Reg.

'To get things for Lyndsey,' I said.

'Although,' said Reg, wagging his tail in an 'if I might remind the jury' manner, 'you specifically said you didn't want to. You don't want to and then you get in the car with me. Ten minutes later it deposits you at the very place you've said you don't want to go. So if you could influence it you wouldn't go there, would you?' said Reg. 'I refer you to my earlier point about your lead.'

'I didn't want to go there but I had to,' I said.

The dog rolled his eyes. 'And I suppose you had to leave me in the car when you got there, didn't you? Admit it, you could only get that window open a crack on the back door and you had to go away and wait until it decided to let you back in. The doors locked without you even touching them!' he said, like Einstein QED-ing a staunch Newtonian.

Outside the League, the flakes were falling like they do in the imagination, Parmesan shavings onto the pizza of our together-ness. I hadn't really eaten, all right?

'He's got an educated accent, not posh but well-spoken, if you see what I mean,' I said.

'Very sweet,' said Lucy, meaning 'stop being such an idiot and concentrate on the job in hand'.

'It's what all the shredding things up was about,' I said. 'He wanted to make it impossible for you to keep him.'

Lucy looked at me harder. 'You're serious about this, aren't you?'

'Yes,' I said, 'and I know about you and Jim too. I don't know how tonight affects that.'

'What about me and Jim?' said Lucy.

'I know you're seeing each other.'

'Did the dog tell you that?'

'He said you . . .' I didn't know how to phrase it, 'get it together sometimes. After dinner.'

I don't know why I added the after dinner bit.

Lucy drew back from me, offended. 'Jim's gay,' she said, 'as gay as can be.'

'That's very gay indeed, isn't it?' I said, chattering, 'but Reg said you . . .' I was trying to choose the right phrase. What did the dog call it? 'You play hide the sausage.' Suddenly the mistake dawned on me, 'You don't perchance conceal food for him, do you?'

Lucy's jaw dropped. 'That's exactly what we do, yes. I didn't want to tell you because I know what you're like about his diet. How did you know that?'

'I told you, the dog talks to me,' I said. 'I've been having treatment for it. The thing is I don't really want a cure.'

The lights went off in the office and I heard Julie and Dan making their way into the car park. Even though Lucy was only inches from me I could hardly see her.

'He's completely barking,' Julie was saying, her voice carrying across the cold air. 'Gave away his dog and then just sat mooning at it in front of the cage.'

'He looks a mess,' said Dan, which was rich from a student.

'If you ask me, the dog probably asked to be put in to get away from him,' laughed Julie. I heard the door of a car open.

'Mind you,' said Dan, 'that lot who took him didn't look exactly stable.'

'He's a psychiatrist,' said Julie. 'He wants his kids to have an unbalanced pet as a challenge. Start 'em early.'

Another car door opened and the lights came on.

'Doesn't he mind if they get bitten?'

'No,' said Julie. 'He says it'll do them good. He'll probably get them to practise restraint techniques. On Christmas morning.'

Both doors slammed and the car started. God, it was cold.

The car pulled away and we were left in darkness.

'Come on,' said Lucy. 'Time for action!'

She scooted down the side of the building, sticking to the wall.

'They've gone,' I said. 'Why are you still hiding?'

'Night staff,' she said.

Sure enough, at the back of the building, well down inside the kennel block, I could see a light still on.

'Why exactly are we going to break in?' I said. I'd not thought to ask before.

'To get the dog's address off the computer,' said Lucy.

'What about the password?'

'It'll be "woof" or "walkies", and failing that there'll be some sort of written record,' said Lucy.

I have to say Lucy seemed in her element doing this sort of thing and, while it made me admire her, it did cause me to consider if I should have paid for a background check on her when I employed her.

We returned to the dark front of the building. Out of the shadows, the light of the moon and some distant street lamps were just enough for us to see that the windows were alarmed – strips of tape across each one.

'There's no direct access to the back of the building,' said Lucy, 'so I doubt the doors there will be alarmed. You can use the wheelie bin to get up on the roof and then shin down the back,' she said.

'Did you learn all this when you were nine?' I said.

'I watch *Is Your Home Security Good Enough? For If It Is Not You Will Surely Be Murdered*,' she said.

'Is that that new one with the Geordie presenter?' I said. I realised that this simply meant that it was on television, everything having a Geordie presenter nowadays.

'You're thinking of *Alack! Alack! Thieves Are Everywhere!*' she said.

'Oh,' I said, eyeing the wheelie bin which, having wheels, didn't look like the best thing in the world to be balancing on when the ground was so icy.

Lucy held the bin while I tried to clamber onto it. Unfortunately my circus days are far behind me and I couldn't make it. I wasn't quite supple enough to get my knee onto the top of it and stood there with one leg in the air like Reg by a tree.

'Oh, for God's sake,' said Lucy. 'Hold the bin.'

I did as I was bid and she shinned up it. The next thing I knew she'd wedged herself up the side of the drainpipe and was on the roof, like some skinny Santa.

Lucy disappeared over the roof and five minutes later opened the front door.

'Loo window was open,' she said as I stepped gratefully out of the cold.

'How did you get by the alarm?' I said.

'The code was 1234, it always is,' she said.

She could see I was looking at her strangely.

'I saw it on *Burglary Today: Misery Is The Reward For Complacency*,' she said.

We went into the office. Far from going at it like rabbits in the last days of rabbit Rome, Julie and Dan had clearly been tidying up. A stray thought hit me. I wondered what the barbarian clean-up operation was like after they'd sacked Rome. Surely they must have tidied up afterwards if they were going to live there but you never see a painting of that. After chaos comes order, I thought. And then some more chaos. I banished these useless musings from my head which is, I've found, far the best line to take with useless musings.

The debris of the party was now neatly packaged in black bags and only the stale smell of alcohol and cigarettes remained from the festivities.

The computer was behind the front reception desk. As I sat down at it I felt a strange tingle wondering how many canine destinies had been decided there. It was the command centre, the Dog Olympus where the Gods of the NCDL decided the fate of Chihuahua, Spitz and Pug.

I booted up the computer which asked for a password. I tried 'woof', then 'walkies' and then 'bark'. None of them worked.

'Try Beckham,' said Lucy.

I did and the computer opened like a flower before me.

It took me an age to find the right files. There were folders marked 'Dogs', 589 of them, folders marked 'Bitches', about the same number, which I thought I could discount, and a promising one marked 'recent placements'.

I opened it to find about twenty documents, each with a family name and a dog's number attached. This was clearly going to take forever.

I noticed my leg was tapping, a sign that I subconsciously wanted to leave. I thought this was a fair bet as I consciously wanted to leave as well.

The money from Mrs Cad-Beauf clearly hadn't been spent on the computer, which was of the steam-driven variety. Each file creaked open with terrible torpor and each file held no information on Reg. 'Topsy – Now called Turvey. Collie X. Placed 12/11. Owners Mr and Mrs Caufield, 4 Brinklow Drive, Fareham, Hants. Family aware of problem with bats and mouth-breathers.' It was all that sort of thing.

File after file revealed no information on my dog.

After about twenty minutes I glanced up. Lucy wasn't there.

I'd seen enough slasher movies to find this vaguely disturbing. It's like with *Jaws*. I know there's a very small chance indeed of a rogue Great White finding its way into Worthing Baths but it doesn't stop me checking the water for fins before I get in.

I went to the back of the office. Through the glass on the back door I could see the faint light from the kennel block. Then a shape appeared at the door and she opened it.

'Where have you been?' I said.

Lucy said nothing. She opened her coat to reveal a tiny black puppy with one white ear.

'Have you gone mad, woman?' I said, hissing rather more than I'd intended.

'You're going to need it!' said Lucy.

'In the name of God why?'

'We haven't got time for this, just take the puppy.'

She handed it over to me and replaced a set of keys on a hook behind the desk. I was still cold from the car park and the dog felt almost hot as she handed him to me.

'Have you found the address?' she said, looking at her watch.

'No, there's no clue to where it might be.'

Lucy went to the computer, looked for ten seconds and tapped the screen.

I followed her finger.

'Nutter's dog,' said the file.

'That would probably be it then,' I said.

We clicked on the file, and with a few whirrs the computer gave up its treasure: '443 Drove Road, Brighton,' said the file. 'Dog Reg now Archimedes.'

'Archimedes?' I said. 'He hates baths!'

'Dr Robinson et Fam. Do not under any circumstances reveal information to former owner D. Barker as he is unstable.'

'Unstable!' I sniffed.

'Papa!' said the puppy.

'Oh, don't you start,' I said.

32

A Family Christmas

Drove Road, I have to say, is an ideal place for a dog. Right on the edge of the Sussex Downs next to the old broken-down bakery for interesting smells and access to acres and acres of prime countryside, viewing recommended.

We walked from the League onto the main road and mobiled for taxis. The Christmas Eve trade had picked up and we had forty-five minutes to wait, sheltering in a bus stop and watching the world turn white while we turned blue.

Lucy was frozen and, more to the point, had her niece and nephew coming to see her so she went the one way and I the other.

I kissed her for luck.

'I wish I could come with you,' she said.

'This is a one-man operation,' I said.

'Where are you going to get the man from then?' she said.

'What did you say about wit not being appropriate to every situation?' I said.

I watched her cab disappearing into the snowy night and something inside me felt how fragile all our relationships are, how they can be taken from us in a moment.

'Are you going to be sick in my cab?' said my taxi driver, winding down his window and returning me to reality.

'No,' I said.

'Is that going to piss in here?' he said.

'No,' I said.

'OK,' he said.

It was nine by the time I reached the Robinson house. It was one of those deep-windowed old Edwardian things of stripped pine floorboards, the *Guardian* Guide and a cat called Andrew that academics tend to aspire to. Four bedrooms, two en-suite, period features, GFCH, stunning views over Downs, a snap at an awful lot of money.

My plan, hatched with Lucy, was simple. I'd just go up to the front door, explain the mistake to Doc Robinson, offer the puppy in exchange and all would be as calm as the snow-heavy day, so to speak.

The one bluebottle in the Nivea was provided by the character of Dr Robinson. He'd wanted a problem dog for his children, according to Julie. I wasn't sure he'd be the type to accept a more appropriate gift.

The cab pulled up outside the property and I was relieved to see the lights were on.

The doctor was too middle-class for net curtains and so the whole front room was lit up in a way that would have caused the Geordie from *Alack Alack!* to give one of his disapproving but cuddly tuts. My mother would have said it was 'lit up like Casey Court', wherever that was.

I went up the steps and rang the bell. There was no one visible through the windows. A large tree dominated the living room, decked out, it seemed, by a brewery. It was this that was illuminating the room, covering the walls with a magic pattern of blues, reds, greens and gold. There were presents under the tree and a piano next to the window, an accommodating sofa and a cavernous fireplace.

I stood for a second like Tiny Tim looking at the goose in the window before reminding myself what I'd come for.

I rang the bell again and waited.

'Papa!' said the puppy, nuzzling into me. I gulped, which I hoped was the sort of thing one does when seeking to harden one's heart.

I rang for the third time. Nothing. If Reg was in there, I thought, he would bark. He could never resist a bell. Even when we went to call on Lucy and I rang her bell he barked. 'Who's that!' he'd say, with his ears at half mast, which was as erect as he could manage.

'It's us, you fool,' I'd say. 'It's you.'

'Then why am I ringing?' he'd say. 'Look out, we are powerful and ready to repel foes!'

'We're ringing because we want to get in,' I said.

'As I thought,' said the dog. 'Invaders! Beware, my teeth are sharp!'

There were some things you just couldn't explain. The dog seemed very opposed to the idea of invading territory, even if it was him who was doing it. In fact, he was so opposed to it that he couldn't see himself as an invader and presumed it must be someone else.

The cold had got right inside me and, since the Robinsons' porch was a charming period feature rather than any good at keeping the weather off, I thought I'd go round the back and see if there was a shed I could hide in until they came back.

There was an alley at the side of the house affording ample access to the well maintained garden and I went down it and opened the security gate with an insurance-approved five-lever deadlock that was open.

There was no shed, just a snow-covered garden, south-facing and benefiting from a cupid emerging from a pond. A pond is roughly the reverse of a shed when it comes to providing shelter so I turned to wait at the front of the house.

It was then that I was struck by an idea. Despite my pretending to Lucy that I was too high and mighty to watch *Alack! Alack!* I had seen the odd episode, seduced by the laddish banter of the genial Geordie into sucking in my breath or quietly shaking my head at the security lapses of the hoi polloi. I particularly enjoyed the 'Asking For It!' segment of the show where they handed out the idiot of the week award.

I can't say that I'm proud of what I did next but I will point out, in my defence, that I was still quite drunk, I was stressed and I was as cold as it is possible to be without uttering the words, 'I may be some time.'

There was, I noticed, a cat flap in the back door. I'd seen on *Alack! Alack!* that various enterprising toughs would reach up through these flaps and undo the locks in order to relieve you of your electronica.

Tucking the puppy firmly into my top pocket, I bent to the flap and put in my hand. The flap was high and the lock was low. To my amazement and pleasure, I felt a key.

I allowed myself a little smile as I turned it and locked the door.

With some difficulty I then found the key again, unlocked the door and went in.

Opposite the back door was a rack of security keys dangling from hooks. All the fittings of Fort Knox and they don't lock the back door.

I'm not a complete idiot, so I went to the front door and put a chair behind it. I thought this would give me the chance to slip out the back if I didn't hear them coming from down the street.

At first I stood in the red-tiled kitchen, looking up at a noticeboard which seemed to have a lot about good works on it – Amnesty This, War on That. I was particularly gratified to see a small flyer with 'Let's keep religion out of Christmas' on it. The Robinsons, I decided, were people after my own heart.

After half an hour I'd had enough of waiting in the kitchen. I was longing to feel Reg's presence, was waiting to have his head on my knee again, to stroke his calming fur.

I gained the front room by increments. First I used the loo, which I couldn't avoid. Then I patrolled the hall, listening for their arrival. I definitely thought I could make the back door before anyone got through the front, particularly if I remained vigilant. Emboldened by boredom I went and sat in the front room.

A Christmas tree is a wonderful thing, laying an enchantment of colour on a room, a faerie fire that seems to deepen the enclosing dark. So no wonder I nodded off, especially as the margaritas, kept at bay by stress, had indicated they'd waited long enough and now by rights were allowed control of my central nervous system for at least a couple of hours.

It was ten by the video recorder when I heard sounds at the front door and still ten by the video recorder when I realised I couldn't find the puppy.

My eyes swept the floor but it was nowhere to be seen. I heard the key turn in the front door.

'Puppy!' I said.

'Papa!' said a voice, inside my jacket pocket.

The door was thumped open and I heard a girl's voice say, 'I can't open it!'

I got to the hall and turned for the kitchen.

'No muddy shoes on the carpet, Chloe. Go round the back!' said a man's posh voice.

'That door's broken,' said the girl.

'You've broken it!' said a boy.

'You can't open it because you secretly don't want to. You don't want to disappoint me by walking mud into the house but you want to assert your independence by trying. It's all very healthy,' said the man's voice indulgently.

The child grunted in frustration, slamming the door shut.

'Go on in, Penny, I'll get him out of the car,' said the voice that I now took to be Dr Robinson.

My legs went one way and then the other. There was clearly no escape. In a way I didn't want to escape. 'I'll get him out of the car' he could only be talking about Reg.

I don't know why but I found myself back by the front door. The back door opened and I heard a woman telling a child to take off his wellingtons as soon as he got in.

Then the front door opened a crack. It was clearly OK for old Dr R to get dirt on the carpet then, just not his kids.

I'd half expected to see Reg's nose round the side of the door, levering it open like he did whenever he was in a lift, but I didn't. The world seemed instantly simple. I was about to see my dog and nothing else mattered. I was having him back no matter what obstacle the Robinsons placed in my way.

The chair was shoved away from the door and there stood Dr Robinson bending over a carrycot and saying, 'Who's a lovely boy then, please don't cry.'

The most logical thing to do, clearly, was for me to – well, that was the problem, wasn't it? There was no logical thing for me to do.

If in doubt, I normally find, go with what you know. I was suddenly in the front room. The sofa was one of those big leather ones with the back at a generous angle. There was just enough room in there for a desperate estate agent and I took it, worming in on my elbows like a Marine under barbed wire.

I heard light footsteps enter the room.

'Ooh, look!' said the boy. 'Presents under the tree, can we open them?'

'Those aren't your presents!' shouted Penny.

'Who are they for?' said the girl.

'Wait and see tomorrow,' said Penny.

'Where are our presents?' said the girl.

'Santa's got them,' said Penny.

'I wish you wouldn't say that, dear,' said Doc Robinson.

'And I wish you wouldn't say that, dear,' said Penny.

'Papa!' said the puppy. There was a silence in the room.

'Come and have some biscuits!' shouted Penny from the kitchen.

I heard the children leave.

I wasn't quite shafted yet, I thought. The family would go to bed within a couple of hours and then I could slip away.

Where I was going to slip away to hadn't crossed my mind but I thought I'd deal with that problem when it arrived.

The radio came on, in French.

'Oh, John, it is Christmas Eve,' said Penny.

'Christmas in French is beautiful,' said Dr Robinson.

'It's also in French,' she said.

'It avoids the religious connotations if the kids can't understand the carols,' he said.

'Who gives an airborne shite?' said Penny.

The children seemed to think it very funny to hear their mother swear.

There's something very comforting in hearing a family settling down for Christmas Eve, even if you are wedged behind their sofa with a less than continent puppy dog asleep on you. The children wondering what presents they've got, the parents trying to calm them enough to get them to go to bed, the setting out of the mince pie and whisky for Santa, the 'testing of the bottle' by the father.

There's a wonderful stillness to a house the second after the children have been put to bed and the adults lie exhausted on the sofa.

'I'm knackered,' said Penny.

'Worth it, though,' said John, as I was now calling Dr Robinson. 'The kids don't often get to see snow. Maybe we can take the dog out there tomorrow if he's up to it.'

'Why shouldn't he be up to it?' said Penny, with very much the tone of voice Reg used to say, 'You're not going out without me, are you?'

'He's been in the home for some time, he might not be fit, he might have problems.'

'This "might", John – how much of a "might" is it?'

'Therapy is my gift,' said John. 'I would like to pass it on.'

'Oh, can't we have a normal dog that we just go for walks in the country with and take down the park? Do we have to have Hannibal Lecter in fur?'

'He's not that bad,' said John.

This filled my heart with some joy. Penny was clearly going to be delighted I'd brought Patch, as I had now taken to calling the pup, in exchange for the sofa-destroying Reg.

'Look,' said John, 'everything is going to be fine. We'll have a wonderful Christmas, the children will have great presents and a project.'

Penny snorted. 'They don't want a project, John, they want a dog.'

'Shall we just put out the presents?' said John.

'OK,' said Penny.

There was some stuffing about outside the room while presents were dug out – from under the stairs, by the conversation.

'Here we go,' said John. 'Do you think it will be safe to leave these here with the lights on?'

'We'll turn the lights off,' said Penny.

'I can see you, Sebastian,' said John.

'Is it Christmas yet?' said the boy's voice from the stairs.

'Not until tomorrow,' said John. 'Now go back to bed.'

'It is tomorrow!' said the child. 'I've been in bed and now I've got up so it's tomorrow.'

'You have to wait until it gets light,' said John and I heard him going out of the room, 'otherwise Santa might not come.'

'Reference to Santa, one nil to the forces of common sense,' said Penny.

'Beh, beh, beh,' said John, distantly.

After five or so minutes, during which my arm went to sleep, he returned.

'Have you been drinking a lot today?' said Penny.

'No,' said John, 'just what I've had since I came in. I've been with you all day, woman, and I've been driving, how could I have been drinking?'

'It's just that there's a very strong smell of drink in here,' she said. 'Would you have a shower before you come to bed?'

'It's not me,' he said.

'Well, I don't see anybody else here,' she said in pretty much the only way there is to say it.

John tutted. I liked John and Penny, I thought, and I hoped they'd invite me in when I explained the mistake.

I had formulated a plan after all. I'd call a cab back to Lucy's, freshen up and return at just before first light on Christmas Day. All would be well with the world, I was sure. If Reg put up his barking display, Penny would be glad of a substitute puppy.

A smug glow ensconced me, as smug as a glow can be when it's emanating from behind a sofa.

'Shall we go to bed?' said John.

'Yes, I'm exhausted,' said Penny.

'What are we going to do about Sebastian? If he comes down tonight he'll open all his presents like he did last year,' said John.

'No he won't,' said Penny. 'I finally found the key to the sitting room yesterday. It's on the mantelpiece.

'Great,' said John.

Half of me wanted to get up there and then but unfortunately it was the right half which was underneath the left half, which wanted to stay where it was.

'Come on,' said John, 'up the wooden hill. Merry Christmas, darling.'

'Merry Christmas, darling,' said Penny and locked the door to the front room.

I was entombed.

33

The Best Present a Boy Ever Had

I'll say this for the Robinsons, their security arrangements are first rate – other than leaving the back door open – but I wouldn't fancy being in their shoes if there was a fire.

I felt very much how the old Egyptian boys who got buried with the Pharaohs must have, surrounded by the treasures of the age but, by any sensible measure, shafted.

The windows were secondary glazed to a high standard and fixed by security bolts throughout. I tried each one but they were all locked shut: I remembered the shelf full of security keys I'd passed on my way in. I'd have to break the inner panel of glass, clear that out and then break the outer panel of glass in order to escape.

I looked at the firegrate – I could probably get through the windows with the poker. But I couldn't do it, could I? I couldn't smash these people's windows to avoid embarrassment. Well, I could actually, but I thought that there was no guarantee the window would break first go and then I'd be into the territory of very embarrassing indeed.

'I can hear Santa! He's leaving the presents!' said Sebastian's voice at the door.

'Go back to bed Sebastian!' said John.

'But Santa's in there, I can hear him!' said Sebastian. Bloody middle-class families with their bloody creaking stripped pine floorboards, desirable period feature that they are.

'Let me see Santa!' said Sebastian.

'If you disturb him he won't leave his gifts,' said John who, after God knows how many years of training as an analyst, had seemingly just woken up to the child control possibilities of Father Christmas.

I tiptoed towards the sofa again, managing to tread on a floorboard that made a creak rather like the introduction of the cello in Stravinsky's 'Rites of Spring'.

'Are you in there, Santa?' said Sebastian. 'Daddy, I can really hear him.'

I heard someone come thumping down the stairs. Before I could move, John had reached the door and thrown it open. All I could do was hold the puppy up in an instinctive movement of defence.

'Look, no Santa!' said John. In one movement he opened the door and closed it again, without looking up. Sebastian, however, for an instant blinked directly at me, before disappearing behind the door again.

'I saw him, I saw him!' said Sebastian. 'He had a puppy dog for me and a great big red nose. He was all scruffy from where he'd come down the chimney.'

I thought that was rather uncalled for but I was prepared to let it pass under the circumstances.

'Good for you,' said John. There was the sound of a child being manhandled up the stairs. All I had to do was get to the door, go out the back and I would be free.

The thumping came back down the stairs.

'Forgot to lock the bloody door!' I heard John saying to

himself, as the key turned and with it my stomach.

It was at this point that I gave up. I'd had my stab at it and I'd failed. The next morning, when the Robinsons came down, I'd explain everything, in detail, take the massive embarrassment and hope for the best.

I let Patch run around the floor for a while until he got tired, which wasn't long, and settled down with him to sleep on the sofa.

Dr Robinson, however, may have been on to something with this subconscious bit because when I awoke with the first light of dawn I found myself behind the sofa once again, with the sort of hangover that reduces the brain to those core functions that are strictly useful solely for propelling a reptile and have no real value for higher thought. The puppy had done something unacceptable on my jacket, on which it was sleeping.

The key turned in the door as ominously as it must to open the cell of a condemned man. Well, maybe not quite that bad, perhaps as bad as someone who was about to be taken to court to face a charge of burglary, something I was sure I might find out all about pretty soon.

'Santa's been!' shouted the girl Chloe as she came running into the room.

Patch sucked at my finger, which at least shut him up.

'Where's the puppy?' said Sebastian, following her.

'Why don't you open your other presents and see what happens later,' said Penny. 'My God, have we left something rotting in here? It stinks.'

'Real pine from the tree,' said John. 'It's an aroma you have to get used to.' He breathed in deeply as I looked at my ravaged jacket.

'A PlayStation!' said Sebastian. 'Oh Dad, thanks for treating me like a normal child.'

'It's OK this once,' said John.

The children were in a high fit of excitement and presents were shredded, gifts exclaimed upon and shown to parents who had bought them and so might have been expected to know what they looked like.

John had bought Penny a lovely bracelet and Penny had bought John a presentation chess set, which were cooed over. There was no sign of Reg, though.

'Right,' said John. 'I just have to go over the road to get our most special present.'

My ears pricked up. He'd been over the road all the time. Had I known I could just have broken in and stolen him.

John went out and Penny told the kids to put any presents they weren't playing with on the sofa to keep them off the floor.

Then I realised that I hadn't taken my pills for the best part of a day. I knew this because, across the flat air of the snow-heavy street, I heard him.

'You've kept me in a darkened room all night which had all the characteristics of solitary confinement, so little did it have to chew, now you drag me out in the freezing cold, ooh, that's an interesting smell. Someone's dropped a mince pie. Don't pull me! I want to go back in the home.'

'Christ!' said Penny, under her breath. She must have heard Reg's shouting as barking and I suppose he must have sounded quite fierce.

'Just wait here, children,' she said.

She went out, closing the door behind her

'John, are you sure this dog's all right?' said Penny, shouting above Reg.

'Never better,' said John. 'Penny meet Archimedes.'

'My name is not Archimedes, it's Reg!' shouted Reg. 'I don't even like baths!'

I could have told them that.

There was more scuffling and quite a bit of thumping and I heard Penny say, 'I think we need to talk, John.'

'Nonsense,' said John, a fine emotion from a man who had made his living through doing just that.

From behind the sofa I could see the door open and John's head come round a little.

'Children,' he said, 'I want you to meet a special friend who has been on his own for a long time.'

'Which is the way I like it!' shouted Reg.

'We need to treat him with very special care if we're going to make him ha— Who the flaming flip are you?'

I realised that the reason I'd got such a good view of John was very simple. I'd stood up.

'It's Santa!' shouted Sebastian. 'I knew it was him. Look, he's got my puppy!'

'There's been a mistake,' I said.

'Santa, can I have my puppy?' said Sebastian.

'Who's that?' said Reg, poking his head round the door.

'I'm from the dog's home and there has been an error,' I said. 'This is the dog you should have had, bit smelly but he'll clean up. That dog is dangerous and needs to be removed.'

I climbed over the back of the sofa, doing God knows what to the presentation chess set. I mean, it still worked as a chess set but I think its presentation qualities were slightly compromised by getting my foot through it.

'Here!' I said, tossing the puppy to John in a way that I'm not proud of. Luckily he caught it. Patch looked up at John and said, 'Papa.' Canine tart.

I snatched Reg's lead, pushed past John and ran out into the street.

'Oh sir,' said Reg, 'I knew if I waited you'd see sense.' We hammered down the steps and along the snowy road.

'Do you forgive me?' I said.

'Of course I forgive you,' said Reg. 'I'm a dog.'

34

Strays

'We're homeless now, you know,' I said as we rounded the bottom of Drove Road and ran down the hill past the racecourse

'Great!' said Reg. 'You mean we're going on a really, really long walk. I am the luckiest dog in the world.'

I'd forgotten his ability to see the positive side of almost anything.

His tongue was lolling in a huge smile as he ran. 'Did Lyndsey agree to take me back?'

I slowed to a walk. 'It was you or Lyndsey,' I said. 'She gave me that decision. I made the wrong one, it just took me some time to see it, that's all.'

'Say you'll never leave me again.'

The snow was still falling and I suddenly realised how cold I was. I'd left my puppy-stained jacket back at the Robinson's house and was only in my shirt.

'I can't say I won't leave you again Reg,' I said. 'I'm afraid I'm in some trouble.'

The dog looked up at me. 'What's wrong?'

'I did a bad thing when I sold the house for Mrs Cad-Beauf,'

I said. 'Now someone's found out and they might put me in a home,' I translated for him. I didn't want to have to spend four weeks describing the concept of prison.

'I can go with you!' said Reg brightly. 'If you got put into Patcham we could both be in at the same time. You get walks in there and the food's not too bad.'

'I wish you could come,' I said.

We walked through the back streets of Southover, down the steep hill towards the centre of town. In the terraced houses, Christmas was sparking into life – the lights on in the homes of the families with children, early risers each.

Once again I was frozen, really cold, dressed only in my shirt and tie. My mobile was in my jacket pocket, which was at the Robinson's so I couldn't call Lucy. I didn't have any money either, as that was in the jacket pocket too. Well, I had 12p, which is nothing, with the added discomfort of subjecting you to the tinkle of cosmic laughter as you rattle the change.

I could walk to her house, I supposed, but seeing as it was in Worthing and a good ten miles away I'd probably be dead by the time I got there. There was no way a cab would look at me in the state I was in. I'm afraid Patch had lived up to his name and caused several on my shirt.

'Explain what happened,' said the dog as we approached the back of the old market.

So I did, going through everything, how I'd talked myself into defrauding Mrs Cad-Beauf, Tibbs and poker at his house, how Miles had come on the scene, how I was now officially buggered.

'I can't forget what I've done to Mrs Cad-Beauf, Reg,' I said.

'Well, that's an easy one, isn't it?' said the dog.

'Is it?'

'Yes. I have a very convenient memory. You're always telling me I forget not to pull and things. So give it to me to remember and I'll forget it for you.'

'I'm afraid it doesn't work like that,' I said. 'I have an inconvenient memory.'

The dog sniffed at a lamp post.

'I've got a better idea then,' he said.

'Yes?'

'Yes. Why don't we just go to Mr Tibbs's house and get all the money back off him. Then you can give it to Mr Cad-Beauf and he won't send you to gaol,' said Reg.

I laughed. The dog's back was now white with snow, giving him the appearance of a mobile Yule log.

'I don't think he'd be very keen to hand it over.'

'I don't see why not,' said the dog. 'All the other people you sit round that table with give you lots of money, why shouldn't he?'

I laughed again, in a teeth-chattery, cold way. Down in the old market was a soup kitchen. A first time for everything, I thought.

'It's a good idea but we don't have the stake to play the Cat for that sort of money,' I said. 'Even winning with your help it'd take me years to get it, by which time they'll have locked me up and thrown away the key. No, Reg, I've decided, it's a life on the road for us, a change of identity, disappear. Maybe we'll get some money from games, maybe we won't.'

'You want a steak?' said the dog. 'I can't blame you, they're lovely. Will there be one here?'

'A stake,' I said. 'It's the same sound but a different word to steak meaning meat. It means a sum of money. You have to show the other person a certain amount of money before they'll give you any of theirs,' I said.

'And Mr Tibbs wants to see quite a lot, does he?' said Reg, exploring a nook near where the fish stall normally stood. I encouraged him to give it up and we joined the queue for soup.

'An awful lot if he was going to risk all that,' I said.

The dog breathed out a wreath of vapour as a kindly-looking woman in a thick coat came towards me.

'Would you like a blanket?' she said.

'Oh yes,' I said.

'You can come and choose one if you like,' she said.

She led me to a large awning, where blankets and duvets of various descriptions were piled on top of a tarpaulin.

'That's my duvet!' I said.

'You like it, do you?' said the woman.

'Like it? I own it,' I said. There it was, my Captain Scarlet duvet, the one I'd had since I was fourteen. 'Where did you get all this stuff from?'

'We collect from a wide area on Christmas Eve,' she said. 'I think this lot came from the villages around Uckfield. Rich people can be quite generous,' she said.

Lyndsey had already started binning my things, it turned out.

'Right,' said the woman. 'As it's so cold you can take the duvet first but I'm afraid I am going to have to ask you to listen to a short speech about our saviour Lord Jesus Christ,' she said.

'Fire away,' I said, wrapping myself into something I think I could quite literally describe as my comfort blanket. In this, I thought, I had just about a chance of making it to Lucy's. Or maybe I could go to a police station, explain that . . . er, I'd stolen a dog. Hmm.

My mind whirred as I listened to the exemplary behaviour of the troubled Job – a biblical case of a guy who did not seem to be able to take a hint – and then I was free to join the soup queue, putting the bottom of the duvet over Reg to stop the snow falling on him.

'I love the smell of this duvet,' said Reg.

'That's the smell of me,' I said.

'Well, I love it, it's my favourite,' said the dog. That, I think, is as near to an expression of total love as I could imagine.

As we waited for soup, the dog froze to his earlier theme.

'What's the reason why you can't just wave those cards at Tibbs and get him to pay you the money?' he said.

'We need money ourselves before we can get any more,' I said.

'Well, why don't you ask Miles Cad-Beauf for it?' said Reg. 'His mum was always very generous to you.'

'Because he won't give it to me,' I said.

'He won't unless you ask,' said Reg. 'You may as well. In my nose that smells like your only hope.'

'It's more complicated than that,' I said.

'Why?' said the dog.

'Because . . .' and at that moment, I really couldn't think. Perhaps there was a way. Miles didn't want a court case that would almost certainly be defended by the Cat. It could drag out for years, taking his energies while the deserving of the world went without. Much better to allow me to get the money back simply and quickly. I wouldn't get it all but I could give him back my £1 million.

'All you need to do,' said Reg, 'is explain that with me you can't lose.'

He was right.

'Minestrone or oxtail?' said the woman in front of me.

'Neither,' I said. 'I'm afraid I have a prior appointment at the Hotel Hotel.'

35

Long Shot

'Miles Cadwaller-Beaufort, sir, I'll just ring up for him,' said the receptionist at the hotel.

I'll say this for Brighton, you have to do a lot to shock, largely because it's full of people who are doing a lot to shock.

The receptionist smiled pleasantly at me as the phone rang.

'May I take your duvet, sir?' enquired a bellhop.

'I think I'll keep it on until I warm up,' I shivered.

'As you wish.' He bowed slightly and retreated.

'Your name?' said the receptionist, and I told her.

'He asks what it's about,' I said.

'Getting his twenty-five million pounds back,' I said.

The receptionist relayed the information down the phone.

'He'll be down in a second,' she said.

She pointed me towards the bar and I headed for it, then decided to hand my duvet in after all.

'I think it's Damien Hirst,' the receptionist was saying. 'Only the very rich dress that poorly. Sorry, sir.'

I passed her the duvet and retreated to the bar to order a cappuccino.

Even though I was in the semblance of smart clothes – suit trousers, a shirt, a tie, I felt I stood out. For the first thing, the shirt was soaked with a variety of substances, snow being the purest, descending through sweat and hitting rock bottom with various puppy emissions.

For the second thing, the Hotel Hotel isn't really my sort of place. It's lovely, that's for sure, but it's just not me, with its self-assured walnut, low-slung leather sofas, inviting half-dark and over-frothed cappuccinos. It's easy on the eye but it displays the Brighton affliction of being slightly too trendy – self-consciously the equal of anything in London, like a precocious little girl slapping on the Clinique and arguing that she should be allowed out with her big sister. Passing for eighteen but somehow not.

I had considered trying out the restaurant here but had rejected the idea. I could never go to such a place with Lyndsey because spending the money – even when it wasn't her own – would bring her out in a rash. Also, to be fair, I didn't like places like this. I'm more a 'go large with this leaflet' man when it comes to eating out.

From the corner of the dark bar was a bright flash. It was Miles Cad-Beauf, dressed in a shirt that even an Australian might describe as 'tasty'. It was one of those that's taken the idea of the Hawaiian shirt and turned the volume up – Hawaii as seen through the filter of unmedicated schizophrenia.

'Christ,' said the dog, 'look at that.'

'I thought you were largely colour blind,' I said.

'There's a limit to everything,' he said.

Miles approached. Even though he was obviously angry with me I could see there was still a little bit of him that was self-conscious about the shirt.

'Mix-up in the luggage,' he said. 'The overcoat's gone to Manila. What happened to you?'

'That,' I said, 'is what I've come here to explain. I'm going to get your money back.'

'How?'

'Playing poker.'

'Goodbye,' said Miles, turning away.

'No, you don't understand,' I said. 'I can't lose, I have the help of this talking dog.'

He shook his head. 'You know what I find unusual about you, Mr Barker?' he said.

'His smell's very high, even for a human,' said the dog.

'What?' I said, guessing it wasn't going to be about my lovely smile.

'That for a crook you do a very good job of appearing like a victim. It beats me how a snivelling wimp like yourself ever got the balls to do a front like this.'

'Well,' I snivelled, 'it's like I said, I didn't.'

'Goodbye,' he said.

'Tell him he had pâté de foie gras with his dinner yesterday,' said Reg at the end of a deep sniff.

'You had pâté de foie gras with your dinner yesterday,' I said.

Miles stopped. 'What's that got to do with it, are you into animal rights now?'

'Tell him his main course was trout followed by a rather obvious choice of the deep chocolate tart,' said Reg.

I repeated Reg's words.

'So you were watching me have dinner. What's this meant to prove?'

'The woman he was with wore a light, musk-based perfume and he spent some time touching her,' he said.

I repeated the words again, almost exactly as Reg had said them.

'Have you been spying on me?' said Miles.

'No,' I said. 'The dog can smell all this on you. He knows what you did yesterday and he can tell what you're thinking now, more or less.'

'He's sweating mildly, probably thinks you're nuts,' said the dog.

'For instance, at the moment you think I'm insane,' I said. 'Am I right?'

Miles nodded slowly. 'I don't think it would take a psychic dog to work that out.'

'He's not psychic,' I said, 'just very perceptive.'

'He's salivating quite heavily,' said Reg. 'I don't think he's eaten. Yes, his stomach's just rumbled.'

'You're hungry, the dog tells me,' I said.

'It's eight thirty and I'm being kept from my breakfast, so that's a fair bet,' said Miles. 'I intend to put that right straight-away, if you'll excuse me.'

'His breath smells acidic,' said Reg. 'It's something rotten in his stomach. Something strange.'

'You won't be having the grapefruit, then,' I said.

Miles looked at me like a bank teller might look at a £50 note that, if you held it in a certain way, appeared to give the Queen a moustache.

'Not with your stomach ulcer and everything,' I said.

'How did you know I had an ulcer?' said Miles.

'The dog can smell it on your breath,' I said.

'This is bollocks,' said Miles, followed by something about 'raw prawns'. He had clearly been in Australia for some time. 'What else can he smell about me?'

'He's wearing the same underwear as yesterday,' said the dog.

I told him, as quietly as I could.

Miles looked at the dog. 'I came down in a hurry,' he said. 'I intend to change it later.'

He sat down on the sofa opposite me.

'You look like a nutcase,' he said. He turned to the dog. 'It's not as important when it's cold. You don't sweat as much.'

'Not how it seems in my nose,' said Reg. 'But it doesn't bother me, I'm a dog.'

'Well, I know I might seem slightly mad,' I said, 'but I've had an extremely hard time of it since your mother died. If you'll allow me to explain, I'm sure you'll see things from our point of view.'

'Who's "our"?' said Miles. 'I hardly wore them yesterday, for God's sake.'

'Me and the dog,' I said. 'Look, it may be madness or it may be that I have developed some weird insight but the fact is that I can hear him talking to me and what he says gives me an edge in my dealings with people. Namely in poker. I've never lost a game when this dog has been with me.'

Reg sat up proudly, even though he didn't quite grasp what a game was, or so it seemed to me.

'How can he say I smell when he's with you?' said Miles. I'd clearly touched a nerve here. 'You stink.'

'I like his smell,' said the dog.

'He likes my smell,' I said.

'And he doesn't like mine?'

'Well, I think you can understand how your old underpants might be an acquired taste,' I said.

'I don't mind the smell,' said the dog.

'They're not old, for God's sake,' said Miles. 'They're clean as a whistle,' he said.

'I wouldn't want that on my whistle!' said the dog, laughing. I thought this was a bit ironic, as he probably would want it on his whistle.

'I'm going to have to think about this,' said Miles. 'I'll say now that forwarding you any more money is out of the question. This dog, however, intrigues me. I was, as you know, brought up with dogs.'

'Any test,' I said, gesturing to the dog, who was looking as proud as if he'd been struck in bronze.

'OK,' said Miles, with purpose. 'I'll think of a test.'

'Deal,' said the dog, out of the corner of his mouth. I'd

foreseen this sort of thing when I'd watched a cowboy film with him one afternoon. I'd been addressed as 'Pardn'r' for a whole weekend and the woods had rung to cries of 'Howdy!' when he met other dogs. I'd only just got the TV off before the Dukes of Hazzard started and we got into serious trouble.

He was no mug, old Miles Cad-Beauf, and in a couple of ticks he'd thought of something.

'Give the dog to me,' he said. 'I want to take him away for a while.'

'How do I know you'll bring him back?' I said.

'Because I have to return to Australia,' said Miles, 'and I'm not a thief.'

The last part of the sentence was said with some emphasis, like he could think of some present whom that description might fit.

'Do you think you could stand me a change of clothes and perhaps a jumper?' I said.

'No,' said Miles. 'You've had enough out of my family already.'

I passed him the lead. 'Are you going to be long?'

'As long as it takes,' said Miles.

He disappeared into the hotel and I sat steaming in the lobby. I did get the odd look from guests but mostly from people I thought were out-of-towners. Brightonians – the trendy ones as opposed to the dirtier hippies – have seen it all and if a man looks as though he's spent the night sleeping in a hedge they're more worried that it's the new look and that they're missing out than that a tramp has wandered in.

This, I thought, is rock bottom. Normally when you hit rock bottom you give something up. 'I hit rock bottom and gave up the booze,' you hear people say, or the drugs. I hadn't anything to give up. I mean, there was the gambling but that was hardly a problem.

I'd done £200,000 in three months, I'd involved myself with

unsavoury elements that had completely screwed up my life but there was an explanation for that. I'd spent hours in the company of people I didn't feel strongly enough about to hate but certainly didn't like. I probably passively smoked around forty a day, in addition to the five that I actively smoked, that was true. And it had provided enough of a diversion from my ordinary life to prevent me from examining my relationship with a girl who was fundamentally unsuited to me. It had also covered up the fact that I didn't really like being an estate agent. But no real harm. The point was that gambling had got me into this mess and gambling would get me out.

I was cold, cold to the marrow cold, cold like I'd been when I'd once ridden from Eastbourne to Coventry on the back of my friend's motorbike in rain-drenched January, cold-for-a-week cold. But I went colder.

I realised that I was an addicted gambler. Even though I might not be one of the raging addicts, the sort that wear holes in their carpets with pacing if they haven't got a bet on, I was an addict nonetheless.

By accident or madness, however, I'd stopped gambling when I met the dog. It isn't gambling if you know you're going to win. Gambling is adrenalin sport. Ninety per cent, maybe more, of the thrill comes from the danger. It's the potential to lose, not to win, that makes it so attractive.

With Reg that potential had been removed, so the little green demon of the decks inside me had looked for another way to get its kicks. That was when I'd decided to go along with defrauding Mrs Cad-Beauf.

I can truly say I didn't do it for the gain, the money means nothing to me. I did it because I thought I might get caught. I needed a bet on in life, and a real bet, one that turns on those hormones that make heroin look about as powerful as sherbet, is one that you can't afford to lose.

I'd blamed Lyndsey and the Cat for getting me into that

situation but when it came down to it it was me who'd done the deed. There were hundreds of ways I could have refused but I didn't want to because I wanted the chance that this would happen, that I would find myself living on my wits, without a blue sou, fighting for my freedom in some over-tasteful hotel.

The inescapable conclusion I was drawn to, as I sat in my stinking clothes waiting for Miles to make a decision that was odds on to send me to gaol, was that I was rather enjoying myself. And, of course, that it had to stop.

A dog has no need for thrills. He likes to run quickly, he likes to catch a ball but when danger looms he's off like, well, the butcher's dog. Only dull people, I'd decided, have the need for excitement. When you can take in a symphony of smells on a tar-stained stone on a beach, when you are sensitive enough to hear the change in someone's breathing or even their heartbeat as they experience pleasure or pain, then you don't need the battering ram of a base jump or a game of high-stakes cards to fire you up.

You don't need to be a dog either. When was the last time I'd ever really listened to anyone, really gauged their reaction, took joy in the difference with which someone saw the world? Reg had started me on that but I hadn't yet extended it to humans.

I'd been fascinated by how he couldn't describe an emotion without a smell, how he couldn't really see evil in the world, how much he could learn from a lamp post, but I hadn't been as fascinated by how my staff saw their lives, how Lyndsey saw hers. Perhaps if I had been I would have made some important decisions earlier.

There's enough thrill in a flower if you're truly alive without having to seek out risks to fire the rusted engine of your senses into motion – real risks, poker and powerboating risks; I'm not talking about bungee jumping at the fair.

I'd turn my back on gambling, I decided. I'd take the dog to the Cat's, if I could raise the stake, not to gamble but to listen to Reg, and then I'd give Miles his money and go home.

That would be it for me and poker, apart from a few games to get myself back on the straight and narrow, natch. Maybe the internet and a few social occasions.

There was a nagging thought in the back of my mind, however. I owed Miles about £25 million. That's £24 million more than would be considered an extremely extravagant pot in England, the sort that would make the news.

But, it occurred to me that my slice was 'only' a million. If Miles would stump up enough wonga, maybe £100,000, then I could get the million back to him. It had to be attractive because there was flip all point in suing me as I was completely, to quote Snake Eyes, boracic.

The only things I owned in the world were the clothes I stood up in and Reg, who I had technically stolen. Even Miles, I thought, wouldn't want a court case which could take months to obtain a dog generously valued at fifty pounds.

'It went all black and then, from the darkness, the greatest gift a dog can know!' It was Reg, who was pulling Miles into the lobby to greet me.

They came over and Miles sat down. There we were in the lobby, the psychedelic Australian (though he was English) and the tramp. We looked like something from a sixties road movie.

'OK,' said Miles, 'what happened in that room?'

'He's already told me,' I said.

'So?'

'I'd say you put a duvet over his head and then gave him a piece of steak.'

I've seen people's jaw drop before, very often on the last card of a hand, as a one in ten chance becomes a one in one. Miles's jaw, however, fell so low that the passer-by might have thought he was inviting me to inspect his teeth if I didn't believe how old he was.

'He drew the curtains first,' said Reg.

'You drew the curtains first,' I said.

'And said, "Let's see what your camera makes of this".'

'And said, "Let's see what your camera makes of this".' I said.

'He also changed his underwear,' said the dog.

'New boxers too,' I said.

Miles sat back in his chair and blew out his cheeks.

'This is a trick,' he said, 'but I can't work out how it's done.'

I drew forward and hit him with my pitch.

'All my money is now in my ex-girlfriend's name. She has no intention of ever seeing me again, let alone giving me a penny, so if you sue me you'll get nothing. Inform the police and I may go to prison. It being a white-collar crime, however, I'll probably cop an Archer in some soft gaol, table tennis, pool, gym, weekends off as long as I don't drink, which I don't normally anyway. I'll even get to play poker.'

'Hold on,' said Miles.

'No,' I said. 'I would like to pay you your money back. However, the amount I personally got from your mum was one million quid. Exactly £999,999 and eighty-eight pence more than I currently have. If you front me enough money I will go to the people who are the chief beneficiaries of your mother's misfortune and I will win it off them. Using this remarkable dog.'

Reg gave a little cough, like a butler disturbing the lady from some flower-arranging in order that she might approve a new tradesman.

'No,' said Miles. 'It's a classic con. Rip someone off and then rip them off again, pretending you're going to help them get their money back. You must think very little of me.'

He had a curious way of speaking, Miles. Part Australian and part Etonian. His last sentence was pure *Brideshead Revisited*.

'Win it off him!' said Reg, who was trying to jam his head under the sofa to get at a peanut.

'Shut up,' I said.

'What's he say?' said Miles. I suppose that being brought up by a mother who absolutely believed that animals had human virtues and vices, down to shredding curtains because they didn't like the pattern, it wasn't much of a leap to believe one could talk.

'He said I should win it off you,' I said. 'He's ignoring the fact that I haven't got a stake.'

The waiter came over and asked me if I'd like any more coffee and if I'd seen the hotel's range of souvenir sweatshirts that could be brought to me immediately if I required.

'Oh, go on then,' I said, figuring I might as well spend as much of Miles's money as I could while I had the chance.

'Actually,' said Miles, 'I believe you have got a stake.'

And he was right, I had – even though I didn't know it. I'll say this, he was no mug, that Miles.

36

Come Play My Game

One card, not to be selected from a pack but to be imagined. Miles would go out into the street, down to the seafront and away from all possible surveillance.

He would write the name of the card on a piece of paper and place it in an envelope. When he returned, the envelope would be placed in the hotel safe.

Then, for a bet of £100,000 pounds, I would, with the dog's help, tell him what the card was.

If I won, I'd get my money to take on the Cat.

If I lost, well. There was something else in the safe.

I was already ahead as I deposited my stake, because I'd persuaded Miles to allow me to take a shower and borrow some of his clothes. Miles was quite a bit shorter than me and the pensioner at Bondi look isn't exactly my favourite, but whatever, it was good to feel clean again.

The hotel manager was a little too busy to help us with anything but the safe stuff but he called in a couple of members of staff at short notice who were pleased to earn £100 each on Christmas Day for what was about one minute's work.

My stake for the game with Miles was simply a signed confession, to everything, naming each of the parties involved.

I missed out Lyndsey, of course I did. The girl hadn't played very straight with me but I was still fond of her. She wasn't driven by greed but by fear – of poverty, of returning to where she'd come from. I wasn't going to send her back there.

The Cat and the Folding Society, however, got a full and frank assessment of their ways, accounting to the last penny for how much they'd stolen from Mrs Cad-Beauf and how much they'd made on top of that. I could make a very good estimate of their profit because I knew how many houses there were on the site and how much they were going for.

I reckoned that, though the site itself had been worth £25 million, they'd made about four times that.

The ten members of the Folding Society had each made around £10 million. Not bad for mugging an old lady.

On top of my confession he also wanted me to avow that I'd persuaded him to part with £100,000 and that I promised to repay this in full at minimum and £1 million should I win in the game. I didn't mind, I could already taste my victory.

The two members of staff were drawn in as witnesses to my signature – though we didn't let them read what I was signing – and Miles, naturally, made sure the whole thing was legally watertight. It might have been an affidavit, it might not. I really wasn't paying that much attention. I was focused where a gambler is most often focused – on his fantasy, and my fantasy was shafting the Cat.

How did I know Miles wouldn't just take my confession and go to the police? I didn't. I had a good inkling that curiosity would propel him to see what the dog could do, but no guarantee. It appeared that my efforts at giving up gambling were off to a bad start.

The writing finished, the witnesses went away with their £100, saying, 'Cheers, mate,' and 'Any more work like that, just let me know,' and then we were alone, he, me, and Reggie B.

'OK,' said Miles, 'what's the card?'

'I reckon it's an old one,' said the dog. 'He doesn't look as if he'd want a new smelly deck.'

'That's not the answer we're looking for,' I said to him.

Miles raised his eyebrows. 'Problem?'

'No,' I said. 'OK, I don't want you to reply to any of the questions I'm about to ask you about the card,' I said.

'Don't worry, mate, I won't,' said Miles, back to the Antipodean accent, which is very good for saying things like that in.

'Is it a heart?'

'No reaction,' said Reg.

'Is it a diamond?'

'Not a bleep,' said the dog.

'A spade?'

'Nope,' said the dog.

Well, it was a club then, wasn't it?

Next round.

'It's a picture or an ace,' I said.

'No,' said the dog.

'It's five or below,' I said.

'No,' said the dog.

'Don't answer any of these, remember that,' I said. 'Only when I say, "This is your card" and write it down, have I made my decision. Eight or below.'

'Cool as a cucumber,' said the dog who was not, as far as I was aware, acquainted with cucumbers, there being little call for them in the doggy milieu.

So it was the nine of clubs, easy as you like and I know you like it easy.

'This is your card,' I said with, I have to admit, some feeling of self-satisfaction.

I was halfway through writing it down when Reg said, 'He's not sweating.'

I scribbled out what I'd written. Rather extravagantly I'd actually been drawing the card, with little flourishes on the clubs.

Why wouldn't he be sweating? Everyone sweats when they're about to lose 100 large. It was then that the awful realisation descended.

'You don't care about money, do you?' I said.

'Not a lot,' said Miles, smiling mildly and sitting back in his chair.

'This, then, could be a problem,' I said.

'What's the card?' said Miles with easy menace.

'What's the card, what's the card?' said Reg, who was amusing himself by chasing his tail.

'Er,' I said.

'That's not a card,' said Miles.

I was in a considerable mess. The dog's ability to read card players rested almost entirely on them having an emotional response to the threat of losing money. If you don't care that you're going to lose it, if you're so rich and pious that you don't even bother to spend the millions you've got but waste your days helping the needy, then you're immune to any canine inquisitor.

'That's it,' I said. 'I'm going to prison.'

'Give up?' said Miles. 'Well, Sight Savers are going to be pleased.'

'Sorry?'

'I decided that if I can waste a hundred thousand pounds on a twit like you I can afford to give it to some more worthwhile cause. You're in gaol, children in Africa have their cataracts removed and are no longer blind, everyone's happy. The money goes to those who need it and deserve it.'

The dog panted up to me, slightly breathless from his tail pursuit.

'Best the children have it,' said the dog, who still hadn't grasped the prison idea. 'It would be very upsetting to think of blind children.'

He was right, it would.

'So what would have happened to these kids if I'd won?' I said. 'Wouldn't you have given them the money anyway?'

'No,' said Miles.

'Why not?'

'I'm a philanthropist not a socialist. You can't give all your money away or you wouldn't have any for yourself. There's a limit to individual responsibility for even the super-rich. I've always thought about giving them money, they're number fifteen on the list. I've got to fourteen so far. This just focused my mind on the fact that I could probably afford it. Well, I can afford it but you have to draw a limit somewhere and one and a half million a year to charity is where I draw mine. Unless I get what I regard as a bonus like this. So this year, thanks to you, Mr Barker, it'll be one point six million.'

'You haven't won yet,' I said. So now I was competing to take money off blind children in Africa. Great. Oh well, I'd just have to win £1.1 million.

'Looks like I have,' he said.

'What would happen if you lost? How would you feel?' I said.

'Since I didn't think of giving it away until I said I was going to then I don't know, I haven't thought about it.'

'How many children's sight could be saved with that money?'

'Tens of thousands, I should think,' said Miles. 'I think it costs about two pounds each.'

'And yet you're prepared to give it to me.'

'I hadn't looked at it like that,' he said.

'No,' I said. 'You're going to throw away the health of thousands on a single card. That makes you rather selfish, don't you think?'

Miles actually blushed, which is not something you expect from a lawyer.

'He's starting to sweat a bit,' said Reg. I didn't need a dog for that, I could see it. That and his evasive eye movements and slightly turned-away defensive posture.

'That's not going to happen, though, is it?' he said. 'You can't guess.'

'Oh, I think we can now,' I said, imagining him in the crosshairs. 'Let's do it again. You just need to know what losing means. If I guess right, the money goes to the game. If I guess wrong, thousands of kids get a chance at sight. Is it a heart?'

'He's pouring with sweat!' said the dog. 'His heart's thumping.'

I felt a bit sweaty myself. I mean. Blind kids. How much of a bastard was I?

'Is it a club?' Just enough of a bastard, it appeared.

'He's calming down,' said the dog.

'So it's a heart,' I said.

'His legs are trembling,' said the dog. I could see that they were.

'It's a picture or an ace,' I said.

'More stress, let's get him!' said Reg.

'Don't be so canine,' I said.

'Sorry,' said the dog.

'King or above?'

'Calmer,' said the dog, 'but not by much.'

'Queen,' I said.

'Woof, woof, woof!' said Reg. 'That's the baby!'

'It's a jack then, the jack of hearts,' I said.

'He's gone much calmer,' said the dog.

Then it was the queen.

I wrote it down, this time just the words without illustration.

'This is your card,' I said.

I didn't need Reg to tell me I was right. I could see it in the pallor of Miles's face. He looked like a chap who had just lost £100,000.

'Well . . . me,' said Miles, the normal swiping, blowing or ruder alternatives not apparently adequate to the job of describing what he wanted doing to him to fit with his emotions.

'I'd say that was the one,' said Reg.

Perhaps Miles had been in the pragmatic southern hemisphere for too long, perhaps the 'my word is my bond' of his public school days had been forgotten, or perhaps he just was quite wise, but I didn't get my money, or even a promise of it, straightaway.

I wasn't in much of a position to argue. It was fair enough, really. He wanted assurances that I could actually play poker – understandable in a man about to put £100,000 on a horse. A horse is what we poker players call someone playing with someone else's money. Why we don't call it 'someone playing with someone else's money' I don't know. I mean, poker isn't the only form of gambling most of them do; what happens if you actually want to put money on a horse?

And a monkey – £500. What if someone had just come into possession of a zoo and actually did bet a monkey? Imagine the confusion as a Barbary ape was handed over.

I digress.

First we ordered up a set of cards from downstairs and I beat him in about ten minutes at a game of Seven Card Stud. 'I had an ace in my hand,' he said, explaining why he'd bet all his matchsticks. 'I thought another was bound to turn up.'

'You don't actually feel like playing for money, do you?' I said. I felt fairly sure I could whip 12p up into a reasonable amount against him, given enough time.

'You haven't got any,' he said.

'Oh yeah,' I said.

Then he insisted that we go down to the hotel's business centre and get on the internet.

You'd think it sad that there might be anyone at all playing internet poker, particularly the practice variety, on Christmas

Day. What is sad is that there are more people playing on Christmas Day than there are on normal days. I should know, I'm normally one of them.

I pointed out to Miles that I wasn't going to be betting with the help of the dog, as he couldn't sniff down the wires of the internet, but he wanted to see that I could play to a reasonable level anyway.

It wasn't too much of a problem. You do occasionally get decent players in the practise rooms but not that often. After three hours I'd built up a theoretical total of about $4,000 from a stake of $100 and Miles seemed reasonably satisfied.

We sat in the sophisticated ambience of the hotel's restaurant, ruining its sophisticated ambience with our clown shirts. Reg had been consigned to the bed upstairs after being sedated with a couple of steaks.

As we ate I could sense the discomfort in Miles. I guessed that I would feel discomfort if I was about to hand over £100,000 to a proven fraud. I decided to try to put his mind at rest.

'I wanted to tell you that I really liked your mother,' I said. 'I might have gone along with this thing but I did my best for her in other ways.'

'I know you did,' said Miles. 'One of the things I found most difficult to understand about the whole thing was why you'd transferred all that money of hers into proper investments without misappropriating any of it. At first I thought I was dealing with some sort of criminal mastermind.'

I was pleased to see he was mellowing.

'I'm afraid not,' I said. 'I just wanted to do well by her. It didn't seem so immoral just redirecting the money away from a dogs' home. I would never have stolen it directly.'

'So you stole it indirectly,' said Miles. I was displeased to see that he was doing whatever the reverse of mellowing is.

I directed his attention back to the dessert card. There was a cinnamon crème brûlée that looked intriguing.

'Look,' said Miles, 'I've been having a think about this and I've decided, why don't we call it quits? I'll give you your confession back and my personal assurance that I won't pursue anything against you and we'll just go our separate ways.'

Suddenly the crème brûlée was very much less intriguing.

I could get my credit card back from the Robinsons, borrow a couple of grand on it, start seeing Lucy. I could probably even give up the estate agent game if I used the dog to make money from poker (wasn't I going to give it up ten seconds before?). I could have a new life. From the depths of despair came the lofty peaks of ecstasy, or so I had once read.

I was free to set up a new life with a new girl and an old dog, free of the spectre of prison, free of Lyndsey, even in some way I didn't understand free of my mum and dad.

'Do you mean it?' I said. It's always best to check, I find.

'Absolutely,' said Miles. 'And I'm willing to sign legal documents to that effect.'

'But what about your money?'

'Maybe I'll get it back off Tibbs. He's at least got money to reclaim. If I don't, it's a bastard but there you go. I won't have lost another hundred thousand.'

'You're on,' I said, 'you really are on. I'm so happy, I can't believe it, I really am. Would you mind if I made a couple of phone calls on your phone?'

'Of course not,' said Miles.

He passed me the phone and I called directory enquiries and then Lucy.

She answered. I could hear a party going on in the background, of the kids' sort.

'Lucy, it's Dave.'

'Did you get him?'

'Yes and he's fine, just like he always was.'

'That's great, Dave.' I could hear her relief pouring down the phone. 'Have you stroked him for me?'

'Right in the prime spot,' I said, 'just behind the ear.'

'And the head, has the head been patted?'

'In the approved fashion,' I said. This strange talk between us had sprung up from somewhere. It would revolt others probably but I took it as a sign that the future was opening to me, warm, cosy. Canine.

'Lucy, can I come round? Things have got rather difficult since we last met.'

'Things were flipping difficult then,' said Lucy.

'I think they're flipping flipping difficult just now. Or they were. In fact things are rather good, despite the fact that I'm dressed like an eighties kids' TV presenter. Things are just fine. But I'm going to need you to pay the cab if I come over, is that OK?'

I was beaming like a chat show host; for the first time since I could remember I was uncomplicatedly, straightforwardly happy. Life had simplified, it had gone into the mixer as squirts of competing primary colours, been shaken up for ten minutes and come out as BK3344904, Dulux Chalky White, the ideal choice in which to paint the bedroom of the soul.

'Fine,' said Lucy, as I heard someone saying someone else was cheating and she was going to tell. 'It sounds like you'll fit in here.'

'I'll be there in ten minutes,' I said.

I passed the phone back to Miles.

I felt that I wanted to thank him so much that I might be in danger of running out of thanks for anyone else for the rest of my life.

'I am eternally grateful. And if I never see you again can I say that you are a credit to your mother.'

'Oh,' said Miles, 'I think we'll be seeing each other again.'

'Yes, we'll need to sign some documents, I suppose,' I said.

'Well, that and the card game,' said Miles.

'I'm sorry?' I said.

'You're going to play, Mr Barker,' said Miles, leaning back in his chair.

'I thought you were really uncomfortable with giving me one hundred thousand pounds,' I said.

'I'm a lot more comfortable now I see you don't want it,' he said.

Somewhere inside me a voice said, 'No!' and somewhere inside me a voice said, 'Yes.' This was progress. The prospect of playing in such a high stakes game, even with someone else's money, would have had me buzzing like a cheap VCR before. Now there was doubt, a little flicker of normality.

He passed me the mobile phone. 'Tibbs' number's programmed in.'

'You've called him?'

'Not yet,' he said. 'Tell him you've got a big backer and you want to play him and his cronies.'

'I should think he'll be suspicious if he knows it's you,' I said.

'Stress the money to him. If I read him right that's what he's interested in. Double it if you feel like it. Make it two hundred thousand. Let's have the bastard.'

I raised my eyebrows. 'You find this gambling thing quite seductive, don't you?'

'Yes, a bit,' he said, flattered that I recognised him as a fellow devil-may-care soul.

'Fancy giving it a go?' I said.

'One day maybe,' he said.

'Don't,' I said, taking out the matchsticks that I'd won and showering them onto the table. Force of habit had seen me pocket my winnings.

'Point taken,' he said.

There were a couple of rings and Tibbs answered.

'Tibbsy,' I said. I wanted to get his back up so he'd feel like putting me in my place.

'Who is this?' he said, in a controlled way which was meant

to suggest, I think, that something inside him required controlling – i.e. a raging and dangerous temper.

'Dave Barker,' I said.

'This is Christmas Day,' he said. 'I was using it to spend some quality time with my bank statements. And I don't think I should be talking to you anyway,' he said.

'Why not?'

'Because I bought that property in good faith. I believed that Mrs Cad-Beauf wanted to sell it cheaply so that it could be developed as a service to the community but now it appears it was all a fraud designed by you in order to make money.'

'Nice one, Tiddles,' I said, 'but don't worry, I'm not taping this. I just have a proposition for you.'

'I've had enough of your propositions, thank you.'

I admired Tibbs for this; he was more than prepared to convince himself that he was the injured party so that he could be all the more convincing when called upon to defend himself before the beak.

'I want a game,' I said, 'Two hundred large in.' Two hundred large always sounds better than £200,000. I mean, there are ways of saying it that don't make it sound like very much at all. Two lock-up garages in Mayfair, for instance.

'We haven't played for that sort of money in quite a while,' said Tibbs, meaning ever. 'Where have you got it from?'

'I have reserves,' I said, 'and I need a little more money to defend myself against our friend so I thought this might be a good way to raise it. If I lose I've got nothing anyway and the bastard can't touch me.'

I felt Tibbs smile down the phone. He clearly liked his opponents desperate.

'Depending on how many you can get to the table, you'd stand to make a couple of . . .' I couldn't remember the rhyming slang.

'Million?' ventured the Cat.

'That's it,' I said.

He pondered for an instant.

'Give me an hour,' he said, 'then you'll have your answer.'

'You need to decide,' I said, 'whether you're a cat or whether you're a pussy.'

'I bet you've been dying to say that for ages,' said the Cat.

'Your powers of observation are as acute as ever, Tiddles,' I said. 'The money's practically yours.'

Miles and I sat eating our puddings in virtual silence for the next forty-five minutes until his phone went.

'You're on,' said the Cat. 'Name the time and your venue.'

'The twenty-seventh,' I said, which was the soonest Miles would be able to get any cash out, 'and anywhere there's a bowl of water.'

37

Pack Animal

This is my plan to convince myself that I know what I'm doing.

I'm going to walk into a room with £200,000 and walk out with a profit of £1 million while the assorted lowlifes I've taken it off pat me on the back and wish me Godspeed with a 'Fare thee well'.

It shouldn't go wrong. I'm not dealing with gangsters. On the gangster scale, they may be nearer Don Corleone than the tooth fairy but they're not *that* near him.

It's worth pointing out, though, that the only thing that stops these people being gangsters is that they're too clever. They've found a way to make a great deal of money without ever really breaking the law.

OK, they may have had a few people beaten up, they may even have had people killed if what the policeman said is correct, but it's not a matter of course for them. They use freelancers, they don't have a standing army that needs to be fed a regular supply of violence and mayhem to keep it sharp. I'm guessing this is what it's like, really, but I think it's a fairly good guess.

So the arrangements for this game were complex as, wisely, everyone trusted each other like timeshare.

Each party books a venue, above a pub, in a hotel, somewhere that's public, preferably has some CCTV – to make any hold-ups at least a little more complicated – and maybe even some security of its own.

Business being what it is, the only possible place to hold a meeting like this was London.

This is for several reasons. Obviously a lot of the people you'll be playing with have interests up there but for a second thing the place is drowned in surveillance cameras should the worst come to the worst. It also means you can get two decent venues quite close to each other so there's no need to start messing around with the sunshine minibus.

Also, in a smaller town there may only really be a few suitable places. A few phone calls could determine where you'd booked.

You need two venues even though, like the loser's ribbons on the FA cup, one will remain unused.

We meet at a bar, flip a coin taken at random in change from drinks to decide which one we use. Then we phone to have our money delivered there. No one's going to carry that amount of folding with them. The money is taken by at least two honoured and trusted acquaintances to the place, where entrance is secured by a password.

These men will inevitably be tooled up in some way – it would be stupid for them not to be. I'm not talking necessarily about guns, though that did cross my mind. I'm talking about maybe some pepper spray or a cosh. Both can easily be obtained by tapping relations' children to go into the right shops when they go on their school trip to France. They're going to do it anyway so you may as well benefit from it.

There'll be a third guy there too, some surveillance bloke from a private detective agency who will sweep the place for cameras and bugs because you never know and sometimes you do know. You never use the guy from a local shop, because they can get to him and bribe him. No, you use someone from an agency in Scotland or the north and you get him to come down.

The money for this you have to regard as part of your buy-in cash. If you want to extract snake venom you have to accept you're going to have to deal with snakes.

My button men, which is what I call them for no good reason other than it makes them sound more efficient and so sets my mind at rest, are Miles – which is far from ideal, though he wants to see what's happening to his money – and Martin the Marine from next door to my old flat.

He was flattered when I called him.

'You are a dark horse, Davy boy, I'll give you that,' he said. This is what he always says whenever he sees me and to be honest it's started to go right through me. Not that I've bothered telling him.

'You were the first person I thought of,' I said. This is what men can do for each other when it's all working well, fan each other's feathers. He was the hardest bastard I knew, I the darkest horse. How could we fail?

Were all these precautions necessary? Probably not. There was no reason to suspect the Cat might pull a fast one. He regularly held big games at his house and other people walked away winners with no undue harm coming to them on their way home. This, though, was the biggest game any of us had ever played and it was the 'probably' that worried everyone. Being gamblers we were unwilling to gamble and so sought to minimise the risk.

The venue I chose was near to Buckingham Palace in a trendy arts club. It was expensive but there was a good reason for my wanting to go there.

First I wanted to put the Cat and his cronies at their unease. They were rich, sure, but they were tasteless. Being forced through a hall of high-mindedness would fill their low minds with contempt, which is just another manifestation of fear and I wanted them scared.

I'd checked it out, and the major exhibition seemed to be an empty room with a chair turned over in the middle of it. This actually filled me with contempt so perhaps it wasn't the best idea after all.

The dog had liked it though.

'It's great,' he said. 'You can run all the way round it going zing zing zing! That's what I call art. And—'

'Not indoors,' I said, pulling him away from the chair.

Also, being near to Buck House, there were a good two hundred coppers and a couple of regiments of guards should anyone get any ideas about relieving me of the winnings. It wouldn't stop them but it would make things more difficult.

On the night of the game I furnished Reg with a new tartan collar obtained after Lucy had gone round to the Robinsons' and got my credit card and mobile back. Luckily Doc Robinson hadn't been in when she'd called and Penny had been only too pleased to hand over my property when Lucy explained what had happened.

'He's still talking about getting the other dog back but the kids love this one,' she said. 'But why did your husband give him away in the first place?'

'He's not my husband,' said Lucy. 'He's just had a lot of problems recently.'

'Well, keep him out of our life then!' said Penny cheerfully as she wished Lucy goodbye.

Reg tried on the collar but didn't like it.

'Why not?' I said.

'Too new,' he said. 'I need something with a smell to it. Can I wear my old home collar?'

'That old thing?' I said, picking up the one he'd been wearing when the Robinsons had got him from the League for Canine Advancement.

'Well, it's more "street",' said the dog. 'They'll feel less inclined to mess with me.'

I clicked it on him, the faded green nylon number, its repeated dog logo scarcely visible beneath the grime.

'Now they'll know they're dealing with a dog, not a pup,' said the dog, stretching inside it like on old cricketer pulling on his favourite jumper just one more time.

We met in the Loco Loco pub at Victoria, which is basically a scale model of a motorway service station but much dirtier.

Four members of the Folding Society were there, the copper, the solicitor, a couple of others, and three stiff-looking City sorts I didn't recognise, which is never a good sign.

'You can't bring dogs in here,' said the bar devil as I approached the group.

I enquired if this was because they might catch something. He said he'd call security. I told him to go ahead. Good, I was right in the mood for the game, firm, assertive, ready to stand my ground.

The Cat was in his leisure wear, which was a truly awful sight to behold for those of us who don't like the pastel shell suit worn over the golfing jumper.

'Still hanging around with that mangy animal?' said the Cat. 'I thought a dog like you would have better taste.'

He seemed to find this mightily amusing, as did the City sorts who looked at each other in a conspiratorial giggle.

'Shall we get on with this?' I said, as Reg took a reference sniff of the Cat. Although the dog has incredible powers of smell and an uncanny ability to read what people are thinking, he does like a base point from which to start. The Cat would be slightly nervous upon meeting me and we did that circling each other growling lightly and sniffing at each other thing but that was OK, Reg would take that into account. He'd be able to read when the Cat relaxed on getting a good card as well as noting when he became more nervous by getting bad ones.

'Can we have a coin please?' said the Cat to the barman.

'I can't serve you when you're with a dog,' said the barman.

'I'm not with a dog, he is,' said the Cat, 'and I'm not asking you to serve me, I'm asking you to lend me a coin.'

'I can't lend anything,' said the barman. 'It's against the rules.'

Suddenly I didn't want to be in England any more, in a place that took a lovely old railway tavern and did its best to make it look like a motorway service station and also tried to tell you that it was an improvement. I didn't want to be a high income person in a low income economy, I didn't want a Boots card or the new shape Astra or to be in a place that cared where dogs went and where they didn't.

Someone in the dead air of that bar I got a feeling of what I did want, something just at the limit of my reach but moving nearer.

'Would you at least point to one person in this pub so we can ask them to flip a coin for us?' I said.

'I can't do that either,' said the barman. 'I just serve drinks.'

It occurred to me that he was less human than the dog. He was simply a means to put the drinks over the bar and the money in the till.

I didn't know where all these thoughts were coming from. For years I'd just done what everyone did – had reasonable friends, been reasonably happy, wanted a reasonable life. The dog, though, had made me see more, that it was possible to love extravagantly, to live without riches but richly, to have an intense, unreasonable life that had nothing to do with all-terrain skateboarding or calling people 'dude'.

'Can I help?' said the security man, giving the dog a pat.

'This gentleman won't leave the bar with his dog,' said the barman.

'Oh, go on, please,' said the security man.

'If you flip a coin for us,' I said.

'Done,' he said, reaching into his pocket and sending a 50p whirling into the air.

'Heads,' said the Cat.

'Tails!' wagged the dog.

It was tails and we were on our way to the arts club. Game on.

The Cat had, as I expected, brought a couple of heavies with him. Disconcertingly, Martin kept referring to them as 'Marys'. The others were light on muscle and the City boys actually had their money with them, or at least their banker's drafts.

I found the sight of Martin and Miles reassuring. Clearly it was good to see that Miles had chimed in with the wonga and it's always good to see a bloke who's murdered a few people with his bare hands turn up to bat for you.

As an observer, Miles would be allowed to sit next to me at the table, but not behind me or any of the other players, for obvious reasons.

Naturally we'd employed professional dealers, two provided by me, two by the Cat. They would deal in shifts throughout the game and one of his would always be watching one of mine and vice versa.

Finally we were in, searched and seated, and the first blinds put in. I'm giving up explaining poker terminology but I will say that blinds are bets.

Various people lit up and soon the air was blue with smoke and expletives as we all showed each other how tough we were.

I'd always been surprised that Reg could smell the sweat and the fear and the gloating through the smoke but according to him the various smokers flavoured their emissions with their emotions, making it easier, if anything, to read them.

Reg sat underneath my chair with a bowl of water ready for him at the corner of the room. This was the medium through which the canine palate would be refreshed, the taste dial set at zero, the lie detector calibrated. Not necessary to the action but so much a part of it – the director's chair snapped out by the runner on a cold movie morning, like all the others though a little bigger and bearing the name A. Hitchcock, Mozart's quill, Churchill's cigar – an incidental feature that seemed to throb with the power of the whole thing.

Beneath my seat the dog wouldn't have an eyeline to the other players but that was OK. You don't have to see someone to smell them and, in fact, many dogs recognise people almost entirely by their smell. He could work just fine from there.

I looked round the table, really looked, I think, for the first time ever.

The Cat, for instance, could I look at him with understanding, really grasp what had made him? I might then want to rip it to bits but I knew that I had to begin by putting myself into his white trainers.

It's difficult not to categorise when you look at another human being, to allow cheap TV and problem page solutions to cloud your view. He's a bastard, she's got a heart of gold, he needs to prove himself, she will never have any self-confidence.

How would the dog see him? He wouldn't, he'd smell him. Aftershave – a little too much of it, wet fur on a dry day and wanting the world in his image, to shape it. These were strange associations but it occurred to me that the Cat was actually quite uncomfortable with himself. Perhaps that's why he was at the table, where cause and effect were so sharply defined.

'You in or what?'

I hadn't even noticed it had started.

I was in and we were off, the dog quickly hunkering down into a groove, busting two early bluffs wide open and steering me clear of one clever trap.

The diamonds rolled, the hearts bled; I dug in with spades and smashed with clubs.

The City boys were out of their depth, so much so that they

didn't even have the brains to realise it and quit. They talked the talk and soon they would walk the walk.

The Cat and the Folders were wiser, of course, keeping their powder dry but not too dry. Even with the dog they were formidable opponents and I knew I wouldn't get their money cheaply.

By the first break I had £800,000 in chips in front of me and only £400,000 to go. We'd had two go home and one ask to borrow money off the Cat. Things were shaping up nicely, especially as having a decent wad makes it much easier to play. The minimum bets were coming up to £500, which to me was only one one-hundred-and-eightieth of my available wealth. To a man down to his last £10,000, it's one-twentieth, which is a lot.

'Will we be off for food soon?' said Reg, chewing a chicken drumstick I'd thrown him.

'You're eating now,' I said.

'Well,' he said, 'you have to plan ahead.'

I could taste the end in front of me, the return to reality. What would I do? I wondered. I didn't know, but with Reg and Lucy about, it seemed that whatever it was I would be happy.

I tickled the dog under the chin. 'You're a very good boy,' I said.

'Oh, I know,' said the dog, stretching up into the pleasure of my fingers.

'You're doing very well,' I said.

'Oh, I know,' said the dog. 'I can feel the warmth of your praise.'

I felt cold eyes upon me and I looked up to see the Cat fixing me as a real cat might a canary. I hadn't taken too much money off him in the game, maybe £50,000. I guessed he'd have brought a serious wad, much more than mine.

'What are you looking at?' I said, somewhat more aggressively than I'd intended.

'I don't know,' said the Cat, his eyes flicking between me and the dog. 'I can honestly say I don't know.'

Session two was more uncomfortable as the Cat began to try to unsettle me.

'How's Lyndsey nowadays?' he said.

'How would I know?'

'She's well, I'll tell you,' he said.

I said nothing, just raised him.

'She's a really lovely girl, isn't she?' he said.

I blanked him again with a 'play your flipping cards, flip-face' look on my face. I was learning from the dog that it was best not to swear, even if you really, really, really wanted to look cool or tough.

He called me and I lost. Caught out chasing one more heart, flushing myself away while he was holding a run. What a mug.

The Cat knew he'd found the way to distract me. I thought at the time that he was implying that he was sleeping with Lyndsey. However, I figured that if he'd actually been sleeping with her he wouldn't have said so.

There's no predicting how someone's going to react to you shagging their girlfriend – she doesn't really get her ex certificate until about six months after you've finished if you've been going out with her as long as I'd been going out with Lyndsey. I didn't know the Cat very well but I guessed he was a physical coward. Given his scrawny build, if he wasn't a physical coward he was an idiot.

'Don't let him bother you,' said the dog. 'Lucy's much nicer. There's no joy in being with a woman who never gives you a biscuit.'

I reached down to pat him. He was no longer under my chair and he had his paws on my knee, as if trying to see the cards.

You'd think the other players would find this distracting but as they've immunised themselves against insults, cigar smoke and bugle-blast farting, a dog comes way down the scale.

'I should think you must be pretty lonely at the moment,' said the Cat, ten hands later.

'I've got a million quid for company,' I said, gesturing to my pile of chips.

I only needed £200,000 more and I'd be home and dry. I hadn't forgotten the blind orphans, of course; there would be £100,000 for them in it.

It was down to him and me again. They say that in poker there are no good hands, only good situations. It's no good having four aces if no one else has got anything. Four aces and him sitting on four kings is a different story.

My hand was a straight – a run from 9 to king. A very good hand. Also, from what I could see, no one had much of a chance of beating me. A chance, but one in five hundred or something like that.

The Cat stared past me, seemingly looking for inspiration from the ether.

'He's very confident,' said dog.

'Excellent,' I said under my breath, as if talking to myself.

'That's good?' said the dog.

'It's an excellent situation,' I said. The policeman rolled his eyes to show his disdain for what he took to be my boasting.

'He's massively confident,' said Reg. 'I can feel the pleasure oozing off him but it's nicer that it's oozing off you,' he said. He looked into my eyes like Scarlett to Rhett and said, 'You're very happy right now, aren't you?'

For a second I thought that the one in five hundred chance was going to come off. But one in five hundred chances don't – well, no more than one time in five hundred and I was sure this wasn't it.

'Boy, is he confident!' said Reg. 'I've never smelled anyone that happy in my life.'

For a second I had a tremble. One in five hundred. It could happen. But it wasn't going to, was it? The Cat was about to pile in on weaker cards and I was going to rake in whatever fortune he decided to try to buy it for.

I looked at Miles and smiled. We were going home.

Then the Cat folded. I was up just the tiny amount on the table, no money at all really.

'I thought you said he was confident,' I mumbled to the dog. The good thing about mumbling to a dog is that they've got very good ears.

'He was confident, sir,' said the dog. 'He still is.'

We played on and I bet conservatively, neither winning nor losing. Two hours later, still one hundred thousand short of my target, we broke again.

I bit on a canapé and chatted to Miles. Martin was still outside the room, as heavies aren't allowed in, though backers are. This is because backers back and may come up with some more money if you're losing, heavies heavy and may come up with something heavy in the same circumstances.

'You're nearly there!' he said, bobbing up and down in his Kaluha shirt.

'Yes,' I said flatly.

'You don't look very pleased about it,' he said.

'This is poker,' I said. 'I wouldn't be nearly there if I was the sort to look very pleased when I'm nearly there.' I quite enjoyed patronising Martin. This I supposed was another benefit of poker, people who never got to patronise anyone about anything got to patronise someone about something.

In truth, I thought, as I swilled my orange juice around my mouth, I wasn't very pleased.

Something in the Cat's manner had changed and a changing manner indicates only one thing – a change. The Cat was thinking about something, I could tell.

Throwing away his cards on the last hand was weird too. If the dog said people were confident, they always went for their bets. Always. And he hadn't.

The Cat stood chatting conspiratorially with the other members of the Folding Society, as he was allowed to do. If a man can't chat conspiratorially with his conspirators then what's the world coming to?

I have to say I didn't like him much, not just because of what he did but of who he was. I didn't like the way he stretched at the table. Plenty of people stretch but not like that. He'd flex his fingers, pull back his cuffs and attempt to look like a concert pianist preparing for a crack at the Dvořák. In fact he always looked to me as if he was about to stick his hand up a cow's nethers.

I didn't like the way he clacked his mouth when thinking, I didn't like his aftershave, I didn't like his expensive trashy-looking jewellery, I didn't like him.

It was as if I could sense an aura coming off him, one of someone with a cheap understanding of the world. I looked at him and saw holidays in conspicuously five-star resorts where he'd complain about the food and bully the staff; I saw him ordering sickly cocktails and tipping only for exceptional service; I saw grey shoes and marinas, a Mercedes, a swimming pool, a yacht that he planned to trade up, a wharf shopping complex and the misconception that the world wanted to be him. On top of that and beneath the aftershave I got a smell off him, like cheap plastic that had been left too long in a hot car. And something else. Like the dog had said about sadness, rain at the fairground, flat soufflé – even though I'd never knowingly smelled a real soufflé – the sweating palms of a stood-up teenager. Disappointment, in a nutshell.

Were these the thoughts of a sane person? If I was losing it even more than I had lost it, I thought, I hoped I didn't lose it completely until I'd won it.

We sat down for session three. Things started to go wrong from the start. When you have a big reserve of cash you can afford to take a few risks, especially if you've got yourself a hard-won reputation for not taking risks.

Anyway, four hands in, my best hand is queen high with more suits than Burtons. I've been holding out for luck but luck has been holding out on me. Why I've gone to the last card I don't know but poker is sometimes a matter of feel and it's only me and the bald solicitor from the Folding Society left in. I decide that I've paid my dues in building up a cautious rep so I act incautiously, slamming £200,000 into the pot, which is all laughing boy has left.

This is not the wisest move in the history of poker but neither is it the most foolish. I wasn't confident, however, and even though I thought my eventual victory was a foregone conclusion, I was nervous.

'Oh no,' said the dog. 'That was a bad move, wasn't it? You're not confident.'

'Your call,' I said to the solicitor, who I could see myself was shaking like a lady on a washing machine and with as much chance of marshalling clear thoughts. He was going to fold, I knew.

Inside I might have been feeling some anxiety but only the dog could pick up on that. Outside I was as cool as a polar bear's sunglasses.

'He's not decided,' said the dog. 'I'm so nervous, will we go into a home if we don't win?'

He was not very good in a crisis, it has to be said, his ears going flat, his shoulders hunching and emitting a low whimper. There was no difference to him between things going mildly badly and the worst possible thing in the world happening.

'Oh dear,' said Reg, 'he's suddenly very confident. Oh no! Help!'

'Call,' said the solicitor and I was a sackload poorer.

Miles turned to me and whispered. 'What happened there?'

'I don't know,' I said. I really didn't know.

I still trusted the dog but it seemed that the emotions of everyone in the room had suddenly started swinging like Glenn Miller at a forces dance.

Another few hands went by and I returned to basics. No bluffing, no fancy stuff, just bet strongly on the strong hands and keep out of trouble on the weak ones.

Then it happened. For the first time in my poker career, I got the best hand possible ever. I drew jack of hearts, queen of hearts. When the next three cards came down they were ace of hearts, king of hearts, ten of hearts. I'd flopped a royal flush, the big one, the once in a lifetime hand, the lottery win, the number one record, what you wish on shooting stars for. It was a time-stopping moment as big as your first kiss, your wedding day and when they say 'It's a girl!' rolled into one. I hadn't been that happy since my balls dropped. Crude, but necessarily so, I feel. This was a feeling that came up from the nuts.

It doesn't happen. It hadn't happened to me before and it has never happened since. It will never happen because it doesn't happen.

I looked over at the fat cop and the Cat. The cop shifted his weight from ample cheek to ample cheek. I'd picked up a tell – a little sign that gave away what he was thinking. He always did the buttock shuffle when he'd got good cards.

What had he got? Two other hearts maybe, there was a reasonable chance. Maybe he'd just seen his third king and assumed he was bearing gifts from the east. Whatever, I was top of the heap, the undisputed winner and since he held good cards and a stack of about £600,000 I was in a position to escort him to Easy Clean and watch him flipping around in the big machine.

The Cat, too, looked confident. With him it wasn't anything as obvious as sliding from cheek to cheek, or in his case blade to blade, but it was just a change in his presence. The hot plastic smell I imagined whenever I saw him got more intense, to a burning and I could almost hear him crackle.

I was right next to the dealer and the obvious way for me to play would have been to buy it. There was a poor chance I had a royal flush and a smaller chance of me having a hearts flush, if one of the other players was looking at one. So I bet small, trying to look as if I wasn't confident.

'Gosh, you feel good,' said the dog, 'and so do those two. Isn't that nice? This is the best I've known you feel.'

'Thank you,' I said, pushing a small pile of chips in.

The Cat stared past me into space again.

His hand hovered over his chips.

'Excellent,' said Reg. 'He's going to give you all those, isn't he?'

'Yup,' I said. The Cat would think I was just trying to distract him.

The Cat gave a big grin and stroked his whiskers.

'Deary, dear, oh deary dear,' he said. I loved the gloating look on his face, he could hardly contain himself, almost on the edge of his seat. The last time I'd seen someone with a look like that it was Sebastian when he'd thought I was Santa.

He reached into his pile, took out roughly £1 million in chips and rattled them between his hands, which is a lot of chips to rattle.

Then he put them back and folded.

First I felt the blood drain from my face then it came back, seemingly weighting my head forward like those drinking birds you used to get in the seventies. I felt like I was going to faint.

The Cat saw my discomfort and, being the Cat, decided to add to it, flipping his cards over to show three tens. A fantastic hand, though not as good as mine.

The cop did likewise on a flush. A brilliant hand, though useless against what I had.

Both of them should have stacked their family silver on that one and neither of them did? Why?

I'd won next to nothing again on the best hand, the best situation of my life – of anybody's life – and it was inexplicable. And worse than that, not only was it inexplicable but my two chief opponents wore the sort of grins that indicated they could explain it.

If they'd had any cameras quickly brought in or if they were getting some way of knowing exactly what my cards were they wouldn't have done that. They'd have used their knowledge like I did the dog, secretively and underhand.

It was more than that, it was as if they knew what I was thinking, which was annoying because that was supposed to be my prerogative.

'You won!' said the dog, as I raked in the miserable antes – the small bets that a couple of players are forced to put in at the start of each hand to sweeten the pot.

'Aren't you pleased?'

'Not really,' I said.

The next hand was dealt and I was relieved to see that I was on an incredible streak of luck.

I won't go into the details but there were two nines in my hand and one on the table, making an emergency number for the other players. Three of a kind. Again.

'We'll get them this time!' said the dog, who was making his comments based on my reactions rather than the cards. I was aware for the first time of a light breeze on the left side of my face.

I looked round and down to see the dog's tail helicoptering away in anticipation of my win.

Again hands paused above piles of chips. The Cat wasn't even looking at me any more, I noticed. He folded. As did everyone else.

'Getting tougher, isn't it?' said the Cat, clacking his mouth.

'Happy, happy, happy!' said Reg, looking fondly into my eyes.

I followed the line of the Cat's gaze. He was looking at Reg. A very specific part of Reg. His tail, which was wagging up a storm in anticipation of us leaving.

I was rumbled and I was dead.

'What?' said the dog, suddenly glum. 'Why are you sad? Is it the home and a life apart for us? Oh no. ' He began to whimper and his ears went flat.

The Cat laughed and shook his head in mild disbelief.

I had a canine tell and there was nothing I could do about it.

38

End Game

We were now on exactly the kind of playing field I didn't like –
a level one.

I tried telling the dog to go under the chair but every time I
had a bad hand and my spirits dropped, even I noticed that he
whimpered, and every time I had a good one and I felt my heart
skip he let out a great pant of relief.

We were too close, he knew me too well; it was as if I'd got a
large, furry loudhailer communicating my feelings to the rest of
the table. The dog knew nothing of cards but everything of me
and, groan by groan, wag by wag, he was unravelling me.

There was nothing I could do to stop him.

What this meant was that, even playing conservatively, drip
by drip I'd be losing money without any real chance ever to win
some.

We broke again at midnight and I was down. Not big but not
small either.

'Not going your way in the last session is it, Rover?' said the
Cat, who had obviously been quite rattled by me calling him
Tiddles. He bent to pat the dog.

'Who's a good boy?' he said. 'Go on, wag your tail, we like it when you do that.' He stood and looked at me. 'Bloody voodoo,' he said, and walked away.

'I don't like him,' said the dog. 'He smells of warm folder.'

I'd left a bunch of ring binders from work in the car once on a sunny day and he'd moaned about the pong for weeks, even though I couldn't smell a thing.

Miles was at my arm.

'What's going on, mate?' I'd noticed that when he was relaxed he was quite the English toff, when he was more agitated the Aussie ocker came out in him.

'We have a problem,' I said. 'I think you should take your stake back and whatever winnings I've made and we should leave it there.'

'That leaves you in prison,' said Miles. Clearly my attempts at bonding had not gone as smoothly as I'd thought.

'Right,' I said.

'What's the problem?'

'They're on to the dog,' I said.

'What do you mean?'

'He wears his emotions on his sleeve, doesn't he? Every time I get a good hand he wags his tail and every time I get a bad one he whimpers and they've picked up on it. We're stuffed!' I said.

'I'm not,' said the dog, 'so if you could just pass me down one of those salmon sandwiches.'

Miles pondered a bit. He'd been quite nervous and, because he wasn't playing, he'd been drinking.

'Can you not wag your tail?' he said to the dog.

'Or sigh when I feel happy?' I said.

The dog wagged his tail and sighed. 'Certainly not,' he said. 'If I'm happy my tail wags and I sigh. That's part of being happy. The only way I can stop my tail wagging is not to be happy. It's not an expression of the emotion, it is the emotion.'

'Rubbish,' I said. 'So if I wag your tail, that's going to make you happy, is it?' I picked up his tail and wafted it from side to side.

'I think that will suffice,' said the dog, very pleased with himself.

'Why are you so smug?'

'Well, you wagged it in a smug pattern,' said the dog. 'That means I feel smug. Do it a bit faster and it'll be an eager-to-please wag. Oh, too late.' His tail made that slight circling motion it always does when he first meets me.

'Couldn't you want me to lose?' I said. I thought that might confuse them, if he started rooting for someone else.

'Never!' said the dog. He looked at his back quarters. 'That's a loyal wag, by the way.'

'I know,' I said. I recognised it, I'd seen it before. 'We're absolutely banjaxed,' I said.

'I have to point out,' said Reg, 'that this is why dogs don't play poker, as a whole.'

He was right, I knew. A dog doesn't act honestly, a dog is honesty.

'There is one possibility,' said Miles. 'You could always play them on your own. Go on, it's worth a punt.'

He was swaying uncertainly in front of me. I have to say that I didn't like the effect my company was having on Miles. He'd gone from being someone whose heart rate increased in horror at the thought of taking money from the starving hordes to a bloke who thought things were worth a punt.

I gulped. I knew that the solicitor was a serious proposition and had come highly placed in the world series. The Cat, too, was a hell of a player, he'd made mincemeat of me when I'd first been to his house.

I may as well, to quote the dog, roll over.

Reg looked up at me. 'Are we ready for the next go?' he said. 'You might slip me chicken this time when I get it right.'

'No,' I said, 'we're not.'

There comes a time when every man needs to stand up to be counted. I had until that moment thought that this time only existed in cowboy films but I'd been wrong. Now it was happening in my life. Was I a man or was I a mouse? And you know what happens to mice in the company of cats.

I went to the door and opened it to where Martin was watching TV.

'Martin,' I said, 'it's very smoky. Can you take Reg for a walk.'

'Even better!' said the dog.

'Oh dear, oh dear oh dear,' said the Cat. 'Got too much for Lassie down there, has it?'

'Yeah,' I said, turning to him, 'but not for me. Let's have it, you feline fuck.'

Poker is a wearying game. The next eight hours, until the sun came up over St James's Park, were spent in the grind, not the spectacular, searing big hands but the knocking it out on the small stuff.

I was in my element. Unfortunately I was also in theirs. It was a hard battle of pairs and aces high and making the best when you'd been given the worst. Poker was, I realised, more like life than I'd given it credit for. Its biggest test is patience. I wanted to be out of there so much, to be back with Lucy, with Reg who was now sleeping in with Martin and Miles, back in the clean air of the next room.

But I couldn't be. If I wanted to enjoy that clean air I had to sit there in the dirty first. For as long as it took.

Flops were flopped, turns were turned, people were taken to rivers in the awful war of attrition that this game can be. And I did OK.

I began to smell the game, to sniff out weaknesses and difficulties, to notice minor changes in skin tone, the way the eyes darted to the right for a bluff, to the left when it was for real, to see the vibration of a hand and know the difference between it and a forced shaking.

The walls between my senses seemed to dissolve, and I stepped onto that strange ground where emotions are seen, felt, heard, smelled and tasted in one so that you can't distinguish one from the other.

The bald cop fell away badly and left while he still had at least some of his money left, going through the door.

The City boys had either too much money or too much pride to pack it in when they should have and left with nothing. The solicitor made his £200,000 back and called it quits there. The two other folders packed up and went, severely down.

In the end it was me and the Cat face to face over the chips.

Hand after hand we went at it, hand after hand we won a little, lost a little.

It was eight in the morning, I had £600,000 and the Cat about twice that. We could have just walked away there and then and sensible men might have. We, though, weren't sensible. The game was coming to its finish, we knew, and it was just a matter of timing the moment when our circling would stop, we'd clash and one of us would lie dead on the carpet.

Cats are not pack animals, they're not cooperative or clever. They just want to be number one and will do anything to get there. This gives them a focus to beware of.

Miles came into the room and sat down behind the dealer.

My cards came down. Two spades, king spades. Not marvellous but where we were there were no prizes for second.

I bet large. I can't remember the amount, only the feeling, pushing the money away from me like an unpleasant past – almost not wanting it back, just wanting an end, any end but knowing that it had to return, that it was the key to everything I wanted.

Any other day I would have walked, but it wasn't an option then.

'I have to say,' said the Cat, pushing an equal amount into the pot, 'that I was surprised when your Lyndsey first came to me.'

I kept up the tactic of ignoring him although I could feel my heart going up to the rate where a hummingbird doctor might advise me to take it easy. Lyndsey had not been to see him, I told myself. But down in my deep heart's core, some animal, wordless understanding told me that she had.

'You see, we'd run out of ideas on how to persuade you.'

'I thought you were going to have me beaten up or killed.' I fronted it. Had I been betrayed? I still didn't blame Lyndsey for walking away but had she engineered it so my attempts at backing out had come to nothing.

'Not my style,' said the Cat, as more cards landed. Seven of spades, king of diamonds, two of hearts. Not bad.

'That's what you implied,' I said.

'Well, exactly,' said the Cat, 'but I don't really operate like that. I don't have to normally.'

'Why not?' I decided to check, bet nothing for reasons I won't go into.

'People are greedy,' he said. 'Every development we've been involved in for the last three years has had some aspect of "turbo profit".'

'You mean you've paid under the odds for developments.'

'Standard industry practice,' said the Cat. 'A few grand to the estate agent here and that's normally enough.'

He checked. Still a big pot on offer.

'I would like to have had you killed but unfortunately we'd have been back to square one with the old lady then, wouldn't we? And to be honest, I'm a bit lightweight for murder and violence.'

I felt myself go into a sweat.

'But you had Lyndsey beaten up.'

'On her suggestion,' said the Cat. 'I'd rather assumed you didn't have a girlfriend, she never seemed to be around when we had you watched. You didn't have much of a relationship, did you?'

I snorted. I couldn't believe his bullshit. 'And you didn't have much of a surveillance team if you couldn't find out I was seeing someone.'

'They're a couple of nightclub bouncers, not Panor bleeding rama,' said the Cat. 'So Lyndsey suggested that she got beaten up. Which I thought was quite ballsy of her. I must say I enjoyed doing it. Bam!' He mimed driving his fist into someone's face, his lips curling back over his teeth at the memory of the enjoyment it had given him.

'You're lying,' I said but I could see that he wasn't.

'Actually,' said the Cat, 'why don't you have a look at this?' He flipped out his mobile phone, turned it on and slid it across the table towards me. It was a top of the range job, natch. 'You'll find the relevant information under messages,' he said. 'I like to keep them for a bit of a record – call me an old romantic. The photos make interesting viewing too.'

I couldn't not look. I scrolled down the messages, all the dates, all the times of my eventual betrayal spelled out in that brutal language. 'RU Free 2nite? L'escargo (sic) @ 6. UR V Bad Cat!' The photos showed, rather sweetly in a way, Lyndsey with her eye already swelling, waving as she got into her car.

I felt a ball of hatred coming up inside me, for him, for Lyndsey. There's only so far you can forgive. If I'd been left to my own devices Miles wouldn't have been robbed of a fortune, Reg wouldn't have gone inside, I wouldn't have been sitting there playing for my liberty.

I peeked at my two hidden cards again. One more spade and I'd dig him his grave.

The next card came out. It was a spade and the Cat was six feet under. I'd turned a flush and I was home and dry. If I strung the Cat along I could be in for some money. It was time to bet big. I knew I couldn't lose. Three hundred thousand went into the pot. The Cat raised his eyebrows.

'Believe what you like,' said the Cat, 'it's you that's going to be the pauper and me the multimillionaire. Have you any idea how much money I'm going to make off the Charterstone deal as soon as we get those tossing hippies out of the trees and the rest of the houses built?'

'A lot, I should think,' I said. I could only picture him beating up Lyndsey. In fact he'd been beating up me. I wanted to take that pain and magnify it, give it him back double.

'The investment alone is greater than the combined profit of my last four projects,' he said. 'When they all come to fruition I'm going to be worth about fifty million.'

He answered my money, the stupid bastard.

There it was, my £1.2 million. I was free of him and his world of people who allow themselves to be beaten up for money, people who will lie and cheat for money, people who will tread on every conceivable moral for money.

'I'm all in,' I said.

'Then show,' said the Cat with a toothy grin.

I flipped it over, my flush. The Cat showed his. A pair of swans, two twos. He was away with the birds betting so big on that.

And then something strange happened. The dealer raked the chips towards him. I looked at him and then back to my cards. There was only one spade in my original two cards. In my tiredness and my stress and my wanting to be out and thinking about Lyndsey I'd misread the queen of clubs as the queen of Spades.

I'd bluffed myself and now I didn't have a penny. I was dead.

'The losers lose, the winners win, and so the world goes,' said the Cat as he sat exchanging his chips for the banker's drafts.

They piled up in front of him, the sheets of paper on which I could have written the story of my freedom.

The air in the room felt heavy, as if in a diving bell.

'I'll be glad to rest,' said the Cat. 'I need to be fresh for taking

Lyndsey out tonight. I expect she'll be ever so pleased with this, you know how she "like de cash money".' I think for some reason he was attempting some sort of New Orleans jazzy accent.

I wanted to punch him.

'It's true, you know, me and Lyndsey. I've given up bluffing,' said the Cat, 'for today at least.'

Something inside me didn't care. I'd done all my caring intensively for a week and didn't seem to have any left. In fact I felt very strange indeed, as if nothing really mattered any more. I had the dog, I had Lucy, I had a hefty prison sentence. So what?

We'd opened the windows in the room and it seemed bright and new, the smoke of the session draining out into the clear morning light.

The Cat clipped the drafts into a briefcase and was about to step outside the room to reunite himself with his heavies to do the formality of having the dealers searched when Miles stood up.

He'd sobered up over the course of the session but he still looked bleary and pale. In the drained air he held up his hand like an end of shift traffic cop stopping his last motorist of the day.

'Could I just have a word?' he said.

'You're having one, aren't you?' said the Cat, clipping down the briefcase.

'Yeah, it was just these other projects you mentioned, the ones that will be going into paying for Charterstone.'

'Housing estates in the Midlands,' said the Cat, 'Commuter belt. Recharging units for the worker drones.'

'They're presumably in your company's name.'

'Yes,' said the Cat. He was no fool, that old moggie, and he'd detected something he didn't like in Miles's tone.

'And you're using them to honour the contracts in Charterstone?'

'Up your wig, law boy,' said the Cat, who was some way further ahead of the game than I was.

'It's just that in light of your confession it seems to me that the Office of Fair Trading and the Serious Fraud Squad might be interested in looking into those.'

The dealers left the room and I could hear the heavies stirring into life behind the door.

'They might be,' said the Cat, 'but they won't find anything to go on. Everyone's got an interest in watching their back.'

'Not everyone,' said Miles. 'In fact David here has no interest at all. A spell in prison would sort out his accommodation problems for the next few years. I think if he actually went to the police with the story he might end up with considerably less of a sentence than you. And of course all your assets from the fraud itself would be returned to the rightful beneficiary.'

'And who might that be?' said the Cat. I could see we had him rattled.

'Me,' said Miles. 'Miles Cadwaller-Beaufort, QC, at your disservice. I came along because I thought it might be good to get hold of your confession.' He lifted up his jacket to show a tape recorder sticking out of his shirt pocket.

'How did you get that in here?' said the Cat.

'Wouldn't you like to know?' said Miles. 'I think the evidence will stand up just fine, particularly when we combine it with Dave's confession. You're looking at losing all your money and spending some time with thugs as sexual partners rather than employees.'

The Cat's face hardened, if you can imagine granite hardening.

'Looks like the stakes are raised,' said Miles. I heard a stirring from the next room. The Cat backed towards the door. 'Darren, Ady, come in,' he said.

The door opened and the Cat's two heavies made their way into the room. Martin followed, but I couldn't see Reg.

'Do you want me to batter this couple of tarts now?' said Martin, who seemingly had a nose for trouble.

'I think that might prove more difficult than you anticipated,' said the Cat. Before anyone could move he produced a silenced gun from his pocket and aimed it at Miles.

'How did you get that in?' I said.

'Wouldn't you like to know?' said the Cat.

I wasn't ready for this. I knew it was only a slim chance that the Cat would kill us but I'd seen enough slim chances come up that evening not to want to bet on it.

'The recorder and the tapes, please,' he said. 'It appears the stakes are indeed raised.'

Time falls to bits after a certain period awake; the hours hum like a computer that's been left on all night and the senses function as if you've spent too long at the screen.

I'll describe the events not in the order I remember them but in the order I think they should go.

'You're eating steak!' said a houndly voice. 'That's the second time you've mentioned it and I'm flipping starving!' There was a tumult of paws against carpet and then I couldn't see the Cat any more.

An arc, the dog had once told me, is the image of life and in the ashtray air of that room it seemed so to me. The gun, which the Cat had been holding rather too gingerly to be entirely convincing, flew through the air, black against the yellow of the electric light and descending to pink, the meaty hand of Martin the Marine.

'Oh dear, oh dear,' said Miles.

'It's a fake,' said Martin, on one movement checking the weapon and casually knocking out the Cat's two heavies with its butt.

The Cat was moaning from beneath the table.

'Aren't you always meant to land on your feet?' said Martin.

'You can have half of the money if you just make him give me the tape,' mewled the Cat to Martin.

'No,' said Martin. 'I couldn't help overhearing some of your conversations of earlier and it occurs to me that it was you that damaged my glasswork, or someone working for you. Plus, it is an established fact that Davy here is a dark horse and I for one know that it's not wise to cross dark horses.'

'Neigh,' I said, 'it's not.'

'No, no, Cat,' said Martin, 'you have been a very naughty kitty indeed and as soon as I can find something to lubricate this weapon, you'll have the most graphic reminder I can think of of the perils of gun ownership.'

'Look,' said the Cat, who didn't seem in much of a position to be saying 'look' to anyone, 'I can't afford to fight a court case at the moment. All the money's dependent on all the other money. I can't risk having any of it tied up. What would it take to get you to drop this?'

'One point two million pounds,' said Miles, 'and the tape's yours.'

The Cat grimaced, as well he might. 'Six hundred thousand,' he said.

'Goodbye,' said Miles.

'OK, OK,' said the Cat. He knew full well it would cost him that and more to fight Miles through the courts, with no guarantee that he'd win.

'Fine,' said Miles. He flicked out the tape and put it on the table.

The Cat pulled himself to his feet stiffly and looked down at it.

His eyes widened, which is something I'd never seen them do in my time playing poker with him.

'You bunch of numpties,' he said. Then, with the sort of miracle recovery only known to devout Catholics and certain German centre forwards, he was gone, hammering down the stairs out of the club.

What happened next I'm not entirely clear. All I know is that someone in the room was something of a mucky pup. I'm not referring to the dog here, of course.

A chicken drumstick had lain unnoticed on the carpet between Martin and the Cat. As the former Marine and present violent maniac sprang forward to retrieve the Cat, Reg sprang forward to retrieve the drumstick, causing the violent maniac to trip over and break his ankle.

To Martin's credit this didn't stop him and he hammered off down the stairs after the Cat on all fours but too late. The Cat was gone, off into the foggy morning.

'At least we have the tape,' I said. 'Why did he run off if he knows we've got that?' Miles flicked the tape towards me. 'Because a million quid's rather a lot of money to pay for the Spice Girls' *Forever* album,' he said. 'Martin was listening to it on his Walkman and I thought it was worth a bluff.'

'I'm getting an iPod next week,' said Martin, blushing or at least going red as he crawled back up the stairs. 'It's just you have to get rid of all your old tapes and I'm a bit sentimental.'

'What are we going to do now?' said the dog.

'Is he talking to you again?' said Miles.

'Yes,' I said.

'What's he say?'

'What are we going to do now?'

'Get you arrested and go about getting my money back the proper way,' said Miles, 'because I'm not very sentimental'.

'Children in Africa, boo hoo hoo!' said Reg.

'Come on, Reggie,' I said. 'We've played and we've lost. Let's take it like men,' I ruffled his ears, 'or dogs.'

'You were going to prison anyway,' said Miles.

'What do you mean?'

'I'm owed twenty-five million, not one. Whatever the outcome of the game, I was going to use your affidavit. A no-lose situation,' he said.

'You're a hard bastard, aren't you?' I said, rather as if I was in *The Sweeney*.

'Hardest there is,' said Miles with a shrug.

'Aren't you going to talk down that tube?' said the dog.

'What tube?' I said.

'That tube on the table, it's shaking.'

I followed the dog's eyes. There on the table was the Cat's mobile phone, softly vibrating.

I picked it up. It was set on silent but that wasn't the first thing I noticed. No. That was the name on the screen.

'Lyndsey,' it said.

39

Waking Dogs Lie

'Hello,' I said, as near as I could approximate to the Cat's nasal southern counties drone. I don't know why I did it, it was just some instinct telling me it was the best thing to do – to deceive her.

'It's me, baby!' said Lyndsey, in something of a state of repressed excitement.

'Yes,' I said, doing that coffin lid creaking open voice of the Cat's

'You don't sound very pleased to hear from me,' said Lyndsey.

'They know everything,' I said. 'Barker spilled the beans.'

The dog looked around. I knew he was looking where these beans might be.

'What do you mean?' said Lyndsey.

'I can't explain,' I said, still down my nose. 'Go to the house, get all the incriminating evidence you can and put it in your car, then await further instructions. I can't say any more than that. I can't use this phone either, I think they've bugged it.'

'Why are you talking about incriminating evidence on a bugged phone?' said Lyndsey, sounding slightly desperate.

'A mistake,' I said, sounding rather too much like Custard the Cat, rather than the Cat.

'Shit!' said Lyndsey. 'That twonk's left me up to my neck in debt now he's nowking up the rest of my life. What's the code for the safe?'

The dog shifted from paw to paw. Four paws. Lucy had said that the code is always 1,2,3,4. It was something to tell her anyway.

'One, two, three, four,' I said.

'Same as your alarm!' said Lyndsey. 'Actually, can't Jenkins do this?'

'I wouldn't trust that twonk,' I said.

There was a slight pause. Then she said. 'Don't worry, Mike, you can count on me.'

'I'll call you later,' I said, 'from a different phone.'

'Love you like crazy,' she said.

'Yeah . . .' I said on a long feline note and hung up.

'Gentlemen and canine,' I said.

'And canine gentlemen,' said the dog.

'We have a glimmer of hope!'

Miles was looking at me as if I'd gone mad. 'I have a great fat wodge of hope,' he said. 'I have your confession in a safe and one of the most feared legal minds in the world in my head. You're shafted, mate!'

I didn't have much of an argument against that one. I looked down at the dog.

'Are you,' I said, 'intent on parting me from my only friend in the world?'

'Yes,' said Miles with a pretty decisive nod.

'Oh don't,' said Reg, butting his head into the side of Miles's leg and looking up at him. 'Give us a pat.'

Miles shook his head wearily. 'What,' he said, 'is your plan?'

'He's not hard at all really,' said Reg, looking up at me.

My mother, when I was a child, used to accuse me, on a semi-regular basis, of 'tearing around like a blue-arsed fly'. In my childish opinion, of course, I was doing nothing of the kind. I was simply responding to emergencies in what I considered to be an appropriate manner. Martians at the front door to be repulsed with water pistol, for instance. Nuclear attack forcing me to dive beneath a table. Destroyers hunting for my submarine, meaning I had to go everwhere in a crouch, holding my nose and saying, 'Bing!' I think the sense of injustice that this bred has seen me, if anything, cultivate an air of languour and steadiness in later years.

However, what I should have told my mother, had I then had the advantage of my present experience, was that in some cases 'tearing around like a blue-arsed fly' is not only right and fitting, it is bleeding essential. This was one of those cases.

Miles still had something to gain: absolute, incontrovertible documentary evidence of the fraud. It was OK having my sworn statement, but 'ladies and gentlemen of the jury, I ask you to believe the estate agent' has never been much of a winner in an English court. We had to move fast, though.

'I don't want to sound like a whinger or anything,' said Martin, holding his ankle, 'but you don't know where there's a hospital round here, do you?'

'I won't take the dog!' said a taxi driver outside the club.

'We'll pay double!' said Miles.

'Then keep him off the seats!' said the taxi driver.

'We will!' I said. It was a morning for exclamation marks, cold and foggy where things suddenly loomed!

Martin was left waiting for a second cab, apologising for being such a tart.

The heavy fog meant there was no way we could make the journey I was planning by car. On the positive side this meant that the Cat wouldn't be going back any time soon. I knew there was no way he'd travel by train – public transport risking contamination by pleb. With luck he'd check into a hotel and sleep until the fog lifted. That gave us time to weave our magic.

Exactly what our magic was I hadn't at that moment decided. All I knew was that, if I could get Lyndsey to shift the Cat's files out of his house, we might be in with a shot. I called the Cat's home number.

'Yup!' said Jenkins.

'Miss Lyndsey will be coming over soon,' I said. 'I want you to let her into my office.'

'Whatever,' said Jenkins.

I didn't think we'd have much trouble there. I could have delivered my words in the style of the late Al Jolson and I think he'd still not have noticed anything awry.

I thought that Lyndsey would probably take the files back to Charterstone. If necessary I could overpower her and take them. Actually, with Martin gone and only me and Miles on the premises I wasn't so sure about the overpowering bit.

Once we were on the train and heading south, I called Lucy. We could do with a bit of back-up, I thought.

'Get her to wait up Bramble Lane,' said Lucy. 'It's just off the A27 heading up to Devil's Dyke. It's really quiet and it'll be deserted up there at this time of day.'

'How do you know?' I said.

'Because I used to do a lot of shagging up there when I was a teenager,' she said.

'Sorry I asked,' I said.

'So am I,' she said.

'I love you.'

'And I love you too,' she said. 'I'll pick you up at Hole Street station and we'll take it from there.'

The train seemed to make the journey from station to station as if the fog were some clogging jelly, a substance notorious for slowing the progress of even the most determined traveller. We moved at much the same speed as a medieval pageant, complete with minstrels singing songs along the lines of 'and on the third day they did rest'. Points failures were as difficult to negotiate as any dragon.

We crept through the fog, the train creaking like some ancient galleon, the dog straining at the lead, as if that would make it go quicker. I knew how he felt, my leg muscles involuntarily flexing as if I wanted to run ahead.

Eventually we drew nearer Hole Street, each ghostly station making the acid bite in my stomach in a stress rehearsal for what was ahead.

Finally, there it was. Like so much in Britain, the name bore no relation to what was there. It wasn't a street at all, just a rudimentary concrete platform in the middle of the countryside. The train only stopped there, I thought, because it stopped at every other bush and pole, and to speed up past a platform, no matter how unused, would have seemed perverse.

Through the mist I could see the lights of Lucy's car. I hadn't even known she had a car and, in a way, I was right. It was an ancient mini van with what appeared to be leprosy, so cracked was the paintwork.

Lucy threw her arms round me while the dog, whose paws had managed to get muddy in record time, soiled her coat.

'Shall I call her now?' I said.

'Go ahead.'

I flicked open the phone. No signal.

Rarely in my life have I attempted to do an impression of self-made southern businessman while standing on top of one of the worst ideas for a commercial vehicle ever conceieved but I made such a good fist of it that I may in future include it as a party trick.

I took Lucy's phone and dialled Lyndsey's number.

'It's me,' I said, like that cat off the advert used to say, 'Tuna!'

'The code's wrong, you muppet!' screamed Lyndsey down the phone. 'It's a five-number code and you've only given me four.'

'Add a five,' I said, my mouth dry.

'Five, five, five,' said Lyndsey. 'Thank God, it's open. Do you want me to take all this lot? All these banker's drafts?'

Code 12345. The one the safe was delivered with. The Cat obviously didn't watch *Up to Our Necks In A Tide Of Crime While The Police Force Concentrate On Rubbish Like Road Safety And Speeding*. Did I want her to take the banker's drafts? You betcha.

'Take the lot,' I said, as if I had cotton wool in my mouth. 'Get Jenkins to give you some bags but for God's sake hurry. I'll meet you at Bramble Lane, do you know where that is?'

'Of course,' she said. 'I used to do a lot of shagging there as a teenager.'

'Right,' I said. 'I'll meet you there in an hour.'

'Love you like crazy!' she said, slightly breathlessly.

'Like crazy,' I said, slapping my mouth like the Cat did.

We drove up onto the mighty Devil's Dyke, where the hills of the South Downs make their stand against the flatness of the Surrey Weald. Slowly we rose above the fog, looking down at it as if upon a giant bowl of soup.

Bramble Lane was a dead end – ironically with quite a few brambles either side of the road, given what I've said about place names bearing no resemblance to the actual place. We turned the mini round and reversed, so the car was pointing down the road, ready for a quick escape.

A couple of teenagers, a boy and a girl, relaxed in the front seat of a max-powered Escort, smoking and looking at us with vacant gapes, like fish from the bottom of a pond.

We had half an hour to kill before Lyndsey arrived, so we got out of the car and I let Miles and the dog out of the back.

'A dog!' shouted the boy. 'That is so sick, man! You should keep dogging to humans.' I had no idea what he was talking about. He started up his car and turned it round, leaving us alone in the lane.

'Have you actually worked out what we're going to do?' said Miles.

It was then that I saw it clearly.

'Exactly,' I said.

Quickly I hopped into the mini van and positioned it further down the lane. We'd get her to go up to the top of the lane, back up, seal her in and then hope that it didn't come to a scrap.

'If it does, me and Miles will restrain her while Lucy unloads the stuff,' I said.

'I don't mind restraining her,' said Lucy, producing a set of Chinese nunchukas from inside her coat. 'They're Jim's,' she said. 'He does Kung Fu.' She held them a little too familiarly for my money. 'He's shown me how to use them.'

'Let's try not to get done for assault here, shall we?' I said.

The half an hour came and went and we waited in the van.

'Phone her and see what's happening,' said Miles.

I did.

'I'm just coming into the lane!' said Lyndsey.

'Here she is,' said Lucy under her breath as the Discovery trundled towards us.

'Pull past this old mini van and park at the top. I can't be seen,' I said.

'OK,' said Lyndsey.

The next part of the operation went like clockwork. The Land Rover stopped at the top of the field and Lucy, who had been disguising herself by giving me a quick snog as Lyndsey drove past the van, hammered the van into reverse, backing it right up to the Discovery.

Unfortunately the bit after that went like clockwork that has been given the full sledgehammer treatment.

It was the dog's fault in a way. Like I've said before, most of the time no one else can hear him speak. Sometimes, though, when he gets particularly excited, shouting at a squirrel for instance, they'll hear it as barking.

So his comment, 'Now we have you, my fine lady!' sounded to Lyndsey like a great big woof. Lyndsey had never been much of a dog fancier but that particular bark held a certain resonance for her, as its owner had already cost her a cashmere sweater. This caused her to look in her mirror and, needless to say, she wasn't pleased with what she saw, a mini van reversing at speed towards her. So as soon as we all jumped from the van she saw who we were and already had her foot on the accelerator. This was OK, I'd factored that one in. It was a dead end and she was stuck.

Or rather she would have been stuck had she been in one of those useless, only good for taking the kids to school 4×4s that clog the roads nowadays. Instead she was in a Land Rover Discovery, full off-road suspension kit, first choice of rescue services everywhere and capable of going up the side of your average suburban semi.

Lucy hit a hard left, going straight through a flimsily tied gate and into the field adjoining the lane. Then, rather expertly bringing the car under control, she crashed through the hedge and back onto the tarmac.

'Come back!' I shouted.

'She won't fall for that one,' said the dog, rolling his eyes. I didn't like this cynical streak he was evolving.

Lucy's mobile, still in my pocket, rang. It was Lyndsey, having hit last number redial.

'Keep on losing, loser!' she said. 'You know, Dave, I don't know how I stuck you for so long. I'm off to my wonderful life. Say hello to the prisoners for me! Aaahhh!'

There was a terrible bang and a scrape and a bang, a dull moan of protest as two things that were meant to be kept apart came together, in this case the side of one of Coventry's finest Land Rovers and the top of one of East Sussex County Council's worst roads.

What the cyclist was doing out on such a foggy day no one knows, nor why he didn't stop after Lyndsey had swerved to avoid him. I might have thought that Lyndsey was imagining it, that she'd lost control of the car simply because she was using the mobile phone and the shock of the accident had caused her to see things that weren't there. I saw him too, though, as we ran down the lane to the Land Rover, or rather the back of him, just a flash of Day-Glo pink and an old-fashioned back light disappearing into the fog.

The Discovery had hit the right-hand bank hard and taken a huge gouge of mud from it; it had then veered across the narrow lane and smacked the other bank, which flipped it onto its side, with the driver's door down to the road.

The tailgate had burst open and a trail of paper led to the car.

'Is she all right?' said Lucy.

'I don't know,' I said, approaching the side of the downed car.

'Shiteing cyclist came from nowhere!' said Lyndsey. 'Get me out, get me out!' She was banging on the glass of the window like an angry sprite trapped in a bottle.

'Er, probably not actually,' I said. 'Lucy, start loading the mini van.'

'Bastards!' said Lyndsey, making a bid to get over the back seat and out of the rear of the car. She'd just got her fingers round the dog guard to pull it out when Reg snapped at them.

Miles and Lucy were already busy picking up the paper and loading it into the car.

In the end Lyndsey just sat crying in the Discovery, the dog snarling every time she made a move to get out.

'I always loved you,' she said. You have to say this for Lynds, she was no quitter.

'No you didn't, Lyndsey,' I said. 'That's why I was with you.'

'Come on!' said Lucy.

'Yes, come on!' said the dog. The Mini van was full and Miles was in the front seat. It was going to be a squeeze.

'Bye, Lynds,' I said. 'Look after yourself. I know you will.'
I turned and opened the door of the mini van
'Drive!' I said, cool as McQueen, getting in and sitting on Miles's lap.

40

The Emotional Retriever

The beaches of the Australian Gold Coast curl against the shore like a dog at the feet of an indulgent master. Like a very sandy dog, admittedly.

Endless sand, a tropical sunset, a Frisbee flying and the canine engine motoring after it. This is paradise.

Miles did sue the Cat, and the Cat was prosecuted over his business dealings in the Midlands by judges he didn't know and coppers he couldn't buy – largely because Miles knew them all and had made a large donation to the Police Widows and Orphans fund just before he asked the chief constable to review the evidence. Lyndsey had done a thorough job on the documents, it was all there. She'd even taken a CD of his emails for the past year. He was screwed.

I should have been cited of course, but I wasn't there. No one knew where I'd gone, in fact, other than Miles, Lucy and the dog.

One of the advantages of owning a Lear Jet, of course, is that dogs are allowed in the cabin.

'Look at those people down there, they look just like ants,' said the dog, staring out of the window.

'They are ants, you fool, we haven't left the runway!' I said.

Our experiences had brought me and Miles quite close to each other and it was nice of his mate to give us a lift down to Aus, even if the dog did have to keep a low profile on the stopover in South Korea.

'They eat dog burgers here,' I explained, as we warily patrolled the airport.

'Burgers just for dogs, how lovely,' said Reg.

'Not quite,' I said.

It seemed that the Gold Coast wasn't quite covered for dogs homes. Miles thought that, given my experience in real estate, I'd be the ideal person to set one up and run it, honouring his mother's wish. We don't get paid much but it's enough.

The money we got off the Cat, £600,000 in banker's drafts – you may call it theft, I call it retrieval – bought a handsome home overlooking the sea, with enough left over to pay us to run the Edith Cadwaller-Beaufort trust.

What happened to Lyndsey? Well, she did all right. She had to spend another two years on the Charterstone estate up to her neck in mud and my debts until the service roads and the excavations grew over.

The Cat's assets were frozen awaiting the outcome of the court case and the road to the A23 was never built. This meant that none of the other houses were ever completed so Lyndsey became the new single lady of Charterstone. I don't know if the Cat ever tried retribution on her. I doubt it. He was in enough trouble already. So Lyndsey got her home, and in a way she got her happiness, I suppose. Last I heard she'd settled down with a semi-professional golfer.

If Miles gets his wish, though, the houses on the estate will eventually be built, split into flats and sold off cheaply to nurses, public sector workers, and the low-paid. So while she'll be living in a lovely house, she won't exactly have the neighbours she would have chosen.

I don't blame her for what she did and I still even love her in a way. She wasn't a villain, she was just doing what she thought was best. Which I suppose is the way that most villains look at it.

So I sit with Lucy, watching the evening sun drop over the sea. I come here every night with the dog to watch him chasing his frisbee in the relative cool of the evening.

Even though the sun comes down quickly in this hemisphere I rarely notice the dropping of the light. Suddenly there are stars above us, strange constellations turning in the deep blue, and the feeling I had all those years ago reverses, the child's address backwards, The Universe, The Milky Way, The Solar System, The World, Australia, The Gold Coast, Penhaligan Beach, the fourteenth dune from the car park, Dave, Lucy and Reggie B, no smaller unit imaginable. Three of a kind.

'I'm happy here,' said Lucy.

'What, happier than in Worthing?' I say, looking along the line of palms.

'There's not as much rubbish here,' said the dog, with a slight tone of disappointment.

Never in my life will I truly fathom dog aesthetics. This was the beast who, on having the work of Damien Hirst explained to him, described it as 'Appetising' and when pressed would only come up with, 'Shark. Yummy!'

'You get longer walks,' I said.

'That's true,' he said, watching a gull make its way sedately along the line of the surf and clearly tossing up whether he should have a go at it.

I feel strange tonight, as befits a man who has spent his life struggling through little rooms when he gets to sit under a big sky.

There seems no future on this beach, no possibility that it will ever change, as if we could sit in this dying light forever, as if it could die for eternity and never be dead. But change it will.

Lucy has a bump in her belly and the dog is getting grey hairs on his chin.

The moments, in their endless procession, will get us in the end, him, Lucy, me and even the baby.

So I watch the night coming down along the beach, the lights of the boats hanging like paper lanterns on the body of the dark sea and I can only think one thing. So what?

I look at my watch. It's poker in an hour but I think I'll give it a skip tonight, just to be with Lucy and Reg. It's only a dollar in anway.

'Are you happy?' I say to Lucy.

'Yes.' She has her head against my right shoulder.

'Are you happy?' I say to the dog, who has his head against my left.

'Woof,' he says, and I am too.

MARK BARROWCLIFFE

Infidelity for First-Time Fathers

'Stunning – even better than his first' Jill Mansell

There's something wrong with Stewart Dagman's life. The party invitations used to read 'Bring bottles and First Aid kit. Eight till police raid.' Now they say 'Ben is one. Help us celebrate. Please leave quietly before afternoon nap.'

Life is moving on, and Dag wants to move with it. All he wants is someone to love, a family of his own and a half-indecent sex life.

So what happens when those dreams come true? Twice. In a week.

It's a tough life, being a modern man, dealing with girlfriends, parenthood, friendship, lollipop ladies, bloodhounds, parents, weddings and 6'8" gangsters called Dave the Lesbian. All whilst finding time for the annual lads' ski-ing holiday, of course . . .

'Mark Barrowcliffe is a master of recognition humour' Sue Margolis

And don't miss Mark Barrowcliffe's earlier bestseller, GIRLFRIEND 44

'I howled with laughter' *Mirror*

'A natural chronicler of the love-lorn male' *The Times*

'Hilarious . . . [Barrowcliffe is] an assured stylist with a lively, wordy wit' *Independent on Sunday*

0 7472 6815 0

review

Girlfriend 44

MARK BARROWCLIFFE

Since he was ten years old, Harry has had one ambition – to find the girl for him. Forty-three women and twenty years later he is no nearer his goal. He doesn't ask for much; just a beautiful intellectual who doesn't mind his constant infidelity.

Harry's flatmate Gerrard did once find true love – but he didn't realise it until the day she left him. Only two women have met his exacting criteria, and he's not hopeful that he'll find another. Even if he does, he isn't sure he can trust her not to grow old eventually. Then they meet Alice.

Alice is the perfect girl. She's the only woman in the world Harry and Gerrard can agree on. Unfortunately, she seems to like both of them.

Gerrard wants Alice for himself, but Harry will stop at nothing to win her. Friendship is forgotten and even a little light poisoning is on the cards.

'A natural chronicler of the love-lorn male' *The Times*

'Sharp and funny' *Loaded*

'I howled with laughter . . . lively, witty and upbeat' *Mirror*

0 7472 6814 2

headline

You can buy any of these other **Review** titles from your bookshop or *direct from the publisher*.

FREE P&P AND UK DELIVERY
(Overseas and Ireland £3.50 per book)

A History of Forgetting	Caroline Adderson	£6.99
The Catastrophist	Ronan Bennett	£6.99
The Mariner's Star	Candida Clark	£6.99
Hallam Foe	Peter Jinks	£6.99
This is Not a Novel	Jennifer Johnston	£6.99
The Song of Names	Norman Lebrecht	£6.99
In Cuba I was a German Shepherd	Ana Menéndez	£6.99
The Secret Life of Bees	Sue Monk Kidd	£6.99
My Lover's Lover	Maggie O'Farrell	£6.99
Early One Morning	Robert Ryan	£6.99
Missing	Mary Stanley	£6.99
The Hound in the Left-Hand Corner	Giles Waterfield	£6.99
God Breathes His Dreams Through Nathaniel Cadwallader	Charlotte Fairbairn	£6.99

TO ORDER SIMPLY CALL THIS NUMBER

01235 400 414

or visit our website: www.madaboutbooks.com

Prices and availability subject to change without notice.